To George and [?]
for all the Good Times
Kerry McCan

GRINGO VERDE

A Novel of Revolution and Redemption

Kerry McCan

SUNBELT EAKIN   Austin, Texas

PREFACE

This novel takes place within the era of the Mexican Revolution of the early twentieth century. Perhaps a quick outline of that conflict might be helpful to the reader who has little knowledge of that bloody conflict.

The Mexican Revolution broke out in 1910, and the cause of it has generally been ascribed to the reelection of Porfirio Díaz, who had ruled Mexico for over thirty years. The leader of the revolt was Francisco I. Madero, a member of an old and aristocratic family from the state of Coahuila, around Torreon. The revolution had genuine popular support and soon toppled Díaz into exile. Madero became president in a quickly following election. In less than two years, Madero was murdered by counter-revolutionaries led by Gen. Victoriano Huerta, who became dictator.

Thus started the second and bloodiest part of the revolution, lasting for more than two years. This phase of the revolution is the background for most of the action described in *Gringo Verde*. There were four arenas of action in this phase, mainly delineated by the revolutionary leaders. The guerrilla war, just south of Mexico City, was led by Emiliano Zapata. In the north, Alvaro Obregón led the revolutionary forces in the west, mainly west of the Sierra Madre Occidental. In the east, Pablo Gonzales was leader; in the central zone, Francisco Villa led the Division of the North.

All three of these forces combined were called the Constitutionalists and were under the overall authority of the first chief, Venustiano Carranza, who, after the fall of General Huerta, became supreme leader.

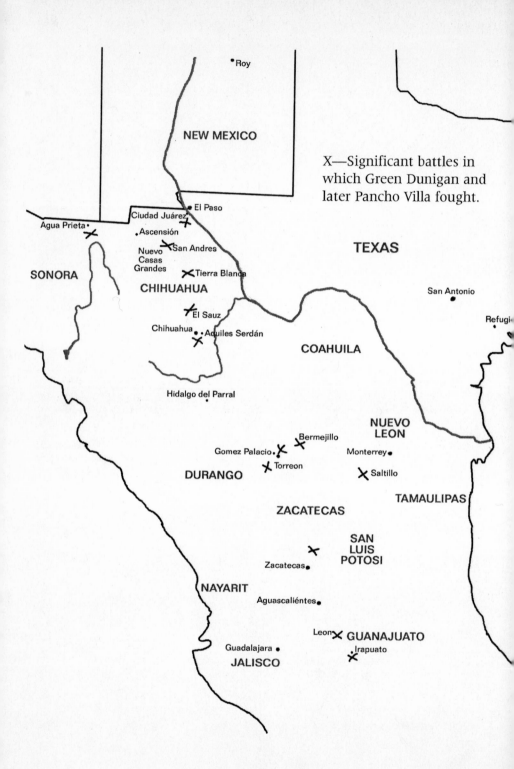

X—Significant battles in which Green Dunigan and later Pancho Villa fought.

The start of the third phase began with a struggle between Carranza (who was able to regain, for a while, the loyalty of Obregón) and Pablo Gonzales on one side and everyone else on the other. Carranza and Obregón won, defeating and assassinating both Villa and Zapata. But the upheaval continued until Carranza was killed, Obregón became president and then was assassinated, whereupon Plutarco Elias Calles became president and the revolution finally ground down. Almost one-third of the population of Mexico perished in this upheaval, and real stability did not return until the election of Lazaro Cardenas in 1936.

Geographically, the war was fought along the north-south rail lines, as the railroads were the only way to move the large amounts of men and materiel in Mexico. This, of course, was not the case in Zapata's territory, but there the war was little more than hit-and-run raids and ambushes, and had little effect on the larger picture in the north and central parts of Mexico.

Details about the cattle industry are reflective of the period 1865-1885 and are covered more completely in my first book, *Brindy Polaris*.

There is one chronological error in the novel. Pascual Orozco was killed in 1918, not 1915, but the circumstances were generally the same. I placed his death in that year because I felt it would fit the story better—and, after all, what good is artistic license if you don't use it? All other events in the novel are fairly accurate, as to times and places and persons, so I hope that my error can be forgiven.

PROLOGUE

South Texas / Christmas 1905

John Dunigan gazed down the table with a great deal of satisfaction. His entire family was present, together, for the first time in several years, all seated at the same table. All, that is, except his grandchildren, who were, according to the custom of the time, sitting at a smaller, second table in an adjoining room, the parlor.

Amanda Dunigan was seated at the foot of the table, and on each side of her were sons Jack and Adrian. Next to them was daughter Kathleen and her husband, William Foster, up from Brownsville. Jack's wife, Lucinda, completed the table.

Seated in the parlor were Jack and Lucinda's twin sons, John and Lawrence, and their daughter Amelia, and the Foster children, Green and Sylvia.

Adrian had risen to propose a toast with the familiar native mustang grape wine.

"To all Dunigans, God bless 'em. May they prosper."

Everyone drank the slightly sweet but rough native wine. An educated palate would have choked, but most Texans didn't drink enough wine to be particular about it. The wine, like practically everything on the table, was made on the ranch. The turkey had been shot by Adrian only yesterday; the sweet potatoes and greens were from the ranch garden. Even the butter had been churned from milk produced by cows kept at ranch headquarters.

Dunigan, the paterfamilias, had made substantial money as a traildriver from '67 to '81. He owned 70,000 acres along the Aransas River in Refugio, Bee, and San Patricio counties, having started with thirty acres as a seventeen-year-old in 1853. In addition, he had over 200,000 acres in a South Texas ranch spanning LaSalle, Dimmit and Webb counties, and had paid cash for all of it. It had been a far journey for an Irish orphaned boy, and every day he thanked God and his lucky star for all he had, including the fine family that was here with him.

Amanda, at the other end of the table, was just as proud. She was connected to an old-line family in Kentucky, until Dunigan wooed and won her, and brought her to the wilds of Texas.

Amanda had given Dunigan three children. Jack, the oldest (age thirty-two) lived on the South Texas ranch, close to the little town of Cotulla, and operated it for his father. Kathleen (now twenty-five) had married William Foster, a cotton broker from Brownsville, seven years earlier. Adrian, who was called by his middle name, Green, had been named for his grandfather, Amanda's father, Adrian Green, from Kentucky. The twenty-eight-year-old bachelor was the most adventurous of all the children. Jack was settled, running the Cotulla ranch, and Kathleen was happy with her husband and two children in Brownsville, but Green was a free spirit, always on the move. For five years he had been taking care of the family's cattle. Fall and winter would find him along the Mexican border, buying steers to stock the Cotulla ranch. In the spring, he generally helped out at the home ranch, and in summer he took care of the steers they had in the Osage (in the Indian territories), and also in the Flint Hills of Kansas.

John Dunigan kept about 1,000 cows at the home ranch, but the rest of his country was normally stocked with steers growing for two or three years, until they were sent north to the Bluestern pastures in Oklahoma and Kansas. Each year he would send 3,000-4,000 steers of an age, usually three years or more, north to be marketed. This involved a lot of travel for Green, as he would cut out the fat cattle and ship them to Kansas City weekly. The operation had been going on since Dunigan had trailed his steers to the Osage in the early seventies, and it had worked well for them since then.

The two brothers got along well together but were very different in temperament and outlook. Jack, the eldest, was all business and ran the South Texas ranch under an iron hand. An able cattleman, Jack Dunigan was well regarded in industry circles, and was well known as a South Texas booster. Green Dunigan was just different. It was not that he was any less efficient or dedicated than Jack, but his whole approach was quieter and kinder. Abel Castro had sort of adopted him when Green was only five, Amanda being pregnant with Kathleen, and Jack being an active eight-year-old who did not resist. John, knowing how much Abel would teach young Green, thought it a good idea.

Abel Castro had been with Dunigan for many years and lived at the headquarters to the north and west of the home ranch. He had been married for some time but had no children. Both Abel and Sulema were especially fond of Green, as was he of them. Sulema was kind and wanted children badly, but evidently could not have her own. It was an ideal solution for everyone, but Amanda did not want it to become permanent, as she was afraid of her children losing all touch with civilization out on the ranch. They had a penchant for this, inherited from their father.

Jack had experienced a similar influence on his life through Lon Castle, who had taken over Jack's education on the ranch earlier. Lon had taught him to ride, rope, and perform all the cowboy skills to the point that Jack, at the age of only eight, was a valuable hand on the ranch.

Kathleen, as a girl, was kept closer to her mother's ways. She was taught to ride, but in an elegant manner, not like her brothers, who rode like half-tamed Indians. Her mother saw to her early education as a well-behaved young lady of quality.

All three children, as soon as they were old enough, were sent to the nuns in Refugio, where they boarded during the week. They would visit the ranch each weekend and on holidays until they graduated. Jack attended the University of Texas for three years, coming home to manage the South Texas ranch. Kathleen was sent to a young lady's finishing school in St. Louis for two years, and Green attended the Texas land grant college, Texas A&M.

As with most land grant colleges, A&M was military, and Green was assigned to the artillery for his training. He had a bent toward mathematics, and his course of study was in civil engineering-surveying. Green was good at it, but he grew bored and left after two years, in 1894.

Because he knew something of surveying, Dunigan had Green work on some abstracts and land titles he thought were a bit weak. After six months, however, Green wanted to do something more productive. All of his childhood spent in company with Abel Castro had taught him to speak Spanish as a native tongue; plus, their hunting and trapping had made him a superb woodsman. As a horseman he was natural-born and could do anything another rider could do. Dunigan thought about letting him take over the horse-breeding and training, but decided it was too limiting. Instead, he sent his son to El Paso to buy steers imported from western Mexico.

Green was too adventurous to stay in El Paso all the time. He made many trips into West Texas, New Mexico, and even into Mexico, buying and trading on his own account as well as for the Dunigan operations. Most of his trips began in San Antonio, where he caught the train for points north and west.

CHAPTER 1

San Antonio, Texas / May 1898

reen Dunigan had never seen San Antonio so busy, or so full of people. He had just ridden in from Refugio, on his way to catch a train for the Indian territories, to see the pastures up there. He stopped at the livery to stable his horse and catch a ride to the Menger Hotel, where he always stayed.

"What's going on here, Pete?" he asked the stable man. "It looks as if all of Texas is here."

"Yep, and a good bit of the next country, too. It's the war with Spain. The army's gathering up soldiers from all over, and if that wasn't enough, there's a crazy Yankee from New York over at the Menger, trying to raise a whole regiment of cowboys. Calling 'em Roosevelt's Rough Riders, he is."

"I hope there's a room left for me there. I'd hate to have to find a place somewhere else this late in the day."

"I'd hurry if I was you, Green. There's all kind of people over there," Pete said. He put Green's bags in the buggy, and they drove over to the Menger.

The front of the hotel was jammed with young men. Green got out, thanked Pete, and took his bags to the front desk.

"Can you fix me up with a room for the night, Walter?" Green asked. Walter, the old-timer desk clerk, knew the whole Dunigan family from years back.

"Green, I can't even guarantee you space at the bar. We're filled—no rooms. And it's that way all over town. I reckon the closest rooms would be in Austin."

Green took this in, and hoisted his bags on the desk.

"Can you take care of my baggage for me, Walter? It looks like I'm gonna sleep with my horse tonight."

"Yes, sir. It'll be here when you want it, Green," the clerk replied.

Green wandered through the lobby, amazed at the diverse group. About half of them were in uniform: blue wool shirts, khaki breeches, and puttees, or boots if they were officers. A portion of the rest were cowboys. Cowboys more or less dressed the same the world over, but regional differences were in effect. Plains cowboys tended to wear wider brimmed hats and shorter boots as opposed to South Texas cowboys. Dunigan knew a number of these men, cowboys and young ranchers he had met on business or in his travels.

"Well, hello there, Green. You coming to join up?" asked Tom Mabry, a young rancher from Uvalde, whom Green had done business with.

"No, I was just passing through on my way to the Osage. What is going on here?" Green asked.

"Haven't you heard? It's the war with Spain. Teddy Roosevelt is forming a volunteer cavalry regiment here. The newspapers are calling it 'Roosevelt's Rough Riders.'"

"Who is Teddy Roosevelt?" asked Green.

"He's a Yankee politician from New York, but he used to ranch in the Dakotas," answered Mabry.

"He's more than a Yankee politician," said a well-dressed young man. "He used to be police commissioner of New York City, and was assistant secretary of the navy, and someday he'll be president of the United States. Hi, I'm Edison Grey, Harvard '95." He extended his hand.

Taking it, Green responded, "Green Dunigan, Refugio. Tell me, is he a Democrat?"

"No, Republican ... but a progressive one," answered Grey.

All the young men were excited and voluble, and Green was

having difficulty sorting it all out. He knew about the war with Spain, but not an awful lot.

"Where are we supposed to fight with Spain? Are they invading Florida?"

One of the young Yankees laughed. "No, we're going to liberate Cuba and Puerto Rico, and maybe the Philippines." He, too, extended his hand, saying, "Henry Fieldston, Yale '97. I'll wager it won't take any time to whip the Dons."

It was like that all over the hotel. Groups of Easterners and cowboys waiting to get in on what looked to be a short and glorious little war. Green was pretty sure from all the stories his father had told him that it wouldn't be, but he was carried along with everyone else's enthusiasm.

Pretty soon he found himself with a group of eight, half of whom he knew, squeezed into a corner of the hotel bar, drinking and singing songs as if they were on a college weekend. This went on for several hours, or so it seemed.

As usual, Green awoke at daylight. He counted eight sleeping bodies in the room, which was usually rented as a single. He had no idea where he was, and very little remembrance of the night before. He quietly slipped out the door and into the hall, which he recognized as the Menger Hotel. Reassured, he went downstairs to the coffee shop for a wake-up cup, and seated at the counter, he tried to reconstruct the afternoon and night before. He vaguely remembered a sort of pudgy man with huge teeth and pince-nez being the hero of the hour. He also remembered participating in a mock bayonet charge back and forth across the hotel bar. Beyond that, he was at a loss.

After nights like these, he had a habit of counting his money, to see if he had been robbed. Going through his pockets, he pulled out a sheet of paper and started to read it. In large letters across the top was emblazoned "Certificate of Enlistment."

"Oh, my God," he said under his breath, which was far from being sweet. "Surely I didn't get that drunk."

It was all there. He had enlisted in the 1st Volunteer Cavalry for the duration of the war, or three years, whichever came first. Down at the bottom were two signatures. One, a bit illegible, was unmistakably his own, and the other, much grander, that of Theodore Roosevelt, Lt. Col., 1st Volunteer Cavalry. He was to report the next day to Fort Sam Houston. On further examination, he determined it was a copy, and not the original, so he was enlisted with no way out. He checked his money and found that he was short some, but figured he had spent some during the night. There was also a newly minted $20 gold piece, which he hadn't had before. He guessed it was an enlistment bonus. The fat was truly in the fire.

During breakfast Green had an idea of what to do. After finishing, he took himself to the offices of Jesse Singleton, an old friend of the family who had done a lot of legal work for his father.

Mr. Singleton had just arrived himself when Green got to his office, and bade him come in.

"Mr. Singleton, I need some advice. I got drunk last night and did something I'd like to undo." With that he handed Singleton the paper.

Jesse Singleton, a deliberate man, took his time reading the document and when he had finished, he smiled at Green.

"Boy, what kind of whiskey were you drinking? You have tied yourself to the army for sure. I could possibly get you out of it, but it would take a lawsuit. And you would probably acquire the reputation of cowardice."

"Well, Mr. Singleton, I don't think that's a very good idea. But hell, I don't even remember signing that. Yet I do have that $20 gold piece it mentions."

"Son, the army has had a good deal of experience enlisting people when they didn't want to, and it would be about what I mentioned to get out of it. I know you're not a coward, but that's the way the army does things."

"Well, I guess there's nothing but to do it. Maybe I'll get to see the Pacific or the Philippines. Daddy ain't gonna be very happy about this. He'll probably have to go up north this year to take my place."

"Have you told him yet?"

"No, and I have no time to. I'll have to wire him."

"I suggest you do that, and then write him a letter all about it. By the way, Green, do you have a will?"

Green looked at him blankly, with the realization that in war soldiers often die.

Jesse Singleton read his expression and said, "Don't worry, Green, I'll fix one up for you. I guess you want to leave everything to your brother and sister. That is, unless you've had an earlier night like last night and now have a wife?"

"No, by God. I don't make a habit of it, Mr. Singleton."

"Come back this afternoon and I'll have it ready for you."

Green walked morosely back to the hotel. On the way he stopped and sent his father a wire that read: "Am going to Cuba with a Yankee Republican. Be back in a year or so. Letter follows."

After he sent the wire, he went back to the Menger, to the room in which he had slept. His fellow revelers were awake and moving about. He recognized Tom Mabry and Henry Fieldston, Yale '97, but had no idea who the other six were. They introduced themselves. A couple of them were from the plains, two from New York, and there was an Indian, an Apache reservation policeman from Arizona. All had hangovers and were hungry, so they trooped down to the coffee shop, where they discussed the night before. None of them remembered much about it after the bayonet charge. And none would admit to any knowledge of his enlistment. After breakfast they went to the bar for a little hair of the dog that bit them, and it started all over again.

CHAPTER 2

Fort Sam Houston, Texas / May 1898

Like all first-day recruits, Green Dunigan was confused. After the medical examination, issuance of clothes and equipment, and barrack assignments, he had received all kinds of information for all kinds of purposes. When the army found out about his military background at Texas A&M, he was appointed a temporary platoon sergeant, but he would be closely supervised by a grizzled veteran sergeant brought in from the 8th Cavalry as cadre. Green's authority was mostly to keep other recruits from getting lost. His latest assignment was to show his platoon how to make up their bunks in a military fashion. Most of the Easterners had no idea how to do it, as there had always been plenty of maids everywhere they had been. They didn't seem to resent having to do any of these things for themselves; it was just that they had never done them before.

A trading bazaar had ensued in the barracks, as no one had gotten the right size in the uniform issue. Their last formation for the day, the evening mess call, had been completed, and their sergeant had left in apparent disgust, as is the way of all sergeants in all armies. He had left acting Sergeant Dunigan to straighten up the platoon. He was trying to do just that, but since their barracks were eight-man tents, Green was kept hopping from tent to tent to show the men how to make beds, store their clothes and other things in foot lockers, and generally how to do things the army way.

Green told them all that reveille was at 5:00 A.M., so they should get things ready for tomorrow. After many obscene replies, Green wished he had kept his mouth shut about A&M. He also hoped his hangover would be gone tomorrow, when he knew things would be busy.

All that week the volunteers were taught basics: close order drill and the manual of arms. The level of intelligence being quite high in the regiment, it quickly was able to put on a presentable show. Roosevelt had been able to equip them with Krag-Jorgenson rifles that used smokeless powder, and they were well ahead of the National Guard units being brought in.

The "Rough Riders," because of Roosevelt, had the best of everything and were shaping up well. Green had been promoted permanently to sergeant and assigned to the scout platoon, mainly because of his mastery of Spanish and general woodcraft. During the second week they were to be issued horses, but orders came for the embarkation port at Tampa, and there wasn't time to become mounted. The regiment was designated dismounted, as were all the regular regiments going, and would remain so throughout the campaign. The orders to pack up and leave for Tampa left little time for organizing the move in a military manner. They got on the train, sat down, and were off.

On June 3 the regiment got off at Tampa and set up camp close to the Plant Hotel. The hotel and railroad to Tampa Bay had been created by Morton F. Plant, a real estate developer, and the hotel had been commandeered as army headquarters. The 1st Volunteer Cavalry, 1st Cavalry Division (dismounted), 5th Army Corps was part of that army. The whole organization was quite informal, as units arrived on their own schedules and were left to fend for themselves. Rations were poor to nonexistent, and foraging became a high art. Individualistic in its conception, the regiment became organized more or less by squads, or tentfuls, and each squad saw to its own needs, extending to expropriations of food from the Plant Hotel kitchen.

Gradually, the regiment took shape. Many, including Green, were surprised to find out that their commander was not Roosevelt but Col. Leonard Wood, a mild-mannered surgeon whose main talent seemed to be staying out of Roosevelt's way.

The regiment did manage to get hold of twenty or thirty veteran sergeants to hold it together, but the officers seemed to have little experience with troops. The entire regiment had only been in existence less than sixty days, and the only thing that held it together was its youthful enthusiasm and the high level of intelligence of its membership.

About half of its members were from New England, New York, and Pennsylvania, the scions of well-to-do families, who had been taught self-reliance from birth. The other half were cowboys from the West, who knew the rough discipline of trail herds and ranches, and there were plenty of natural leaders among them. Without this peculiar makeup, and a lot of luck, it could have been a great disaster.

The scout platoon was used to carry messages between regiment, division, and corps headquarters, so Green was able to meet and observe all the commanders. The cavalry division commander was "Fightin' Joe Wheeler," a diminutive ex-Confederate general, and the 5th Corps was commanded by the 300-pound General Shafter, who was suffering badly in the heat of Tampa. Wheeler, on the other hand, was a dynamo of energy, as was Roosevelt, but both were held in check by the ponderous Shafter. So many messages were sent that Green soon knew each commander personally, and had come to the conclusion that Shafter was the only one who had any idea what he was doing.

At midnight on June 7, orders came down to board the transports. After wandering around all night in search of transport, Roosevelt and the Rough Riders commandeered a coal train to take them to the pier of Tampa Bay. The regiment was assigned to the steamer *Yucatan* as transport, and they beat two other regiments to it, as it was every regiment for itself. The Rough Riders held the *Yucatan* until the regiment was loaded. Then, as they had some room, four companies of the 2nd Regulars were placed on board and put out into the roads, to await the formation of the invasion convoy.

The weeklong wait in Tampa harbor was quite unpleasant, what with the heat of June in Florida, the humidity, foul rations, cramped quarters, and nothing to do. Some of the soldiers tried out their weapons on shoaling marine life, turtles, and other targets of opportunity, until orders came down to quit it. During this wait, Green composed a letter of explanation to his father and mother.

11 June 1898
Dear Mother and Father,

You have always warned me of the evils of strong drink, but I never would believe what it got me.

In San Antonio, I joined what seemed to be a party of Gay Blades in the Menger Hotel. Most of these boys were Easterners from Harvard and Yale, bankers and such, and we had a high old time, I guess, for when I woke up the next morning, I was enlisted in the army. I don't remember a lot about that night, except for a fat little fellow, with the biggest teeth I have ever seen. It turns out that he is Theodore Roosevelt, of the "Rough Riders." We are a cavalry regiment but no horses, so we are the 1st Volunteer Cavalry (dismounted). These Easterners are all awfully high on Col. Roosevelt. They say he will be president someday, but I don't quite feel safe with him. All my eastern friends also say this will be over soon as we land in Cuba, but my experience with Mexicans is that they don't roll over dead very easy. We may have a tough time, as the whole expedition is very confused.

I have been promoted to Sergeant Scout, and I am to be a runner between Roosevelt and General Wheeler's headquarters. Wheeler, by the way, was a general in the Confederate Army, so at least he has some experience, which is sadly lacking in our regiment. Being a Sgt., I am in charge of a scout platoon, and have acquired one friend I can count on. His name is Etienne de la Garza, and is from south Louisiana, Cajun country. He says he is a descendant from some of LaFitte's pirates, and by the looks of him, I wouldn't doubt it. We are in this set up because we both speak good Spanish, and should be able to get around good in Cuba.

I am enlisted for the duration of the war or three years, whichever comes first. I hope we can get this over with soon, but at the rate we are moving, I don't think so.

Father, I am really ashamed of myself for getting in this mess, and letting you down. I did talk to Mr. Singleton, but he said I just about had to do it. He knows all about it, so if you need to know anything more about it, talk to him. Also I left my horse at the livery in San Antonio, so if you have a chance you might send him back to the ranch.

Don't worry about me. I'll be alone or with Etienne most of the time, and can escape most of the fights, I hope. Etienne and me are the only democrats in the whole regiment, I guess, but most of these boys seem all right. I know everything will be all right.

Sincerely, your obedient servant, Sgt. Green Dunigan 1st Volunteer Cavalry

The mail cutter came by to pick up and deliver almost every day, and Green was able to post his letter before departing. They lay at anchor for five more days before the flotilla set sail for Cuba and Green's great adventure.

CHAPTER 3

Daiquiri, Cuba / June 22, 1989

he Rough Riders, courtesy of Theodore Roosevelt, who commandeered a steam launch from a naval officer who had once been his aide, got to the beach before almost anyone and were forming up when Wheeler arrived. He had spotted a fortification overlooking the beach and told Roosevelt to take it. Roosevelt sent some men to climb the hill, and about thirty minutes later the Stars and Stripes were raised on its flag pole. Green was following Wheeler around on the beach, just keeping him in sight, but not getting close enough to be sent on errands.

Henry Fieldston, a member of the platoon who had been taken in tow by Green, asked, "Shouldn't we stay up with General Wheeler? He might need us for something."

He was answered by Etienne de la Garza, who understood the army. "Don't worry, boy. He'll have us busy sooner than we're needed."

Green noticed that Roosevelt's constant companions were myriad newspaper reporters, and he figured that was about what this operation was all about. It didn't do much for Green's morale. Richard Harding Davis of the *New York Journal* seemed to be the leader. He was a trim, almost natty, individual, dressed in a suit, sun helmet, and hiking boots, and was somewhat deferred to by the others.

The debarkation was much like the embarkation—every man for himself. Individuals and units got there any way they could; there was no order on the beach whatsoever. But as the unit commander finally got their outfits together and picked up stragglers, things began to take shape.

About that time, General Wheeler signaled to Green, and Green ran over to him.

"Sergeant Dunigan, get all the regimental commanders up here for a meeting, and you and your platoon stand by. We are going on a reconnaissance after the meeting."

Green sent runners off to get the regimental commanders, and moved out of the way.

Wheeler spoke with his subordinates for about fifteen minutes, at which point they all returned to their units. Wheeler then called Green. "Dunigan, bring your platoon and let's go," he said, and off they went, west along the trail to Siboney, another beach closer to Santiago.

Siboney was abandoned when they arrived, except for a naval beach party that was surveying the beach as a supply post for the army. Word was that General Lawton, the ground commander, was on his way, but there was no sign of him. Just north of Siboney, a few Spanish soldiers were observed in the woods, so Green's platoon was sent to flush them out. Green's fears were realized when one of his men was killed and two were wounded. The five or six Spanish soldiers were put to flight, except for two, who were killed. Green observed that the Spanish rifles were accurate and effective, so he expropriated one from a dead Spaniard, along with a bandolier of ammunition.

The weapon proved to be of the new mauser design, about 7mm caliber. It was much superior to the Swedish Krags that the Rough Riders used. Green exchanged with the fallen Spaniard, figuring he could pick up more ammunition the same way.

Green buried his dead, treated the wounded, and left them with the navy beach party. Wheeler instructed him to send runners back to Daiquiri to bring up his regiments first thing the next day, and to load as much ammunition and food as they could carry.

General Wheeler and his staff moved north off the beach and

set up camp to wait for the rest of the division. Green and the eight men he had left there spent the night with them.

On the morning of the 23rd, Wheeler designated bivouacs for the formations coming up. Green furnished the rest of his men as guides to take the regiments to their bivouacs and sent them down the road to Daiquiri. Then he, Wheeler, and the staff intelligence officer found the road to Santiago, as well as a trail in the jungle parallel to it. Where the two came together, they observed some Spanish soldiers apparently forming a defensive position, so the little party stole away unseen back to Siboney.

At Siboney, the regiments began arriving, led by the guides to their bivouac areas. As usual, Roosevelt's Rough Riders, followed by the reporters, led the way. General Lawton had arrived and set up his headquarters and was trying to organize his troops. This was not easy, as Wheeler was senior to him in rank but junior in command, and getting "Fightin' Joe" in hand was difficult at best. Wheeler knew where he wanted to go, and the way to go, but Lawton was ignorant of the lay of the land. Green decided that his best interests would be served by keeping his mouth shut.

Wheeler had managed to get the Rough Riders and two squadrons of regulars to Siboney, but Lawton had blocked the trail with the rest of his division, so that no more cavalrymen could be expected until the next day.

That night Wheeler issued a warning order. The Rough Riders would slip out of camp at 5:00 A.M. and take the parallel trail to meet the two regular squadrons at Guasimas. The regulars would take the Santiago Road, also being careful to slip away unnoticed by General Lawton.

With Green and Etienne de la Garza acting as scouts and guides, the Rough Riders left at the designated hour and proceeded up the trail. The regiment was thrashing its way through the jungle, unable to see more than ten yards in any direction, but still making progress toward their objective, when they began to hear small-arms fire from the direction of the Santiago Road and the regular squadrons. It was only a little while later that the sharp report of the mauser rifles was heard and some of the blue-shirted volunteers began to fall.

With no maneuvering room in the jungle, Roosevelt drew his sword and urged his men forward. They finally broke out of the thick underbrush and linked up with the regulars just in time to see the Spaniards debouch from their breastworks and retreat. Lawton had sent an infantry regiment to extricate them but arrived to see the enemy retreating.

The casualties were high, considering the numbers engaged, and included one reporter, his spine being smashed by a mauser bullet. The rest of them ran back to file their stories of the glorious victory at Guasimas. As the troops watched the dead and wounded being carried back to Siboney, they knew they were in a war. It came as quite a shock to the gallant young men of Roosevelt's Rough Riders.

Wheeler and Lawton's division took position on a ridge five or six miles from Santiago. They had only gotten a bloody nose, but they still had to breach the defenses of that city. There were no college songs that night.

CHAPTER 4

Before San Juan Hill / June 30, 1898

O n the ridge overlooking the San Juan River, 5th Army Corps had set up their lines, pending orders to attack, but did not move out for almost a week. There was no offensive action from the Spaniards, and the scout platoon was kept busy, searching for information and weakness in the Spanish lines.

By this time, Green was being utilized by Shafter's headquarters, reporting directly to the general himself. He had secured five horses, so that his scouts were generally more mobile and efficient.

Green and three of his men rode into corps headquarters at 8:00 A.M., after spending all night surveying enemy lines. He approached the general to report.

"Sergeant Dunigan reporting, sir."

"Ah, Dunigan ... have you found anything for me to use?"

"No, sir. The wire is pretty well in place all the way to El Caney, and the trenches are well dug. The good thing is that there doesn't seem to be any Spanish guns in the lines. We did kill three sentries in listening posts, and that should worry them some, but we didn't find any weak spot. It's going to be a hard nut to crack."

"Thank you, Sergeant. Get your men some rest, for I'll be sending out orders later."

General Shafter had a conference with his division commanders, and orders were issued. The approach march was to begin at 3:00 P.M., with the general advance in the morning. Lawton's division was to attack El Caney first, then one infantry and one cavalry division were to attack San Juan Hill and Kettle Hill. The lack of roads for the approach march, as well as the lack of cover for deployment, ensured that there would be plenty of confusion—and there was, especially when the Spaniards started firing on the approaching troops.

The battle began at 7:00 A.M., with the artillery firing at El Caney. Billows of white smoke poured out of the cannons and obscured the vision of the gunners, who could not then adjust the fire. It had the further effect of pinpointing the guns for the Spanish artillery, who returned fire and silenced the American artillery. Green, riding forward with a message for Lawton to get moving, observed all this and wondered why his troops didn't have smokeless powder.

The battle developed from bad to worse. Lawton's division remained bogged down before El Caney. The cavalry and infantry got mixed and clogged on the trails to San Juan Hill, and when they finally deployed they faced the Spanish lines on more than 500 yards of open uphill terrain. Casualties were being taken from the deadly mausers, but every soldier realized that to retreat was to run into advancing columns that clogged the trails, so they turned to advance on the Spanish lines.

Green was returning from General Lawton to General Shafter when he ran into a battery of Gatling guns commanded by a Lieutenant Parker, sent up with vague orders to help out.

"Is there a place where I can get my guns into action and help out?" Parker asked Dunigan.

"You bet, Lieutenant, just follow us." He and de la Garza led the battery out to the San Juan River, dismounted, and helped them into action. The effect of the battery's fire on the Spanish lines was immediate. The Spanish troops fell back on Santiago, firing as they retreated.

The attack then carried San Juan and Kettle Hills, but Green was struck in the upper leg by a bullet as he was helping the Gatling gunners. Green fell by the guns and was pulled back by Etienne and one of the gunners to a depression that sheltered him, and Etienne bandaged his wound.

"Ugly hole, Green, but don't seem like no bones broke. You try standing."

Green tried, but the pain made him cry out and fall down.

"Maybe bone is broken, but hole is clean, not shattered. I got it good and clean. You be all right," comforted Etienne, just as Green passed out.

In the early hours of July 4, Green awoke in Clara Barton's Hospital at Siboney. He asked the nurse changing his dressing, "Lady, where am I, and how did I get here?"

"Sergeant, you are in Miss Clara Barton's Hospital at Siboney. Further, you have a nasty bullet hole in your thigh and your thigh bone is fractured. You were delivered here by an irate corporal who brought you here on what appeared to be an Indian travois, behind a horse. The corporal then proceeded to threaten dire consequences if you died or lost your leg." The nurse paused, then continued.

"I am happy to report that neither of those calamities appears to be in the offing. That corporal, who spoke with a French accent, stayed until all seemed to be well. He had done a good job of cleaning your wound and stopping the bleeding."

"Good old Etienne. He probably saved my life," said Green.

The nurse smiled. "You'll probably be sent back to Florida soon, as we have many casualties here who really can't be moved yet."

"That'll be just fine with me. By the way, nurse, when do we eat around here? I'm kinda hungry."

"We'll be bringing breakfast soon," she said as she walked off on her rounds.

Green was given crutches the next day and was taught how to use them. The following day he left Cuba behind, on a boat to New Orleans. He was feeling a bit feverish but figured it was just part of his being wounded. It wasn't. His feverishness was a full-blown case of malaria, and he traveled unconscious most of the way to New Orleans. On arrival his fever had broken, and he was transported to the Military Hospital in New Orleans for recovery.

CHAPTER 5

New Orleans / July 20, 1898

Lying in the enlisted ward at New Orleans Military Hospital, Green was still weak from the malaria and did not try to get up and use his crutches. The hospital was activated to take the overflow from Florida, and none of the yellow fever patients had been sent there. There were nine other men and six empty beds in the ward, so all were pretty well treated.

By the 22nd Green had rested well and felt he had gained some strength. But the nurses wouldn't let him do much moving on his crutches, for fear of a malarial relapse, and put him back into bed any time he tried to move.

"Nurse, since you don't want me moving around, could you get my barracks bag for me? I want to check my gear and see how much I have left."

The nurse brought his duffel bag to him, and he was surprised to find all his things, except the uniform he had been wearing when he was shot. Even the mauser rifle he had expropriated was there, as was his money.

Green worried that his family might have gotten a wire from the War Department saying he was wounded, so he wrote a message to tell them that his wound wasn't life threatening, and where he was. He put $5 in with it and asked a nurse to send it.

"The War Department has already informed your family. It is entirely unnecessary," she informed him.

"Nurse, you know how mothers worry. I just want to be sure they know I'm all right, and out of harm's way."

"Yes, and the next thing is that your whole family will be here, disrupting my ward, Sergeant."

"I won't let them. You can rely on it."

"Oh, all right, but if they show up here, I don't want them stirring anything up," she added.

Three days later, Green was able to stand on his crutches for the colonel and general who came to award decorations. Green was decorated for his wound and for meritorious service, as he had been mentioned in dispatches for his part in guiding Lieutenant Platt's Gatling guns and getting them into action. Everyone in the ward got at least one medal, and several, like Green, got two.

As his medal was being pinned on, Green asked, "General, how goes the war?"

"It goes well, Sergeant. Cuba is taken, the Philippines and Puerto Rico pacified. All we need now is a treaty. The army is going to be expanded. There'll be plenty of room in it for a soldier like yourself, Sergeant."

"Thank you, General, but I've had all of it I want. Do you have any idea when the volunteers are going to be demobilized?"

"Pretty soon, I think. You really ought to consider staying in. With your record and your backing, you could probably count on being commissioned an officer. You do know that General Shafter himself wrote the recommendation for your medal?"

"No, I didn't know that, and I am proud that he did. But General, I am a cowboy at heart, not a warrior, and I want to get back to my old life."

"Well, best of luck to you, Sergeant, and come to see me if you change your mind."

Green got back into bed when the officers left. He wasn't too agile on crutches yet, and was even weaker than he thought from the malaria, and he immediately dropped off to sleep.

When he awoke it was late afternoon, and John and Amanda Dunigan were beside him.

"Well, I'm glad to see you are still alive, Green," his father said, as his mother embraced him, shedding tears.

"Green, what has happened to you? How badly are you hurt?" asked Amanda.

"Mother, I just got shot in the leg and it's broken, but not badly. I've had malaria, too, but that's over now. Dad, if you can work it, I'd like to go home as soon as I can. I've had all the soldiering I want."

"Well, I don't really know what I can do, but let me see. I used to know lots of army people. Perhaps some of them are still around," Dunigan said.

Green caught up on all the news from home in their visit that lasted more than an hour. As they were leaving, Amanda said, "This is the first time I have been in New Orleans since our honeymoon, when your father got involved in a duel with that horrible man. I hope there aren't any warrants lying around."

"Amanda, all that was over twenty-five years ago. Don't let it bother you," John said.

They left, saying they would be back in the morning.

However, John Dunigan did not come back with Amanda the following morning.

"Son, your father has gone to army headquarters to see what he can do about getting you out," she explained. She had brought him a pair of pajamas, as she disliked the issue nightshirts worn in the hospital. She also brought him a robe and slippers. Green was pleased with these gifts, but the hospital nurses were put out. All things needed to be equal in the hospital, in their view, and individuality was, if not forbidden, frowned upon. Nor did Amanda endear herself to the nurses, trying to do everything for her son. The other ward residents got a laugh out of the nurses' discomfort and envied Green his mother's care. All of the patients in the ward were battle casualties, and Amanda talked to them all, making them feel that she cared about each. The regular nurses were highly incensed but were not about to confront Amanda.

John Dunigan joined them in the midafternoon. Green was especially anxious to hear what he had found out.

"Well, there is something good. The army, it seems, wants to return the National Guard back to their respective states, but they are not quite ready to release the volunteers. I got the idea that

20

Roosevelt wants to have a good victory parade in New York City with them. Ain't that just like a politician."

"I can't march in any parade. My leg's broken, and it's not healing any too fast."

"It won't heal as long as you move around so much, and malaria doesn't do much for bone growth either," volunteered the ward nurse, in defense of her profession.

"How can anything heal in this Turkish bath?" asked Green. "I've never sweated so much in my life."

"Green, get back into bed and stay there. Getting upset is not going to help," Amanda commanded, trying to keep things from getting out of hand.

The other ward patients, having heard all of this, were highly amused and glad to see the authority of the despotic ward nurse challenged. None of them was ready to join the rebellion, however, and things quieted down.

John Dunigan regained the floor. "I think I may have found a way, but I'm not sure I want you to do it, Green." He paused then went on. "If you sign a release from all claims on the army, they may let you go, but I don't think your leg has healed enough to do that yet."

"It's just this cast, and the malaria. If I could get back home to breathe good air, I know I would be walking in no time. Besides, you and Mother didn't see the yellow jack. It killed more of us than the Spaniards did, and the longer I stay around, the more likely I am to come down with it," explained Green.

This really upset Amanda. She turned to Dunigan in anguish, for, contrary to what Green thought, they both had read of the horrors of yellow fever among the troops.

"Please, John, get my boy out of here," Amanda begged.

It was settled.

John Dunigan acted as Green's agent and was able to get him released several days later. Green had to give up any future claims but could claim against them for his wound. Although they tried not to, John demanded they give his son his back pay and mustering out pay, amounting to over $800.

Green was released from the hospital on August 1. He and his parents caught the train that evening and arrived back at the Aransas River Ranch on August 3. Green was feeling woozy as he fell into bed upon arrival.

CHAPTER 6

Dunigan Ranch, Refugio County, Texas /

August 10, 1898

hen Green awoke, he had almost no recollection of anything since arriving home August 3. It was early, but he
could hear activity in the kitchen. He started to get up to
get a cup of coffee but was so weak that he couldn't even throw the
bed covers off his body. He called out, and quickly Amanda appeared at his bed.

"Mother, have I been sick? I am as weak as a newborn calf."

"Green, you have been out of your head for almost a week. The
doctor said it was a recurrence of the malaria you had from Cuba,
but your fever broke yesterday, and you are going to be all right. We
all thanked God that you were allowed to live."

Amanda was haggard and bedraggled, a condition he had never
before seen. Green guessed that his mother had not left his bedside
the whole time he had been ill, and he was right.

"I'll bet you're hungry, aren't you?" Amanda asked cheerfully.

"No, Mother, all I want is a cup of coffee and maybe some soup,
if there is any."

He was helped to a chair to drink the coffee and soup, and the bed was made up with fresh linens. His mother and the house maid then changed his pajamas and washed him, much to his embarrassment.

"Mother, get out of here! I'm naked. You and Juana can't do this," he protested.

"Who do you think has been doing it for the past week—John Dunigan and Abel Castro?"

Trying to stand, the pain from his broken leg hit him, and he collapsed into the chair, where he submitted to the ladies' ministrations. After they finished, he was put back into bed, where he slept until the next morning.

Green Dunigan's recovery took a long time. By Thanksgiving his wound had healed over, and by Christmas he was able to move about with crutches. In March he began to walk about with the help of a cane, and the day after Easter he rode a horse, although he had to be helped on by Abel Castro. Abel took him home with him for a week of Sulema's cooking, and Green felt stronger. It was the first time he had eaten the food that he had grown up on in over a year, and it tasted like heavenly ambrosia to him. Frijoles, tortillas, and as a surprise, roasted kid (called *cabrito*), all cooked with plenty of grease to, as Sulema said, "make you pretty." He rode back at the end of a week, a little fatter, but still unable to mount without help. A mounting block was installed in front of the house, and an extra stirrup was added to his saddle to facilitate Green's ability to mount a horse. A scabbard for Green's cane was added to the saddle as well.

All these things helped, but mostly it was Green growing stronger every day. He still was not fully recovered, but he even helped out during the spring shipping, if not with the rough work. Mostly, he handled records and bills of lading to cover the cattle that were being sent to the Osage and Flint Hills pastures.

By June, Green was nearly recuperated, though still conscious of overexerting himself and bringing on another relapse of malaria. He did not go north that year with the Dunigan steers but continued with his rehabilitation in Texas. Pete Roussell, the Aransas ranch foreman, who had handled that job before Green came back from college, went instead.

Green visited the Salado Creek Ranch two or three times that year. He and his brother Jack were very close, even as different as they were, and Jack's wife, Lucinda, was as solicitous of Green's health as his mother. The twin boys loved their uncle and spent a lot of time with him. The Dunigan family ties had always been very tight. Green also visited his sister Kathleen and her family. Kathleen had tried matchmaking with some of the belles of Brownsville, but Green wasn't too romantically inclined, as he was still recuperating.

Green made an effort during this period to keep in touch with two of his comrades-in-arms, Henry Fieldston and Etienne de la Garza. Fieldston had become a banker in New York with the J. P. Morgan interests after he was mustered out, and Etienne, a natural-born warrior, was just passing time until the next war. Green invited them both to visit, and Etienne promised to "when de muskrats lose dey hair." Fieldston was less committal, saying he was busy financing great empires and trying to get in position to help Colonel Roosevelt become president, which was all he really talked about.

By the end of summer, Green felt strong. He was fully recovered, and able to get about without a cane. All that remained was an ugly scar on his thigh and a slight depression where he had lost some muscle. He felt whole again and became fully active in his old activities. Amanda would not agree to him leaving the ranch until the spring, but she knew she couldn't hold him back after that. Green attended social functions in San Antonio and Corpus Christi that fall and winter, and cut a fine figure as the handsome, decorated hero from Cuba.

CHAPTER 7

Osage Indian Reservation, Indian Territory /

July 16, 1900

There was great sorrow in the Osage village. The old chief, Black Deer, had died early that morning, and there was much lamentation. He had become chief sometime during the Civil War and had led the village wisely and peacefully until his death.

Green Dunigan had ridden down from Kansas to look at the 1,500 steers summering on Osage grass, as they had been for about thirty years. He had come to the village to recruit some help to cut out and drive north about 300 fat steers that would ride the railroad from Wichita to Kansas City.

On arriving at the village, he was told of the old chief's death. Green, of course, delayed his cattle work and participated in the funeral ceremonies. The rites went on for two full days, because Black Deer had been chief for so long and was truly beloved by the village.

The Dunigans had summered fewer and fewer steers through the years on the Osage. The Kansas Flint Hill pastures had better rail transportation and were closer to the market at Kansas City, but the real reason for the thinning of herds in the Osage was that officials from the Indian Bureau had become more and more intrusive. The Dunigans had always paid for pasturage in beef, thus assuring the food supply for the winter. But the Indian Bureau objected, as their friends had lucrative trading posts on the reservation, so Dunigan began to pay in cash.

Other harassments were used to disrupt this long-standing arrangement, but finally Black Deer turned away from the Indian Bureau and made his deals directly with John Dunigan. The bureaucrats tried to disrupt this, but Dunigan used countervailing pressure from Texas office holders in Washington who had no Indian Bureau influence. Still, the Osages had lost land to the Oklahoma land rush in 1889, and as Oklahoma approached statehood, the pressure of in-state ranchers to use the Indian pastures all combined to cause Dunigan to move the bulk of his operation into the Kansas Flint Hills.

The day after the funeral of Black Deer, a strange white man appeared in the village. Dressed in a three-piece suit, and wearing low quarter shoes and a straw boater, he was definitely not a cowman. Green was still recruiting his outfit when this man walked up and introduced himself.

"I am Robert J. Folsom of the Indian Bureau. What are you doing on this reservation?" he asked.

Green replied, "I am getting some help to drive my steers to Wichita, Mr. Folson. Have you come to pay your last respects to Black Deer?"

"Well, yes. But I also want to know if you have filed with the bureau to do business here. If not, I can't allow you on the reservation."

"Mr. Folson, my family has grazed steers on the Osage lands for thirty years. We have enjoyed a mutual benefit with Black Deer's people, and the Indian Bureau has been no help to either side. We have our own deal. So why don't you just let it alone?"

With that, Folson pulled out a notebook and pencil. "What is your name and who do you represent, young man?"

"My name is Green Dunigan, and I represent the Dunigan Cattle Company of Refugio County, Texas," Green replied evenly.

"Do you have a grazing permit from the Indian Bureau?"

"We have several permits, but the one we operate under is the permit from Black Deer."

"How many cattle do you have here?"

"We have 1,500 steers, 300 of which I intend to move to market tomorrow, leaving about 1,200."

"Well, I know you don't have our permit, and I will be back tomorrow to confiscate the steers that are here," Folson replied.

"If you try to move one of the steers on this place, you'd better come armed, and with plenty of help," Green told him.

"Are you threatening me? I'll have you arrested right here!" screamed Folson. He looked around for the tribal police and spotted two of them looking on. "Here, you two, come here. I want you to arrest this man. I am Indian Bureau Agent Folson, your superior," he yelled.

The two Indians were indeed the legally constituted authority on the reservation, but their authority had been from Black Deer, not the Indian Bureau. One stepped forward and said to Folson, "We not arrest him. Dunigan cattle fed us every winter, and he is our friend. He no steal like Indian agent."

"You are no longer reservation policemen unless you arrest him immediately," shouted Folson.

"Black Deer make us police. New chief keep us or not, not you."

Folson turned on his heels and bellowed, "You haven't seen the last of me," as he walked away.

That night Green met with the village elders. He was qualified to do so, as both he and his father had been adopted into the tribe several years back. Green was worried about the Indian Bureau agents trying to confiscate his cattle during the interval between Black Deer's death and the establishment of a new chief powerful enough to keep the Indian Bureau at bay, as Black Deer had done.

"My brothers, I do not want to lose control of our steers here. I think that I had better move them now. I want to pay you for a full season, as we have in the past, and I want to leave here with a title to them, two steers for each hundred as rental, thirty in all, but I believe I should move the balance now," Green told them, and waited for comment.

"My brother Green," started Prairie Dog Tom, one of the elders. "You and your father have been the only whites who have treated us fairly, and we want to do what is right. But the wages and fees that you pay our people have sustained us, and we hate to lose these moneys."

"I know that, and if this is straightened out, I want to come back next year. However, I fear the Indian Bureau could keep my cattle for years, and it would be a great hardship on us both."

Green did not want to participate in the choosing of a new chief and wanted to get his business over with first, but the Indians discussed the matter for almost two hours. Finally Green agreed to leave forty steers if he could start the next day. The elders agreed, and Green gave them two bottles of whiskey to help their deliberations.

The cattle were gathered and on the way before noon the next day. It would be a short drive. The equipment they would need had been left on the reservation during the years the Dunigans had used the Osage grass, and the Indians were well-trained drovers, so no difficulties were expected.

About 4:00 the next afternoon, Green saw a small dust cloud to the southeast. Green figured he was all right, as he knew the trail well enough to know he had passed into Kansas about five miles back. Also, he had two of the tribal policemen with him for further protection. They had traveled about three miles further into Kansas when an Indian policeman on a well-lathered pony rode up to Green.

"Stop these cattle and turn them around," he ordered. "They are the property of the Indian Bureau, and you have no right to move them. You will turn them around and drive them back to the Osage reservation, and await Agent Folson's pleasure."

"Do you have a warrant?" Green asked softly.

"I don't need no warrant. I am a Creek policeman. I am White Wolf," he announced.

The two Osage policemen had moved to flank White Wolf on each side by that time, so Green asked him again, "Have you any paper or authorization to take these cattle?"

White Wolf took a paper out of his tunic pocket and handed it to Green. It was an order for impoundment of 1,500 steers signed by one Abner Robin Feather, a justice of the peace of the Creek Nation, countersigned by Agent Folson.

"This paper is only good on the Creek reservation. The Osage tribe does not recognize it," Green said as the two Indians nodded in furious agreement, "and it is certainly invalid in the state of Kansas, where we are now. You take this paper back to Agent Folson and tell him to stick it up his ass."

White Wolf's face fell almost to his knees. He was gently but firmly escorted by the Osage policemen back to the trail to Oklahoma. One of them remarked how he had always wanted a Creek finger, but they harmed him none.

The next day, as they passed the little town of Wellington, Green rode in to send a wire to Bob Wilson in Emporia. Wilson was the commission agent most Texans used to locate summer pastures. Green outlined his problem, saying he would be shipping 300 steers the next day, and that Wilson should find a home for the other 1,200 for the balance of the season. He rejoined the herd and they drove on to Wichita, arriving about 10:00 the next day.

Green cut out 300 steers and shipped them to Kansas City for sale.

"Mr. Dunigan, I have a wire for you," called the railroad agent, just as they finished.

The wire from Bob Wilson related that he had found pasture for 1,200 steers with Sol Clagett just up the line at Bazar.

Green asked the agent, "When can I ship these steers to Bazar?"

"You can load them this afternoon, if you want, and they'll go first thing in the morning. Get to Bazar about 3:00 tomorrow."

"That'll be fine. Will you send a wire for me to Sol Clagett to expect them?"

"I surely will, Mr. Dunigan, and I'll be ready to load at 3:30."

"Fine. Can I leave them in the pens until then?" Green asked.

"Sure can. If you'll come by about 3:00, I'll have all the freight bills ready for you."

"I'll be there, and I'll be going with the cattle, and taking my horse."

Green penned the herd, paid off his Indians, and wished them well, saying he would see them in the spring. He asked for their assistance in loading the steers before they left.

The cars came on time, were loaded, and Green rode the caboose to Bazar the next morning.

Sol Clagett and his crew unloaded the steers, and he and Green settled on a price for the short season. Green found out he could catch a local to Kansas City that night, so he and Clagett shook hands and Green was on hand when his fat steers sold in the Kansas City yards the next day. He thought he ought to inform his father about all this, so he sent him a wire:

Black Deer died. Trouble with Indian Bureau agent. Moved 1,200 steers to Sol Clagett, Bazar, and sold rest to market. Letter follows. Green

The following week Green tended to the cattle scattered throughout the Flint Hills, numbering almost 3,500 steers even after the early shipments made in July. More steers were shipped that week, as shipments would continue into September, until they were all marketed. The cattle had done well because of timely rains and a good market. The profits generated to Dunigan weren't like those in the '70s and '80s, when cattle and grass were free, but they were adequate.

Green enjoyed what he was doing, working cattle in the country early each week and then watching the cattle sell later in town, either in Kansas City or St. Joe, in Missouri. He had made a lot of friends in Kansas but was careful not to infringe on their sensibilities, as some of the Texans did. There was still a lot of hostility between Texans and Kansans left over from the Civil War and early trail-driving days, exacerbated by the fact that most of the cattle were owned by Texans but tended to by Kansans. One had to span a fine line if one wanted to be acceptable to both groups, as Green was.

CHAPTER 8

St. Louis, Missouri / August 21, 1900

reen had shipped, or arranged to ship, all of the steers fat enough for slaughter off the Flint Hill pastures. He would have a residue of about 500 steers that would be sold to farmers for further fattening on their corn crops that winter. Green had come east in search of buyers for them and had been visiting an old family friend and banker, Gerard Alton, in St. Louis. Alton and his wife, Genievieve, were the oldest of friends, going back to the '70s with the Dunigan family.

Of course, Aunt Ginny, as Green called her, was delighted to have him as a guest. She was a born matchmaker, and with a genuine handsome, wealthy war hero in her presence she was having a fine time trying to market the belles of St. Louis. She wasn't getting much cooperation from Green.

"You are just like your father, Green Dunigan, I am trying to show you the cream of St. Louis, and, as your father before you, you won't get serious," said Genievieve.

"Well, Aunt Ginny, you must admit, Father's choice, when he made it, was superior. Maybe I ought to travel over to Kentucky, like my father did," he teased.

"You know how much I love both your parents, but that doesn't mean there aren't plenty of eligible, fine young ladies here. There is a ball tonight, and Eve Lampson and Claire Dumont will both be there, so you be ready and dressed before 8:00," she commanded.

Green winced at the idea of putting on tails for the second time that week. He countered, "Maybe Mr. Alton can help me find a farm around Hayes, or Garden City, and I'll find me a farm girl who can pack plenty of water and marry her. Then I can sit on the porch and grow rich selling irrigated tomatoes. Could you do that, Mr. Alton?" asked Green.

Gerard Alton could barely keep from bursting out with laughter, but contained his mirth and replied, "I dunno Green, that land is bringing pretty good prices, and the supply of stout farm girls seems to be dwindling. A whole bunch of young fellows must have the same idea."

Genievieve Alton was not going to stand for both of them teasing her, and she gave them absolute orders. "Both of you go put on your dress clothes and get back downstairs before 8:00, as I don't want to be late. You can get a snack in the kitchen if you want, but there will be a late supper at the ball after midnight."

Alton and Green grabbed a quick sandwich in the kitchen and went up to prepare. When they came back down into the parlor, Genievieve was awaiting them, a gold-headed walking stick in her hands.

"Green, I want you to use this. Amanda wrote me that you had a horrible wound and that you used a cane. Besides, it'll make you look very dashing."

"Genievieve, quit trying to peddle him, will you? It's bad enough having to wear these clothes and go to these balls," protested her husband.

"Well, you could use one, too, as creaky as you are getting. I have one for you, too."

Both men shut up and started for the door in case Genievieve had secured capes and opera hats for them.

The ball was elegant. All the girls were quite beautiful in their new Paris finery. Green danced with most of them, and they did find him quite dashing. He suggested a buggy ride and picnic in the country or a quiet dinner at a downtown hotel, but he could get no takers. None of them wanted to be caught alone with him. Seduction was not nearly as high on their list of priorities as it was on Green's. He did dine with one of the young ladies, but she wasn't buying either.

Green went home with Genievieve and Alton at about 1:00 A.M. The younger ones stayed on until the wee hours, but Green begged that he needed some sleep.

Rising early, he crossed the river to east St. Louis and went to the stockyards. He was known at this place, as he had marketed steers there in the past, and he visited with a commission agent he had dealt with previously. Some traders were looking for steers to be fed, and he talked to them. All of them were a bit wary of South Texas cattle, but most of them knew the Dunigan cattle by reputation. He sold the steers to a trader, agreed on price and delivery, collected a down payment, and went back across the river to deposit the money in Alton's bank. On the way he stopped at a telegraph office and wired his pasture men to have all the cattle at Matfield Green Railroad pens on September 15 for delivery. He also wired his father to tell him what he had accomplished.

Green sat down beside Gerard Alton's desk to do his banking. Gerard had been president of the bank for over ten years and ran it absolutely, and one of the reasons for his position was his successful relationship with John Dunigan. So when he talked to Green, he was dealing from a strong position.

Green handed him the down payment, with a synopsis of the trade, and sat back.

"Green, you know this bank has had a long and profitable history with your father. I was thinking maybe you'd like to get started with us while I'm still here."

"Mr. Alton, I'm mighty flattered that you'd want me as a customer, and I'd like to be one. Looking at it from my point of view, I might like to start with someone closer to my own age, as you might just be thinking of retiring. I know my father has nearly turned over everything to Jack and me, and he is younger than you," Green replied.

"You're absolutely right, and I was going to introduce you to one of our bright young bankers, name of Ben Davidson. His folks have a pretty good-sized ranch in the Nebraska Sand Hills, and I think you two would get along good."

"Mr. Alton, St. Louis is a long way from Texas. I wonder if we could set up something that we could kind of handle with a bank closer to home, say in San Antonio or Victoria?"

"We have a correspondent bank in Victoria, and perhaps we could set it up with them handling up to a $50,000 line with us backing it up with a $100,000 line. How does that sound?"

"That sounds about like what I'd like to do. I know some of those Victoria bankers, and they are all right. The Welders, O'Connors, and McFaddins all do their banking there, and they know all about cattle finance."

Green hesitated, and then continued, "Mr. Alton, I'll need to put up some money, won't I? I have some cash and some bonds that I could put up as collateral. Would $10,000 in Victoria and $20,000 here be enough? That'd be twenty percent."

"I think so, Green. We would,be willing to do it without that, but we'd probably then be depending on your father, and so would Victoria. But I think you want to do this on your own, am I right?"

"Yes, sir, you are."

"Well, we're in agreement on that. Let me get Ben up here and we'll go to lunch and discuss it."

Ben Davidson walked into the president's office with some trepidation. He had only been with the bank about six months and had not handled any loan bigger than 100 acres of wheat. He knew Gerard Alton but had never been called to his office. He saw the young man with him and said to himself, "Probably another hog-feeder. I came to this bank because they financed big cattlemen, and the closest I have come is a milk cow."

When he saw Green's Stetson on the hat rack, he reconsidered.

"Ben, this is Green Dunigan. As you may know, we have done business with his father for a long time, and Green wants to get on with us. I thought maybe you might be the one to handle it," said Alton.

"I certainly would, sir," he extended his hand. "Glad to meet you, Mr. Dunigan."

"Call me Green. Mr. Dunigan is my father." They all chuckled at that.

Alton said, "Come on, you two, let's get some lunch. My club all right?"

"Yes, sir," Ben and Green said in unison.

Ben knew about the Dunigans, both from history with the bank and their general reputation in the cattle business. Dunigan was a name to be reckoned with in the cattle trade. A man who handled that many cattle was legendary, especially one who had broken trail with 5,000 cows to Montana in the early seventies.

The three of them had a nice lunch at the city club and discussed details of the line of credit. Green told them that he had from time to time put out Mexican yearlings on some ranches south of Raton in New Mexico for summer grazing, and that was what he would do with this credit line.

"I know this country by reputation only," Ben said, "but I would like to see it sometime before we finance cattle on it, if it wouldn't be too much trouble. You know how some of these tightwads are on that loan committee, Mr. Alton. And although I know it has your approval, I don't want any talk about being the boss's pet," Ben explained.

"I'd like it that way, too, Mr. Alton," echoed Green.

"Well, now that you both have done away with me, can I at least make the arrangements with the Victoria Bank?"

"Of course, Mr. Alton. I wouldn't know how," said Ben.

"Ben, I'll be in El Paso after New Year's. Suppose I meet you in Raton about January 15. You can see the country then. It won't be in its Sunday clothes, but you might be able to get some kind of idea about it," Green suggested.

"If the bank will let me get away," he glanced at Gerard Alton, who nodded, "I can find more out about the country just talking to the natives, if Billy the Kid didn't kill them all."

"Well, that kind of wraps it up," said Alton. "I'll get in touch with the bankers in Victoria, and Ben, you take care of the papers. Green is going to be here two or three more days, so we have time to get it all moving. After he sells his steers in Kansas on September 15, we can tie it all up then."

"Uh, Mr. Alton, could Ben meet me in Kansas and kind of see me in action? We could finish up everything down there, and I wouldn't have to backtrack. I could go straight home."

Gerard Alton sat back in his chair. "You boys are going to do this on your own and move me all the way out, aren't you? Well, it's time I was getting out anyway. But Ben, you do it right for the bank, you hear me?"

"Yes, sir, Mr. Alton, it'll be done right. You can rely on me."

And Gerard Alton knew he had chosen the right man.

CHAPTER 9

Matfield Green, Kansas / September 15, 1900

reen delivered the tail-end steers on the agreed-upon date. Ben Davidson had come down from St. Louis and was delighted to be working with the cattle. He helped with sorting and loading and anything else there was to do. Dressed in western clothes, he was indistinguishable from the Kansas cowboys.

After the cattle had been loaded and the train left, Green and Ben went to the boardinghouse where they had rooms, to finalize their banking business.

"Mr. Alton fixed up everything with the Victoria Bank. You might just get your dad to deposit some money there. That's what they would really like, although they didn't require it. They want all the cattle bought on bill-of-sale drafts, but so do we. All you have to do is buy the first 50,000 on their bank, and the rest on us. You need to sign chattel mortgages for both banks, and also notes. The interest rate is seven and a half percent for both banks, which is a little high, but you know how banks are," Ben explained.

Green signed all the papers and gave them to Ben, along with the check for the steers they had shipped that day. The check totaled almost $20,000. "Not bad for a bunch of tails," said Green, and Ben nodded agreement. "My father would say that the whole bunch wouldn't have brought that much in the 'good old days.'" Green laughed, and both expressed the opinion that the "good old days" probably never were.

After they had finished their banking, Green asked, "Ben, instead of Raton, just stay on the Santa Fe and get off at Springer when you come in January. Most of the pastures that I generally use are within a half day's ride from there. I'll meet you and get you a horse, or a buggy if you prefer?"

"A horse will do just fine, Green."

"You like to hunt, Ben? If you do, those ranches out there always invite me to kill an antelope or mule deer or maybe even an elk. Maybe you could bring a rifle and I'll get a pack horse and we could spend a week or so. What do you think?" Green asked.

"Sounds like a lot of fun, Green," replied Ben. "I can bring my old .44."

"Maybe you ought to get something more modern, Ben. I use a 7mm mauser I took off a Spanish soldier I killed in Cuba, and it's a lot better than those old Winchester calibers. The shots are longer, you know."

"Yeah, Green, we have antelopes in Nebraska, and most people use a .30-caliber nowadays. Those old .44s were good at short ranges, but when they are running over the prairie at 200 yards, they are not near as effective," countered Ben.

"Why don't you plan on spending about a week out there? You can get a good idea of what that country can do, and we can have some fun."

"Sounds good, Green. I'll make arrangements to meet you on January 15 at Springer."

Both went their respective ways the next morning; Ben back to St. Louis, and Green to Texas for the fall roundup.

Springer Station, New Mexico / January 15, 1901

Green had been in the little town for two days, securing supplies and gear for his expedition. Etienne de la Garza, who had been visiting in Refugio, had agreed to come along to do the cooking, if he could hunt also. Green readily agreed. He and Etienne had secured seven horses, tentage, and cooking utensils for the trip and figured they were all set. Whether Ben Davidson was properly equipped was a matter of conjecture.

Green had plotted the course of the hunt, making sure that Ben would see all the country and be able to talk to all of the ranchers who usually pastured yearlings for Green. That was what Ben was really coming for, and Green wanted to make sure he saw it all.

Green and Etienne met the train at the Santa Fe line station at 11:00 A.M. Ben dropped off onto the platform with his baggage.

"I brought a lot of stuff because I really didn't know what to expect," said Ben.

"No problem. We can sort it out and anything you won't need, we can leave here. Ben, meet Etienne de la Garza, an old Cajun friend of mine from the army. Etienne is between wars right now so he's coming along. He's volunteered to do the cooking."

"Glad to meet you, Mr. de la Garza. We gonna have etouffe on this trip?"

"Call me Tim, Ben ... we get along better, not so much formality. We got no shrimp, but I bring plenty good roux." Etienne smiled.

Ben, dressed in trail clothes, left the valise carrying all his suits with the railroad agent. Ben had done this before and was pretty well equipped for this type of hunting expedition. He even brought one of the new pump-up gas lanterns and proudly showed off his new .30-caliber self-loader, purchased because of Green's advice. Green and Etienne had brought their expropriated Spanish mausers from Cuba.

With two pack horses and two spares, the little party headed generally west, toward the mountain.

Green explained, "First, we will hunt antelopes here on the plains. They stay here in the open, depending on their speed afoot for their safety. Later, when we are in the foothills, we will take deer. They hide in the brush for safety. Higher up the mountains we may find elk, for that is where they stay."

"Will we camp every night, or have we invitations to stay at some of the ranches?"

"Yes, we have. But we should exercise judgment and only visit rather than stay the night, so as not to be a nuisance."

But that would not happen. The northeastern part of New Mexico was sparsely populated, and families there craved visitors of any kind. The three of them spent almost every night in a warm bed, and it was very cold there in January.

The hunting was very good. All three men killed at least one antelope and one buck deer each, and Ben killed a large bull elk. There were eleven trophies taken in all, and Etienne did wonderful things to the game meat with the help of his roux.

The group gradually moved back to the plains from the mountains on their way back to Springer. The day had turned off warmer but very threatening—muggy, very cloudy, with a high east wind. As they left the foothills, Ben seemed ill at ease as he kept looking to the north.

Green approached him. "Ben, I guess you must have had a good time. You act like you don't want to leave."

Ben looked at him grimly and said, "Green, it's not that I don't want to leave. It's just that I have seen this same weather before, and I don't know whether to be scared or not."

"What do you mean, Ben?" asked Green.

"I remember a spell of weather just like this at the ranch about ten years ago, and right on its heels came a blizzard that lasted for three days. My older brother got lost between the barn and the house, and we found him frozen to death not twenty yards from the front door after it broke. It wouldn't be good to be caught out here on the prairie."

"I don't know much about storms like that, and neither does Tim. Do you think that might really be coming?"

"I can't be sure, of course, but it seems like all the bad winter storms I remember were preceded by conditions just like this."

Green called Etienne over and told him. After some discussion, a retreat to the timber was thought to be wise. It would only cost them a day or so in travel, and if they got caught in the open by a blizzard, they would all die.

They turned around and headed back to the shelter of the trees in the higher ground, and when they got there, Ben searched for a draw or ravine that would provide shelter, in case it lasted some time.

They heard him before they saw him, from the west. He appeared, waving his arms.

"Over here, boys! I've found a good place here!" he yelled.

Green and Etienne moved to him, and he showed them a narrow defile that had plenty of timber for firewood.

Etienne set up the camp and tents, Green took care of the horses, and Ben gathered dead wood for the fire. After Green got the horses settled, he strung a rope from the camp to the small mott where he had tethered the mounts. The horses would need constant care if a blizzard came, and the rope would keep them from getting lost, although the mott was only thirty feet away.

The northern sky continued to look ominous, and the storm, if it was a storm, was getting closer. They had gathered a huge pile of firewood and hoped it would be enough. All of them cut leafy branches to use like brooms to sweep away the snow, and they strengthened the tents with more poles because the snow could accumulate enough to cave in the tent on them. Ben had taken over leadership of the group, as he was the only one who knew anything about cold weather storms. He set them to cutting grass for horse feed, and they had accumulated a good pile of it when it started snowing. Big, wet flakes fell at first. Green and Etienne marveled at it, as neither one had ever been around snow much.

About two inches of snow was on the ground and the wind had started up by the time they ate supper. Green and Etienne both entertained the idea that coming back had been a waste of time. They felt certain they could have gone on through this weather. But they had no idea that the three hours of camp preparation before the snow fell was all that was between them and an icy death.

Ben was a disciplined leader. He made sure the horses were checked every two hours, sweeping the snow off their backs and making sure their nostrils didn't freeze from condensation. He also swept the tent free of snow.

By midnight, the wind was almost to gale force and the snow was so thick that seeing things two feet away was next to impossible. The snow got heavier and the wind hadn't slackened by morning.

They all tended to the horses, figuring they had cut enough hay for three more days, and if they kept the horses' muzzles clear and the snow swept off, they would be all right.

When they got back to the tent, Ben took the axe to cut down some trees close to them. He tied a rope around his waist and told Green to keep a hand on it. They could not even hear Ben chopping with the axe only twenty feet away, so loud was the wind howling. Ben came back in less than an hour. It was all he could stand away from the fire. Green and Etienne then took their turns as axemen, each for an hour at a time. They eventually cut down and chopped up four trees, providing more sweeps which were in constant use. Ben kept everybody busy all the time, for the snow had built up considerably during the past night and day.

The horses seemed to be getting along all right, but Ben worried what their condition would be when the storm blew itself out. How long that would be was anybody's guess, so they curtailed the hay ration a little, hoping it would last. Water wasn't a problem, seeing that much of it was piling up around them as snow, but the grass couldn't be found under the snow, which, even under the sheltering trees, was at least a foot deep.

It was becoming harder to do anything in the freezing wind. The snow was icier than before, and no one could tell if it was still snowing or just blowing down on the north wind. Green and Etienne deferred completely to Ben's orders, figuring he had saved them from the very beginning. Ben tried to keep them constantly moving to keep from freezing, but the cold sapped their strength so much that none of them knew if they would last another day.

They did—but not by much. Late on the fourth day, the wind lay and the snow stopped and the sky started to clear. Ben knew they had to move the next day or they wouldn't make it. The hay had been exhausted at midday. They did what they could for the horses, made up their packs (discarding anything that wasn't an absolute necessity), and prepared to move east at daylight.

The last piece of firewood was used that morning for breakfast and the little party left the woods, just as the first rays of the eastern sun peeped over the horizon. They had survived the blizzard. But they still had the snow-covered prairie to traverse.

CHAPTER 10

Mora County, New Mexico / January 20, 1901

he party came out to a sea of white snow, covering the prairie. All three men despaired of going very far on their gaunted horses, but it was the only way. They again equalized the loads and led their horses, following one rider who broke trail. All day they headed east across the trackless snow, seeing no sign of habitation until midafternoon, when they spotted a thin plume of smoke directly east. They hurried along and, atop a small hill, spotted several buildings and corrals. The three beat a path to the door of the house from which the smoke was coming. Clearing the snow, which had drifted around the door, they knocked.

"*Quien es?*" someone said from inside, and the door was pulled open.

A small, wiry Mexican, about sixty years old, stood in the doorway, regarding the three apparitions before him.

"*Entranses, caballeros, mi casa es suya.*"

"Our horses," said Green, pointing.

"We have a secure barn with hay just there," the man said, pointing across the snow-covered yard.

They took the six horses to the barn and unsaddled them. One horse had given out just about midday and had to be left behind.

Unpacked and unsaddled, the horses rolled on the bare ground in the barn, as the riders put out hay and water for them before returning to the house.

The Mexican was stoking the fire and his wife was at the cookstove as the small party entered.

"I am Ramon Ojedo, and this is my wife, Josefa. You are at the *rancho* of Don Sebastian Santos. How in the world did you get here?"

"Señor, we were hunting north of here and got caught by this blizzard. We have come this day from the mountains. My name is Green Dunigan, and this is Ben Davidson. That big fellow there is Etienne de la Garza," Green explained.

When the name Santos was mentioned, Green knew they had drifted farther south than they had realized. Having used neighboring ranches of the large Santos grant in the past, he had an idea of where he was now.

"You are lucky to be alive. To be out in such a bad storm is very dangerous," said Ojedo. "Come, my wife has cooked some food and you must be very hungry and cold."

"Señor, we gladly accept your hospitality. We hate to inconvenience you, but we are nearly all in."

The travelers sat down and devoured the stew, beans, and tortillas put before them.

Ojedo was familiar with the name Green Dunigan, as he had known of his steers on the neighboring ranches, but he was especially perplexed by Etienne.

"Señor de la Garza," he asked, "where are you from that you have both French and Spanish names?"

"I am from the bayous of Louisiana, a descendant of the pirates led by Jean Lafitte, who were of all races and nations," he answered with a grin.

Earlier, they had explained Ben as the one who had saved them with his knowledge of winter gained in Nebraska.

"Señor Davidson, you are a banker from St. Louis, yet you left the *rancho* of your family in Nebraska. Why did you do so?"

Ben grinned and answered, "Señor Ojedo, I left because it was so cold there, and banks are usually warmer."

"Ah, yes," said Ojedo, and they all laughed.

"Señores, we have a spare room in the house here, but only one spare bed. I am sorry we do not have more, but I am here only to take care of this end of Don Sebastian's *rancho,* and this is all we can offer."

"Señor Ojedo, we understand and do not like to put you out, but we can manage. We have bedding of our own to use, but we gratefully accept the offer of your room, but only for tonight," said Ben.

"Señores, it would be madness to leave before it warms, and some snow melts so you can find the roads. You must accept the hospitality of Don Sebastian and myself until then," Ojedo said, and they knew he spoke the truth.

That day they spent inside, except for a trip or two to see if the horses were doing all right. Ojedo got to know each man, his antecedents and his business and locale, as they did with him. His was a far more interesting story.

"My family used to own a *rancho* south of here, close to Santa Rosa, but after the war with Mexico the *gringos* took it because they said we owed much taxes. I was a little boy then, and it happened to many Mexicans. We fought but we were few. My family was killed. I came here to Don Sebastian Santos, who had always been a friend of my father. Don Sebastian had more money and was able to keep some of his properties. At one time he had vast holdings, but now he has only about 70,000 acres. You know, as I get older I no longer blame the *gringos.* I realize that the reason was simply that we lost the war, and to the victor belongs the spoils. Besides, now we all get along together. We have to, to fight the common enemies, the weather, and the *politicos.* It is the same everywhere, no?"

They nodded in agreement, and Green added, "You got it right, but I don't think I would be as forgiving as you."

"You will be when you get older."

There was general agreement on that as well.

At the end of the second day they could see patches of brown where the snow had melted or blown off and they spotted the outlines of roads and fence lines stretching over the horizon. They decided that they should go on the next day, as both men and horses were sufficiently rested by then. They wanted to leave a present for Ojedo but could not decide what to do until Ben said, "I'll leave him my rifle. I don't think I'll need it a whole lot, and by the time I do, there'll be something better on the market."

"Etienne and I will pay our part in cash to you if you do that, Ben."

"No need. If I need a rifle any time soon, I'll just borrow your mauser. I don't know what I would use it for."

"Now, Ben, you're not going to forswear hunting just because of a little storm?"

"There wasn't anything little about that storm, Green, and you know it."

"If dey was, I never see it," said Etienne.

It was settled. They gave Ramon Ojedo the autoloader, and all left notes of thanks to Don Sebastian Santos. Green said that he would try to visit the next time he had cattle in the area.

The three left with the sun the next morning, arriving in Springer about 3:00 in the afternoon. Ben caught a train north at 5:00, and Green and Etienne had to wait until the next day for the southbound.

Before Ben left on the northbound train, the three friends stood and shook hands solemnly.

Etienne said, "I doan know bout you fellers, but I never be de same after dis."

They all nodded, knowing that out there in the blizzard each had seen the end of his mortality and realized that living would never again be anything but a serious matter.

When Green and Eitenne returned the horses to the livery, the stable owner was surprised to see them.

"I didn't think nobody would be back from that storm," he said. "It's the coldest, worst weather since '86. We lost some folks here. How'd you make it through, with the horses and all?"

"We had a fellow from Nebraska with us and he told us what to do and made us do it. It was all that saved us. We lost one of the horses, though," answered Green. "We also stayed at Ramon Ojedo's place a couple of days."

"He's a nice old man, isn't he? Never bothers nobody, just stays out there and looks after the old Santos place."

"We'll pay you for the horses, but we'd like to trade some things in on what we owe, if you're of a mind?" ventured Green.

"Shore I will. What you got to trade?"

"A tent, a couple of axes, a couple of shovels and tools, and some pots and pans."

They unloaded the packs and started trading. In the end everyone was satisfied, and Green and Etienne went off to find a room.

Both slept soundly until dawn, and they caught the southbound at 9:00 A.M. for El Paso, arriving home two days later.

It was late by the time they made it to the ranch house. Not wanting to wake his folks, Green took Etienne to the bunkhouse and they slept there that night.

They were finishing breakfast at the camp kitchen when John Dunigan walked in.

"I sent you a wire from Springer, Dad, did you get it?" Green asked.

"Yes, son, I guess you couldn't have let us know sooner, but your mother was sick with worry. We read about that storm in the papers and since we hadn't heard, we were afraid you had gotten caught out in it."

"We were caught in it, and if it wasn't for Ben Davidson knowing about blizzards and taking care of us, we wouldn't have made it," said Green soberly.

"Well, you two damn sure don't know anything about snow storms, so I'm glad someone did."

"We do now, Dad, much more than either one of us ever wanted to know."

"You'd better go over and tell your mother that you're back. She is still worried," ordered Dunigan.

"Right away, Dad," Green said, and they saddled their horses and rode over.

As they approached the front door, Green called out, "Mother, we're home!"

The front door flew open, and Amanda Dunigan flew out to embrace her son. Green could feel the tears on his neck as she clung to him desperately. She finally released him and wiped her eyes.

"Green, you don't have any idea how worried we were that you would freeze to death. Your father especially, as he knows how deadly those storms can be."

"Mother, to tell the truth, you weren't any more worried then we were. We had an ace in the hole with Ben Davidson, in that he had been in some blizzards in Nebraska. He took over and really saved our hides, but it was scary. Why don't you invite us over for dinner tonight, and we'll tell you all about it? Right now we have some errands to attend to, but we'll have ample time at dinner."

"All right, Green. I'll wait. It seems like all I do is wait to see if you Dunigans are going to make it back again."

Green and Etienne arrived at 6:30. John and Amanda were waiting, along with Pete Roussell, for them. They had a drink and proceeded to relate the story of the blizzard. The young men were still somewhat gaunt and wind-burned from their ordeal, but there was something else about them that seemed quite different.

As they related the tale of their narrow escape, John Dunigan realized that everything about Green had changed. There was no longer any trace of the happy-go-lucky cowboy, the dashing young horseman. His son, in the space of a few weeks, had become mature, serious, and accountable. That storm had truly changed him overnight. Amanda realized the change, too. Her baby was a grown man, ready to shoulder any and all responsibilities that could conceivably be put on him. Looking at him, she realized that he was as strong a man as his father had been when he broke trail to Montana.

CHAPTER 11

El Paso, Texas / December 16, 1905

reen Dunigan dismounted and gave his reins to the stable boy at Ratigan's livery, across the street from the Paso del Norte Hotel. He was dusty and tired, having ridden forty miles that day up the old Santa Fe Trail from Chihuahua City. In the prior two weeks in Mexico, Green had purchased over 1,500 steer yearlings from Mexican ranches, mainly from those between Chihuahua and Parral. Another two weeks would pass before he would return to drive them out, and he wasn't looking forward to it.

Stopping by the desk, Green picked up his room key and his mail. He could hardly wait to crawl into a hot bath and rinse off what seemed to be half of Mexico.

As the hot water washed away the dirt and his fatigue, Green gazed out at the mountain that lay just to the east of El Paso. Green had always been mesmerized by it. The mountain looked like solid rock, but after heavy rains, it seemed to turn green.

"Everything turns green here, if and when it rains, I guess," he mused.

He got out of the tub, toweled himself dry, and shaved off four days' growth of beard. The bath had relaxed him, and he lay on his bed, resting for a few minutes before starting to dress for a dinner engagement in the hotel dining room. His whole body ached from ten uninterrupted days in the saddle. He caught himself just before he fell asleep, and rose up from the bed to dress.

Green looked into his closet and found that the tailor had delivered his new gray suit while he had been away. He also saw that his best boots had not been polished, and he called down to the valet to take care of that. Having decided to wear his new suit, he put it on, admiring the fit.

"That Chinaman is a pretty good tailor. I'll have to give him more trade," he said to himself. In the last few years Green had indulged his vanity and wore very stylish, good-looking clothes. To a stranger on the street, he could pass for a successful young lawyer, rather than the cowman he was. It was his only vanity, save that of firearms. He always kept a pair of dark blued, stag-handled, Colt single-actions, but rarely wore both of them at the same time. He figured he could handle one gun well, rather than two sloppily.

He finished dressing, slipped on the highly polished boots the valet had returned, and went down to the lobby to join his dinner partners, Don Anastasio Herrera, his wife Doña Marisol, and their daughter, Mercedes.

The Herrera family was in the lobby when Green walked out of the elevator. He greeted them and they went into the dining room, where they ordered wine and began to chat before ordering food.

Green had known Herrera for about three years and had been a guest at his *hacienda*, "Herradura," several times when he had brought the steers they had for sale.

Don Tacho was an archetypical Mexican *ranchero*. Tall, straight, sunburned, the color of old mahogany, with white hair and goatee, he had a touch of Indian ancestry. He ran Herradura as an extension of himself and his family. Doña Marisol was of pure Spanish blood with pale skin, blue eyes, and jet black hair, and was originally from Guanajuato, where her family had owned silver mines. Mercedes, the youngest of five children, was a lovely girl of twelve, with green eyes, black hair, and her father's dusky skin. She had just arrived from school in Washington, D.C. for the Christmas holidays.

Noticing her as they sipped their wine, Green thought that in a few years she was going to be stunning.

"Green, Mercedes is my tomboy. At Herradura we can't get her to wear dresses. She is always horseback and can ride like my va-

49

queros. She is a better vaquero than Tomas and Vicente, but maybe one day she will turn back into a lady. They told me they could do that at the school in Washington," said Don Tacho.

"Tacho, don't encourage her. She is becoming a young woman, and she should act like one," added Doña Marisol.

"Well, I sure agree with all that. Maybe you'd better get her a *duenna* to protect her from the boys," said Green.

Mercedes, blushing, countered, "Maybe I should start fainting all the time, like Teresa Recendez. Then you all would be satisfied."

"Teresa Recendez can't hold a candle to you, *mi chica*." It was obvious that she was Don Tacho's favorite child and she loved it.

They ordered from the menu and continued the small talk. Green had the trust of Don Tacho and was treated almost like a *gringo* cousin to the family. He had been buying the Herradura steers for three years and was well regarded by the Herreras.

Herradura was one of the finest properties in northern Mexico, consisting of 250,000 *hectarias* along the Rio Concho, west of Parral, in Chihuahua. Established by Don Tacho's grandfather in 1822, the property consisted mostly of range lands, but they did farm about 500 *hectarias* in the river bottoms. They grew alfalfa, corn, wheat, and beans, and other foodstuff in their irrigated fields. Herradura had imported blooded cattle in the 1860s from Britain and the U.S., and the herds were among the finest in Mexico. The headquarters itself was a fort, enclosing about fifteen *hectarias*. It had cannon and Gatling guns for protection from the raiding Yaquis, Apaches and Mayos, and all its people could retreat within its walls when danger threatened. There were silos for grain storage, a blacksmith, tannery, and grist mill, and a place to butcher and process beef, hogs, and chickens. In short, even under siege, Herradura was self-sufficient. The few essentials that the *hacienda* didn't produce, such as cotton and wool cloth and clothing, could be purchased at the commissary, as well as iron pots and cooking vessels.

Herradura was unique for two reasons: its almost total self-sufficiency and the presence of its owner at almost all times. Most of the large property owners lived in the valley of Mexico, visiting once or twice a year, and they were only interested in garnering adequate amounts of money to support a regal lifestyle. The Herrera family was different. They had come into a wild country, claimed and tamed as much of it as they could hold on to, and lived on it, making it their personal crusade for civilization.

Although their system was feudalistic and paternalistic, the people of Herradura were treated well and had a great deal of loyalty to Herradura and the Herrera family. That Herradura was a *latifundia* was undeniable, but the rule of the Herreras was benign and compassionate, and for that they commanded great loyalty. The "Herraduros," as they called themselves, were mostly vaqueros and cowboys, and only a few worked the *hacienda* fields as peons. More than forty vaqueros could be mounted at any one time, but many people were needed to hold the *rancho* against raiding Indians and bandits of the Sierra. Field labor was always scarce, as all the children of the peons aspired to be vaqueros, and most succeeded. As with all frontier outposts, justice was administered by the strongest, in this case, the Herrera men, but no one went hungry or lacked for clothing or shelter. From the *hacienda's* ample herd of fine horses, mounts were provided for everyone who wanted them. There was a school with a teacher, and attendance was compulsory through the age of fourteen. The *hacienda* also had a chapel, and mass was said at least once a month by a traveling cleric. A well-stocked infirmary was in place, and a doctor from Parral visited weekly. Herradura was a complete, well-ordered world to itself, and many of its citizens had never left it in their entire lives.

A few of the vaqueros lived in outlying stations away from headquarters, but most lived within Herradura's walls and went about their daily lives as they had for the last fifty or sixty years. There was no indication of the gathering storm that was to break over Mexico five years later; indeed, there was little sign that such a thing would affect the *hacienda*, as most of Mexico's troubles had affected it little.

"When will you be coming back to Herradura, Green?" asked Doña Marisol at the end of the meal.

"Probably six weeks, maybe two months. I will start from there, picking up steers on my way north. I have told my vaqueros to be around Parral around the tenth of February, Doña." Green used a group of Mexican drovers about four times a year to drive his cattle to the border. They were all experienced vaqueros who didn't mind fighting if they had to. There were plenty of bandits in the Sierra who made a living stealing cattle, but Green had lost none so far.

Green had stolen a march on the rest of the American traders by trading with the owners in Mexico before the cattle came to the border. The cattle didn't cost him any less, but he got the quality he needed by going into the interior. He never paid for the cattle until they were in the U.S., and then he deposited the money in the Mexican ranchers' accounts. He usually bought steers for the Dunigan ranches in the fall. The cattle that came in the spring he either ran himself, in New Mexico, or sold to other traders. A few traders had tried to emulate Green's tactics, but most weren't as successful. They weren't as simpatico as Green, not having grown up with Mexicans, as Green had.

"How long are you staying in El Paso, Don Tacho?" asked Green.

"We are leaving tomorrow for Parral, Green, and it should take us no more than two days to get to Herradura. Mercedes only got in this morning from Washington."

"Mercedes, how do you like your school in Washington?" Green asked.

"It is awful. The girls there are so silly. We have to wear little sailor dresses all the time. They used to tease me about my accent, but they quit. I don't have any friends there. The only good thing is that they have horses there, but they are so old and fat that it is like riding burros, and we have to ride sidesaddle."

"As all proper young ladies should, I might add," said Doña Marisol. "But you remember the *charreadas,* and all of the *charras* ride sidesaddle, and beautifully, too."

"Yes, Mama, but the *charras* ride horses, not burros," said Mercedes.

"Don't worry, *chica,* when we get home you can ride your horses any way you want," said Don Tacho reassuringly.

After finishing their coffee, the Herreras left for their hotel. Green thought that since he had been in Mexico for two weeks, he might go to the bar to catch up on the latest trades. Only two of the border traders were in that night, as things had been slow for the last two weeks and some had gone back home for the Christmas holidays. Green had nothing coming for the next six weeks, so he decided to go home, too. He would spend a fine Christmas with his parents, his brothers and sister, and their families.

CHAPTER 12

Parral, Chihuahua / February 16, 1906

reen arrived at Parral on the noon train. After retrieving his horse at the livery, he started hunting his drovers. Two of them were at the livery, knowing that would be his first stop. One of them was his *segundo*, Cesar Dominguez, and he had a line on the other eight men in Parral. Three others would be awaiting them in Herradura.

They all rode south to Herradura, arriving at the headquarters about two days later. There they found the other three drovers, and all moved into a vacant house, except for Green, who was a guest at the main house. Don Tacho and his wife met him at the door with warm greetings, and then Green excused himself to rest and clean up before dinner.

When he returned at 7:00, Green joined Don Tacho and Doña Marisol, the two younger Herrera men, Tomas and Vicente, and their wives, and another daughter, Otilia, a pretty twenty-year-old. She had just returned to Herradura from Mexico City for a respite after the social season, which she pursued with her aunt, Doña Marisol's sister. Everyone was having a glass of wine, made from Herradura's vineyards. Green took a glass and found it to have a robust, if slightly rough, flavor. That was as good a characterization of Herradura as he knew, so the wine fitted the place.

When they went into dinner, Green was seated beside Otilia and chatted with her quite a bit. She was fairer skinned than the other Herrera children but had the same blue eyes and black hair. Green asked her about the balls and soirees she had been to in Mexico City, and wondered about the latest news in the capital.

"Señor Dunigan, I am just a woman, and know nothing of politics. I know only that Don Porfirio Díaz is still the president and is loved by all Mexicans, because of the peace and progress he has brought to us. He is the reason for the splendor of the balls and parties of the capital, and everyone says that as long as he is in power, Mexico will continue to prosper."

This was more than Green had asked for, but he took it as it was given. He glanced around the table to see how Otilia's statement had been received.

Doña Marisol, looking tentative, seemed to nod in agreement, while Don Tacho glared at his fork, saying nothing. The rest of the family stared in shock.

Tomas was the first to speak. "Otilia, have you not seen the poor on our cities' streets, begging for a tortilla? Have you seen the great *ranchos* of Hearst and Green here in Chihuahua and Sonora? Don Porfirio has sold most of Mexico to the *gringos,* don't you know that?"

General argument broke out around the table, and all participated except Doña Marisol, who felt ladies should not talk about politics, and Green, who knew it was none of his business. The younger Herreras, other than Otilia, were opposed to Díaz, and Don Tacho grudgingly allowed that "Don Porfirio has brought peace and order to Mexico, and that is no small matter."

Green, who was sorry to have initiated the subject, was amazed at the opposition to Díaz inside one of the great families of Mexico. Later he would find that this was the case in northern Mexico, but that the reverse was true in the south.

Don Tacho soon stopped the argument and took the men to his office for cigars and cognac. No more politics was discussed—only cattle and horse matters.

The next morning, Vicente took Green and his men to help gather the steers. Vicente, the eldest, was sort of *mayordona* of the *rancho* and was in charge of most things to do with the cattle, while Tomas dealt with everything else but spent a great deal of time overseeing the horse operations. Both were of an age with Green, and got along well with him, Tomas to the extent of giving Green one of their most promising young horses.

Vicente and Green were riding together, pushing the steers toward the headquarters, when Green decided to probe further into Vicente's politics.

"Vicente, I noticed last night you didn't agree with your sister about the worth of Don Porfirio. Your family has prospered under his rule, hasn't it?"

"*Sí*, Green. We have prospered, but mainly from our own efforts, and the fact that the government hasn't confiscated our properties. It is an involved question, Green, one that has no easy answers. First, Mexico is unique in that it is the only country of the Spanish empire that isn't dominated by the Gachupines, the old Spaniard political leftovers, or the Indios. Mexico's meztizos, the mixed bloods, occupy, if not a dominating position, at least a strong one."

Vicente paused, then continued. "My opposition to *porforismo* is that in the name of economic progress they have sold most of Mexico's assets to foreigners, instead of helping to finance the native entrepreneurs, who would keep the profits here, for more development. There is a place for foreign investors in Mexico, but what is happening is that the interests of the nation are being subordinated to the interests of other nations. Also, the fact that we have no say in our government, I am opposed to. We want effective voting for all, and I think a no reelection position is not bad. The *científicos* running the government have not done a really bad job, but they have gathered all power to the capital and left the rest of the nation with no say in the government. You must realize, Green, I am no friend of any kind of communism, but we must have more power given to the outlying people, so everyone can get his say. I don't want to have a revolution. I just want the central government to relinquish some of its power to the states and the *municipios*. It is true that Mexico has prospered under Díaz, but the fruits of that prosperity have all been eaten in Mexico City, or London, or maybe San Francisco. Do I make myself clear, Green?" Vicente asked, and Green nodded in the affirmative.

"Vicente, you have education and appreciation for such affairs, so you would naturally have a better approach. But what do the small ranchers, vaqueros, and peons think about this?" asked Green.

"Well, they are being squeezed, especially by the bigger places, but I think that there is a lot of resentment by the more thoughtful people, especially about the lack of voice in government. I don't think the lower classes think about it much. You know, there is a proverb in Mexico that expresses it well. It says, 'There are three kinds of fools in Mexico: the man who marries for love, not money; the dry-land farmer; and the *politico* who doesn't steal.' Overall, I think it is easier to stir resentment up over the land you *gringos* stole than over the quality of government in Mexico."

Green grinned at that, and so did Vicente. There was no animosity between them.

All thousand of the steers were gathered by noon, and after lunch, Green headed his herd northeast. He would pick up an additional 500 from two *ranchos* before he crossed the railroad at Julimes. From there on he would follow the river to Ojinaga and load the steers across the river at Presidio. The drive should take five to seven days at the most, and Jack Dunigan would unload them a couple of days later and they would be home.

Green's outfit consisted of ten cowboys, with Cesar Dominguez as *segundo,* and Cesar's wife as cook. All of the cowboys were able, experienced drovers who did this five or six times a year for Green. They worked as day help for the smaller *ranchos* the rest of the year. He paid them well, as there were enough bandits around that from time to time some fighting might be called for. Otherwise, it was just like the old trail drives—dusty and boring.

CHAPTER 13

El Paso, Texas / May 5, 1911

reen was to meet four of his trader pals to cross the river and enjoy some dinner and entertainment in Juárez. They met at the hotel bar at 5:00, and one of them, Bill Summers, had just come from the Mexican side.

"Boys, I don't think we want to go across tonight. It's like a tomb over there, and it's Cinco de Mayo, their holiday. Most everything is shut up. Even the whores are out of sight," he said.

"Well, what's up?" asked Green, who had just arrived from South Texas.

"Haven't you heard? There is a revolution down there, and they are fighting all over," retorted Tom Rogers, another trader.

"Tom, there is always a revolution in Mexico somewhere, but they don't shut anything down for it," Green said laconically.

"That's right, Green, but there's fighting all over now. And to top it off, Pascual Orozco and Pancho Villa have Juárez surrounded. They are fighting under one of the Maderos, you know, from Coahuila. This one is a grandson of old Don Evaristo. He was the one with all the cotton around San Pedro, east of Tomeon. His name is Francisco, Francisco I. Madero," explained Tom.

"I went out of Chihuahua one time, and there must have been

thirty or forty *rurales* hanging from telephone poles along the lines. They said that was Orozco's signature. I also heard of this Villa— they said he used to be a Sierra bandit," said Pete Burns, another trader. "It ain't Little Bo-Peep there in Juárez, is it?"

They discussed what they knew of the troubles in Mexico for a couple of hours and then went out for a steak at an American restaurant, deciding that discretion was the better part of valor. This was the first indication to Green of how widespread the revolution had become. It had not been reported in the interior of Texas up to this time.

While eating breakfast the next morning, Green heard a popping sound, seemingly coming from Juárez. He went back to his room on the fifth floor and glanced out the window toward Mexico. There were clouds of dust and smoke over Juárez, and while Green was watching, a building blew in a big explosion, with accompanying smoke and dust.

"Well, I guess it's starting," he mused.

The cattle trade in El Paso had become nonexistent in the last week, so Green did not think a trip to the customs yard would be worthwhile. Instead, he wrote his brother, Jack, and his father about the revolution, telling them not to expect any cattle for a while.

Downstairs he posted his letters and walked out toward the railroad tracks, which traversed the high land next to the river. Coming to the tracks, he could see lots of people standing on top of boxcars, watching. Green did the same, clambering up to watch the show.

From the top of a Southern Pacific boxcar, Green could see that the *federales* were defending the town from trenches, barricades of wagons, and even from buildings. There was very little in the way of big guns, only small arms. The *federales* had a couple of machine guns, while the rebels were armed with rifles, .30-30s mostly, judging from the low boom, but they also were using a great deal of dynamite. Mostly, it was the rebels making rushes from strong point to strong point, with the *federales* falling back in pretty good order. A lot of rebel horsemen were rushing around, throwing dynamite at the *federales*.

The rebels, attacking from the west and south, were winning mostly by dint of manpower, but the *federales* weren't beaten yet and were retreating in an orderly fashion, inflicting casualties on the rebels.

From his vantage point, Green watched the battle progress. Having been a participant before, he had never really seen war from an overall perspective. Occasionally a sharp crack would mark the passage of a stray bullet, but no one seemed to have been hurt. Engrossed in the actoin, he watched the progress of the revolution all day and did not return to the hotel until after 6:00.

Green would watch the battle from atop a boxcar until it was over, on May 10, when General Navarro surrendered. Many of his troops had run or crossed the river beforehand and were interned by the U.S. Army, which was mobilized along the border. The news from Mexico was of battles breaking out from the Baja Peninsula all the way to the Yucatan. The day after Navarro's surrender, Díaz sent peace commissioners to Juárez to meet with Madero, and it seemed to be over.

After three days living vicariously as a soldier, Green felt he had to get back to work. The trouble was there weren't any cattle coming out of Mexico, and not just at El Paso. No cattle were coming to Presidio or Eagle Pass in Texas, nor Columbus in New Mexico, nor at Douglas or Yuma or any other of the crossing points in Arizona and California. There were no cattle coming to the U.S. from Mexico. Green talked to everyone he knew who might know what was going on across the river. His business was built on his presence in Mexico, but it would not continue at the risk of his life.

CHAPTER 14

Juárez, Chihuahua / May 20, 1911

reen had been idle too long, waiting for the dust to settle across the river. He needed to buy some cattle. From what he had heard, Díaz was out and Madero was in. Madero was very visible in El Paso, going to parties and dinners every night. Green had been unable to meet him but had seen him. He didn't look like a conqueror or ruler of Mexico. He was a short, neat little man who always wore the red, white, and green tricolor on his hat. Green had heard that even though Madero was no soldier, he was fearless.

Green thought that Villa probably had more to do with things in Juárez, as he was from Chihuahua, and that maybe his best shot was to talk to Villa. He knew that several merchants had gone over, and they seemed to have gotten satisfaction.

Green dressed in his trail clothes, got a horse, and rode across to Juárez. Villa was headquartered at the municipal building, so he rode there, tethered his mount, and walked in. Fierce-looking Mexicans wearing bandoliers of bullets across their chests were all over the building. Green walked up to a desk and asked the soldier behind it to see the general.

"*Gringo,* I don't know if the general will see you now, or ever, but write your name and business and maybe I'll see."

Green wrote his name and "Pasaje a Parral" on the paper, and passed it back, along with a ten-dollar U.S. bill. The soldier pocketed the money and took the sheet of paper through a door back of his desk. Green took a seat on a bench opposite the desk. A few minutes later, the soldier came back and sat down.

"Maybe the general will see you after a while."

Green watched the comings and goings for two full hours. Most of the people who went in looked like vaqueros, but some were dressed in fancy *charro* outfits, with silver buttons, and most were addressed as Major or Colonel. One or two old women, with black shawls covering their heads, went in and came out smiling, apparently having gotten what they asked for.

Shutting the great man's door behind one of the supplicants, the soldier said, "Okay, *gringo*, you can see the general now."

Green entered. Villa was standing by a window, looking out. He was bigger than Green had supposed—fully six feet tall and powerfully built, with almost reddish hair and a big mustache.

"Why you want to go to Parral, *gringo*?"

"You speak English, General?" ventured Green gingerly.

"*Sí*, American smelting and refining, *y* sonofabitch," said Villa, cackling.

Green chuckled, too, and continued. "General, I want a paper from you so I can get to Parral to bring out steers."

"You know that all the cattle in Mexico belong to the revolution."

"General, I have bought the cattle of Rancho Herradura and its neighbors for some years, but I will pay for them to whoever I am told to," said Green, feeling his way.

Villa turned to an aide and said, "Go get Vicente and bring him here."

The aide left to do his chore and Villa motioned for Green to sit down. He offered his visitor a cold beer.

The door opened and an officer walked in. Villa said, "Señor Dunigan, do you know Major Herrera?"

Green was dumbfounded, as was Vicente Herrera, but each recovered and hugged each other, then shook hands.

"Major Herrera, this man wants to go to Herradura to buy cattle. Is he legitimate?"

"*Sí, mi general*. Green is an old friend and has bought our cattle for some years and has always treated us fairly."

"Well, I will give him his pass," said Villa.

"General, I don't think he can get the cattle out unless we help him. The railroad is torn up between here and Chihuahua, and all the vaqueros from Herradura and the rest of the *ranchos* are here, mostly in my troop of cavalry," said Vicente, seating himself.

"Señor Dunigan, since half of the money from the cattle goes to support the revolution, maybe we could let you have some help. Major Herrera, can we do that?"

"*Sí.* Since we are no longer fighting, we could lend him some vaqueros, but you know that there are still *federales* in Chihuahua and we would have to go around it or fight them."

"Major, I will leave it up to you. You provide the men and see to it. Just be sure we get the money and that the men are paid. Señor Dunigan, nice to have met you. Maybe we can do more business in the future. It looks like the revolution is over."

Vicente Herrera led Green out of Villa's office and across the street to a *cantina,* where they had lunch. Over tamales and beer they renewed their old relationship and then got into particulars.

"Green, you know there have been few cattle sold in the past year. There are a lot of steers to come out, but we would have to gather them and drive them all the way to Columbus, I think, to be safe. Ojinaga is closer, but we would pass too close to Chihuahua and I wouldn't feel safe. Anyway, Columbus is only about a three-week drive. Will that upset your plans?"

"I can deal with it, Vicente, but how many cattle would come? I have to arrange finance."

"Maybe six or seven thousand, maybe more. Will that break the market?"

"No, because nothing has been coming in. I can sell them all easily if you want to come with that many, and the market will absorb them all right, especially if I can work on some before we go. By the way, Vicente, when do we go?" asked Green.

"The sooner the better. I need very little time to arrange things. I will bring about thirty of my men and make them leave their women here. That will leave Tomas with fifty or so. We'll have to ride, but we can make a fast trip because there are plenty of remounts at Herradura, and we can take the train about halfway to Chihuahua. The tracks are torn up from there on. Will you need anything, Green?"

"Is Cesar Dominguez in your troop, Vicente? If so, I really want him and his wife, also. She's a good camp cook. I'll need a pass to bring my guns across, and I'll be ready to leave in the morning. Where should I meet you?"

"Meet us at the railroad yards at 7:00. I'll have all the men, horses, and equipment that we'll need and will arrange for a train. Are you going to bring anyone with you, Green?"

"No, I won't need anyone, if your men will be along and I can have Cesar. How far can we get down the tracks, Vicente?"

"A little over a hundred miles I think. I'll get all the passes we need and I'll leave one for you at the bridge."

Vicente and Green departed to make their arrangements. Green returned to El Paso and sent wires to his father and Jack, asking if they wanted any older steers that would be coming out of Chihuahua. He wrote a letter delineating all of this and asking them to write him in care of Samuel Ravel at Columbus. He told his father he would handle all the yearlings on his own. Next, he wired the banks to expect drafts in about a month, and he wired his agents in New Mexico to secure pasturage and to contact him at Columbus with what they could get.

With all this done, Green went to the hotel bar to get on with some trading. Most of the border traders were there, as was customary, and after a drink Green announced that he would be bringing out substantial numbers of Mexican steers at Columbus in about a month. All the traders wanted to buy immediately, but Green told them he didn't know how many or of what class he would be coming with. The traders' response assured him that he could sell any or all of the cattle he might want to.

The next morning, the horses were being loaded into two stock cars as Green rode up. He dismounted and handed his reins to Cesar Dominguez, after exchanging greetings. Green knew most of the men there and enjoyed rekindling old acquaintances.

In addition to the two stock cars there was a locomotive and tender, a passenger car, and a flat car in front of the locomotive that carried a machine gun and its crew, a necessity of the times. Some minor difficulties in loading were quickly overcome by the experienced horsemen, and everyone boarded the train. A few men rode on top of the cars as guards, but there was room inside for all the women who came.

The train moved through the Chihuahua desert at a good clip, with no stops, until it stopped at a small village and water station called Sueco, where they unloaded. Two miles south the tracks had been demolished to prevent the reinforcement of Juárez from Chihuahua City and they could go no further. It was midafternoon and the outfit disembarked and set out quickly, going southwest to give Chihuahua City a wide berth because of the undefeated federal troops there.

They camped that night almost due west of the city, planning to make Herradura the next night. Fires were kept small, even though they were shielded by the Sierra del Nido, taking all precautions against discovery.

They rode into the fort at Herradura just after nightfall the next day and were pretty sure they hadn't been reported to the *federales.* Nothing could move in Mexico without being seen, but the Sierra Indians were mostly partisans of the revolution and in no way trusted the central government.

Vicente saw to the needs of his men before he and Green went to Don Tacho's house. Don Tacho and his house servants were armed and ready, as they had heard the group ride in and were taking no chances. When he saw who it was, Don Tacho grabbed Vicente in a crushing *abrazo,* and did the same to Green.

"Come in, come in. I bet you are hungry. We were just starting dinner. Your mother will be overjoyed, Vicente."

They walked up and joined the elder Herreras in the dining room. Doña Marisol was indeed overjoyed to see her oldest son home from the war. Vicente's sister, Otilia, was also there. Questions flew at them during dinner, making it difficult to eat.

"Well, how goes the war, Vicente?" asked Don Tacho.

"It goes well, Papa. As you know, we took Juárez, and the word is that Díaz is going to leave and Francisco Madero will be president. There is a peace commission from Díaz in Juárez now, and Madero is leaving in a few days for Mexico City. Abraham Gonzales has been made governor of Chihuahua. Tell me, Papa, how is it here? Have you had any trouble?" asked Vicente.

"No, it is known that Herradura supports Madero, and is under the protection of Villa. We do not have enough people to do the needed work, is all, with everyone in Villa's army."

"Green, are there many *gringos* fighting for Madero?" Don Tacho asked.

Vicente answered for Green. "Papa, Green is not fighting. He came to buy the cattle, but there are some *gringos*. Major Garibaldi, from Italy, and Viljoen, the South African from New Mexico, to name just two, but there are many."

"We have no way to gather the cattle, Vicente. We have many to sell but no men to bring them in," explained Don Tacho.

"Papa, we have brought enough men back to gather the cattle and also to help at Pajaritos and Halcones, our neighbors," explained Vicente, and then proceeded to tell his parents all about Green's deal with Villa and the help Villa sent from Juárez.

"Green, there are many more steers than you have ever bought before at one time. Have you brought enough men, and can you sell them without terrible effects on the price?"

"Don Tacho, very few cattle have come across the border this year. We can probably sell them easily at a good price. As for men, there are over thirty of us from Juárez," answered Green.

"Vicente, how do you like working for that bandit, Pancho Villa?" asked Otilia with some malice.

"Francisco Villa is a patriot, Otilia, but I work for the revolution, for Madero. Aren't you forgetting that Herradura and all the Herraduros are under the protection of 'that bandit,' and your own well being as well?" sneered Vicente.

"Children, no more politics during meals. You may argue among yourselves, but do not do so in front of your parents," commanded Doña Marisol.

"*Sí,* Mama," they obeyed meekly.

"Vicente, you have told us nothing of Tomas. How is he, what is he doing?" asked Don Tacho.

"Tomas is fine. Right now he is commanding our company, the Herraduros, in my absence. Juan Silvestre and Hector Montana were killed and Luis Gomez was wounded in Juárez. The rest you know," answered Vicente.

"You said you would take not only our cattle but those of our neighbors and friends. How do you intend to do that?" asked Don Tacho.

"We will gather and take their cattle along with ours, if they agree that half of the proceeds go to the revolution. If they don't, we

65

will not take them. The expenses, wages, and food and such will come out of the revolution's half. I had hoped you would make the arrangements with the other *ranchos,* Papa."

"I will be happy to, Vicente. Most of the *ranchos* here support Madero, but for those who don't, I will try to keep this drive quiet, so that the *federales* don't find out. They probably wouldn't do anything anyway, but it will be better if they don't know. Do you intend to help gather the cattle for the others, as all the *ranchos* are short-handed?"

"Yes, we will help gather, but if they have any vaqueros, ask them to send them over. We will start here tomorrow afternoon, on Herradura. We should be finished in five or six days, if we work hard and steadily. You can tell our neighbors that."

CHAPTER 15

Hacienda Herradura, Chihuahua / May 28, 1911

Green swung the gate closed on the last of the steers. There were over 9,000 of them, culled and sorted, to start the drive on the following morning. He couldn't think of a time that he had worked harder in his life. Everybody concerned had put out maximum efforts for the last week. Now he and Vicente had to plan the drive.

As they unsaddled their horses at the corral, Green spoke.

"Vicente, can you and me sit down somewhere and sort out what we have to do?"

"Sure, Green, let's go to the big house and get Don Tacho to help us."

"First, why don't you get old Diego Yanez to set up the rolling stock? I think we'll need two wagons, maybe three. We can have a common kitchen, and Amalia Cisneros, Cesar's woman, and the other women who come with us can probably take care of the feeding, as long as they have enough food, don't you think?"

"*Sí*, Green. I was thinking that we need to keep the herds close for common defense, no?" said Vicente.

"That was my idea. You get Diego working on the wagons, and I'll start with your father."

"Fine. I'll be there as soon as I can."

The major-domo let Green in, and Don Tacho came into his office to see what Green wanted.

"Don Tacho, Vicente will be here in a minute, but I wanted to ask your advice about the drive."

Don Tacho, who was very tired, haven ridden as long and as far as everyone else, said, "Green, I don't think I can make the drive. This last week took it all out of me. I am close to seventy years old now, you know."

"Don Tacho, if it hadn't been for you driving us all, I don't think we could have done it. But we can take it from here. What we want is some advice on how to do it. Didn't you drive steers to the border before the railroad came through?"

"Oh, yes, I did many times—usually to El Paso, only once to Columbus, and I always drove them close by Chihuahua City, which you don't want to do. But I can make a map showing the waterings and it should not be a difficult drive, because we have had a lot of rain this winter and spring. There should be plenty of feed as well. I may have one of my old maps . . ."

Vicente came in just as Don Tacho pulled a map out of his desk. It didn't look old to Green. He figured the old man had drawn it up for them in the last few days. All three sat down at a table, spread the map, and studied it for some time.

After a while, Green spoke. "I have never driven a herd for more than a week's drive, but my father has told me about his drive to Montana so many times that I have almost memorized the story. I'll need to draw from that, because some of it was similar to this one."

"That drive was the best and hardest I have ever heard of. I would like to hear the whole story someday, but go ahead, Green," said Don Tacho.

"First, we have too many cattle to keep in one herd. I think three herds is about right."

Both Vicente and Don Tacho nodded in agreement.

"Second, we need to stay close, because of the *federales* in Chihuahua City and also the Sierra bandits. My father told me he separated into two herds but made up a bunch of scouts to give early warning. What I propose is that we have two herds of the older and bigger, and they are already sorted that way, and one herd of yearlings. I also think we should have a common camp in the middle, with a common remuda, to save hands, and that we drive the herds in a wedge, one forward and two back and out to the flanks. What do you think?"

Vicente spoke first. "I had come to about the same conclusion, Green. We will be a little short-handed, if we have even a small group of scouts, so it is important that we have good men in charge of the herds. The cattle are gentle enough, but ten men to 3,000 steers is a little short. Your ideas about the remuda and camp are mine, too, but I would like to hear from the Maestro."

Don Tacho cleared his throat and said, "I agree with both of you. You have the right idea. I suggest that Vicente, because he knows the country best, take the scouts, and I will let you have Diego Yanez to drive one of the herds. He is old but is well experienced. Also, my observation of Cesar Dominguez, Green's *segundo,* is that he is quite capable. The third herd Green could handle, the yearlings, and I suggest you give him a few extra men, until they become accustomed to the trail, three or four days at the most. Two or three of the young boys from here can handle the remuda. I suggest Ramoncito Perez and José Menchaca, as they have been working around our horses, under Tomas. Does that sound about right?"

"I wouldn't change a thing," said Green.

"Ni yo, tampoco," echoed Vicente.

"Bueno, it is all agreed. I shall help Green when we leave. We have only two men left here until the others get back, and we will help get you started." Both Green and Vicente noticed that the old man had slyly assumed control, as he should have, being the most experienced.

"One more thing," said Green, "as far as I am concerned, Vicente is the overall boss, and I am under his order, until the cattle are paid for." Both Vicente and Don Tacho nodded agreement.

Vicente then left them to give the orders to his vaqueros. With the help of Diego Yanez and Cesar Dominguez, the cowboys were assigned to each herd. All details they could think of were taken care of, and everything was ready.

May 29, 1911, dawned bright and clear as the herds left Herradura for Columbus, New Mexico.

CHAPTER 16

The Chihuahua Desert / June 15, 1911

The drive had gone off without a hitch. There had been no trouble from Mexican federal troops, and as most of the Sierra bandits were in either Villa's or Orozco's armies, none were seen. The herds were within four or five days of Columbus on the Maria River, just south of Santa Maria Lake. They had made good time and were resting for a day before driving through to Columbus. Most of the vaqueros were in camp when a dust cloud was spotted from the east. Green and Vicente, although wary, did not think there was danger. They had plenty of men to fight off a band of what looked like no more than fifteen men. Nevertheless, they arranged a defense before riding out to meet whoever it was.

The group appeared to be a band of revolutionary soldiers, as there was no uniformity in their dress and they were heavily armed, but as they came closer, Vicente said, "It is Villa. No man alive sits a horse like he does, and the number is close to the men in his personal guard. There is no danger."

They rode forward to meet Villa and escorted him into the camp. When he approached, there were shouts of *"Viva Villa," "Viva Madero,"* and *"Viva la Revolucion,"* and friends greeted the newcomers.

70

"It is good to see you, *mi general*. What is the news?" asked Vicente.

"Much news, Vicente, good news. But I am very dry. A cup of coffee and I will tell you all the news," said Villa.

Coffee was passed around as Villa sat down with Vicente and Green to bring them up to date.

"Díaz has resigned as president and has left the country for Europe. Leon de la Barra is the interim president, and elections will be held next fall. Señor Madero is sure to be the president. Instructions are on the way to disband the revolutionary forces."

"*Mi general,* can we demobilize while the *federales* are still in place? The army could then overturn the revolution, if they were to come out for Felix Díaz or one of the others," said Vicente.

"*Sí,* Vicente, and for my part, I am going to go slowly, but I do not trust Pascual Orozco to disarm, so I am going to keep an eye on him and keep my rifle near me," said Villa, nodding solemnly.

"What do you think, Señor Dunigan?" Villa asked, turning to Green. "How do you like the news of Mexico?"

"General, it is great news, both for me and for Mexico. I am like you—I think Señor Madero will make a good president, and I can get back to my business."

"You aren't a soldier, so you call me Pancho," said Villa, grinning.

"All right, Pancho, but you call me Green. And by the way, I have been a soldier in Cuba."

"With Roosevelt, huh?" He tried several times to say Green's name, but it came out wrong—as *gring.* "Is your name like the color, *verde?*" Villa asked.

"*Sí,*" explained Green.

"Good. I shall call you 'Gringo Verde,' no?"

"*Muy bien,* Pancho."

"Where do you go now, *mi general?*" asked Vicente.

"Vicente, there was nothing going on in Juárez since Madero left so I thought I would go with you to Columbus to watch my investment, if you don't mind. Besides, Orozco came this way yesterday and I thought you might need some help if he wanted to steal our cattle. I was a pretty good vaquero some years ago. May I go with you?"

"Certainly. You can take over Green's ... uh, Verde's herd, when he leaves to go to Columbus to sell the cattle," said Vicente.

71

Villa grinned and gave Green a hug, saying, *"Mi caporal* Verde, Pancho Villa *a sus ordenes."*

The good-natured banter between the soldiers and the drovers continued through supper. After supper Villa, Vicente, and Green separated themselves and talked. They talked of their hopes for Mexico and the revolution. Villa was eager for the reforms to be put in place by Madero and expressed genuine affection for the little man. Vicente, being more sophisticated, knew that Madero had many barriers to cross, even to make a dent in the system. After all, it was basically the same system that Cortez had brought to Mexico nearly 400 years ago, plus the fact that the machinery of government had not been dismantled by the revolution and was still in place, as was the army. Each of the two nights that Green stayed in camp, he gained insight into Mexico and her problems. He felt he could see the soul of Mexico in Villa's eyes and the brain of Mexico in Vicente's. There was a serenade every night, the men singing songs of the revolution, broken from time to time by songs of unrequited love, the universal topic of Mexican music. Villa, the man who could not read or write, spoke of providing schools for all of Mexico, now that they could vote. Vicente, the large landowner, wanted stabilization of Mexico and justice for all, as well as land for those who would use it properly.

Green mused to himself that these good men could bring justice and progress to Mexico, but that politicians would be the ones who ended up with the power.

Green gained a great deal of respect for Villa during those few days. He admired his forceful personality and his compassion. He became truly fond of him.

When they were within two days' drive of Columbus, Green turned over his herd to Villa and rode in to make the sales and shipping arrangements. Villa insisted on sending someone with him and assigned Andres Gomez, saying, "Don't you let nothing happen to our Gringo Verde. You watch his back all the time."

Gomez nodded. He was one of the Dorados, Villa's personal bodyguards, who were distinguished by the gold lacing on the brim of their hats. Green knew he was in good hands.

CHAPTER 17

Columbus, New Mexico / June 18, 1911

reen and Andres rode across the border and on into Columbus an hour before dusk. They went to the hotel, where Green got rooms while Andres saw to the stabling of their horses. Across from the hotel, Green saw a store sign that proclaimed, "SAM'L RAVEL, GENERAL MERCHANDISE," and he went directly there.

A man was locking the door as Green came up. "Mr. Samuel Ravel?"

"Yes," the man answered.

"I am Green Dunigan, Mr. Ravel. I hope you have some mail for me."

"Yes, I do. If you'll wait a minute, I'll get it for you. But if you want anything from the store, you'll have to wait till tomorrow," Ravel explained.

"No, sir, the mail will do fine," Green said as Ravel reentered the store. He came out with three letters and handed them to Green, who took them and thanked him. "Mr. Ravel, I'll have a bunch of steers here day after tomorrow, and as you will be handling most of the money, I'll need to see you sometime tomorrow. By the way, you'll be happy to know that General Villa came with us. But I wouldn't tell anyone just yet."

"That's just fine, son. I'll be in the store all day tomorrow. Come when you get free."

Green crossed the street just in time to pick up Andres and go up to their rooms. There Green opened and read the letters. The first was from his father, who told Green he needed 2,000 steers for Kansas—the bigger the better—and since it was late, he should ship them direct to Matfield Green, Kansas.

The second letter was from Green's agent in northeastern New Mexico, who related that he had secured pasturage for 1,000 yearlings around Springer, and the third was from a New Mexican rancher who had talked to the agent and badly needed 500 yearlings for which he would pay top price. Green knew this rancher and knew his request was genuine, so 3,500 of the 9,000 already had a home. The remaining 5,500 he could readily sell. Deciding to test the market, he went down to the saloon across from the hotel, where the traders usually hung out every night.

Green pushed aside the swinging doors to Sanchez Bar and Grill and walked in. All the border traders he had ever met were sitting around tables in the saloon. Green immediately realized that his steers were the only game around and could trade accordingly.

"Hey, Green, glad to see you made it in. Are the steers here yet?" asked Bill Summers.

"No, but they'll be here day after tomorrow."

"How many did you bring, Green?"

"There are 9,000 coming, but I have commitments for 3,500, so there's still 5,500 for sale—4,000 big cattle and 1,500 yearlings. All horseshoe steers, or just like them," Green said, referring to the horseshoe brand of the Herrera cattle.

"I'll take all the yearlings," yelled Pete Burns.

"No you won't, because I need a thousand," yelled another trader.

"Boys, boys . . . Give me a chance. Let me sort off mine and shape the others, and then you can buy them. Why don't each of you write down on a slip of paper what you want, and I'll try to sort them to suit? Remember, there are 4,000 twos and threes and 1,500 yearlings. You'll have to judge the weight for yourselves."

He thought for a moment and reconsidered. "No, I'll sort and weigh the steers, the best I can to suit what you want, and then you can bid on them. I want to warn you, however, that part of these cattle belong to Pancho Villa, so if anyone tries to stiff us for payment, Villa will probably track you down and maybe feed your liver to those pie-dogs in Juárez. I'll have everything done and the cattle ready for bids right after noon, day after tomorrow, at the customs pens, and that's the way I'm going to do it. So don't come around trying to make deals beforehand," said Green, with finality.

Green sat down at a table with Bill Summers and Tom Rogers and a couple of others and got a drink before ordering supper. All of the Americans dropped by to ask questions about what was going on in Mexico, and Green answered to the best of his ability.

"Is the revolution really over, Green?" asked Tom Rogers.

"Well, Madero is on his way to Mexico City and is ordering the revolutionary army to disband, but Zapata hasn't quit, and I don't think Orozco and Villa are going to turn in their guns. It may be settled, but everyone is keeping his powder dry."

"You said Villa had an interest in those cattle. What is he doing with an interest in the Herraduras?" asked another.

"Well, the Herrera family gave the revolution half their cattle proceeds, and Villa kind of guaranteed their protection. He's with the cattle right now—said he wanted to get away from Juárez and all the politicos, but he may be watching his investments. Besides, both the Herrera boys, Vicente and Tomas, commanded troops that were under Villa," explained Green.

"What is he like, this Pancho Villa?" asked one of the older traders.

"I've kind of gotten to know him lately, and I'm not sure I can really tell you what he really is like, but I'll try. Pancho Villa is like Mexico—wild, unsophisticated, but plenty shrewd. What he wants is really a fair shake for Mexicans, whether in dealing with the U.S. or *gringos,* or with their own government or the politicians. All he really wants is a reasonably square deal. I don't think he wants to be president or hold any other office, or even to be a general. He has very little personal ambition. He was a bandit, without a doubt, but he may be like us, no other avenue of enterprise open to us."

They all laughed at that and thought about what Green had explained.

After he had dinner, Green returned to his room to compose wires to his father and the people in New Mexico. It was late when he got back, but he noticed that Andres was not in his bed.

Rising, Green ate breakfast at the café down the street. Some of the traders were there, and all of them tried to buy his breakfast. One finally got hold of his tab, but Green told him, "You're still going to have to bid for the steers."

Green went directly over to the railroad depot and found the freight agent. "I've got a bunch of cattle coming in here tomorrow and I'll want to ship them out right away. Have you got a handle on any cars close around?"

"How many cars will you need?"

"About sixty or so to Kansas and thirty or so to Springer, but there's more cattle, and I'm sure they'll be shipped out. Let's see, about a hundred twenty-five to go east, and thirty more north, so a total of two hundred seventy-five ought to cover all of them," explained Green.

"Well, I don't think there's over forty or fifty cars at Douglas, but there ought to be plenty at El Paso. Let me get to work on it. When do you think you'll want to load?" asked Jenkins, the agent.

"I can load tomorrow afternoon, and the others should be ready next morning," said Green.

"I'll get back to you, Mr. Dunigan. Where will you be?"

"At the hotel, or at Ravel's store."

Green went to Samuel Ravel's store, a general merchandise store stocked with everything from food and clothing to harness, plows, and windmills. Ravel came from the back of the store to greet Green.

"Ah, Mr. Dunigan, your mail was satisfactory?" he said.

"Yes, sir, Mr. Ravel, it was. I need to discuss with you the payment for and disposition of about 9,000 steers."

"You must be doing business with my esteemed friend, Francisco Villa. Tell me, how is he and what is he doing?"

"He will be here tomorrow with the cattle, Mr. Ravel. Right now I'll need to tell you the disposition of the cattle and the proceeds," Green said.

"Mr. Dunigan, I have heard of your trading here for some time but have not had the pleasure of doing business with you personally. I presume you know the 'rules' of the border trade."

"I do, Mr. Ravel," replied Green. He went on to explain the whole thing, including price, his noncompetitive purchase, and Villa's interest.

Ravel said, "Usually Pancho took all the money, but we sold the cattle surreptitiously, and for a lower price. This deal sounds like it's a good bit cleaner. Now that the revolution is over, I wonder what he'll do with the money. I have a lot of arms here for him. I guess I'll have to sell them elsewhere."

"I don't think he'll want that. My impression is that they are all waiting to see what happens, and they are keeping their arms oiled and working."

"Yes, I suppose that is so. It would seem to be the prudent course, wouldn't you think?"

"My business is cattle, Mr. Ravel, not revolutions," answered Green.

"I understand, Mr. Dunigan. I just wish my life was as uncomplicated. Now, how should I bill these cattle out?"

Green proceeded to detail all the instructions for payment on the cattle he was buying, together with his plan to sell the balance. Ravel understood the transaction.

"I'll talk to Pancho about what he wants to do with his share, but from what you say, he'll probably just stockpile more ordnance," said Ravel.

"I'll tell him to come see you tomorrow, when he gets in."

Green found the freight agent for the railroad, Mr. Sykes, who informed him that there would be 100 cars available the next day and up to 200 the day after.

"If you load your own cattle tomorrow, they can go out together," the agent explained. "The Santa Fe will pick them up in El Paso, and probably the same train up to Springer, arriving the next day. The Kansas cattle should arrive three days later if nothing happens."

"Well, I can work with that. Thank you very much. I'll let you know if there is any change," said Green.

Green hurried off to send telegrams to his father and to his agent in New Mexico, detailing arrival times and approximate numbers. That afternoon he visited with the customs officers to make sure everything was in readiness for the arrival of the cattle.

It was after all this activity that Green remembered he hadn't seen Andres Gomez all day and started hunting him. He found him in the livery stable.

"Andres, have you eaten?"

"*Sí, jefe, comi a las ocho de la manana.*" (Chief, I ate at eight this morning.)

77

"Did you sleep here last night?"

"*Sí, jefe.*"

Green realized that Andres was not accustomed to a comfortable bed and probably rested better in the stables. "You gonna sleep here tonight, too?"

"*Sí, jefe.*"

This one is as bad as my old friend and teacher, Abel Castro. Both very economical with words, mused Green to himself. "You need anything, Andres?"

"*No, jefe.*"

"We'll leave here at daylight tomorrow."

"*Sí, jefe.*"

When Green left the hotel lobby at daylight, Andres was waiting with saddled horses. They struck a lope and reached the lead herd under Diego Yanez, who was told to pen the cattle and get them ready to be sorted. Green would be back in about an hour.

Next he found Vicente Herrera and told him to tell the other herds to wait until the lead herd was sorted. They would be sent for in turn.

Green sorted 2,000 steers out of the first herd to send to his father in Kansas as they were the biggest cattle. He brought in the second herd and cut them into three pens of 1,000 each, plus the leftovers from the first herd, which made four. Then he sorted the yearlings—1,500 for himself and three pens of 500 each. Green's cattle were put aside next to the loading ramps, awaiting the arrival of the train. By that time it was noon and everyone rode to the camp, about half a mile south. Besides the drovers, ten of the traders were there, plus Samuel Ravel and Sykes, the freight agent. Green introduced everybody and explained how he was going to sell the cattle to Vicente, Villa, and Ravel.

After lunch, Green held his sale at the pens. It was over quickly, as the traders had had a good look at the steers earlier. Ravel got all the money and divided it up for the various owners in Chihuahua and the revolution, represented by Villa.

By that time Green's cars had arrived, so his cattle were loaded, finishing about dusk. The traders' cattle would be loaded the next day. The traders asked Vicente and Villa if they could use their men.

"Yes, if you pay them," replied Villa.

78

All the new owners agreed, and Villa said, "We will be here when the train comes in tomorrow."

Villa led everyone but the traders back to camp for supper. Later he spoke with Green and Vicente.

"You know, Verde, I felt better driving that herd of cattle than I have felt in years, and I didn't even have to steal them."

"Yeah, it's really nice to do something that you enjoy, and do it well. I have to say that you are a first-class trail boss, Pancho. You can drive my cattle any time you want!" said Green.

"General, what are you going to do now that the revolution is over?" asked Vicente.

"I'm not sure it's over, Vicente. I'm going back to Chihuahua City and be a butcher of cattle and hogs, but I'll be watching Mexico City and Presidente Madero, and I'm going to keep all my guns," said Villa.

"General, can we go back to Herradura from here, or do we stay under arms?" asked Vicente.

"You may take all your men back and I will send the others home when I get back to Juárez. But Vicente, hold yourselves in readiness for my call. I may need you again."

"*Sí, mi general.* We will stay prepared."

Green said goodbye to everyone and left for his hotel. Villa went with him, saying, "The easiest way to Juárez is on the U.S. side, on the train."

They departed the next morning—Villa for El Paso and Green for Springer, New Mexico, to see to his yearlings there. Then Green would move on to Kansas to his regular duties with the Dunigan Cattle Company.

CHAPTER 18

Hacienda Herradura / April 20, 1913

It had been two years since the drive to Columbus, and Green was back in Mexico, buying steers. He had purchased 2,000 yearlings from Herradura and the neighboring ranches that he was preparing to drive to Columbus, starting the following morning. On this night he would, as always, dine formally with the Herrera family at the big house. He always enjoyed these times because the Herreras treated him like family.

In the main room of the big house he enjoyed a glass of Herradura wine as small talk ensued. Present were the older Herreras, Don Tacho and Doña Marisol and Mercedes, the youngest daughter. The two sons, Vicente and Tomas, were off with the Division of the North, Villa's army, but had been there earlier to help gather and brand the cattle that Green was receiving. Villa was starting to rebuild his forces after the campaign against Orozco, under Huerta, and his subsequent incarceration at Santiago Thaltelolco, near Mexico City. He had escaped just before the assassination of his beloved Madero and reentered Mexico only a month before, issuing calls to his former troops, who were now gathering at Ascensión in northwestern Chihuahua. Armed clashes had ignited all over Mexico since the death of Madero, each day becoming more ominous.

Huerta, the de facto head of Mexico, was marshaling his forces to crush the various revolutions, while Carranza, nominal head of the Constitutional forces, was uniting the forces of Villa in Chihuahua, Obregón in Sonora, and Pablo Gonzales in Tamaulipas under his umbrella. No one really trusted Venustiano Carranza, but the leaders needed some coordination. This left only Zapata in the south, independent of the combined movement, but Zapata trusted no one and was enough of a problem by himself.

All the talk at dinner was of the *decena tragica,* the ten days of the palace revolt in Mexico City, ending with the execution of Madero and his vice president, Pino Suárez, and the real showdown between Huerta and the Constitutionalist forces, which would take place probably in the next year. The Herreras, backers of the Constitutionalists, were elated that the armies of Villa and Obregón were growing fast and were well equipped, but there was word that Pascual Orozco had returned to Mexico and was allied with Huerta.

"Well, Green, we have had two good years without any fighting, but it looks like this time it will be a hard war. If Huerta is one thing, he is a soldier—and the *guerrilleros* will not have an easy time with him, no matter how many men they have," said Don Tacho.

"Yes, and with that savage Orozco beside him, it will be bloody and no one will be safe," echoed Doña Marisol.

"With most of the men of Herradura with Villa, we may not be able to put up much of a fight. I wish Mercedes was still in the U.S., but when we planned her return it was pretty quiet," said Don Tacho.

"I wouldn't have stayed even if you had told me I couldn't come home," Mercedes said, her green eyes flashing. "I was sick of those *gringas* and the teachers and the place that was wet all the time. I couldn't have stood it one more minute. Here in Chihuahua, I can breathe free and see the horizon. Here I can ride astride and gather the cattle and hunt and do all the things I love. Don't worry, Papa, as long as I have my .30-30, nobody but Herraduros will come through that gate."

Green studied her for a moment. It had been over seven years since he had seen her. Tall, about 5'7 and willowy, but with an aura of strength, both physically and emotionally, she had become an incredibly beautiful woman with her dusky color and jet black hair. Green had no doubts that she would exact a heavy toll on any invaders. He saw both of her parents shiver at her display of bravado, and Green shivered, too, because he had seen a village that had resisted Pascual Orozco and what had happened to it, as the older Herreras had. Don Tacho most certainly was thinking of getting her out of harm's way.

"Don Tacho, Orozco knows Villa protects Herradura, and he knows Villa hates him. He would not bother this place, would he?"

"Huerta does not fear Villa, and he is just as bad as Orozco. Our only real protection is our remoteness, and I fear we will be right in the middle of the fighting. You know that Huerta had Abraham Gonzales, the governor of Chihuahua, thrown under the wheels of a moving train only a month ago. No, Green, we are really not safe here, but I have to stay," said Don Tacho.

As the men moved to Don Tacho's office for cognac, he had a request to make of Green. "I am so afraid for Mercedes to stay here, Green. It has all happened so fast that I was unable to send her anywhere. Can you take her to El Paso on this drive? She can stay with friends there until the trouble passes."

"I would be proud to be of help. You have treated me like one of your family, so let me respond in kind. Let me send her to my family in Refugio. I know they would like to have someone as beautiful as Mercedes, and they have no more children at home. She would like it there, too. She is one of the few women I know who prefer life in the country. If she doesn't like it she can stay with my sister in Brownsville. Please, Don Tacho, let me repay you for all of the things that you have done for me and get Mercedes to a safe place until this is over."

"Green, I have friends in El Paso, and also in San Antonio, and I have plenty of money in banks across the river. Just get her across the border and she can go where she wants, either with your people or whomever she chooses. Just get her there!"

"*Sí*, Don Tacho."

"Now, let us rejoin the ladies and tell them what has been decided."

"You tell them, Don Tacho ... I'm scared!" whispered Green.

The two men entered the parlor and Don Tacho cleared his throat.

"Mercedes, we have decided that you should accompany the cattle to Columbus with Green. We want you to stay there across the border until this trouble is over. You can stay with the Cantus in

El Paso, or the Filesolas in San Antonio, and there is plenty of money for you. Green has also invited you to stay with his family at their *rancho,* if you would like."

Doña Marisol hugged Don Tacho and said, "Thank you, Tacho ... You don't know how much better I feel."

"Well, nobody asked me how *I* feel!" bellowed Mercedes. "Papa, you need me here. You are very short-handed, and I can do much more than all the *viejos* you have left. No, I stay here. If you are not running, neither am I."

Don Tacho frowned. "Young lady, we are your parents and you must obey us. It is the duty of all good Mexican children to obey their parents, and you have always been obedient, as a properly raised lady must be. There will be no more discussion. You will go with Green and that is that." He and Doña Marisol stood together and glared Mercedes down.

"*Sí,* Papa, I will obey, but I will not like it," said Mercedes.

To break the tension, Green spoke to her. "Mercedes, be sure to take some clothes that are very plain. If need be, we may try to pass you through as a common peon woman. You know, black shawl over a white blouse, that sort of thing."

"I will take such clothes along, if you insist, Green, but I will be working as a vaquero and will dress accordingly."

"That'll be fine, Mercedes. Just have someone take your baggage over to the camp wagon before we leave or I'll send someone to get it."

"Do not worry about it, I'll see that it gets done. If there are no more orders for me, I have to attend to my packing."

She dutifully kissed her parents good night, bowed deeply to Green, murmuring, *"Mi jefe,"* dripping with sarcasm, and left the room.

"Don Tacho, I sure think we got out of that easy. Of course, it hasn't all happened yet," said Green, with obvious relief.

"She is a strong-willed girl, much help in these uncertain times. I want her to survive, to be able to rebuild Herradura after the revolution. She loves it more than all the others, but I want Herradura to be like Mexico, just enough left to rebuild on a good foundation after all the destruction."

"I hope it can be so, Don Tacho, for it is a good thing to be built upon."

In the morning, Green thought at first that Mercedes was not there, but he spotted her just before putting the herd out. She was indistinguishable from any vaquero, except for a mass of black hair disappearing under her sombrero.

Mercedes took station just behind the point as the herd moved out to the north. Green watched her ride expertly back and forth, alternately squeezing and relieving pressure to keep the herd going in the right direction.

"She was right," Green said to himself. "She knows what she is about around cattle."

Green had talked to his vaqueros before the drive, telling them to treat her as they would any vaquero as his mission required anonymity for her. Most of the men knew her and respected the importance of her remaining unnoticed.

The drive followed basically the same route that Green had followed with Villa's people two years earlier, swinging wide to avoid Chihuahua City, then straight north to Columbus. No difficulties were encountered along the way, and after two weeks they were within a week of Columbus. They had seen almost no one along the trail. Green felt pretty safe because both sides of the revolution tried to stay clear of the U.S. border, so as not to provoke the colossus of the north. The U.S. had been very unpredictable all through the revolution, first backing Díaz, then friendship with Madero, then hostility to Huerta, even landing at Vera Cruz and Tampico. Green thought the policy was dictated by nervous businessmen, trying to protect their investments and concessions.

Three days out of Columbus, Green spotted a group coming east, probably out of Ascensión. Because he knew Villa was forming his troops there, he wasn't too worried, and Vicente and Tomas were with him and knew Green was taking their cattle to Columbus at about this time. Just to be sure, though, he had Mercedes pull a neckerchief over her face and throw dust all over herself.

As they drew near, Green was reassured. He recognized Pancho Villa at the head of the group of only seven or eight men. Green rode out to meet him and cried out, *"Pancho, mi compadre!"*

"Aieee, es el Gringo Verde, with some more of my cattle," said Villa, grinning.

They all joined in driving the cattle, distributing themselves around the herd. Villa, always observant, remarked, "Verde, you have got a pretty little vaquera with you this trail, eh?"

84

"*Sí*, she is a good hand," Green said, not sure how much he could trust Villa around a beautiful young woman. "These past few years you have had all the men away fighting, so women at times have taken their places, and many are pretty good with cattle. My little Juanita is one of the best."

Villa smiled. "Oh, I see ... my little Juanita. Don't worry, Verde, I do not poach another man's woman. There are plenty to go around."

"That's good, Pancho, but would you tell your men hands off also? I don't want any trouble—because she is also a good cook when I need one," said Green.

"You should marry her, Verde. I always marry my women. They like it legal."

"How many wives have you got, Pancho?"

"Oh, maybe twenty, twenty-five. I don't keep count, except for the first, Luz," answered Villa.

"What's legal about that?"

"It's legal to them. I am the sinner."

Green thought through the tortured logic and guessed it made as much sense as anything else in a revolutionary setting.

During the afternoon Green was able to ride with Mercedes to explain what was happening. "Mercedes, I told Villa you were my woman, to protect you from him and his men. Tonight make your bed beside mine so it'll look right."

"Gringo, I'll do that, to make it look right, but if you so much as put one finger on me, I'll cut off your *cojones* and feed them to you for breakfast," she said, her eyes flashing.

"Mercedes, I'm just trying to protect you."

"Make sure that's all you do, Green," she said, whetting her knife on her leather leggings.

Green rode off, glad he was unmarried and confused as ever about women.

CHAPTER 19

Columbus, New Mexico / April 25, 1913

illa and his men were a great help with the cattle the rest of the drive into Columbus. As they rode along, Villa asked Green, "Verde, you told me one time you were in the army in Cuba. Did you have any experience with guns, artillery?"

"No, we were dismounted cavalry, infantry. I did some artillery training in college, though, and I remember enough so that I think I can still lay and fire guns. Why do you ask?"

"I have captured some guns and bought some, too, but I have no one who knows how to shoot them. Could you help me train some people?"

"Pancho, I told you this revolution was none of my business. I am a cattle trader, not a soldier, and I don't want to change."

"Verde, I only want you to train some people, not fight. I could make it worth your while. You could have all the cattle I bring up to the border, cheap."

"Let me think about it, Pancho. I'll give you an answer when we get to Columbus."

The days into Columbus were uneventful, but the nights were bad. Green had to make it appear that he and Mercedes were lovers, but without touching her. She wasn't particularly cooperative, and that made it even worse.

Arriving in Columbus, Green shipped the yearlings to his pastures around Springer and paid Ravel—half to Herradura and half to Villa's revolution. Villa took Green's drovers aside and told them he needed them to drive cattle for him, and they agreed to stay with the revolution.

Green and Villa were talking after the train pulled away.

"Come with me, Verde, I want to show you something," ordered Villa, and Green followed obediently. They went to Samuel Ravel's warehouses, where Villa showed Green his arsenal: cases of mauser rifles, machine guns, and two shiny 75mm artillery pieces, complete with caissons and harness.

"Can you shoot these guns, Verde?" Villa asked.

Green had never been around such weapons, but they seemed to be simply more modern and more powerful versions of the pieces he was familiar with from earlier days. He then made a momentous decision and said, "*Sí, mi general,*" and Villa enlisted him.

Green stopped by the telegraph office to send his father a wire:

Have been kidnapped by Villa. Will be back after the revolution. Let me know in care of Samuel Ravel, Columbus, New Mexico, when you need steers, and I will send them. Letter follows. Green.

At the warehouse, Villa had already sent some horses for teams to pull the guns and had sent many horse-drawn wagons to transport the rest of his arsenal. His men were loading rifles, machine guns, and ammunition, and Green saw to the harnessing of the eight horses that Villa had chosen, four to each gun. He also saw to the loading of each caisson, with its proper loads of ammunition and of the resupply into several wagons.

Villa said, "Verde, you are my artillery. I make you a captain. Go take these guns to Ascensión and train my people to use them. After that, you can go about your business as you see fit."

"I will do so, *mi general,*" Green responded, knowing he was trapped. He was still going to try to get Mercedes across the border, and on to his family, and the guns would go along with the rest of the wagons that were still loading, so he thought he had time.

He found Mercedes around the camp at the railroad pens. "Get your things," he said. "I can get you on a train to my folks' place in two hours."

"You act like you are not going, Green. Did you get a chance to steal some more Mexican cattle?" she asked.

"I told your father I would get you to the U.S. safely, and I have done it. If you want to go to El Paso or San Antonio, that is fine, but you are taking that train out of Columbus ... today!"

"Let me tell you something, Gringo. Both of my brothers are fighting for Mexico, and even you are now, so it appears. What do you expect from me? You think because I am a woman I am not a patriot? I will stay and fight also!"

Green felt nauseated. He couldn't break his word to Don Tacho or her brothers, but he knew he could not keep her out of this. She would just come back when he was gone. He stared at her, all dusty in men's trail clothes, glaring at him. He had never seen any woman as beautiful or desirable, but she could never be his. He threw up his hands in disgust.

"All right, you break your word to your father if you must, but if you try to become a common *soldadera*, I will get Villa to carry you to El Paso. You just pretend to be my woman like we've been doing, and stay out of trouble."

"If you acted like a man instead of a *maricon* (homosexual), it might be easier," Mercedes snapped back.

Green was at a loss. Was she inviting him into her bed, truly, or was she just lashing out in anger? He was going on the assumption that it was anger, but still he was badly confused. How would he be able to carry on this charade, with her in her present state of rebellion?

Villa had witnessed the whole exchange, and in fact had known the whole story, even to the identity of the beautiful señorita. He had extracted it from one of the vaqueros, and now was choking with laughter. He would confront Green later, but it was just too much fun to spoil for now.

Green was assigned two experienced teamsters to take the guns to Ascensión, and he put them on the caissons with much instruction on how to keep them out of ditches. Satisfied that all was well, he put them on the trail to Ascensión, with himself and Mercedes as outriders, their personal baggage tied onto the back of the caissons.

When the time came to make camp, Green had decided to treat Mercedes just like all the soldiers treated their women. He took her horse and told her to make supper. Green and the teamsters led off the horses, watered and hobbled them for the night, then returned to the fire for supper.

The beans were burned, the bacon was black, and the tortillas were hard as china plates and just as tasty. The teamsters looked at Green and shook their heads. Green didn't look at anybody. He knew that common practice dictated a beating for a woman who put out such food, but he figured her reaction would be so violent as to expose her, so he just kept quiet. He knew he had lost a lot of face with his teamsters, but he didn't know what else to do. The teamsters wandered off, probably in search of a decent meal.

He approached Mercedes. "Can't you cook any better than this? I can't pass you off as a *soldadera* if you can't do any better. They'll all know you as a *caballera*, a gentlewoman, in no time."

"You don't deserve any better, Gringo. If you don't like the food, don't eat it. What's wrong with it anyway?" she spat.

"It was all burned up! Didn't you learn anything about cooking in that fancy school?"

"Young *gringas* don't cook. They have servants to do it," she said, still boiling.

Green gave it up and unrolled his blankets. Mercedes did the same, next to his. She had her hand on the haft of her knife, and she told him plainly, "One move, and I'll serve you your *cojones* for breakfast." With that she rolled up in her blankets, as did Green a few minutes later.

CHAPTER 20

Ascensión, Chihuahua / May 25, 1913

As soon as they were settled in Ascensión, Green set about recruiting his gun crews. Villa had two more of the 75mm guns that he had captured from the *federales*, complete with teams, harnesses, and caissons. He would need five men for each crew, including a gun captain and four others. The captains would need their own horses, while the others would ride two of the team horses and two could ride the caisson. One or two of each crew would need a little mathematics to be able to work the sights and aim the gun. Green had brought the instruments needed for alignment from Ravel's warehouse, along with extra ammunition, so he could begin as soon as he recruited his crews. He started with Villa.

"*Mi general,* I will need about twenty-five men and most all of them need to be able to read, write, and do some figuring to shoot these guns and be able to hit the target. I'd like to pick them myself, if you don't mind."

"Verde, come with me. I have someone I want you to meet who can probably solve your problem." Villa took him to his headquarters and called out, "Colonel Medina, can you come out here? I have my artillery *gringo* here."

A tall Mexican, neatly dressed in the federal uniform of a colonel, appeared in the doorway.

"Colonel Medina, met *Capitan* Verde. You two will handle all my artillery."

Medina grasped Green's hand warmly and said, "Very glad to meet you, *Capitan*. What experience have you had?"

"Very little, I'm afraid. I had two years of training in college and I am a licensed surveyor."

"Do you have your instruments here?"

"Yes . . . instruments that Ravel had in Columbus. I think we can adequately service a four-gun battery with them."

"Medina, Verde asked for twenty-five men who are educated to service these weapons. Do you really need that many?" asked Villa.

"General, we will need at least one hundred of such men. Four guns is all we have now, but we must have trained crews for many more. These you will get for us from Huerta's forces," explained Medina.

"All right, Colonel, I will provide the men, and you provide the bombardment. I will send them tomorrow. Where do you want them?"

"General, with permission, we will establish a separate camp for the artillery. *Capitan* Verde and I will find it and report back to you tonight."

"*Bueno* . . . I'll be here until supper," said Villa.

Medina took Green and they walked off toward the gun park.

"Tell me," he said, "is your name really Verde?"

"Colonel, my name is Green Dunigan. General Villa had trouble getting his tongue around that, so he translated it and now I'm called 'Verde' or sometimes 'Gringo Verde,' at least around here."

"Well, I can say Green and Dunigan, but for the sake of uniformity, I will officially address you as *Capitan* Verde," said Medina, smiling.

"Colonel, we will get along good," answered Green.

They came to where the guns were parked and Medina inspected what they had. Then he and Green got horses and rode off to look for a camp for the artillery. As most of the camp was on the east side of the lake at Ascensión, naturally they thought to move to the west side. A little group of abandoned adobes sat on the northwest end of the lake. The plains beyond, toward the distant sierra, would make an ideal firing range. The adobes would serve as headquarters and living accommodations.

Green started moving the guns and the people associated with them, Mercedes among them, to the spot they had picked out. Medina went to report to Villa so he could send the prospective gunners in the morning.

Green had the teamsters harness up and move the guns, while he and Mercedes rode over and took over one of the adobes.

"Fix it up to suit yourself. I'm going to try to find Medina, and we'll be back at dark. Fix enough for everybody," Green told her.

"Your wish is my command, my Lord," said Mercedes, with a deep bow. Green got out quickly before she started throwing things.

Green wandered through the camp that was growing every minute. He was looking for Vicente or Tomas Herrera to get their help with Mercedes. Perhaps one of them could handle her.

There were 700 to 800 men in the camp and more coming all the time, with no particular organization.

"I guess Villa knows where everything is, but I don't see how," Green mused to himself. He asked about for the Herraduros, but nobody seemed to know. Finally one fellow seemed to remember that they had been sent to scout the way to San Andres, to the south, and would return in a few days. Green quit looking and continued to Villa's headquarters to find Medina.

He came upon them outside the headquarters adobe.

"Ah, *Capitan* Verde, Colonel Medina and I were just chatting about you. We want to ask you some questions."

"Ask away, *mi general.*"

Medina spoke. "You said that you had learned artillery in school. What kind of a school teaches artillery? Did you go to Chapultepec?"

"No, nor to West Point, the U.S. military school. I went to Texas A&M, a land grant college. Most of the land grant colleges have an army officers' training corps, but I didn't finish. I only went for two years. I had a little experience with guns in Cuba. I was a scout-messenger with the Rough Riders of Roosevelt. A couple of times I was commandeered to help with the artillery. I was a sergeant there. That is about all my military background."

"Compared with most of these men you are a grizzled veteran," commented Medina.

"Colonel Medina, I have taken one of the buildings for myself. Do you have anyone with you, or will you stay in the headquarters?" asked Green.

"I have a wife and family in Coyoacan. I may find a *soldadera*, but only to cook for me. I will stay in the headquarters building."

"*Bueno,* Colonel, and I will await the arrival of our recruits in the morning, if that pleases General Villa," said Green.

"It pleases me, *Capitan,* but if it doesn't, you will be the first to know," said Villa, the menace in his words was understood, if unspoken.

Medina walked back to the artillery camp with Green. They mostly talked of the revolution and what drove men to participate. Medina, an educated man from an upper-class family, was very candid with Green.

"Most of the men here, the vaqueros and *campesinos,* are here because their lives are dull. For them it is better than working for a miserable existence, and the prospect of looting is a powerful magnet. A few of us, like Villa, want a better future for our nation, and others want a better future for their children. But for all of us, and I include you, it is an escape from a dull existence to the promise of adventure. Only a few have any real ideals in this revolution. Madero was one, and so is Zapata. The intellectuals, such as Flores Magon, and some of those with Zapata, Paulino Martinez and Díaz Soto y Gama, are trying to articulate goals to edify the soldiers, but to the vast majority, fighting in the revolution is simply more interesting than working. But it had always been so, in all the revolutions—the peons die and the intellectuals mouth slogans."

Green thought about that for a while as they walked in silence, then spoke. "You're right, Colonel. When I was with Roosevelt, he talked a lot about liberating Cuba and bringing democracy to the Cubans, but we never saw any of his blood, only our own. Then he got to be president of the United States and we got little tin badges. But it was an interesting trip."

They arrived at their camp just at dusk. Mercedes was tending her pots of food, but the few men there had finished eating. Guitar music and soft singing peremeated the evening.

"Colonel, come and eat with me and Juanita. I told her to fix plenty."

"Thank you, Green, I will," Medina said, and they sat down to eat. The beans were better and the tortillas pliable, which was much improvement. Green smiled at her and she stuck out her tongue at him. He decided that even silent communication with this *virago* was useless. Maybe her brothers could do something with her, but he doubted it.

The men Villa sent over started arriving about 8:30 the next morning, and Medina and Green started culling them into roughly equal numbers of gunners, loaders, and teamsters. Medina took the gunners off to probe the mysteries of the gun sight, while Green set the teamster group aside and showed them where he wanted corrals for the horses and sheds for everything else, and sent them to scrounge material and tools to build them with. Then he took the loader group and started teaching how to handle the shells, to cut fuses and charges, and other skills.

When they broke for lunch, Medina came over, followed by a big, bushy bearded cutthroat.

"*Capitan*, this soldier said he was with you in Cuba. You know him?"

Green peered at the smiling giant a second, then cried out, "Etienne! Etienne de la Garza! You've found another war!"

They hugged and danced around each other until Green finally addressed Medina. "Colonel, I think we have found our gunnery sergeant. He was the one who saved my life in Cuba when I was wounded."

"Do not put so much authority on me before you know what I can do, Colonel," said Etienne soberly. "Green may be overestimating me."

"Don't worry, I make up my own mind. But you seemed to catch on quick, and starting from scratch, we will make do with what we have. You are a temporary gunnery sergeant as of now, but we will demote you if you can't do the job. Have no fear of that, Sergeant de la Garza," said Medina.

"Come on, Etienne, we have lots to catch up on over the years, no?"

"*Sí, my capitan*," answered Etienne, and both Green and Medina realized that their newly appointed sergeant was putting proper military usage back into the relationship, as proper noncommissioned officers usually do. Green took this subtle reprimand to heart and said, "*Bueno*. Now come on, *Sargento*."

"I look forward to meeting your green-eyed *haciendera, Capitan.*"

"How do you know this?" Green demanded, suddenly frightened by the fact that the identity of Mercedes was known.

"It is talked about around the campfires, *mi capitan.* There are no secrets in armies. But don't worry, no one pays any attention. Mostly they are jealous because she is so beautiful," answered Etienne blandly.

"I had some doubts about your Juanita, Green, and if there is something secret or dangerous here, I think you'd better tell me about it," Medina said.

"Well, Colonel, my little Juanita is actually Mercedes Herrera of the Hacienda Herradura, south of Parral. Her father asked me to take her to safety in the United States, and I did, but she refused to stay. So I had to bring her here. Her brothers, Vicente and Tomas, are the leaders of a troop of cavalry, but they are off scouting San Andres for the general. I don't know how long I can keep this thing going, for she is a willful and headstrong girl, besides being a beauty. I just have to find a way to get her safely across the border. She is playing the part of my *soldadera,* and I have not laid a finger on her, I swear."

"That being so, I will keep your secret," vowed Medina.

"Thank you, gentlemen, and I really mean it," said Green.

Training for the artillerymen started in earnest that afternoon. Medina took one gun and started training all the gunners. Green, with Etienne helping, took three guns, the teams, and equipment and trained all the rest in moving and emplacing the guns for firing. Gradually the two groups were integrated, and at the end of three weeks the three instructors had trained crews for eighteen guns, and thought that their men could expand to serve many more if they could capture them. They organized "*Batteria* A, Division del Norte," from the four best crews and fired some practice rounds out on the plains. Medina pronounced the battery combat ready and so informed Villa.

"Good, Colonel. I will try to find some more guns for you. Maybe Huerta has some, no?" said Villa, grinning evilly.

Gradually, over the next ten days, they organized Batteries B, C, and D and did some live firing. Lacking officers and reliable sergeants, Medina went back to recruiting. He had very little luck, as no one wanted to be a gunner without a gun, but he did get B and C partially staffed. The four batteries had been fully equipped with all the horses, harnesses, wagons, and tools they would need. All that was lacking were guns and caissons and more ammunition, but they were ready to capture those.

Gradually, Mercedes' cooking improved, and Juan Medina and Etienne de la Garza became regular diners. Green felt comfortable with both of them, but his relationship with Etienne was deeper.

One night after a supper that only Etienne had shown up for, he and Green sat around the fire with a bottle of tequila.

"We've been so busy that we haven't had time to catch up with ourselves, have we, Etienne?"

"We have been very busy, but I think we have done well."

"What brought you here, Etienne? Why did you come to fight with Villa?"

"Green, I wasn't doing much of anything in the bayou country—a little trapping, fishing, and guiding hunting parties. I got to drinking and fighting and I was thrown in jail a lot. Nothing serious. But one morning about a year ago, I woke up in the parish jail and made up my mind to follow my instincts. I am a warrior, and the only time I really feel good is when I am in danger and fighting. And I'm good at it. So I just found the closest war, and here I am."

"Well, I, for one, and I think Medina for two, are glad you came. We could never have organized this outfit without you."

"What about you, Green? What brings you to this war? You are a good soldier, but not warrior."

"That's a hard question. You know, I've been trading on the border most of my life. A couple of years ago I got involved taking cattle from some old friends and customers to help the revolution. I got to know Villa. He asked me to help train his artillery and I came. I haven't been able to figure out why, except that I like it here in Mexico, in the desert, and I like the people. I don't know what my folks think. I haven't been much help in the family operation, except that I get first crack at all the best cattle coming out, and that will make us some money. Maybe that's why I'm still here."

"Maybe your *chica* there has something to do with it, eh?" said Etienne, nodding at Mercedes, who was washing the plates off to the side.

"Maybe so, but I don't think so," Green countered. "Which reminds me ... I have to get a hold of some people and I need to write my father and mother to bring them up to date."

The next morning, Green begged off the training sessions for the day and went to look up Vicente and Tomas Herrera. The encampment at Ascensión had grown to over 1,000 fighting men and sprawled over 100 acres, including pastures for the livestock, wagon yards, and everything else that was allied to an army.

After asking around, Green located the area that contained the Herraduros and found Vicente and Tomas, as well as some others he had known. They embraced him vigorously and invited him for lunch.

During lunch he remarked, "You'll have to come over for supper some night. My *soldadera* is a pretty good cook, and she is from Herradura originally."

"Oh? Maybe we know her. Who is she?"

"Mercedes Herrera," answered Green quietly.

Both men stared at him with steely black eyes, not knowing what to think. Green waited for them to speak.

"What are you doing with our sister? It is bad enough that she is here, but as a *soldadera*?" queried Vicente.

Green laughed and told them the whole story, including her threats to amputate his manhood. The brothers laughed, but it was a nervous laugh. Both knew Green had a tiger by the tail and neither had a solution for him. They would prefer that it remain Green's problem.

A change of subject was made by Green. "Weren't you scouting San Andres? What did it look like?"

"Well, we shouldn't be telling you, but it looks pretty easy. There are some guns there that could give us trouble, but I think we can take it and so does the chief," said Vicente.

"Listen, we want to get those guns and we have the crews to get them. Can you make me a sketch of the layout?"

Tomas looked at Vicente and then addressed Green. "You'd better talk to the chief about this. He knows we need artillery, but he isn't going to let you run the operation. I will tell you that there are four guns there and two of them are well placed, but you see the chief about the rest."

"All right, I'll get Medina to talk to him. But we need maps of that area and I thought you might have one. I've got to go now, but you come by for supper tomorrow."

When Medina talked to Villa about the guns at San Andres, Villa said he knew about them and showed him a map of the federal position in that area. Medina persuaded Villa to allow them to try to capture the most dangerous guns so they could turn them against the *federales,* and he asked that a cavalry squadron be assigned to work with him. Villa agreed to it and even assigned him the Herraduros.

Green was overjoyed when Medina reported back. He said, "Colonel Medina, Tomas and Vicente Herrera are coming for supper tonight. They command the Herraduros and have been scouting San Andres for Villa just recently. If you join us, we can talk about our plan."

"That sounds good, *Capitan.* I'll be there."

It was about dark when they all arrived at Green's adobe. He had scrounged a table and some nail kegs for chairs, resulting in an al fresco dining area. A bottle of tequila and one of fairly decent *aguardiente* awaited his guests.

Vicente and Tomas came first. They poured a drink and sat down, without even acknowledging the presence of their sister. When Medina arrived, he was introduced all around, as was Etienne.

Medina asked them about the environs of San Andres and told them they were to be detailed to him to capture the federal cannons. Everyone was interested in the upcoming operations, and a lively discussion ensued until "Juanita" announced that the meal was ready to eat. The guests moved to the cooking area to fill their plates with stew, beans and rice, and sat down to eat. Neither of the brothers had paid the slightest attention to their sister until Vicente said, "*Chica,* bring me more stew, if you please."

"*Sí, Major,*" she replied dully.

As she served him more stew, Vicente said, "Green, I like your *mamacita,*" and with that he pinched her on the bottom and grinned widely.

A lot of things happened then. No one could recount them accurately later, but certain surprising things did occur and with astonishing rapidity.

Vicente was on his back with the stew bowl covering his face. His attempts to remove the stew from his face and clothes brought

98

gales of laughter from Tomas and Green, astonishment from Medina, and a quiet strategic retreat from Etienne.

Vicente, trying his best to salvage some dignity, glared at Mercedes and then at Green.

"If she was my woman, I would beat her good," said Vicente.

"She didn't hit me with the stew," said Green, choking back a guffaw.

"You gonna beat me, Señor Major Herrera?" purred Mercedes beside him, with a butcher knife inserted between his legs.

Tomas' head was on the table, choking with laughter. Etienne was chuckling just at the edge of the firelight. Vicente had turned white. Green pulled Mercedes away and took the knife. Colonel Medina took all of this in with a blank stare, comprehending nothing, but knowing there was more here than met his eyes.

Finally, Vicente realized the humor of the situation and started laughing, whereupon Green and Mercedes got some wet towels and wiped him off. Medina was still amazed at the performance. He knew any *soldadera* who hit an officer with a bowl of food would have been badly beaten, and here were these fools laughing.

Vicente, Tomas and Green, in order not to appear complete fools, felt they should let Medina in on the fact that Vicente and Tomas were the brothers of Mercedes. After he had been informed, he chuckled along with them. The brothers and Green felt that their secret was safe with Medina and Etienne. Mercedes thought differently.

"You men always talk about women gossiping. You talk more gossip than those *gringas* I went to school with. I think I would be better off staying with the rest of the *soldaderas* and take my chances."

They all reassured her that their lips were sealed, and the subject was dropped in favor of the upcoming operation at San Andres.

Medina brought out maps of the area, which the Herreras had originally drawn, and they all looked them over. Everyone came to the same conclusion. There was a federal gun position that could cause many casualties to an attacking force, but it was vulnerable to a surprise attack from its right rear. Medina's plan was for the Herraduros to attack it just before the main assault, accompanied by Battery B, the trained cadre that didn't have guns. After taking them, they would turn the guns on the federal lines in support of the main assault. This plan had Villa's stamp of approval, but there was something missing.

"What's to keep the federal reserve from meeting and turning back our attack on the guns? Don't they realize the position is important and vulnerable?" asked Green.

"Just right, *Capitan*," countered Medina. "Battery A will mark the attack by fire and protect the assault as its primary mission, and I will promise you I will protect you until you can consolidate your position, as I will command A personally."

For Vicente's and Tomas' satisfaction, Green said, "That is good. I have seen Colonel Medina shoot. He can certainly protect us by fire during and after the attack."

So the plan of attack was agreed upon, with only details to be settled. All knew that traveling orders had been cut to go in two days. Medina would command Battery A, and the rest of the ungunned gunners and Green would have Battery B to service the guns they planned to capture. Medina had asked that Etienne stay with him, as A Battery's performance would be crucial in the operation. Green understood and agreed. He set out to pack up and prepare his unit for the operation.

CHAPTER 21

San Andres, Chihuahua / August 25, 1913

olonel Medina, Green, and the Herrera brothers walked away from the headquarters after the briefing on the upcoming attack. They were to have their units in attack position before dawn and had to make a wide detour to be able to attack from the right rear of the federal line, so they would have to leave soon.

Medina was to open fire on the left flank of the objective at 7:00, thirty minutes before the general assault. This would enable the Herraduros to take the position at about the same time as the advance started and be able to support the assault with their captured guns.

Signals were arranged to shift fire ahead of these attacks, so as not to have friendly fire falling on the attackers. Medina's plan was to keep the *federales'* heads down until the Herraduros were about to attack the position, then shift fire to the reserve, to keep them from reinforcing. Green would take the guns and shift fire onto the main federal line before Villa hit it with his main effort.

Villa's plan was simple. He would hit the federal line straight on, with a wild cavalry charge, followed up by his infantry. This was his basic tactic, and he relied on it heavily. It had worked in the past.

They all pulled out as soon as they rounded up their troops and equipment and marched all night, arriving at the jump-off point at 4:00 A.M. to begin deployment. Green and some of his men were horseback, but the bulk of them went in wagons which carried their equipment and some extra ammunition for the guns. Green would not start until the Herraduros had taken the position, but he would be there to consolidate it. The attack plan was similar to Villa's in that it started with a wild cavalry *golpetazo* (mighty blow), but the similarity ended there.

Most of the men had brought along snacks of cold beans rolled in cold tortillas, so they ate as they waited for dawn, behind a masking hill. Vicente and Green had crawled to the top of it and spied the campfires of the *federales,* about a half mile away. All seemed normal, both sides waiting for the battle to start. The *federales* had 1,300 men and the advantage of numbers, Villa's forces numbering less than 1,000. But Villa's advantage was the speed and ferocity of his attacks, which usually carried the day.

Promptly at 7:00 A.M., the artillery began to fall accurately on the infantry line to the left of the artillery, and Green saw that it was very effective, chewing up the defensive line and isolating the gun position. The Herraduros had covered about half the distance to their objective and were well deployed for the attacks. Green then started the wagons of Battery B, to be there to take over.

The gun position was immediately overrun. Green arrived with his men, and they quickly shifted the guns ninety degrees to be able to put fire on the center of the federal line. The Herraduros occupied positions to protect the artillery, and everyone took their horses and the captured *federales'* horses out of the line of fire. Within ten minutes of his arrival, Green was laying fire down on the federal line, whereupon Medina shifted his battery to support Villa's charge.

Green had a ringside seat for the performance. His battery was firing now to immobilize the federal reserve, as was Medina's, but he was able to watch the fury of Villa's assault on the main federal lines. Upwards of 500 horsemen, in three lines, hit the line breaking it, and Green could see the *federales* running away. Cavalry and infantry turned toward the flanks, rolling them up quickly, and the Herraduros were soon busy keeping the *federales* from their position. Not that they really wanted it; they were more interested in getting away from the storm of bullets all around them. By this time, close to 8:00, the Herraduros were making bets on killing individual *fed-*

erales streaming past their position, on their right. A train came flying out of San Andres, headed north to Chihuahua City, quickly outdistancing a troop of pursuing riders. Green shifted his fire to it, bracketing it once but not scoring a hit. It was the federal commander making his escape. The Battle for San Andres was over, and Villa had won. All that was left was to add up the loot.

And there was a lot of it. Eight more 75mm guns were captured, plus over 700 mauser rifles, 20,000 rounds of ammunition, and nearly 1,000 rounds for the guns. Two Herraduros among the thirty-two *villistas* were killed. A total of 236 *federales* were captured and shot by order of Carranza, who had invoked the Juárez Law of 1862, but Villa had been killing them all along. He had them lined up four deep, so one bullet would kill four *federales* at a time.

It was nearly 11:00 by the time Medina and Battery A showed up. Green greeted him by saying, "Great news, Colonel, you now command a battalion. There were eight guns here altogether, all undamaged, except for one with a broken wheel, for which we had a spare. We have three full four-gun batteries, a full battalion of guns, with plenty of ammunition, all harness, teams and assorted equipment, fully equipped. I am in the process of gathering everything up and bringing it here, so you may activate Battery C and the battalion. Also, I want to congratulate you on the fine performance of A Battery. You did some very accurate and very timely shooting."

"Green, you trained that battery . . . I only shot it," said Medina.

"Well, for whatever part I had, I am proud of them."

Green had hidden his prisoners from the *federales* artillery, and they all wanted to join Villa, including a lieutenant from Sinaloa. He told Medina, and Medina talked to them all, after which he called a sergeant aside and shot him. When Green asked him about it, he replied, "He was a Huertista pig. I knew him. He joined us to save his hide, but he would desert the first chance he got."

This incident raised Medina's stock with everybody. It proved he wasn't a blood-thirsty savage, and that he valued loyalty both ways. Green had seen some of the prisoners being shot, and it had sickened him—mostly because it was a waste. Most of the soldiers had been dragooned into the *federales* and should have made good recruits for Villa anyway, and many of them would have deserted to the revolution when they got the chance.

By dark, all of the camp followers had arrived, and fires glowed all over. Juanita had hers going and there was plenty of food, owing to the captured supplies. Green had gotten all the guns and equipment to their area and assigned Battery C to its positions.

Green asked Medina, "Colonel, why don't you ask General Villa to visit us in the morning and we'll arrange a parade of the battalion for him?"

"I'll go try, but you know he captured seven trains here. That's quite a haul, and he may not be too excited about eight more guns, although they'll do him more good."

"Don't tell him what it's for. Let it be a surprise. He may know about the guns that were captured, but I don't think he'll realize he has a fully manned and operational battalion of artillery, so let's surprise him," said Green.

"All right, *Capitan*, but don't promise anything you can't deliver," cautioned Medina.

Green had already eaten when Medina returned. Juanita gave him a plate as he sat down.

"He's coming," Medina reported. "He'll be here at nine in the morning. He was pleased by our part in the action and wants to show it, but I didn't tell him anything about a review."

"Colonel, I have it all fixed. I even got a color guard with a battalion flag. You lead the battalion, and I'll lead B Battery, if that's all right. The women are making the flag right now. Do you think we should call it the 'Ascensión Battalion' or 'San Andres'?"

"We formed and trained at Ascensión, but we proved ourselves at San Andres, no? I favor San Andres. What about you, Green?"

"That's what I had them sewing on the flag. I like it."

"San Andres it is, then."

Green had his gunners stirring early, making them all shave and dress in their best clothes, which varied from white peon shirts and trousers to captured federal uniforms, to three-piece business suits, and everything in between. By 7:30 he had them on the ground practicing the review. Just after 8:00 they took a break, dusted everything off again, and lined them up for inspection.

Villa arrived at 9:30 with three staff officers and Maclovio Herrera, a *guerrillero* who had come in that morning with over 1,000 men. Medina led them on an inspection of the troops and equipment; then Medina led the battalion in passing in review, three batteries, four guns abreast, four wagons following each battery, all headed by a color guard with the battalion flag and a Mexican flag just behind Medina.

Villa was simply delighted. It was very precise and very military, as becoming a great general. After the battalion was dismissed, Green and Medina joined him and the other officers.

"Maclovio, didn't I tell you I had a proper army? You see my artillery battalion? We are soldiers, not *guerrilleros*."

"*Sí*, Pancho, but can they fight?"

"We beat the hell out of a brigade of *federales* yesterday," Villa said pugnaciously. He turned to Medina. "Colonel, you need an assistant battalion commander, don't you?"

"*Sí, mi general*. I might suggest *Capitan Verde*."

"A good choice, Colonel. Congratulations, Major Verde."

"I thank the general," said Green, smiling.

"Colonel, if you have any other officers to be named, give me a list. I want the San Andres battalion to be up to the mark."

"I have a few, General, but we will be wanting more men to train to staff another battalion when we capture the guns."

"Just tell me what you need. Your unit did brave work yesterday," Villa said, and he was gone.

After Villa left, Medina called the men together and announced some promotions to sergeant and corporal, and promoted Etienne de la Garza to sergeant major. He congratulated them, but warned them to be ready to leave the next day. There were too many *federales* in Chihuahua City, and they would be moving south to Jimenez.

Villa sent a squadron of cavalry south to Jimenez the next day. The day after that, he loaded his division on the seven trains he had captured and they moved off toward Jimenez. There were no *federales* there and no resistance developed, so the move to Jimenez was without incident. Some raids to the east and west netted more loot and equipment. And in Jimenez, Villa was joined by another rebel force, the Morelos Brigade under Villa's old comrade-in-arms and fellow bandit, Tomas Urbina.

CHAPTER 22

Jimenez, Chihuahua / August 31, 1913

illa's Division of the North was growing by leaps and bounds, and a period of reorganization was desperately needed. Jimenez offered many advantages for this kind of thing, the principal being its distance from Orozco's forces at Chihuahua City. To Colonel Medina and Major Verde, the most welcomed new recruits were former *federale* officers, disgusted with Huerta's heavy-handed rule. Many of these officers had varying amounts of knowledge of the workings of artillery and some even brought their guns with them. Medina now had enough guns and trained men to put two battalions of artillery into action, with a reasonable assurance of effectiveness. Fire coordination was a problem, as they still had no one who could run a fire direction center, but a recently defected federal major showed promise.

Colonel Medina was part of Villa's operations staff now, but he still helped and was in overall charge of the artillery. The rumor mill was very active at this time, as is the case in any army, and most of the guesses centered on Chihuahua City as Villa's next objective, with Torreon running second.

Medina favored Torreon because the main north-south railroad lines met there, as well as lines from the east, and since the focus of the war in central Mexico was the railroads, it seemed natural, or so Medina had confided to Green.

The question was answered two days later, as Villa moved south in two columns.

The night before departure, Green wrote to his mother and father in Texas:

Dear Mother & Dad:

I feel badly about writing you so late, to explain my seemingly irresponsible behavior of late. I know I have not upheld my end of the work and responsibilities of the ranches, but there were good reasons. Don Tacho Herrera put his daughter, Mercedes, in my care to get her to safety. I was unable to do so, as I was drafted by Villa to train his artillery, but Mercedes is still with me and undiscovered, as my soldadera, Juanita.

I must remain here until I can find a safe way out for the Herrera girl. I owe a lot to her family and they are good friends. It will not be a total loss, however, as I have first pick of all the cattle sent to the states by Villa, and believe me, it is a lot. We get them under market. I have already sent 1500 to Jack as you know, and there will be more. I haven't been back to Columbus, so I haven't gotten any messages, but continue to send them to me there and I will try to get them forwarded.

I am now a major, commanding an artillery battalion in Villa's army. It looks like we are headed toward Torreon, but we will probably not operate outside of the state of Chihuahua, so don't worry about me. We are well equipped and in a high state of morale, having just won a decisive battle against superior forces at San Andres. The war here is waged on the railroad lines, as they are the main supply routes, and distances here are large and the only way to move with any speed is on trains. Villa has got seven of them so we have good mobility.

I know that the United States papers label Villa a bandit, and he was, but he is a good man and a good general, with many fine people fighting for the principles of Francisco Madero, who started all this. Just to name two, Vicente and Tomas Herrera are here. You remember the Herrera cattle, with the horseshoe brand.

Here in northern Mexico, the overriding reason for the support of the Revolution is to break up central control of the Republic by Mexico City. In other parts it may be over land expropriation, or other issues, but here many of the best, oldest families support the revolution. Villa's army is not a blood thirsty rabble—it is a well organized, effective military organization and I ought to know, as I have been in several.

Guess who I found here? Etienne de la Garza is here with us! He is currently our Sergeant Major and is doing a great job. The Mexicans aren't quite sure what to make of him yet, but some of the federal officers who have deserted to us speak French to him. He is happy just to find a war.

Dad, you have always had first call on me. If you need me, I will come anytime you say, but I am trying to carry my weight through the cattle I buy and send to you.

This thing is really just getting into high gear, but I think it will be over soon; but I will come anytime you say. My agreement with Villa was to train his artillery, not to fight it, so I can really leave anytime.

Tell Abel and Sulema that I am all right and doing well here.

Your loving son, Green

The Division of the North moved south to Torreon, with the Juárez Brigade, under Maclovio Herrera advancing along the north bank of the Nazas River toward Gomez Palacio and Lerdo. Villa's columns, with the Morelos Brigade under Urbina protecting his right flank, followed the south bank of the Nazas to the federal position at Aviles, directly fronting Torreon. Green's artillery battalion supported Herrera's brigade, and the rest of the artillery commanded by Medina supported Villa's columns.

Villa took Aviles quickly, while the Juárez Brigade took two days to clean out Gomez Palacio and Lerdo, and the final assault on Torreon was well planned and coordinated. Villa led the final charge and Torreon, with immense amounts of supplies and military ordnance, was theirs.

The effect of the fall of Torreon was significant in that it cut the rails to Chihuahua City and Juárez, destroyed a well-equipped federal army, and relieved pressure on Obregón's forces to the west and Pablo Gonzales in the east. It was the beginning of the end for Huerta.

The fall of Torreon also brought many recruits to the Division of the North. Enough so that Villa could now think about attacking the large federal garrison at Chihuahua City and clear the whole of Chihuahua of federal troops. Villa had over 20,000 well-equipped troops with plenty of rolling stock to move them.

After stores and men had been replenished, Villa loaded his division to move north to invest Chihuahua City. The division was unloaded at Camargo, some 130 miles south of the city, and began the approach to invest Chihuahua City. Villa telegraphed the federal commander, his old nemesis Pascual Orozco, to surrender, and in reply Orozco wired for him to "come and get it."

In about two weeks after leaving Torreon, Villa had placed Chihuahua City under siege. Villa was not using his *golpetazo* method of attack here. He would carefully prepare his objectives with his artillery and then attack, but could gain no foothold. Orozco was a good commander and was well equipped.

After three weeks, Villa could see the only result from this would be more casualties, so he devised a plan to draw them out. He withdrew most of his mobile forces, infantry and cavalry, and left a small force to continue besieging the city. Green was left with two battalions of artillery to carry on shelling as before. With the bulk of his forces withdrawn, Villa stopped a coal train from Juárez and had the conductor wire Juárez that the train could not get to Chihuahua because of the besiegers. Villa unloaded the coal, loaded his soldiers, and ordered the conductor to return to Juárez. At each station the conductor, with a pistol at his head, wired his progress to Juárez. Arriving about 4:00 in the morning, Villa's forces controlled Juárez before dawn.

The shadow forces besieging Chihuahua City were quickly withdrawn north, and Villa, with a modern iron trojan horse, had isolated Orozco and Chihuahua City with few casualties at all. Villa was a celebrated hero in El Paso, especially after, under the advice of Medina and American Gen. Hugh Scott, he let the prisoners live, either by joining him or crossing to the United States. Some were killed, but the practice of executing prisoners was stopped—at least by Villa.

CHAPTER 23

Juárez, Chihuahua / November 18, 1913

As soon as he was settled in Juárez, Green crossed the river to settle accounts with Sam Ravel. All the cattle he had sent had been paid for correctly, and his accounts were all in order. On his way back, he sent wires to his family, telling them he was fine. He also bought a fancy box of chocolates to give to Mercedes, hoping he could persuade her to leave the revolution.

Green had not really been around her much since they had left Jimenez, his duties being too close to the fighting for her to see him. When he got to the house where he was billeted, she was cleaning and putting things in order. Green asked her to go outside with him, as he had something for her.

"I'll be out in a minute, *mi major,*" she answered.

When she came out, Green said, "I brought you some candies ... sweets for the sweet."

She looked at him suspiciously and took the box, sampling some of its contents. She smiled and said, "Oh, they are so good. I haven't had anything like this in so long. Thank you, Green." She reached up and kissed him on the check.

Seeing that she was not hostile, Green brought up the subject of her going to Texas.

"Are you going back there?" she asked.

"I am, just as soon as we get organized, for I only told Villa I would train his artillery, not fight it. And I have been doing that— more than I agreed to do."

"I will go when you do, then," she said, and went back inside to resume her housework.

Green made up his mind that he would see Villa the next day to ask for demobilization and get out of a revolution that was none of his business. After all, Villa had a full regiment of artillery that, thanks to Medina and himself, was well trained and efficient, and he had competent officers, even some *gringos* to fight it. He felt Villa would let him go.

That night, Vicente, Tomas, and Colonel Medina came for supper, and Green told them what he intended to do. Vicente and Tomas looked relieved. They had worried about their sister.

Colonel Medina frowned and said, "Green, we received information that Orozco is on the march north. Villa sent that cutthroat Fierro to wreck the tracks and slow them up, but even so, we will meet them in battle in a very few days. I can't do without you when we do battle. Orozco is bringing over 5,000 troops, and he is well equipped."

"Colonel, there are plenty of good men to do this job. You don't need me." Green knew Villa would not let him go unless Medina approved.

"I promise you, Green, that if you stay, we will destroy Orozco once and for all, and then you can go and I will recommend it to Villa."

Green turned to Mercedes. "I will put you on the train tomorrow, and I will follow just as soon as we beat Orozco."

"I told you, I am a *maderista*. I have more stake in this revolution than you do, *gringo*, and I am staying," Mercedes stated.

Tomas, Vicente, and even Juan Medina all tried to persuade her to leave, to no avail. They gave up and left for their quarters.

Marching orders came the next day. The Division of the North moved out for Tierra Blanca, about one-third the distance to Chihuahua City, and began digging in a strong defensive position with over 6,000 troops. Villa's men had a whole day to make their position strong. On November 23, 1913, Orozco's *federales* showed up, and the battle began.

Orozco had to attack over a desertlike, treeless landscape before he could reach Villa's position on the Tierra Blanca ridge. He, like Villa, favored the *golpetazo* tactic and launched attack after attack at Villa. Green, with his guns, was blowing gaping holes in the federal charges before they could get into Villa's lines. It was a terrible slaughter, but Orozco had guns, too. Green was adjusting fire for Battery F when Orozco's guns got the range, overturning one gun, and killing three cannoneers. Shrapnel hit Green in the arm and chest and knocked him down, but he was still mobile. After being bandaged, he started about getting the battery back into action, when the remnants of some federal cavalry hit their position and were in it. Fierce hand-to-hand fighting was going on in the gun position, and Green had shot at least three men before he was hit in the chest by a bullet. He shot another *federale* but was unable to dodge his sabre, which hit Green on the side of his head. The last thing he remembered was *villista* horsemen coming to their aid and pushing out the *federales*.

Green woke up that night in the hospital train, hurting all over. A nurse was passing by and he grabbed her arm.

"Did we win?" he asked.

"It is not over, Major, but all say we are winning. From what I see being brought back here, it is costing us heavily."

Green didn't wake up again until he was taken to the hospital in Juárez. Mercedes was sitting beside his bed when he opened his eyes.

He recognized the hospital as being in Juárez and asked, "How did I get here? What's wrong with me?" His eyes scanned his body, looking for missing arms, legs, or other parts.

"Be quiet, Green, you are going to be all right. You were hit several times. No bones broken, but you are weak ... you lost a lot of blood. I saved this for you." She held up a mashed piece of steel. "This bullet came out of your shoulder. They say you were very brave and that you killed many *colorados* and that you saved your guns from them," she said slowly. "I was so scared that you would die. You were all blood and stitches when you got here." Mercedes held his face between her hands. "Green, I will go with you now. Let's go to your *rancho* right now."

"Mercedes, I don't think I can sit up, much less walk, but we will go as soon as I can. That I promise you."

During the desperate fight, Tierra Blanca had left over a thousand *federales* dead in front of Villa's lines, but it cost him dearly, too. After the second day, Orozco broke it off and retreated, not to Chihuahua City but southeast to Ojinaga, opposite Presidio, Texas, with his back to the Rio Bravo. Villa detached Panfilo Natera to deal with him and moved the Division of the North to Chihuahua City, its natural home. He later had to take more men to Ojinaga, and Orozco and his men were driven across the river. Villa had at last made all of Chihuahua free of federal troops. He met with the American commanding at Presidio, General Pershing. They got along well, as Villa had put an end to troubles along the Chihuahua border, from Eagle Pass, Texas to Douglas, Arizona.

The first week in December 1913, Villa was back in Chihuahua City, organizing the government. At the end of the week, word came that all but the most severely wounded would be taken to Chihuahua to recuperate, before rejoining the division. Green, who was still weak, raised all sorts of hell to stay in Juárez. But as all his friends were south, he was taken in Villa's new hospital train, sparkling clean, with trained nurses and well staffed with doctors, to the hospital in Chihuahua City. Mercedes, who never left his bedside, was there when Colonel Medina came to visit.

"Colonel, you promised to get Villa to let me go, and they brought me here. I want out, Colonel, and you promised to get me out. So do it."

"Green, I know all about that, but I didn't know they would move you. You are here now, though. I will try to get you out, but it will be more difficult. I have, however, great news. Carranza has sent General Felipe Angeles, the best soldier in Mexico, a fine man and a real Maderista, to us. We now have two full regiments of artillery with two new batteries of 120mm guns. We are forming into an artillery brigade, and I have recommended to General Angeles that you be made brigade major. He has agreed."

Green winced at this and Mercedes narrowed her green eyes. When she spoke, her voice was husky and menacing. "Colonel Medina, Green doesn't want to be a brigade major. He has given more time and blood to this revolution than most Mexicans. You promised he could go in Juárez. Are you a man of your word, or are you a lying dog?"

Medina knew better than to tangle with Mercedes and told her,

"Señorita, I will keep my word, but the decision is up to General Villa. I will do my best, but I also know that we need Green more now than before. Angeles and Villa both know that, but I will keep my word and do my best."

Mercedes did not change her expression. "I can ask no more, Colonel."

Green healed quickly, and on January 2, 1914, they released him from the hospital. His wounds were nearly fully healed, and though he had lost about twenty pounds he felt strong and could move about on his own.

From the time he had been brought from Tierra Blanca, Mercedes had been with him, nursing him, making sure no sepsis set in. She would change his bandages, wash him, and feed him. Paying no attention to his appeals for privacy, she knew his body intimately now, though not through love. She had secured a small house near the center of town for them and had her brothers bring furnishings for it.

Their relationship had subtly changed. No longer did she defy him and act as if there was nothing between them. She was fiercely protective of him, as she had been of herself, and she did all that was to be done for him. On the other side, Green had changed toward her. If anything, after seeing the blood and destruction of Torreon and Tierra Blanca, he was more determined than ever to get Mercedes as far as he could from the revolution. He knew that she was no shrinking violet, but he wanted her away so she wouldn't be harmed. He began to consider her precious to his life.

Vicente and Tomas came for supper that night. He knew they had been scouring the country south of Chihuahua, and they seemed to be soberly preoccupied that night.

While Mercedes was with them, eating supper, Vicente said, "We have some very bad news. Tomas and I have been to Herradura. It was raided by Orozco's *colorados* before Tierra Blanca. Orozco himself led the raid, and only old Mercadio Gomez and his woman survived. Everyone else was slaughtered, and some pretty horrible things were done. Then it was burned."

Mercedes blanched. *"Mama y Papa ... ?"*

"Yes, Mercedes, everyone's dead. I guess Pascual Orozco did it because we were supporting Villa and Madero ... but it is all gone. Most of the buildings, because they were stone and tile, did not burn down, but everything else burned to the ground. All that is left are graves."

Mercedes burst into tears and left the room. Tomas started after her, but Green stopped him.

"Tomas, she must grieve for herself. Let her do it and get it over with."

No more words were spoken, but each swore an oath to himself. An oath of vengeance for Pascual Orozco.

Vicente and Tomas left for their own camps soon after. Green found Mercedes standing in a corner of the room, tears streaming down her face. He took her in his arms and held her tightly for a long time. Finally, she was able to talk.

"Will you promise me that Pascual Orozco will not live another year, Green?"

"Your brothers and I have sworn such to one another, and one of us will see to it, if it is our last act. You have our word."

"Green, my whole life is destroyed. I loved my family, but I loved Herradura as my reason for life. Nothing will be the same ... never again."

"Mercedes, Herradura will endure—it will be rebuilt. But the land and the buildings were not its soul. It was the people who are buried there, who worked it, and made it. The Herraduros will rebuild it after the revolution. It won't die, because you won't let it."

"Will you help me, my Gringo Verde?" she asked.

"I am not a Herraduro, but I will do what I can."

"I will make you a one!" she said with conviction.

Feeling tired from standing, Green let her go and sat down on his bed. Mercedes helped him off with his boots and tunic, but when she started on his other clothes, he told her, "I am no longer an invalid, Mercedes, I can undress myself."

"Hush, Verde, I have been doing this for too long."

Over his protests, she completely undressed him and put him under his blankets. Then she shed all her clothes and stood naked in the moonlight, watching him, as he watched her. He had never seen anything so lovely. The moonlight on her long, lean body, her small but firm breasts, her jet-black hair tumbling over her shoulders composed an image that would have made Venus hide her face in shame. She moved to his bed and lay down on his body, kissing him tenderly. Green was too shocked to do anything, but well

115

knowing that this was the time both admitted their love for each other.

Mercedes slipped under the blanket beside him and pulled him on top of her. She pulled him into her and wrapped her legs around him tightly. They made love for a time, and then, exhausted, they fell asleep in each other's arms.

Green awoke at first light and was startled by Mercedes in his arms. She stirred, and hugged him to her again. After a while, she arose to fix breakfast. Still weak from his wounds and their love-making, Green was slow in dressing. She was putting his food on the table when he went to eat.

Mercedes quietly said to him, "Verde, I am now truly your woman, your *soldadera*. I have wanted you for so long and now I have you, at least for a while. I feel like a wild bird, released from a cage."

"Mercedes, I feel the same, but I think it is not for a little while. I believe it is forever, for I have loved you for a long, long time."

"Think about what you are saying, Verde, for if you say it again, I may believe it," Mercedes said with a twinkle in her eyes.

Puzzled as ever by the female species, Green thought it best to eat his breakfast and keep his mouth shut.

CHAPTER 24

Chihuahua City, Chihuahua / March 3, 1914

The Division of the North had been reequipped and reorganized with the loot from Juárez and the addition of the gold reserves of the Banco Minero, whose location was secret until it was coaxed out of Luisito Terrazas, the scion of the Terrazas clan. Villa's division was now the pride of the revolution: 12,000 men, two regiments of artillery. Villa had even bought thousands of pairs of American shoes for his soldiers. There was more uniformity of dress now, and with the addition of Felipe Angeles as artillery brigade commander and division chief of staff, there was more vigorous training and discipline. Man for man, it was more effective than any regular army formation.

Green had met Angeles in mid-January, when he returned to full duties, and was very impressed. Angeles was probably the finest soldier in Mexico at that time. Tall, handsome, and aristocratic, he was completely dedicated to the revolution and the principles of Madero's plan of San Luis Potosi. Villa was somewhat in awe of him and even considered turning over command of the Division of the North to him, and to take a subordinate command, but neither Angeles nor the other brigade commander would hear of it. Actually, Angeles had examined Villa's campaigns and felt he was a great commander, but he knew he could help Villa, especially in the area of artillery deployment and support. Angeles arranged to inspect the artillery soon after he came and was surprised to find it so well trained and efficient. He called all officers and senior NCOs in and told them so.

General Angeles told Green and Colonel Medina how he would have to depend on him a great deal as he and Medina would be spending most of the time during the battles advising Villa, and that Green, although junior to the two regimental commanders, would really be the brigade commander. Green was not quite sure about this arrangement, feeling that the regimental commanders were quite competent and able to command their regiments. Angeles agreed but felt Green was the only one, beside himself and Medina, with the experience to coordinate the brigade in battle. Green reluctantly agreed, knowing he was being committed to at least one more battle.

He reminded Medina of his promise, to which Medina responded. "I have pleaded your case to General Villa, as you asked. He has told me that the next campaign was too important for you to be absent. He understands your position and will let you leave as soon as you can be spared. As a reward for your service, he has promoted you to lieutenant colonel."

"And what is this next campaign that I am so essential to, if I may ask?" Green asked testily.

"We have decided to retake Torreon, and then Zacatecas. After that, Huerta should be beaten forever. By the way, rumor has it that Pascual Orozco is back in Mexico and is operating south of Zacatecas."

Well, that does it, Green thought. *At least I'll have a chance to fullfill my vow to Mercedes.*

This wasn't easy to explain to her, and she did not like it. Not withstanding his pledge to kill Orozco, she felt he had done enough. It wasn't his country after all, but he had made the vow of vengeance and he would keep it. He had become very much a Mexican. Knowing it would be futile to try to dissuade him, she quit trying.

The next two weeks were busy for Green, developing his position between the regimented commanders. Medina and Angeles were working with the artillery brigade, and the two regimented commanders were really unaware that Green was going to be the defacto commander, as all of the orders from Angeles and Medina came through him. When they went into action, Angeles and Medina would be in Villa's headquarters.

It didn't take long for Green to acquire a deep respect for Felipe Angeles, a man whose character commanded respect. His knowledge of military affairs was unsurpassed by anyone on either side. He maintained strict discipline in his brigade but was not a martinet, and his coolness and equanimity under fire was legend. The only person Green had ever known remotely like him had been General Shafter in Cuba. However, Angeles was not only a good commander; he was also a leader. Green felt extremely confident serving under him and was able to make Mercedes feel it also.

When marching orders came down, Angeles called an officers' meeting to brief his brigade. They were to load the following day with the whole division. When loading was completed, the trains would pull out for Escalon. Villa had sent troops ahead to secure the rail line that far. When the first train reached Escalon, the advance guard reported that the line was secure as far as Bermejillo. So the division kept moving toward Bermejillo, where they finally detrained.

The Division of the North would be fighting over familiar terrain this time. Villa and Angeles had planned all phases of the battle meticulously. First Sacramento was taken, followed by Lerdo and Gomez Palacio. Final preparations were finished for the assault on Torreon itself. It would not be an easy task. The best of Huerta's forces had retaken Torreon from a revolutionary garrison in December and, having expected a counterattack since, were well dug in. But Villa had about 15,000 men who were now quite well equipped, well trained, and well organized. Villa told the Division of the North they would take Torreon with their teeth, if necessary.

With Angeles at Villa's elbow, it was a masterful battle: artillery preparation ahead of cavalry charges, followed by infantry mop-ups and occupation. The *federales* fought ferociously until April 2, when they began withdrawing. The next day, the Division of the North was in control of Torreon and with it the important cotton-raising district of the Laguna. The cost had been high—500 dead and 1,500 wounded on Villa's side—but many more *federales*. The artillery was commandeered for three days to haul bodies out of town and bury or burn them.

Green missed most of those events when he took two battalions of artillery to support a brigade commanded by Angeles attacking San Pedro de las Colonios, northeast of Torreon. A strong federal garrison was completely destroyed, and very few were able to get away to join the survivors of Torreon at Saltillo.

Before and during the ten-day battle, Villa had repeatedly begged Gen. Pablo Gonzales, head of the Constitutionalist forces of the northeast, to move south to cut the rail line connecting Torreon and Saltillo. To have done so would have prevented the escape of the federal army under Velasco to Saltillo. Now there were some 9,000 troops to be beaten again. Repeatedly, Villa asked that Gonzales attack Saltillo, as it was in his zone of operation. Gonzales waffled, and Villa appealed to Carranza, the first chief. Carranza also refused, then ordered Villa to make the attack. Villa would obey.

Back in Torreon, Green wandered through the destruction that had been Torreon. Most of the dead had been removed, but the hard fight had left most of the city in rubble. Increasingly, Green was led to wonder if it was really worth it. Could Mexico be cleansed by blood and fire, or was it an adventure for the benefit of the participants? For most, he concluded, it was better than working or stealing, but he would never be sure.

Green was given a new job upon his return. He was to oversee the shipping and sale of 100,000 bales of cotton that was part of the booty of Torreon. Another *gringo,* Maj. Tomas Mix, was detailed to help, as both knew Sam Ravel and had worked with him often. Mix was young and had been with Villa a long time, almost from the beginning. Formerly a cowboy and rodeo performer, he was now quite a good troop leader, and was a *dorado,* one of Villa's personal guards. Their work took them to El Paso, to deliver the cotton and take delivery of more munitions' uniforms and supplies, in addition to coal that was needed to fuel Villa's trains.

Green and Tomas Mix returned to Torreon in time to join Villa and Angeles on a visit to Carranza in Chihuahua City, to plead the case for an attack south to Zacatecas instead of Saltillo. They were ushered into an imposing structure on the edge of town. There Don Venustiano Carranza received them, but they would get no satisfaction from him. He told Villa to take his orders from Obregón, which did not go down well. Then he launched into a tirade about the *gringos* taking over Vera Cruz.

Villa replied, "They have shut off all of Huerta's supplies. Nothing could be better for us."

"They have challenged the sovereignty of Mexico, which I will not let happen!" Don Venustiano declared, drawing himself up to his full height with a majestic scowl.

The meeting fell apart from there. Carranza would give Villa no freedom of action and appeared to be against all the purposes of the revolution. Villa left in disgust, but not yet in disobedience.

Traveling back to Torreon in their car, Villa was silent for a long time. Finally, he said, "Carranza does not really want to do the things Madero would do to save Mexico. He wants to replace *porfirismo* with *carrancismo*—just change who is in power. If it turns out that way, we will have bled Mexico white for nothing, and I'll never be able to stop fighting!"

Angeles spoke up then. "I have known this every since I met Don Venus. He has always wanted to rule as an emperor, and that is the reason he causes so much trouble. He wants no one with enough strength to challenge his rule."

"Well, that won't happen as long as Francisco Villa lives, I can promise you that."

Green and Tomas Mix looked at each other, wondering how two *gringos* got mixed up in this Mexican standoff. The rest of the trip was enveloped in silence.

Green found a little villa on the outskirts of Torreon, knowing it would not be long before Mercedes and the rest of the *soldaderas* arrived. Then he went looking for the Herraduros, as he had heard they had endured some heavy action. He found their compound and asked for Vicente.

"He is not here, Colonel. He has gone to find horses to replace the ones we lost."

"Is Tomas here? Maybe I can talk to him."

"You did not hear, Colonel? Don Tomas was killed on the third day of the battle, defending a position we had just taken against a federal counterattack. It failed, but we lost our friend and leader, Don Tomas Herrera."

Green came away very sad. Another tragic loss to a dear family who had given so much to Mexico. And considering the revelations of their interview with Don Venus, maybe it had been for nothing.

Green rounded up Etienne de la Garza to tell him of Tomas Herrera's death. Etienne was saddened because he had liked the brothers. Etienne knew they were preparing to move and wanted to know where the division was going.

"I don't know, Etienne, and I probably couldn't tell you if I did."

"Well, two battalions went with Medina to Saltillo, but that shouldn't take long. I guess it's either Durango or Zacatecas, or San Luis Potosi. But San Luis would leave Zacatecas in our rear . . . that goes for Durango also."

"Panfilo Natera and the Arrieta brothers have taken Durango and are headed for Zacatecas now," said Green.

"Do you think they can take it, Verde?"

"No, but I'm not the chief. We could take it, or San Luis, but we'd have to move everybody to Saltillo to bypass Zacatecas."

The two of them talked for a while and decided that since they wouldn't be making the decision, there was no need to speculate. They would know where just as soon as the decision was made.

Etienne was brigade sergeant major by this time. They had offered to make him a captain, battery commander, but he refused, knowing that a good sergeant major was as powerful as a whole troop of captains, and he didn't want to be an officer in any course.

A good amount of equipment was captured at Torreon, making the Division of the North not only the largest but best equipped unit of the revolution. Clothing was now almost uniform throughout the division.

Mercedes finally arrived to set up housekeeping in the little villa. During supper on the day of her return, Green told her about Tomas.

"The Herraduros told me he died a hero, defending a position against a federal counterattack. I can believe it. The *federales* here were good troops, and well led by Velasco. It was very bloody."

Strangely, Mercedes did not weep. He knew Tomas to be her favorite of all the family, but he guessed that she had no more tears to shed. He dared not tell her of his fears for the revolution in the hands of Carranza.

That night she made love to him—almost in desperation, it seemed. Afterward, as they lay in each other's arms, she said, "We

122

have to get out of here, Green. This revolution is going to kill everybody before it is over. If you were to be killed, I would die myself. Let's go to Texas ... now," she pleaded.

"I told Villa I would stay until Zacatecas, and he agreed. Besides, Pascual Orozco's back in Mexico, and I believe he will be at Zacatecas."

"You and Vicente. Your thirst for vengeance will kill you both."

Mercedes held on to him throughout the night. He awoke once and could feel her sobbing, and he held her tighter.

CHAPTER 25

Torreon, Coahuila / May 21, 1914

reen was appointed regimental commander of the 3rd Artillery Regiment and was given three battalions of new 90mm guns from Belgium. Because he had been in El Paso selling the cotton, he was able to secure very good equipment for his new regiment, including brand new French field telephones. He chose his regimental and battalion officers and NCOs from the existing brigade, but got his junior officers from all over the division. In two weeks the regiment was performing tactically as well as, or better than, the older two regiments. He contacted General Angeles and asked him to bring General Villa for a formal review followed by a field exercise with live fire, which was scheduled three days later.

Villa arrived with Angeles, Medina, and Tomas Urbina about 10:00, and the review was held. The unit performed beautifully, Villa taking the salute as they passed. The regiment looked especially good in that Green had also obtained a full supply of uniforms with Texas hats.

After the review, with the regiment in traveling columns of battalions moving east across the flat laguna country, Green pointed out to Villa an abandoned adobe about three miles away. "You see that *jacal, mi general?*"

"*Sí*, Verde, what are you going to do, shoot at it?"

"Just watch closely and use your watch to time us from right now."

Green ordered the regiment to the gallop and it thundered out on the plain. Then he ordered the regiment to deploy for firing. Each battery turned out of line, went into firing positions, dug in, registered, then placed the fire of every gun in the regiment on that lonely adobe. It was all done in twenty-three minutes.

Green was puffed up like a peacock as he asked, "How did you like that, *mi general?*"

"Magnificent, Colonel Verde. I am impressed."

Angeles added, "Colonel Verde, you can be justifiably proud. I have never seen better deployment and fire. Did I see some old stakes out there in the battery areas?"

"There may have been something out there, *mi general.* I do know my battalions rehearsed in this area yesterday," Green replied, smiling.

"*Ay*, Chihuahua. Pancho, let me have this regiment for my brigade," pleaded Tomas Urbina.

"*Mi general,* the regiment thanks you for your kind words. May I have a word with my general?" asked Green.

"*Sí*, Verde, what do you want?" asked Villa.

"Over here, *mi general.*" Green indicated they should walk out of earshot, and Villa complied.

"General, you said I could leave after Torreon, and I want to leave. I have trained my regiment well, and Colonel Bustamante is well qualified to command it. Let me go, please."

"Verde, I agreed to let you go after I took Torreon and Zacatecas, and I will. You don't know all that has been going on. Carranza has been trying to render the Division of the North impotent. He has sent Panfilo Natera and the Arrieta brothers to Zacatecas, and they are about to lose the battle. I won't go through all of it, but we have had a big fight with Carranza and will be moving tomorrow. Natera has been thrown back to Fresnillo, and we will join him there. We are going as the Division of the North, under command of Francisco Villa. Natera and the Arrietas will fight under us. Not even Don Venus can change that, and we will take Zacatecas. I will need you to command your regiment this one time, and if you will, I will see to it that the Herreras get to keep most of Herradura. Will you do this for me, Verde?"

125

"I will do it, *mi general,* but only until Zacatecas is taken. Then you will allow me to leave ... agreed?"

"Agreed," said Villa, and the bargain was struck.

When they joined the others, Angeles said, "Colonel Verde, you will load your regiment day after tomorrow. See Major Fierro or Major Mix for details."

"*Sí,* I will be ready."

"General Urbina had requested you to support him, and as far as the division is concerned, that will be done. Any objections?" asked Angeles.

"The third regiment will be proud to fight with the brave Morelos Brigade," answered Green.

"Don't bullshit me, *gringo.* You just fire the guns right," grinned Urbina.

CHAPTER 26

Veta Grande Mine, Before Zacatecas /

June 22, 1914

reen's regiment was with the bulk of the artillery at an old abandoned mining property called Veta Grande, north of the city. The 3rd Regiment was to support the assault on the hill named El Grillo on the western edge of the city. The attack was slated to start at 10:00 the next morning. The regiment was well sited, but because of the rocky soil was not deeply dug in.

Just after 9:00, Green began firing on the federal position on top of El Grillo. He gradually brought all his guns to bear, and this seemed to work well as the assault moved up the hill. Green had gone down to precisely adjust the fire of B battery when the federal counterbattery fire arrived. Battery B took the brunt of it, but Green observed where the fire was coming from and was moving the 3rd Regiment fire to the federal artillery site.

Just before the 2nd counterbattery fire fell on the federal batteries, the last of their counterbattery fell on Battery B. Green was hit in the leg and in the shoulder with shrapnel, the latter shard breaking his collar bone, and both wounds were large and bloody.

He was bandaged but refused to be moved until he saw the federal battery silenced and Urbina's troops swarming up the heights of El Grillo.

"Colonel Bustamante, you are now commanding the 3rd Artillery Regiment," Green said, wincing, as they placed him on the litter. "I'm going down to the train to get some sewing done. Make sure Urbina gets on top, or he may come shoot both of us. *Adiós.*"

It was nearly dark when Green awoke to the noise of "Where is the *gringo* Colonel Verde?" He peeped over the edge of the bed to see the enormous figure of Sergeant Major de la Garza, his arm bandaged, coming down the aisle of the moving hospital train.

"I'm here, Etienne," he called, and his friend came and sat on his bed.

"You don't look so bad. It was worse at Tierra Blanca."

"What happened to you, Sergeant Major?"

"Just a scratch, Colonel, but we are headed back to the hospital at Torreon, wounded heroes." The huge Cajun grinned wolfishly.

"Is it over, Etienne?"

"Yes. Urbina took El Grillo just after you were hit, about 1:30. By 4:00 we had broken through everywhere, and not many got away. Villa had ambushes all along the canyon south and most of them didn't make it. We lost a lot of people—over a thousand."

A nurse came up and asked, "May I get you something to eat, Colonel?"

"A cup of coffee will do me. How about you, Sergeant Major?"

"That's all I want, too, sister."

She brought them a pot of coffee and cups, and they proceeded to drink it and talk.

"Etienne, I'm getting out. Villa promised that I could go after he took Zacatecas, and I'm going to hold him to it. You want to come with me?"

"You ought to get out. The next time you're gonna get killed. You stand up too much in fights, Green. This is the third time you been shot since I met you," commented Etienne. "No, I believe I'll stay here. I'm a brigade sergeant major now. And besides, I finally found me a good woman. She takes care of me."

"Well, it's about over. Between Villa, Obregón, and Gonzales, Huerta's on his last legs. They'll have Mexico City inside of two months," said Green.

"That's right, Verde, but Villa's gonna fight Carranza before this thing is over with. You know it and I know it."

"Hell, Etienne, they're all liable to fight one another before it's all over with! Come on out with me ..."

"No, I want to stick around awhile. Besides, there ain't no other war going."

The hospital train pulled into Torreon at 8:00 in the morning. Green was transferred to the hospital; Etienne had his dressing changed and was let go. He obviously went straight to Mercedes and told her of Green's wounds, because she got to the hospital, demanding to see him, before 10:00. A nurse tried to stop her, was shown a large, sharp knife, and let her have her way.

"Where are you hurt, Green? I don't want to cause you pain." He indicated his shoulder and leg. She bent over and kissed him. "You see, if you had taken me to El Paso, you would not have been hurt again. If Villa won't let you go now, I will kill him myself."

"Calm down, *mi alma,* they are only flesh wounds and a broken collar bone. I've been hurt worse by colts. Besides, I talked to Villa, and he agreed that I could leave after Zacatecas."

"You called me your *alma,* your soul, Green. Did you really mean that?"

"Yes, my love. Why don't you find a priest, and we'll get married—right now."

"I will marry you, certainly, but not here. We will go to El Paso, and we will be out of this bloody mess. Then we will marry."

Villa's conquest of Zacatecas was the beginning of the end. Obregón took Guadalajara, and then Pablo Gonzales took San Luis Potosi. Huerta's forces were shattered. On July 15, he resigned and fled the country. While Gonzales and Obregón were on a rampage, taking town after town, Carranza had effectively shut Villa down. Arms and ammunition, coal and fuel never arrived, and without coal for his trains Villa could not move the massive Division of the North. This shutoff of supplies confirmed that Carranza meant to isolate him from the success of the revolution and from having any voice in the reconstruction of Mexico. It also confirmed to Villa that Carranza meant to rule Mexico as a new Porfirio and to let the needed political reforms be forgotten. Maderos' Plan of San Luis Potosi was to be dumped for Carranza's Plan of Guadalupe. Villa tried to contact Obregón and Gonzales to build a common front against Carranza, but got nowhere. His only potential ally seemed to be Zapata, but he was a slim reed to build upon. Emiliano Zapata was an effective guerrilla leader, but he knew his own limitations. He never left his mountain stronghold south of Mexico City, and trusted no one. Against Obregón and Pablo Gonzales, Zapata would be a liability, except in the Morelos area that he knew so well.

All of this was immaterial to Green. The revolution was over, and Mexican politics was really none of his business. His last remaining obligation in Mexico, pertaining to Pascual Orozco, had even changed. Orozco had been defeated by Pablo Gonzales at Leon, in Guanajuato, and had fled north, back to Texas. Green felt he had better inform his family of what was about to happen, so he wrote them:

Dear Mother & Dad,

Well, I am back in the hospital at Torreon. I took a couple of pieces of shrapnel at Zacatecas, nothing serious, but that, along with the collapse of Huerta's forces, had ended my career as a Mexican Revolutionary soldier. I am coming home to Texas for good. I am sure you think, and I agree, that it is high time.

I am a colonel now, but expect to retire in about two weeks. Something else has occurred in my life that is quite important, and I think you will, like me, be very happy about. I have fallen in love with a wonderful woman, and intend to marry her as soon as I get to El Paso. I have written to you about her before. She is Mercedes Herrera, the daughter of Don Tacho Herrera, of Herradura, close to Parral. She is the girl who I was trying to get to the states, out of the way of the revolution. I never did get her out, but I, along with her brothers, certainly tried. One of her brothers, Tomas, was killed at Torreon, but the other, Vicente, is still alive and kicking, leading a squadron of Villa's cavalry.

You need to make plans to come to El Paso for the wedding. I think it will be in about two weeks from now, but I am not sure of the exact date, so much remains to be done. Bring all the family and plan to stay about a week for all the festivities.

It would be nice if you could get to know Mercedes before we are married, but that doesn't seem to be possible. So let me tell you a bit about her. I first met her with her parents in El

Paso. She was home on vacation from a girls' school somewhere around Washington, D.C. She was about 12 years old then, and she is about 21 now. She is beautiful beyond description, black hair, green eyes, and a lovely dusky complexion. She is slender and graceful as the tall grass on the Kansas flint hills. Not only does she possess all the social graces, she is at least as strong willed as mother. She can ride and knows cattle as well as the best vaqueros in Mexico, and she loves me almost as much as I love her. She nursed me when I was shot up at Tierra Blanco, and I owe her my life, which I freely give to her, as she does to me.

Dad, you may realize how happy this makes me, and I hope you are pleased. Except for her brother, Mercedes is an orphan, as her parents were slain, along with everyone else at Herradura, in a raid led by Pascual Orozco. I think we will make our home in El Paso, at least for the time being, as there are a lot of details needing to be resolved. I hope I am still employed by the ranch, under our old relationship, which I want to continue, as does Mercedes.

Mother, I know I have not been a very good son lately, but I really want to get back to being a close family again. With that in mind, I hope that you will make an effort to get Jack and Lucinda, and Bill and Kathleen and all the children, if possible, to come to the wedding. I have sent word to the manager of the Paso del Norte Hotel to block off enough rooms for all of us. If you would, please get word to the Altons in St. Louis, and also Ben Davidson and his wife, and urge them to come.

Dad, I have one favor to ask of you. You remember me telling you of Pascual Orozco. I don't want to go into details, but the things he did at Herradura, and particularly to Don Tacho and Donna Marisol Herrera, were horrible. Vicente and I are sworn to kill him, and I won't rest until I do. He has escaped and is in Texas now, and I know you still have a lot of friends in the rangers. Could your ranger friends be persuaded to keep him in Texas until I take care of him? I know vengeance is a two-edged sword, but I must do this, not only for Mercedes and her brother, but for my own peace of mind. The Herreras always treated me almost like a family member, and being so, I can never rest until that man is dead. He is a completely evil man, and he must die for what he has done. Just get the rangers to keep him there until I can take care of it.

I should be discharged here soon, so any further messages send to the Paso del Norte, or to Sam Ravel.

Do your best to get everyone to El Paso.

Your loving son, Green

Villa went back to Torreon from Zacatecas on July 16, after the news of Huerta's flight. At the hospital he visited the wounded, Green included. Zacatecas had been costly. Over 4,000 casualties, including two generals, but only about 500 *federales* escaped out of a total of 9,000. Villa was almost in tears by the time he got to Green.

"Ah, Verde, look what has happened to my fine division. So many dead and maimed, and we are stopped by Don Venus, after our greatest victory. Mexico is bled white and may be all for nothing."

"*Mi general,* it had to be done. And there are many good men who will not allow it to have been done for nothing. You will see ... the leaders won't allow Don Venus to become another Don Porfirio."

"I hope not, Verde. I don't want any more killing of Mexicans by Mexicans. But there must be justice produced by all of this blood."

"There will be no more blood of mine. You agreed to that. I am going to El Paso to get married, *jefe,* and you must let me go."

"Villa gave his word, and Villa keeps his word. Are you going to marry your *soldadera,* the pretty *hacendada* of the Herreras?"

"How do you know that? How did you find out?"

"I have known from the very first, Verde. You can't fool Francisco Villa. I was listening when she told you to go to hell at Columbus," said Villa, grinning. "The reason to keep it a secret was right, but I knew the Herreras as good people too long to let their daughter be harmed. If it had come to that, Pancho Villa would have protected Mercedes Herrera himself."

"Well, if you are so interested in her, you will be glad to know that I am going to make an honest woman of her in about two weeks in El Paso. I would be honored if you could be in attendance, *mi general.*"

"I will be there, with my best suit on. We shall make it a memorable occasion. I have told you before it is best to marry a woman, even if you are married already. The women prefer it that way," said Villa, smiling.

"Well, I have never been married and intend to marry only this time. I may be a *pendejo,* but I am marrying Mercedes because I love her and cannot live without her."

"I told you I would get most of Herradura deeded to the Herreras by the revolution, and I will. Trust me, Verde. That way you won't be as big a fool as you think you are."

Green was released from the hospital on August 20. He and Mercedes figured they could make the arrangements and get married the last day of August, a Saturday, so he invited most of the Division of the North to come. Vicente would give his sister away, and Angeles, Medina, and Etienne de la Garza would stand up for Green.

CHAPTER 27

El Paso, Texas / August 23, 1914

reen and Mercedes arrived at the Paso del Norte Hotel at 10:00 A.M and Green asked the desk clerk to call Richard Bender, the hotel manager, to talk to him about arrangements.

"Ah, Green, it's been a while. I got your wire about rooms, and I believe we will have enough. As a matter of fact, your mother and sister checked in last night. You can count on Paso del Norte to accommodate you in all respects," said Bender.

"Thank you, Dick, I know you will do your best. But I have invited most of the Division of the North to my wedding, so it may crowd you a bit. By the way, I think you know my fiancée, Señorita Mercedes Herrera."

"Señorita, it is indeed a pleasure to see you again. I had no idea that you were the lucky girl. Most of Green's friends thought he would never get caught."

"Well, I caught him, and I intend to make sure he doesn't get away, Señor Bender," Mercedes replied with a smile.

All border areas have a certain ambience, and the Texas-Mexico border at El Paso was no exception. All of the important people on both sides knew one another, and the social arbiters were usually the hoteliers and restauranteur, who could make the impossible happen. Richard Bender was one of the best, but this task would test even his talents.

"Dick, you say that my mother and sister are already here. Could you put Mercedes next to them, so they may begin making arrangements right away? The wedding is planned for a week from tomorrow, and that doesn't leave much time."

"I've already done that, Green, as a matter of fact. You have no idea how much has already been done. The church is arranged for, with the bishop presiding, and Señora Luz Corral de Villa is awaiting the señorita with dressmakers. I have been told that Samuel Ravel needs to confer with you as soon as possible, although I don't know about what. He seemed to have a great urgency."

"First I would like to speak with my mother," Green said.

Bender rang Amanda on the house phone and gave the instrument to Green.

"Mother, how are you?"

"I'm just fine, Green. Kathleen and I came ahead of the others, but they are all coming. We are just having breakfast. I'll order some more if you want, and you both come up here so we can get started."

"Yes, Mother. We're on our way."

Green had their bags taken to their respective rooms, secured the keys, and took the elevator up to his mother's suite.

Amanda and Kathleen greeted Mercedes warmly before they sat down to breakfast. Mercedes was still dressed as a *soldadera*—white blouse, white skirt, and black shawl. It was all she had. Amanda and Kathleen started right in on getting her some clothes.

"Mother, I'm sure Mercedes wants to get fixed up with clothes. She has been wearing the outfit of a *peona* for two years. But could we finish breakfast first?" Green pleaded.

"Of course, son. Please excuse us, but we had about given up on getting you married and we are justly excited, particularly since you bring the family such a great beauty," said Amanda, hugging her prospective daughter-in-law.

"Green, there is a Samuel Ravel that needs to see you immediately. I would take care of that first, if I were you. We will see to the trousseau, and I have talked to Mrs. Villa, who is arranging for the wedding dress to be made."

"Looks like you have everything in hand, Mother. You might

135

even be able to handle the bride, but I doubt it. I'd guess I better go see Sam Ravel, to see what he is managing," said Green with a semi-snarl.

"Don't worry about us womenfolk, Green, we'll do what is expected of us," stated Kathleen.

"By the way, when is Dad getting here?" Green asked.

"Your father is getting here day after tomorrow, along with Jack and his family, and Kathleen's also. He contacted Gerard Alton and the young banker, Ben what's his name, and they will be here, plus a lot of our friends around Texas. The wedding will be well attended, so I want to make sure everything is done right," answered Amanda.

Green left Mercedes with his motehr and sister and caught a trolley to Sam Ravel's store.

Sam looked up when he came in. "Green, I hear you are here to marry the Herrera girl. I have had definite orders from Chihuahua about what to do. There are a lot of them, but the most important is that Villa himself insists on throwing the reception. Urbina will furnish the champagne. As many places that he has looted, there ought to be plenty. We'll have it at my place, you know, the place on the edge of town. There is plenty of room there. I guess that this will be the only social event for the Division of the North, so Villa is going to make the most of it. Also, I have your wedding suit here. Villa ordered it for you. It is the uniform of a full colonel of the Mexican Army, and I have been ordered to have similar dress for everyone attending."

"Between my mother and Pancho Villa, everything seems to be worked out. Mercedes and I have little or nothing to do with it, I suppose. Sam, I'll need some money. How much do I have on account with you?"

"You have about 80,000 here. The Herreras have something like 200,000. You might want to bank most of it," answered Ravel.

"Sam, I'll want 20,000 cash and I'll get my banker to take care of the rest. The Herreras' money belongs to the Herreras. Just because I am marrying their daughter doesn't mean I control their money."

"Who then? Weren't they all killed by Orozco?" asked Ravel.

"Vicente Herrera will be here to give his sister away. You can ask him."

"Now, Green, don't get testy. I really thought they were all dead. But even so, they could do worse than having you handle their business. I should have known, though, because Villa ordered a uniform for Vicente Herrera for the wedding. You and Mercedes also have a huge gift here from the division. It is about 350 pieces of beautiful silver. I don't know where it came from—probably from one of the great *haciendas*. It is not engraved, but it is complete: knives, forks, pitchers, and everything to make a complete set. I suspect a lot of the loot out of Torreon, Chihuahua, and Zacatecas will show up at this wedding, including Urbina's champagne."

"Well, I guess it's all right if we get it. God knows there was enough to go around. Tell me, Sam, who all did Villa order dress uniforms for? I'd like to know who is coming."

"Well, you and Vicente, and Angeles, Medina, Urbina, and Maclovio Herrera. A colonel named Bustamante and about ten others that I didn't know. Oh yes, a Brigade Sergeant Major de la Garza. I am ordered to spare no expense for the wedding. Where are you going to be married? Can I help with that? I'm pretty tight with the clergy here, even being a Jew."

"I'll send Mercedes and my mother, Amanda Dunigan, over here to coordinate with you on that. Did you know that Villa has his wife, Luz, doing Mercedes' dress?" asked Green.

"Yes, the message came through here. Luz is quite a lady, don't you think? She is Pancho's first wife and only legal one."

"I've never met the lady, but she must be something special. Especially if she knows about the other wives."

"She knows, Green, but it doesn't worry her."

"You can set up all the stuff with the ladies and show them the silver. I'll be back in a couple of days for the cash. By the way, you got a good diamond ring?"

"Got several . . . Come on in back and take your pick."

Green picked out an engagement ring with a 1.5-carat stone for Mercedes, for $3,500.

The ladies had gone by the time Green had returned to the hotel, so he went to see the manager.

"Dick, I need a little help, as I've never gotten married before. We'll be going on a honeymoon, and I want to go to a big city. We've been in the country too long. You got any suggestions?"

"You have come to the right place, Green. That's what hotelmen

137

do best. How about San Francisco? It's a great town. Lots to do. I used to be assistant manager at the St. Francis, and I know a lot of good places there."

"That sounds fine, Dick. Fix us up. And can you get me train accommodations?"

"I'll have you leave on the special that goes Sunday morning at ten," said Bender.

"The reception is going to be at Sam Ravel's place out on the edge of town, but isn't there something like a rehearsal, that the groom is supposed to do?"

"Your mother has already talked to me about it, and it is pretty well done. We'll need some more names is all."

"I might have known. Well, good. I can use this time to rest," Green said and left for his room. He lay down on his bed and slept until 5:00 in the afternoon.

When Green arose, he walked down to his mother's room and knocked. He could hear the women chattering inside, and a voice asked, "Who is it?"

"Verde," he answered without thinking.

"Who?" more chatter and laughing until Mercedes opened the door. "You think you are still in Mexico? Your name is Green," she admonished.

"I forgot, *chica.*" He kissed her lightly.

"*Gracias, mi colonel,*" said Mercedes, lovingly.

"I have a present for you." He gave her the box with the ring in it.

"Oh, Green, it is so beautiful! Where did you find it?"

"I got it off a *federale* I shot at San Pedro de las Colonias."

Mercedes' eyes narrowed and her smile clouded. She closed the box and handed it to him. "I want nothing more with blood on it," she said, handing it back.

Green knew he had made a big mistake. "*Amor,* please forgive me. I just made a bad joke. I bought it this morning. It has no blood on it. Please, put it on. It seals our engagement to each other. Please forgive me."

She took it and placed it on her finger. The air in the room turned brighter, and all the women admired the ring. Mercedes kissed him again.

"Did you see Sam Ravel? He has some arrangements for you to approve," Green mentioned.

"Yes, we saw him. He told us all about the reception and showed us the silver. It's really beautiful, Green. Really fine old Sheffield," said Amanda.

He looked at Mercedes. "Did he tell you about the uniforms, and who was coming?"

"Yes, he did, and I can live with that, but you'd better tell Villa to watch Urbina and Maclovia Herrera. Their party manners are a little rough. But I guess that they are really Mexican patriots."

"Mother, would you see to it that General Scott at Fort Bliss and General Pershing at Presidio get invited? They are old friends, especially of Villa's, and he needs to be on their good side."

"Consider it done, son. Anyone else?"

"I don't know of anyone. Did you and Sam get straight about what church and what priest?"

"Yes, Sam is going to get the bishop from Juárez to do the ceremony in the cathedral on this side."

"Does that please you, my love?" He looked at Mercedes.

"Yes, Green, I think it is a nice touch. And I have known the bishop for many years," answered Mercedes. "Oh, Green, we did not tell you about our visit with Luz Villa. She is such a fine woman, unlike many of the other Señoras Villa, and she is making the most beautiful dress for me! I just love her."

"Other Señoras Villa? I don't understand," Amanda interrupted.

"Mercedes will tell you about it later, Mother, but there are forty or fifty more. He won't bring anyone but Luz to the wedding."

"Mercedes, I asked Dick Bender to make reservations for our honeymoon, which we can spend in San Francisco, unless you want to go somewhere else. Let's take about a month off, before we come back to the ranch, all right?"

"Green, that sounds marvelous! I have always wanted to go there, and now I can go there with my man," she smiled sweetly at him.

"We will leave Sunday morning, and you can get most all your new clothes there."

"Green, I will need some money. Will you take me to the bank my father used? I know he made some arrangements for me."

"I have enough money for your every need, love. You don't need it."

"But I would like to have a little money of my own—and it's mine. It's just sitting in some bank doing nothing."

Green's sister, Kathleen, chimed in, "Green, every woman needs some money of her own, even if it's only to buy her man a present. If it's hers, take her and make the arrangements. Take it from an old married woman."

"All right, we'll do it first thing in the morning. But I'll account for it to Vicente."

"Vicente is *my* brother, not yours, Gringo," spat Mercedes.

Green felt better after that, seeing Mercedes recover a bit of bad temper. She had been too sweet and demure the past few weeks. It also awoke him to the prospects of a wife who had too much money. *Let it be Vicente's problem,* he mused.

CHAPTER 28

El Paso, Texas / August 27, 1914

The last three days had been busier for Green than he could ever remember. Besides seeing to the details of the wedding, Villa was sending cattle every day.

Green was his designated agent for the cattle, which he wanted to keep being, but it was a very time-consuming job. He talked to Sam Ravel about the problem, and Sam suggested he bring in an agent to help him and to do the whole job when he was gone on his honeymoon. Green knew a man he could trust, and would see him in a day or so.

John Dunigan had arrived in El Paso the night before, and he and Green had a long visit over lunch, after they had looked at some cattle Villa had sent in.

"Green, you asked me to contact the Rangers about Pascual Orozco. It seems you weren't the only one interested in him. A William Buckley, who used to be a deputy sheriff in Duval County, had also contacted the Rangers, with much the same objective as you. I think Buckley had been in Pablo Gonzales' forces somewhere around Tampico. Anyway, the Rangers agreed to take him out of circulation in Texas, and they tried to arrest him. They found him in San Diego, just southwest of Alice, but he put up a fight and was

141

killed. If this helps any, feel free to inform your friends that the Rangers took care of it."

"Dad, that's great news. It will please a lot of people. We owe the Rangers a vote of thanks. If they need anything in northern Mexico, just tell them to get in touch," Green responded.

"I met your intended this morning and I am impressed, Green. She is some woman. Very independent and strong-willed, I would say. I wouldn't recommend you put her in daily contact with your mother, even though they are getting along dandy right now. If they live in close proximity, sparks will eventually fly. I guess that's what's in store for us for marrying good women who have minds of their own," John said somberly.

"I have no intention of moving back to Refugio soon, Dad. I've been fighting for a year and a half for something that I think is very little of my business, and I've been shot up pretty good twice. I have Villa's confidence, as you can see by the number of cattle arriving here consigned to me. This is worth a lot of money—not only to me, but to you and Jack as well. I would be crazy not to keep it going. Also, my yearling deal in New Mexico has been quite profitable and I intend to expand it. May even buy a place out here if I can find a good one. Villa has sworn to me that the Herreras get most of their place back, and I may be involved in that. So there are many reasons for me to headquarter around here somewhere when I get back from the honeymoon. I'll probably get a place to live here in El Paso."

"Well, it sounds like you're pretty well committed out here, and that's all right. But I had kind of counted on you coming back to Refugio. You know I'm getting sort of long in the tooth and so is Pete. Thad is doing most of the work anyway, and he's no spring chicken."

"Neither am I, Dad, but I don't want to put Mercedes in contact with a new life all at once. It was pretty rough the last year or so down in Mexico. I'll tell you all about it when we can sit down and have a long talk."

"I understand, Green, and we can do without you for a while yet, but for God's sake, don't get involved in this war that's starting in Europe. If they try to get you back in our army, let me know. I still have lots of friends in Washington."

"Don't worry . . . I've had enough fighting for three lifetimes, and I won't do it anymore. Unless the Huns land in Copano Bay. And I might not even then."

They talked of things at the ranch; rain, markets, all those things of prime interest to cowmen. The senior Dunigan was reasonably pleased with his operations and told Green that his purchases had had a good effect on them. He asked about Green's New Mexico deal, as he had had no contact with it, but wondered if maybe Green wanted to fold it in the overall operation.

"I have enough cash to buy a fairly good sized ranch out here from what I hear about prices, and you'd not need to go into debt to buy it, but I'll leave that up to you, Green, but remember, Jack is going to get the Cotulla place when I die, and to be fair, maybe I ought to do the same for you."

"That's an awful tempting offer, Dad, but let me look around after all this is over with. I'm much too busy to do anything like that now."

"I know, son. I just want you to know that I'm willing and able to do this, and feel like I should before I die."

"You don't look like that's going to happen anytime soon, so quit talking about it. Besides, I don't even want to think about what Mother would do in that happening. Case closed. Let's talk about something else."

"Where are you two going on your honeymoon, Green?"

"We're going to San Francisco ... spend about a month. I think it'll be time to sell my yearlings in New Mexico by then. Mercedes and I are looking forward to it. We need rest."

"I hope it turns out better than mine," John Dunigan said. "I had to kill a man in a duel when Amanda and I were on ours."

"I don't think you ever told me about that, Dad ..."

"It's a long story, son. We'll wait until we have time and you can tell me about Mexico at the same time. When we came to get you out of the hospital in New Orleans, it was the first time we had been there since our honeymoon. That's how strongly your mother felt about the town."

Both Green and John Dunigan had chores to do, so they paid the bill and left on their various errands. There was going to be a party that night in Juárez, given by old friends of the Herreras, in honor of Mercedes.

Green went by the railroad office to bill out the cattle he had sold to various people and arranged for the loading. At the pens he was informed that another 600 steers were there consigned to him.

Oh Lord, won't it ever stop? Green thought.

At 5:00 he left the pens and went back to the hotel. When he walked through the lobby, a dirty vaquero who looked familiar from the back was arguing with the clerk. Green went over to check it out and sure enough, it turned out to be Vicente Herrera. They shared a big *abrazo,* as Green reassured the clerk that Vicente was Lt. Col. Vicente Herrera, who had reservations.

"*Amigo,* you look well. How is my little sister?" asked Vicente.

"She is fine. You will see her in a minute. Your room is just down the hall from her. You need to get cleaned up, for there is a big party in Juárez tonight, given in her honor by the Fernandez family."

"I can't go, Green. I don't have any clothes for parties. I was hoping to buy some here, but I don't think I have time this evening."

"You have clothes, Vicente. The chief has seen to that. He has had Sam Ravel get them for everybody," explained Green.

"We'll go up to see Mercedes. Has anyone else come up yet?"

"No ... most will be coming tomorrow. Angeles, Medina, and Etienne will be here tomorrow, but the chief, Urbina, and some generals will not be here until Saturday morning. Maybe Bustamante will come tomorrow, too."

The two went upstairs and knocked on Mercedes' door. She opened the door, dressed in a pretty cotton frock that she had bought, and threw her hands to her face.

"*Quel horror!*" she said in mock terror. "This cannot be my brother, the great revolutionary. It must be a bandit, come to rob and destroy me." They laughed and kissed in welcome, Mercedes saying, "Vicente, go get cleaned up. You would scare a horse thief!"

"I didn't think that *soldaderas* of the Division of the North scared so easily. It's nice to see you in ladies' clothes again. I think even your sister Otilia would approve."

"I doubt if Otilia and her *chocoloteros* even think about us anymore, unless they wonder about getting some money out of Herradura! They are too busy with balls in Madrid," she said with obvious distaste.

"You look delicious, my sweet. You should wear such clothes more often. They become you," said Green.

144

"Well, if you were around more, you would see me wearing nice clothes. The only time you are around is at dinner."

Green could see this conversation getting out of hand. "I have to take Vicente to his room now. We are all supposed to leave the hotel for Juárez at seven. I'll be by to get you."

"Just make sure you do," she said, and slammed the door.

Green and Vicente walked down to Vicente's room. Green checked the closet to see if any clothes were there and found only the dress uniform.

"*Mi colonel,* you have only a dress uniform to wear tonight, but that'll have to do. You will be very handsome in it. It even has some nice medals. Better call down to the valet to get your boots shined, however. I'll see you downstairs at seven."

At 6:45, Green knocked on Mercedes' door.

"*Quien es?*"

"*Su novio,*" he said.

"One minute, I am already ready." Mercedes opened the door and walked out in the hall. She was dressed in a magnificent scarlet gown. A sapphire necklace set off the dress but did not quite match her eyes. He gazed at her for a moment, having never seen such a lovely woman. She looked like a princess royal.

"*Mi amor.* You are the most enchanting woman I have ever seen! Is this the *vaquera,* my *soldadera,* or did you just come from the court at Madrid? Your sister would be ill from envy."

"Green, my sister Otilia is a traitor to Mexico. Please don't mention her to me anymore."

Green took her arm and escorted her to the lobby, where the others had gathered. Vicente had made himself known to the Dunigan clan, and the whole gathering was awestruck when they saw Mercedes. She was enjoying the attention she was getting, but even Amanda and Kathleen, by no means plain women, were truly taken aback by Mercedes' beauty. All the men in the lobby stared at her in admiration.

Amanda was the first to recover. "Mercedes, you look wonderful. The sapphire necklace matches the dress very well, but it does not quite match your eyes. I wish they were emeralds."

"It is of no consequence, Amanda. It will be fine, and I am so

145

proud to be wearing your wedding present from your husband," said Mercedes.

Vicente suddenly said, "Green, is there time for me to run up to my room? I forgot something."

"Sure, Vicente, we've got plenty of time."

After five minutes, Vicente returned with a small bag in his hand. He held up his hand for attention.

"Maybe the Herrera family can remedy this situation. You recall, Mercedes, that Tomas and I were the first ones to Herradura after it was raided and burned. We knew of a hidden safe in the house and we found it, as the raiders had not. In it were your mother's jewelry and some money. I had meant to give them to you, but I never found the right time. I think now is that time. I brought down only the emerald necklace and matching ear clips. I'll get the others to you tomorrow. Now, let me see if I can do something about the clash of colors ..."

He took off the sapphire necklace, looked at the Dunigan women, then put it on Kathleen, as it matched precisely her blue gown. Then he took out the emeralds for Mercedes, which matched her eyes precisely. Vicente stepped back to admire his handiwork. It was just the right touch.

"Madam Dunigan, I would love to do something for you, but such beauty as yours needs no adornment. I can only hope that these girls can someday match your beauty."

Vicente had ensured his popularity with the group by his courtly speech. He took Kathleen by the arm to escort her to their transportation.

The party was hosted by a group of families. The family of Octavio Fernandez, as leader of the group, was most elegant, if somewhat nostalgic. Almost all of them were large Chihuahua landowners who had fled the revolution to first Juárez and then El Paso. Many of them had supported the revolution to some extent, but almost none were active participants. Many could be said to be supporters of Madero, as opposed to Díaz or Huerta. Now these people mostly supported Don Venustiano Carranza, rather than Villa or Zapata, and were looking forward to returning to their properties now that Huerta had fled.

The Dunigan group entered the old Juárez casino to be greeted and introduced to these families. For the two Herreras it was a reunion of old friends, although Green also knew many of them as former customers.

All the men were in evening clothes, and the women were resplendent in lovely gowns and blazing jewels. The only discordant sight was Vicente Herrera in his uniform, but there were others. The American generals, Scott and Pershing, were there, as was the Mexican commander in Juárez. Mainly it was a reunion of the old Mexican landed families of Coahuila and Chihuahua. Most of them had long operated their *haciendas* and were pretty tough, having fought Apaches and Yaquis for years. But they had gotten out of the way when the revolution became organized warfare and the fighting total and widespread. Most of them were *maderistas*, because he was one of them, their main bone of political contention being the central control exercised by the government in the city of Mexico over all phases of life. There were no avid supporters of land distribution there.

Amanda Dunigan made a point of meeting Generals Scott and Pershing and inviting them to the wedding and reception. She also invited such aides and staff assistants as they wished to bring along. She told them that General Villa and Angeles would be there as well as some other Mexican generals. They assured her that they would try to attend.

Green knew many of the people, and of course, Mercedes knew them all from childhood on. Because of her exquisite radiance, she alone was the star of the party. A few guests had an acquaintance, at least by reputation, with John Dunigan and were very cordial. Vicente was still being very attentive to Kathleen, but he did not neglect the young ladies from Mexico when the dancing began.

The lovely party, very civilized, did not break up until midnight. Vicente did not return to El Paso with the Dunigans, saying he would be along later. He was last seen in the company of a beauty from Durango.

When they returned to the hotel, Mercedes went to check for a message at the desk. Green waited for her, as the others went on to their rooms. There were no messages, so he escorted her to her room.

"Green, I want to ask you something. Please come in."

He came in and sat on her bed as she had occupied the only other chair in the room, taking off her new emeralds.

"*Chica,* what was it you wanted to talk about?"

"Green, I want to know if you want to have children," she stated, rising and undoing her dress.

"Of course, darling, and I want them all to look like you."

She sat down beside him on the bed and pulled him down to kiss. The top of her dress slipped down, revealing her breasts. Green kissed and caressed her, and slowly they stood up and undressed each other, touching, kissing and caressing, then falling back on the bed to make love. It didn't last long, and was not entirely satisfactory, so they tried again. The second time was much better.

Green slipped back into his room a bit after 4:00 A.M., exhausted. It seemed he had slept only two minutes when he was awakened by a knock at his door.

"Green, wake up! Let's have breakfast," said John Dunigan, who was always an early riser. Bleary-eyed, Green looked at his watch. It was almost 6:00.

"Dad, I'll meet you in the coffee shop just as soon as I get dressed."

"Time's awastin', youngster. The coffee already boiled," continued Dunigan as he left.

Mumbling to himself, Green pulled on his clothes and went down to the coffee shop. He found his father and sat down. They were on their second cup when Vicente entered, still looking like a bandit.

"Green, I've got to get something to wear. That uniform is stiff and hot, and what I'm wearing scares people. They think Villa has invaded."

"We'll get something this morning, Vicente, but from what I saw last night, that uniform did not slow you down much. It sure impressed that young lady from Durango."

"Green, do not discuss young ladies before I have had my coffee," he grinned.

"Well, Vicente, at least you got up all by yourself. I had to wake Green this morning," said John Dunigan, chuckling.

Green was too tired to think it very funny. About 8:00 A.M., Green stood up and said, "Come on, Vicente, I think the stores are open now," and they left John Dunigan on his own.

Making their way through the various shops and stores, Vicente was well outfitted by noon. After a beer and a taco for lunch, they went to Ravel's store to see what was happening. Green found that Villa had sent in 300 more steers to him.

"Is Villa going to sell all the cattle in Mexico to pay for his army? Will it never end?" asked Green.

"It probably won't end very soon, judging from the orders I'm getting from him for ammunition and ordnance," answered Ravel.

"Sam, I have to get somebody to handle this deal for the next month. You got any suggestions?"

"That young fella from Kansas, Jimmy Berger, might be all right. He certainly has the contacts, and he is a hard worker," Ravel said.

"Well, I kinda picked him, too. I'd better talk to him. He seems to be a good cowman, although he is a little lacking in Spanish. Should pick it up pretty quick."

They parted, Green making his way to the customs pens and Vicente back to the hotel.

At the pens, Green found Jimmy Berger sorting steers.

"Jimmy, can you talk to me anytime soon? I may have a deal for you."

"Right away, Mr. Dunigan. I'm about through here," he said.

Jimmy Berger was about twenty-five, a thin and lanky red-head with blue eyes and freckles. Originally from a wheat farm in western Kansas, he had worked for several of the larger outfits that grazed calves and yearlings in that area. Bright and hard working, he soon gravitated to trading and had good contacts and a reputation for honesty, as far as Green knew.

Jimmy ambled over to Green and said, "Mr. Dunigan, you and Pancho Villa are sure keeping us busy here. There are more cattle coming into El Paso, Presidio, and Columbus than I have ever seen. 'Course, I only been here two years."

"That's what I want to talk to you about, Jimmy. I need some help handling it all. Would you like to work up a deal to kind of partner with me? I'm gonna be gone about a month, but I really don't want to trade here full time, and the deal with Villa shouldn't last too much longer."

"Mr. Dunigan, I'm just a little trader and I ain't well enough financed to handle all the cattle you're getting. But if we could work out something, where you did the finance and I just collect commission, I'd sure take a crack at it."

"I can do the financing, and I can give you a list of customers that is exclusively mine, because I want them taken care of. My banker will be here Saturday for my wedding, and you and he could meet on Sunday to work out the details. I'll not be here, but we have a good understanding and he could fold you in. I don't really want to think about a permanent situation yet, but I think it'll be worth your while to handle this for a month while I'm gone. When I get back, we can set it up properly. I think it can work because, as I understand it, you need to be in Kansas in the winter and spring, and I need to be gone more in the summer and fall. Sam Ravel is handling the money now, so you can work through him until I get back. Sam is Villa's main agent, so you can work with and through him. I'll have him available on Sunday also, to meet with you and Ben Davidson, my banker, from St. Louis. I'd also like you to come to the wedding reception, which will be at Sam Ravel's place, you know, on the edge of town. You can meet everybody there. I want to emphasize, Jimmy, that the first month of this deal will be on a handshake basis. I believe I can trust you, and maybe you can trust me."

"Mr. Dunigan, I trust you and I won't let you down. My word has always been my bond."

"That's what I've been told about you, Jimmy. The only thing is this Mexican cattle trade is tricky on both sides, and the trickers always get caught, at least on this side."

They shook hands on it, and Green left, saying, "Be sure to come to the reception. Even Pancho Villa's going to be there."

On his way back to the hotel, Green stopped by Ravel's store to inform him. "Sam, I'm going to kinda partner with that Berger boy, for at least a month, and I'll arrange a meeting on Sunday with him, my banker from St. Louis, Ben Davidson, and you. I want to handle this just like we have been doing, and I want you to handle all the money. Will that be all right?"

"Sounds good to me, Green. I can't see any objection. I suppose it's going to be your money he is operating on."

"Yeah, Sam, he hasn't enough to do it. And you and Ben can arrange all that in the interim. I'll be back in October to tie it up on a permanent basis."

"We'll handle it, Green."

CHAPTER 29

El Paso, Texas / August 31, 1914

The day broke bright and clear in El Paso and promised to stay that way. Green was still in need of sleep when he went to breakfast after 8:00. He was joined a bit later by Medina, Bustamante, Vicente, and his brother Jack Dunigan. They had all been there for the "last party" the night before. General Angeles was also there, but he was not an early riser, and he had not been with them when they all made a tour of the seedier places in Juárez.

"May a sergeant major join this gathering of high officers, or would that be forbidden?" asked Etienne as he walked up to the table.

"Join us, Sergeant Major. The Division of the North does not discriminate," said Medina, the senior of the group and the one most likely to object, being a former regular.

Green spoke, mainly to Vicente. "I have some news of interest. I had asked my father to see if, as an ex-Ranger with many friends, they could detain Pascual Orozco until I could have time to deal with him. They went us one better. Orozco started to shoot it out when they tried to arrest him, and the Rangers killed him. I had hoped to kill the sonovabitch myself, but it's over and done with."

Vicente smiled grimly and spoke slowly, "I hope they gut-shot him and he took some time to die."

"This is a time for joy and happiness. A wedding of two of our favorite people. Let's not ruin it with thinking of revenge," Juan Medina counseled. "Let's just be thankful that the world is rid of that savage and that we have a reason for joy."

"Amen," said Etienne de la Garza, and they all finished their breakfast.

"Why are you looking so somber, gentlemen? Seated here are veterans of all kinds of wars and disasters who should be happy that they are still among the living." Ben Davidson had come to the table unnoticed. Green and Etienne jumped up and hugged him and introduced him as the man who had saved them from the blizzard.

"Etienne, you have not changed except for a bigger mustache, which suits you better," said Ben.

"Ben, it's awful good to see you. It's been at least five years, I think. Did your wife come? Did Mr. and Mrs. Alton come?" Green asked.

"Yes and no, Green. My wife is here. But the Altons couldn't come. As you know, both are getting along, and Genevieve has had a sick spell. Nothing real serious, but she is too weak to travel."

"I'm sorry to hear it, and Dad will be, too. Can you stay Sunday, Ben? I want to get you together with Sam Ravel and a young trader, Jimmy Berger, who are going to handle my deal while I'm on our honeymoon. There won't be any changes. I just want you to know how it will be handled."

"That'll be fine, Green."

The men began to talk about past exploits and future concerns, broken up by gales of laughter focused on the prospective groom. Green didn't mind, for it was good to see such good feelings emanating from these men who, in Green's own experience, had witnessed so much death and pain and misery for such a long time. He felt proud of his comrades-in-arms who had endured so much and yet could still be as lighthearted as college boys. Their attitude reflected an optimisim for the future.

Green asked, "When is the chief coming? I'd like to thank him for all he's done."

"Everybody else is arriving about half past twelve, on the train from Chihuahua. They will go straight to Ravel's to get dressed and then to the church," explained Colonel Bustamante.

"Don't worry, Green, everything is going to go right. If it doesn't, the chief will make it go right. Trust him," said Vicente.

"I don't know why I would not. I've trusted him with my life, my *cojones,* and even my soon-to-be-wife, for almost two years, and I would do it again if I had to."

Ben Davidson was amazed at the utter loyalty to Villa from such a diverse group. Ben, who had heard that Villa was no much better than a bandit, realized he must be much more. This group of men were not peons: they were worldly and sophisticated. If they were this loyal, Ben surmised, then Villa was a lot more than a bandit and revolutionary, whatever the general opinion was.

Their banter went on until almost 1:00, when everyone went to their rooms to get dressed for the wedding. They were due at the church at 2:30. Green packed everything he could, so as to be ready to catch the train the next morning. He had already told Mercedes they would spend the night in his room.

He bathed and dressed in his dark blue dress uniform with much gold braid and a dark crimson sash. Then he walked down to the lobby to join his party that consisted of Angeles, Medina, and Etienne, all of whom were dressed similarly. Vicente, who was giving his sister away, would bring her, along with Green's family. His group got a carriage and went to the cathedral, entering by a rear door, where they were met by the bishop who was to officiate. Everything was going along on schedule—a tribute to Angeles, who enjoyed a high reputation as an organizer.

In the interval Green asked Angeles what was going on down south.

"Well, Don Venus entered Mexico City like a conquistador on a fine white horse. Gonzales and Obregón finished off the revolution, as we were stuck in Zacatecas with no coal and a hundred miles of ruined track in front of us. I hear there is to be a meeting in Aguascalientes next month to sort everything out. Every leader is supposed to be there. Maybe we can settle everything, but I am convinced that Don Venus intends to be president of Mexico whatever happens, and Zapata won't agree. I don't think Villa will either. He may be able to keep Pablo Gonzales with him and probably Obregón, so we may have to go to war again. Many of us are opposed to Don Venus, and no one wants an unelected president. But maybe we can agree. After all this fighting and dying, there have to be some basic reforms in Mexico."

"Doesn't sound good, General. I hope the fighting doesn't start again. Even though I am through with it, Mexico needs to heal," said Green solemnly.

"Amen," intoned everyone in the room, including the Bishop, who left the room to officiate the ceremony on cue as the music started.

Soon they heard the sounds of the wedding march. Green cracked the door to see Mercedes coming down the aisle on Vicente's arm. Her dress seemed to glow through the lace that covered it completely.

"My God," he exclaimed, and the others also peeked out.

"I not only have never seen, but there has never *been* a woman that beautiful," said Angeles. The others were dumbstruck.

They all went out to their places as Vicente gave Mercedes to Green. After the short ceremony, Green lifted Mercedes' veil to kiss her; he thought he was kissing an angel. As he took her arm to retreat down the long aisle, he noticed that of the three pews full of dress uniforms, only one was left. He wondered where the others were, and as he passed, he recognized Villa, Urbina, Herrera, and Mix among others, all grinning. Walking through the vaulted archway of the cathedral door, he was surprised to see another archway of crossed sabers that they would have to pass under. Holding those sabers were sixteen officers of the 3rd Artillery Brigade, with Colonel Bustamante the last in line.

"That's where those two pews disappeared to," murmured Green to Mercedes. "It's a nice touch. Villa will be proud of it, and I guess I am, too, as all of them served under me." Mercedes, who was fast becoming allergic to anything military, said nothing.

They got into a Packard to go to the reception, and on the way Green spoke. "Mercedes, you must be tolerant of Villa. He has never been close to polite society before, and as he is tremendously successful as a military leader he wants to show off with all of this, which I think is very generous."

She glowered at him and said, "Maybe you should marry Pancho Villa."

"I don't love Pancho Villa ... I love Mercedes Herrera, and I mean to spend the rest of my life with her."

With that, her eyes misted over and she kissed Green. She lay in his arms, as well as she could in the back seat of a Packard.

"Mercedes, I know this is your show and neither Villa nor the division can really take it away from you, and they know that. They just want to share it with us, as they have many things in the past."

"Well, as long as it is the last I see of them, I guess it's all right. It is our day and I don't like to share it, but I'll do it."

Mercedes headed the receiving line in her most gracious and charming manner, and all who went through it forgot about wars and uniforms. Villa and Herrera were enraptured by her, as Urbina gazed at her with ill-disguised lust. The line went on for over an hour. When the music started, they finally got away to have the first dance. When it was over, Vicente was there for his sister, followed by Angeles, Medina, and many others. Green, already well oiled by Urbina's fine champagne, drifted toward the mariachi music with its inevitable quatrains of "La Cucaracha." He knew he would find Villa there.

"Verde, I never saw such a beautiful woman as your Mercedes. I do not remember her being so, for I think I would have fallen in love with her myself," said the widely grinning Villa.

"Pancho, you fall in love with too many women," admonished Luz Corral de Villa at his side.

"Señora, I can't tell you enough about the beautiful wedding dress that you made. It is magnificent," said Green.

"It is an ordinary gown. What makes it beautiful is the one who wears it," responded Villa's first and only legal wife, looking quite handsome herself.

"Verde, I want you to meet these people," said Villa, introducing Generals Scott, Pershing, and General Pershing's aide, Lt. George Patton. Also there were Villa's brother, Hipolito, and Sam Ravel, whom Green already knew, and young Col. Tomas Mix.

Villa was having fun. He had a sixteen-piece mariachi all to himself, and they played his favorite songs and *corridos* continuously. He laughed and yelled "Ah, Verde, they even made up a verse of 'La Cucaracha' about us. Listen."

"En los altos de Zacatecas
Pelea el valiente Gringo Verde
Mata tantos colorados
Por su jefe, Pancho Villa."

Villa laughed and sang with them, as did Urbina, Hipolito, and some others, singing many more verses of the song and others of the revolution. Scott and Pershing were having a good time, too, but were bravely holding on to their dignity. Patton said nothing, taking it all in, until there was a break in the gaiety, and he came over to talk.

"Colonel Verde, I heard you were a decorated veteran in the U. S. Army. Is that true?"

"I guess so. I was a sergeant in the 1st Volunteer Cavalry, and I was wounded in Cuba, but that's all. I was in less than two years," explained Green.

"Where did you learn about artillery? I am told you are an accomplished gunner."

"At Texas A&M, where I went to college."

"Well, I understand now," said Patton.

"Do you, Lieutenant?" asked Green piercingly. "Do you know that what they taught you at West Point or VMI is gone with the first bullet that whizzes close by you?" Green stopped, knowing that this young officer had to learn that himself, and probably already knew it.

Patton acknowledged experience with a nod of his head and went to provide his general with whatever he might need.

Green sat down next to Villa and said, "*Mi general,* I had asked my father to have some of his Ranger friends to delay Pascual Orozco long enough for me to take care of him. This they tried to do, but he made a fight of it and so the sonovabitch is dead. I thought you would want to know."

Villa heard the news gravely and said, "I'm sorry they did it. I wanted to kill him myself. But so did a lot of people. It's good that he is dead, no matter who did it."

"Chief, I'll be leaving in a while. Any cattle you send, I have made arrangements for. I'll be gone about a month, but then I'll be here if you need me. But I'm not going to fight anymore ... and hopefully that's over anyway. What I want to say is, thank you. Thank you for all you've done for me and thank you for letting me be a part of the Division of the North. I'll never forget."

Villa got up from his seat and said, "Verde, you can ride with me anytime." And with that, they hugged each other for what seemed a long time. There were tears in the eyes of both men when Green walked away. He would fight no more, but he would never break the ties that bound him to Villa and the Division of the North.

CHAPTER 30

San Francisco, California / September 20, 1914

The newlyweds had been in San Francisco for almost three weeks, and the time had passed quickly for them. They had gone to the best restaurants and shows, Mercedes had bought clothes, and they had made side trips to interesting places. They had even made friends with some San Franciscans and visited their homes. It was a time of languor and rest, and of cleansing the dirt and blood of the revolution.

But Green couldn't quite separate from it. Each day he read the newspapers about what was happening and tried to keep abreast. Mercedes didn't want to know about it. She seemed happier than he had ever known her to be.

And she was. They had had time to get familiar with each other without worrying about whether he would return from the coming battle. Green was safe now, and she'd never let him go back to war. Whenever they made love, she felt they were building something of value that wouldn't flow off and dry in the sand, like most of the blood that had been spilled. Mercedes tried to forget Mexico. She was an American now, married to a man she loved and who loved her. Yet several times each day Don Tacho, Doña Marisol, and Tomas spoke to her, and she knew that she would never be anything if not a Mexican from Herradura. She could not deny her heritage. Despite this reality, she would continue to look at Green and feel serene.

Having been in one place too long, Green was getting bored. He talked to the hotel manager and arranged to take an excursion boat down to San Diego. The manager got them reservations at the Hotel Coronado, and they would enjoy the sights and tastes of southern California.

Green felt like a whole man again and was anxious to get back to El Paso and resume life. After a week they caught the train to Yuma and then the S.P. back to El Paso. When they crossed the desert it was cooler and greener. At Yuma, where they were to transfer to the S.P., there was a four-hour layover. Green got off and walked around a bit. Stopping at a coffee shop, he met some of the big farmers of the Imperial Valley. These men complained of the unsureness of the market for their vegetable crops. They told of times when spinach or carrots were in such supply that it didn't pay to harvest them and they just rotted in the field. Green asked why they didn't turn livestock in on the fields and graze them. The farmers' answer was that they were in the cash segment of farming and didn't run livestock, and there wasn't much supply, except out of Mexico, available when they could use them.

Green said, "I'm a cattle trader, dealing mostly in Mexican cattle. Maybe I can figure out a way to help this situation. Give me your names and addresses and let me think on it. By the way, how is the packing situation out here?"

"We have packers, and I think we have enough capacity to even expand the market to supply meat on this side of the mountains, but I don't know much about the particulars," ventured Jack Martin, one of the farmers.

"Listen, maybe I can make something out of this deal. Let me do a little scouting around and I'll be back in touch," Green replied.

They all agreed it was something to think about. Green knew what they said was true about cattle being available in California, and he knew he could supply that market with cattle from Mexico, but he didn't have any idea about numbers that would be needed to fill it. He determined to find out.

During the month following their marriage, Mercedes had subtly changed, becoming calmer and much less prickly in her manner. Green thought it was the disappearance of violence and uncertainty from their lives. Whatever the reason, Mercedes was no longer even occasionally waspish, and when she called Green a *gringo,* she did it with affection and tenderness.

They debarked from the train on the evening of October 2 and took up residence at the hotel until they could rent a house and furnish it, which they set about doing the following morning with the help of Sam Ravel.

"Green, I need to talk to you about all these cattle and everything that is happening down south," Ravel said, watching Green haul furniture into the house.

"Sam, as soon as we're moved in, I'll have plenty of time for that."

"But Villa says—"

"Sam, I am a retired soldier. No one commands me anymore."

He tried again. "Your accounts with Jimmy Berger—"

"Is anything wrong there?" Green asked.

"No, but they need to be sorted out."

About that time, Mercedes came through the door with fire in her eyes. "Mr. Ravel, can you not leave us alone even to start a home? Do you think Pancho Villa's revolution is of any importance to us now?"

Sam was not going to go up against Mercedes when her dander was up. He just held his palms up and said, "It can wait, Señora."

Green was surprised to see her temper appear, especially since it was directed toward someone beside himself. But just in case, he moved the furniture faster so she wouldn't turn it on him.

After two frantic days of moving furniture, Mercedes decided that they had a home. She had hired a young girl to help there, as the house was large. There were still curtains to hang and a few other things to do, but they felt settled. Mercedes cooked supper and they went to bed in their own room, their own bed that night. Their lovemaking was particularly satisfying to them.

Afterwards, lying next to him, Mercedes whispered, "Green, I think for the first time in my whole life, I am truly content."

CHAPTER 31

El Paso, Texas / December 3, 1914

reen sat in Sam Ravel's store, going over his accounts in a little room he had rented for an office. Sam Ravel came in, and
Green noticed that Ravel looked worried.

"What's the matter, Sam? Don't tell me that business is bad . . .
I know better," Green said, tapping his ledger.

"I'm worried about Villa. Angeles was here yesterday while you
were in Columbus receiving Villa's latest herd. We had a long talk
about everything, and Angeles is really worried."

"Why, he has just finished chewing up Pablo Gonzales. He has
more men and equipment than ever before. He represents the
whole revolution through the Aguascalientes convention. He is in
charge of everything," retorted Green.

"Felipe says he is sending half his artillery to Zapata, who has
agreed to fight Obregón. Felipe says Zapata will lose, and Villa will
be crippled. He says Zapata's men cannot fight a battle, that they
are only guerrillas and will not stand up to disciplined troops."

Green looked down at his hands a long time and said, "Felipe is
right. They are only peons from the hills. In a real battle they will
run back to their hills. Zapata is not dumb—that is the reason he
never would fight outside of their own backyard. I've seen them,

160

Sam. If they run up against a real soldier, they'll blot out their minds with marijuana. Felipe is dead on target. Villa isn't going to send the 3rd Brigade. My god, I've got to stop him," Green jumped up from his chair, ready to go and find Villa.

"Relax, Green. You can't do that now. Villa *did* send the 3rd Brigade, but it's no longer yours. Besides, it's already gone, and if Angeles couldn't convince him you certainly can't. And remember, if you went, Mercedes would cut off not only your *cojones* but mine as well, and that scares me more than anything Villa or Zapata or Obregón could do," Ravel said, grinning.

"There must be something . . ."

"If the chief won't listen to Angeles, nobody can convince him. Felipe told me that Villa thinks Zapata is a great patriot, and of all the revolutionaries, only he and Villa really know what to do for Mexico. And he wants him to have a great victory to enhance his stature and power to help dictate the new constitution."

"Where is General Angeles?" asked Green.

"He went back to Torreon. He thinks Villa is going to send him to Washington, to keep the U.S. on his side."

The supply of cattle coming to the border had slowed down considerably, consisting now mainly of lighter and younger cattle. Green was sending some of these north to the corn belt, and to wheat fields in the warmer areas, but there weren't that many coming in. Jimmy Berger had left for Kansas. He still had some open orders, but generally the trade was slow. Green and Mercedes had planned to go east, to spend Christmas with the Dunigans at Refugio, so he planned to close up shop until after the first of the year. Mercedes had finished furnishing and decorating their house, so she had time on her hands as well.

Green spent a lot of time with Villa's brother, Hipolito, who lived in El Paso and was his principal agent in the United States. Hipolito was a very good agent in that he knew all the gossip and some secrets that pertained to the revolution. It was Hipolito who had really explained Villa's attitude toward Zapata and also the changing attitude in the United States toward Venustiano Carranza. The endless violence on their southern border was grinding on American nerves, and they were looking around for a leader who could stop it. Villa still had his champion in Gen. Hugh Scott, while others were starting to look Carranza as the man who could pacify Mexico.

But Green knew Carranza was the one man who would not pacify Mexico. He would keep the revolutionary chiefs at each other's throats until they declared him president for life, and Villa and Zapata would never agree to such a thing. Don Venus knew that he could never make peace with Villa, so he confined himself to scheming and promoting various leaders and elements against his main enemy, Francisco Villa.

Again and again, he brought up the Benton affair. Benton, a Scot rancher, had been killed by Fierro, under Villa's orders, and was a cause célébre to the British and somewhat to the Americans. Carranza also made common cause with the labor unions, which gave him a source of soldiers.

The convention at Aguascalientes did not really solve anything, so Villa and Obregón tried alternative solutions. Zapata had sent a lawyer, Díaz Soto y Gama, whose fiery speeches insulted everyone, and Don Venus would not attend, nor would he recognize it as legitimate. Villa and Obregón almost came to an agreement which would have ended the revolution, but Villa's suspicion of his ambition had prevented it. Carranza was in Vera Cruz with General Velasco, whom Villa had defeated at Torreon and had proclaimed the capital to be wherever he was. Although Villa still had the strongest army in Mexico, Green did not like the looks of it. Too many things were working against his leader.

Green made a point of visiting Villa's wife, Luz Corral de Villa, at least once a week. She knew Villa better than anyone, and their visits gave Green a lot of insight into the inner workings of the man.

"Pancho is a fine man, and a real patriot," she said. "He would knowingly do nothing to hurt Mexico, and everything he could to help it. The trouble is that he is an uneducated man and may not know the difference. He is also a gifted soldier, and that brings him great power, but he knows nothing of politics. I wish he would pay more attention to Felipe Angeles. He is also a true son of Mexico, but he is educated about the things that matter. Still, I know nothing of politics, Verde, and I don't like to talk about it. Tell me, how is your beautiful wife, Mercedes? I know you have a nice house because I have visited there. She has lost much to the revolution. It is sad, but she seems to be happy."

"I think she is, Señora. She has put the revolution out of her mind and will not talk of it. She worries about her brother, Vicente, but her defense to all the horror that has happened is not to consider it and to get on with our lives."

"She is very wise for her years," said Luz Villa solemnly. "Listen to her."

Green made arrangements to shut everything down for the next three to four weeks while he and Mercedes visited the elder Dunigans at Refugio. The train trip across Texas would take nearly two days.

CHAPTER 32

Dunigan Ranch, Refugio, Texas /

December 20, 1914

reen and Mercedes alit from the train platform in Refugio, to be greeted by John and Amanda Dunigan. John Dunigan had brought his new Packard and a wagon for the baggage.

Green noticed his father was using a cane but did not rely on it heavily. As he would be eighty his next birthday, Green thought he looked remarkably spry, as did his mother. It was a joyful reunion— Green's first visit home in almost four years—and Mercedes was most genuinely welcomed.

Arriving at the ranch, Green and Mercedes were put up at the big house. There was plenty of room, as none of the Dunigan children or grandchildren were coming until New Year's. A sort of *fiesta* was held that night, and all the ranch people came to meet Mercedes.

Pete Roussell and his wife were glad to meet Green's bride, but Abel and Sulema Castro took her over and wanted to know everything about her, as they had had so much to do with raising Green. Michael O'Grady and Thad Scott were on hand, and told the newlyweds they had trained a horse especially for each of them. Thad and Michael had handled the highly regarded Dunigan horses for years but lately had retired from breaking them. There were lots of new faces at the ranch and many of the older ones marked by crosses behind the headquarters. When the party broke up about 10:00, but Green promised the Castros that he and Mercedes would come and visit in two days.

Back in their room, Mercedes' eyes were dancing. "Green, this reminds me so much of the old days at Herradura. All the wonderful people—just like it was there. It's almost the same to me."

"*Querida*, give it time and it will be. These are great people who had great times with my father when they trailed cattle north. Tradition here may not be as old as at Herradura, but it is just as strong. I will tell you all the old stories as you come to understand our people."

"Oh, I feel at home here already. But enough old stories. I have something better to do," said Mercedes as she wrapped her arms around him.

Green was awake before dawn and walked to the camp kitchen at headquarters for coffee, where he encountered all the Dunigan outfit, including John Dunigan. He conferred with Thad and Michael about the horses.

"Don't worry about Mercedes—she can ride anything and certainly does not ride side-saddle."

"Sure, Green. Your horses will be up at the big house before ten," said Thad.

Over coffee with his father, Green told him that they planned to ride over parts of the ranch for the next few days. "Why don't you come with us, Dad? You know it better than anyone."

"Green, I don't ride much anymore. I'm so broke-down that I can't hardly get on a horse anymore, and if I do, I can't get out of bed the next day. I'm about ready to retire to the cookshack."

"That'll be the day when you give up running ranches," Green said, smiling.

His father looked very serious then and spoke, looking directly at Green. "I told you at your wedding about maybe buying a ranch for you in New Mexico, to kind of balance out with Jack. I've done some investigating through some old friends that have operated out there for many years, and I have found a likely place. You probably know the ranch. Part of it was the old Mora Grant. It borders the CS on the south and runs along the Canadian nearly to Roy. It's about

130,000 acres with some winter country in it, mostly in the breaks of the Canadian. Known as the old Bagwell place. If you think it's all right, I'll buy it, but I'll own it and leave it to you, as I'll leave the Cotulla ranch to Jack. The Cotulla ranch is bigger, but the carrying capacities are about the same. I'm going to leave this place to all three of you, and even it all up with cash and securities to Kathleen. What do you think?"

"Dad, I really don't want to think about you dying, but I think you have probably done it right, unless you haven't made any provisions for mother."

"Of course I have, and quite handsomely, I might add. But what I want to know is what you think of this place in New Mexico."

"I know the place, Dad. I pastured some yearling on it two seasons and have been all over it. It is right in the heart of the best country out there, and my cattle did all anyone could expect. The ranch has plenty of water and is well improved. Some of the River Vega could even be farmed, I think, if one was of a mind to. You calculate pretty close, because there wouldn't be a mite of difference between it and Cotulla that I can think of. What surprises me is that it is for sale. The Bagwells are good people and pretty well fixed, and they have a son a little older than me with a good reputation as a cowman. Why would they sell?"

"What I was told, Green, was that their son got divorced and remarried to a girl from San Francisco. She got him mixed up in a bunch of real estate deals in San Francisco after the earthquake and fire, and he lost a lot of money. I think the old folks are selling to bail him out, rather than mortgage it and maybe lose it all. One of the stipulations is that the two of them get to live there for eight years, or until they die. They have a burial plot that's not in the deal, only about a half acre."

"That won't be a problem. I know the old folks, and they are first-class people," said Green.

"Well, I'll get started on it, unless you want to have a look to reconfirm your recollection?"

"No, those people are operating all right, and even if they've overstocked a year or so, it'll come back. One thing I'd like to suggest to you, Dad, is that you draw the division lines here, in case we want to divide, and make sure Kathleen gets the part with the big house. She really loves it."

"That's a good idea, Green. I'll do that and it will save any family fights, I hope."

When Green got back to the big house, Mercedes was ready, looking quite fetching in cowboy clothes. Amanda had packed a picnic hamper for them, and Green gave it to Michael O'Grady to tie on his saddle. Then he and Mercedes mounted their horses and rode off toward the river.

Mercedes was captivated by the amount of green grass and the size of the brush, as opposed to the land at Herradura.

"Is it always this green here? It's almost like what I have heard of England, except for the big mesquite and brush," she said.

"No, sometimes it gets very dry. It's only green now because the cold weather is late this year, and we've had no frost. But it does rain here, usually, and where you have to give a cow fifty or sixty hectares, ours live on four to five."

"Ah, that's it. I had thought from the number of cattle we had seen that you must have over 600,000, but it is because you can put many more on the land, no?"

"Exactly, *chica*," said Green with affection.

He took her along the river to show her the big oaks and cottonwoods that towered to forty feet or more, and she was fascinated by the beauty of the place and the immense amount of sky visible, because there was nothing to block the view.

In midafternoon Green stopped under a huge live oak tree. "Let's have our lunch here."

They dismounted and unsaddled the horses, Green taking care to tell Mercedes to leave the bridles on, as the Dunigan horses were trained not to wander off as long as they had bits in their mouths. They spread the saddle blankets for their picnic and also spread their leggings to sit on as they ate their picnic. Amanda had even included bottle of wine for them, and they pillowed their heads on their saddles as they finished the last of it, gazing at the sparkling blue winter sky.

"Green, this place is truly beautiful, so green and fertile. I may never want to leave."

"Oh, yes you will. You will miss the desert, just as I do from time to time, and you know how beautiful it can be right after a rain."

"Yes, that is true. But it rains so seldom, and here it rains a lot."

Mercedes propped herself up on one elbow and began to pick at

Green's shirt buttons. She bent over and kissed his chest, then began to unbutton his pants. He did the same for her. This process took some time, as it was interrupted by kisses and caresses, but eventually they were both naked.

"You're quite a randy little slut, aren't you?" he murmured.

"Yes, and you have such a sweet *pico*. Show me what you do with it, *mi colonel*," said Mercedes, rolling over on the blanket.

Bodies warmed by the bright sun came together for some time, and when it was over, they lay back drowsily, almost sleeping.

"Oh, Green, help me!" screamed Mercedes suddenly.

Green sat up and looked into the big brown eyes of a brindle cow that had just walked up and licked Mercedes on her naked belly. The cow looked from one to the other, and then walked off back to a small bunch of cows that were remarkably like her.

Mercedes had pulled a saddle blanket up to shield her nakedness, and Green started laughing.

"What is so funny, *gringo?* That cow nearly gored me."

"Mercedes, you have been given the Dunigan stamp of approval. You were in no danger whatsoever, but you are now a full-fledged member of the Dunigans. I think I told you of the cow that was called Brindy Polaris, which led the herds to Montana. Well, that is one of her descendants. I know, because we keep them separate. All the rest are pretty much Herefords now, but we keep Brindy's line pure, and that was one of them. She licked you to welcome you to the ranch. I don't know that any of us have had that intimate stamp of approval. Usually they just come up and say hello, but she licked your belly! You are really a part of everything now." Green took her in his arms and kissed her and then she rose, dropping the blanket, and walked naked to the cow.

Mercedes said, "Thank you for taking me in. I will come back to see you again, and I will address you as 'La Reina Gauteada'."

It was a solemn moment. The new "Brindle Queen" wagged her head in response to Mercedes and then wandered off.

Because they were both naked, there was an element of comedy to this invitation, but as Green thought about it, it might have been an omen, a sign that Mercedes carried the Dunigan seed where the cow had licked her. Time would tell.

They hurriedly dressed and continued their ride around the ranch. They visited the *manada*, the broodmare band, but the mares were still two or three months short of foaling, so there wasn't much to see. To make up for it, Green showed Mercedes that year's foals, which had been weaned some time before and were being halter broken and handled mainly under the supervision of Michael O'Grady and Thad Scott. She liked this better and would squeal with delight at some particularly well-behaved foal. Green explained how they were all descended from Kentucky stock that was his grandfather's wedding present to his parents.

Mercedes was like a child in a candy store. Each new vista brought her delight, and she thought it all most beautiful. Green saw little beauty in the coastal winterscape; it was old hat to him.

When they returned to the big house, Mercedes asked Amanda if she should dress for dinner. Amanda told her that she had been forced to introduce formal dining into the household when her children were young.

"If I hadn't, all of them would have grown up as wild as coyotes! The Dunigans have an inclination to be feral, and you will find out, when you have children, that their natural state is untamed. You'll have to do somewhat the same thing, unless you plan not to let them loose on polite society. Or do you even plan to have children?" Amanda asked.

Mercedes laughed merrily and said, "I plan to have at least fifteen, Amanda."

"I don't know if that is possible, but it is an admirable goal. However, in view of Green's age, I'd set my sights a bit lower."

"I really have, but I like to tease Green with that."

"Well, that's good, but you must keep a tight rein on these Dunigans. They revert quite easily to a wild state," cautioned Amanda.

Dinner was quite nice. The men wore coats and ties and the ladies dresses. The table was covered with a white damask tablecloth and matching napkins, silver utensils, and china. There were three courses: soup, entrée with vegetables, then dessert and coffee. Mercedes could detect some irritation on the part of John and Green, but on the whole it was a pleasant interlude. She thought that Amanda was right—this was a painless way to maintain civility.

The next day, Green and Mercedes rode off to spend the day with Abel and Sulema Castro. It was a pleasant two-hour ride to their house on the far end of the ranch. The country was a little different here—a prairie with intermittent mottes of brush and oak, a savannah-like environment.

Abel and Sulema were very glad to see them. Both were in their seventies and liked living where they were. The mini-headquarters had working pens and barns and sheds. About a third of the cattle on the ranch were worked at the place. The outfit would move in and stay about a week at least twice a year. The outfit would camp there, so housing wasn't a need, but horse corrals and traps were. The house that Abel and Sulema lived in was small but neat, with a porch across the front and the yard swept clean of grass.

Nothing was said, but Green knew that the Castros were proud that he had married a Mexican. They asked Mercedes about Herradura, as they were from a similar property in Coahuila.

As Mercedes described life at Herradura, Abel smiled, recognizing the similarities to his childhood on Hacienda San Francisco, where his father had been a vaquero in southwestern Coahuila.

Green told Mercedes he had spent a lot of his boyhood here, and thought of Abel and Sulema like an aunt and uncle. Abel had taught Green much of his knowledge of cattle and ancillary crafts, such as working rawhide, woodcraft, and training horses. Since they were childless, they held Green in the esteem that he held them, and were in the process of taking Mercedes into their hearts.

After lunch, they rode around with Abel to the portion of the ranch under his charge. His area was mostly stocked with steers that would go to Kansas the following spring. Mercedes even saw and pointed out some steers from Herradura that Green had sent a year earlier.

Sulema had a reputation as a *curandera* and midwife and was invariably paid in livestock, so there were numerous pigs, chickens, geese, goats, and even rabbits around. Mercedes was enchanted by their attentions, as they were enchanted by her.

Mercedes and Green headed back for the main headquarters late that afternoon. Sulema gave Mercedes a small, mysterious leather bag to take with her. Green figured it was something like *asfoetida*. He asked Mercedes.

"It's for babies, Green," Mercedes offered, and would say no more.

"We don't have any babies," he said.

"Well, maybe we'll have some later," she said, just as mysteriously.

Green was surprised to find that Mercedes had some faith in *curanderas*.

Green's brother and sister and their families came to Refugio to celebrate Christmas and the New Year. All the grandchildren were there, and Amanda played the Queen-Bee-Grandmother to the hilt. There was a *fiesta* in Refugio, at which both Jack and Green won prizes for roping. Mercedes wanted to do something but was firmly told that it was unladylike in the U.S. for women to rope and ride wild broncos. This did not deter Mercedes from putting on an exhibition of trick riding done in the style of the Mexican *charras*. Her riding was well received by the audience, and was an object of much interest to the many ranch women in attendance. The whole Dunigan family were quite proud of their new but full-fledged member—especially Kathleen, who was remembered as a much accomplished horsewoman.

The time passed quickly for Green and Mercedes. Mercedes was entranced with quail hunting, and went out with Kathleen and John on a hunt. She was also busy with Michael O'Grady, training a black filly she had picked out for herself.

Mercedes felt happy to be part of a large family again, and Green was glad to reestablish himself as a family member after so long a time. But soon both thought that it was time to return to El Paso.

Green made arrangements to leave on January 23, taking the black filly, "Minerva," back at the same time.

CHAPTER 33

El Paso, Texas / January 25, 1915

ercedes had left before Green awoke, having gone to the livery stables down the street to check on Minerva. Green had finished breakfast when she returned. "Did Minerva pass the night well, my love?" he asked.

"Yes, she is quite content. I'm going to let her rest for a day before we begin training again. What are you going to do today?"

"Just catch up. I'll be at Sam Ravel's all day finding out what is going on. I'll be back for dinner."

At Ravel's, Green first went through his accounts and then questioned Ravel about the events in Mexico.

"Outside of Obregón's fulfillment of Angeles' prediction, there is not much fighting," Ravel reported. "Angeles begged the chief not to depend on Zapata, but he did, and sent him half of his guns. Obregón, when he got organized, beat up Zapata at Puebla, just as Angeles predicted, and got half of Villa's artillery. The *zapatistas* just ran back to Morelos and left it. Villa did take Guadalajara, but I think he is back in Chihuahua. The convention—no one knows. Euladio Gutierrez left for the northwest, but no one knows where. Carranza refuses to recognize any authority except his own, and he has Pablo Gonzales and Obregón with him still. Villa still is the strongest militarily."

"Doesn't sound too good, does it Sam?" said Green sadly.

"No, but if the chief would just listen to Angeles and Medina, like he used to, Villa could sort it all out. I don't think he will, though."

"Well, enough about wars, Sam. From the books, it looks like the cattle finally have about run out in northern Mexico. I guess it will be a while before any number start crossing again, probably late summer. Sam, you know anything about the Bagwell place, up north of Roy?"

"It's damn good country, Green, but I think it's being sold. I think the old folks have to bail out a bad marriage. Why?"

"Oh, I'm looking for a place where I can put all my steers on one property so I don't have to travel so much. Being sold, huh? You know how much, Sam?"

"No, but it ought to bring a premium, maybe five or six bucks an acre," answered Ravel. "Why, you thinking about buying it?"

"No, but I may want to rent it, maybe as a headquarters place to keep my steers, so I can put that operation on a permanent basis."

"Hell, Green, I got all kinds of places closer to El Paso that would be better. Let me show you some of them."

"Sam, those places are too far south. The really good country is in the northeastern part of the state, and that's where I want to be. Where I can make the cattle do something, not just trade. Trading is fine and profitable, but I am a family man now. I want to slow down and smell the flowers, you know what I mean?"

"Yeah, I know what you mean, but I don't agree. I have made a lot of money trading on this border for almost forty years and I've seen cattle traders come and go—mostly go. You are about the best I have seen here, not even counting your deal with Villa. You can make plenty of money here as long as you want, and as long as you're willing to work at it. I have also seen plenty of people do just what you want to do, and all they did was slowly go broke on those ranches. Don't do it, Green. Don't go out and vegetate on some ranch. You're too valuable to the trade," Ravel pleaded.

"Oh, come on, Sam. That boy Berger is as good as anyone on the border, and there is plenty of talent here. I wouldn't be missed ten minutes."

"Some of them may have your talent, but I saw—not once but almost every time—when you came up from the revolution, the market would jump by a dollar a hundred."

"That's mighty complimentary of you, Sam, if a trifle exaggerated. But I'll tell you one thing—I'm not needed right now. There's nothing to do. I should be in Mexico, trying to see if there's ever going to be any cattle coming, but Mercedes won't let me," Green said as he left for his house.

Green had bought an automobile, and both he and Mercedes had learned to drive it. That night, over dinner, he told Mercedes that while things were quiet he would like to drive up and take a look at the Bagwell ranch. He asked if she would like to go with him.

"How far is it, Green? What do you want to look at a ranch for? You have seen plenty of them."

"It's a pretty long way, almost 400 miles. I'm thinking about renting it to put some cattle on, and I want to see what it looks like."

"Well, I'm not doing anything. Maybe a motor trip would be fun. Minerva is doing fine, and doesn't need to be worked every day. So I'll go with you. But you have to promise me that you will tell me what is really on your mind." She had read him like a well-thumbed book. There wasn't any reason to deny it.

"I will, *mi alma*. We'll be leaving day after tomorrow, and it will be nearly a week before we get back."

"I'll be ready, *gringito*," she replied, impishly.

They made the trip from El Paso slowly, as the roads were not too good and the country was not well populated. Filling stations were few, but Green had a good map. They had wired ahead so they would be expected.

When they arrived, they were warmly greeted by the senior Bagwells. Green had put out yearlings on that ranch, so he knew the people. The Bagwells treated them like honored guests. Green felt it was because the Dunigans were well respected. If these people had to sell their ranch, he knew they would rather sell it to cattle people than eastern investors.

Green had told Mercedes of his father's plan, and she thought it to be fair. She had some hesitation in moving to northern New

174

Mexico, but it wasn't all that different from Chihuahua. And except for the snow, its general topography reminded her of Herradura.

Over dinner that night, Green told the elder Bagwells that his father was thinking about purchasing the ranch and he was just appraising it for him. Green asked them exactly what Dunigan would be buying.

"You'll be buying everything here. Plus or minus 130,000 acres in fee title. There's only three milk cows and about twenty-five horses. There's three barns, five hand houses, a foreman's house, and two sets of working pens, plus a bunkhouse. There are forty-seven windmills with troughs and storage, and I don't know how many miles of fence. It's cut into twelve pastures and about twenty traps. This house after we're gone, or eight years, whichever comes first. The house is nothing grand, but it's comfortable and we've been here so we don't want to move. Where would we go? I guess if you want it, we could make some deal, but I hate to leave," said Bagwell.

"Mr. Bagwell, we don't need this house, and you're welcome to stay as long as you like. I would like to hire most of the people here to stay on and work for us. They know the country and we don't. If I need a place to stay, I can make do with one of the hand's houses. One thing more, Mr. Bagwell, I got caught in a blizzard west of here about ten years ago and it scared me pretty bad. I wouldn't want to go out looking at the ranch if anything like that was in the offing."

Bagwell laughed and said, "Green, I wouldn't either. I think we can expect clear weather for the next few days, so we can probably see everything."

The next three days were spent looking at the place. Bagwell, although in his seventies, still rode everywhere. The ranch, still short from last summer's grazing, had adequate moisture to bring on the coming year's grass, so at least part of a good season was guaranteed.

"Mr. Bagwell, this is an awful nice ranch, and you don't want to leave. Unless you owe an awful lot of money, the rent should make you plenty. Why do you really want to sell?"

"Green, it isn't any of your business, but because you can understand, I will tell you. Marva and I have only one son, and he is dear to us. He came along late, and Marva had a lot of trouble carrying him. He is twenty-eight now, and a real hand. About three years ago he married a girl from San Francisco—society girl, supposedly well-off and well-connected. She talked him into living out there. It turned out that she and her well-connected friends weren't so well off, and she got Jim, that's his name, into a bunch of deals out there that were phony. He owes over $150,000, mostly to her society friends. He still loves her and won't leave her. Since this ranch is really for him, I am going to pay off those leeches and leave him what cash is left over.

"I'm seventy-seven, and Marva is seventy-one and is ailing some. So, that is what we decided to do. I haven't run my own cattle for a couple of years, as you know. I sold them to pay off for my boy, and I'll be glad to see an owner who will stock this place with his own cattle. You can winter about 1,000 cows in the river breaks here, and summer an additional 5-6,000 yearlings or about 8,000 yearlings for the summer alone. I hated to sell those cows. They were all nearly pure-bred Herefords, and they, with the heifers I had saved back, brought nearly $100,000. I really hated to do it, but I guess it was the best thing for everybody." When Bagwell finished, he looked off in the distance, saddened by his confession.

"Mr. Bagwell, that's a lot commoner story than you think these days," said Green, and they rode a long way in silence.

Toward the end of the second day they had seen most of the ranch, and turned for home.

Green said, "Mr. Bagwell, I reckon I have seen most everything that I need to, so why don't we get into price?"

"You're right, Green. It's painful, but we need to get along with it. Tomorrow there are a few places to see that I have been saving. Thought we could take a buggy and bring the ladies. We could pack a lunch to see some of the real pretty spots, but that has very little to do with the worth of the place. We might as well get to the meat of the deal."

"We might as well, Mr. Bagwell," Green said with finality.

"Green, with what exceptions I've talked about, us staying here and being buried in the cemetery back of the house, I'll sell the whole kit and caboodle for $500,000, the place and everything on it, including the hands, and I'll guarantee the title."

"You want it all cash, Mr. Bagwell?"

"I'd like $200,000 down and $100,000 a year for three years, if that's okay?"

"It's a reasonable deal that I can recommend to my father, Mr. Bagwell. If he agrees, I'll be back in thirty days to close on it, and I'll wire confirmation."

The following day the tour was by buggy and in the company of by the ladies. Mercedes had been chafing about not being allowed to inspect the place and was only partly mollified by Green's verbatim description of the country and all conversations. The tour generally took familiar roads to pretty spots around the ranch. They stopped for a picnic lunch next to a cottonwood-lined creek—fast-flowing, clear water coming out of a small canyon about a half mile from the Canadian River. It was a warm, clear day for early February in New Mexico, and it made everyone, even Marva Bagwell, feel good. She and Mercedes had gotten along well during their stay. Although she was sad about selling their home, Marva felt it was going into good hands.

That night over dinner, Green mentioned in passing that he had spent some time with Villa in Mexico. The Bagwells were most interested and wanted to know more about the revolution.

"Tell me, Green, is Villa the great general, or is he just a bloody-minded bandit?" asked the old man.

"Depends on who you ask. Although he was certainly a bandit before Madero, in my experience with him, I take him to be a Mexican patriot and a very effective general, less greedy and corrupt than most other leaders down there," answered Green.

"It seems like they have been fighting forever. When will it be over?" asked Mrs. Bagwell.

"The fighting up to this time has been to get rid of the dictators. First Díaz and lately Huerta, and that is just over with, but I feel that the fighting is going to start all over again between revolutionary factions, the people who follow Carranza, Obregón, Zapata and Villa, and this will be over who is going to be president, or at least be in control of Mexico. I am very glad to be out of it—this year may be the bloodiest of all."

"Who will win, Green?" Mrs. Bagwell asked.

"Villa is the strongest, and his Division of the North is the finest, but Villa has put a lot of faith and ordnance into an alliance with Zapata, who either will not or cannot fight outside of his own backyard. Villa gave him half of his artillery, which was a lot, and Zapata lost the battle for Puebla and all of Villa's cannons at the same time.

If Villa will listen to General Angeles, who is the best in Mexico, Villa will win. If he doesn't listen, and lately he hasn't been, it will probably be Obregón and Carranza, but in no case will it be Zapata."

"Well, I just hope it will be over soon. Mexico has been bled white already," Mr. Bagwell said.

The Dunigans left early the next morning, driving back to El Paso. The days were cool and dry, and the trip was not too arduous, although auto travel in 1915 was a strenuous activity. On the way home, each had plenty of time to ponder the possibilities of the ranch that would soon be theirs.

CHAPTER 34

San Bernardino, California / March 20, 1915

reen had been in the California desert for three days, meeting with the farmers he thought would buy cattle. What he had ended up with was an arrangement to sell steers when there were surplus vegetable crops in the fields and buy them back when the grazing was over. Green didn't particularly like the arrangement, but the farmers had no experience with cattle and were scared to try jumping into the business head-first. They wanted and got a sort of stop-loss deal from Green, whereby he agreed to buy the steers back, at a certain price, when he sold them. Green had figured he could eventually get the farmers to retain the cattle, once they were used to the working of the trade, but to get them started he had to go this way. He also knew that he was going to have to find partners for some of the cattle when he got them back. Most would be fat enough to kill, but there was always an end that wouldn't get fat. He would find either a market or some grass for them, but he could figure on about ninety days for the cattle to be in the farmers' hands, and he had a built-in profit at the buy-back price.

Green thought he might get Jimmy Berger to work out the details of this operation later. He left California with signed commitments of 5,000 steers to be delivered sixty days hence.

On the way back to Texas, Green visited ports of entry points at Tijuana, Mexicali, Yuma, Nogales, Naco, and Agua Prieta. He found that the bulk of Mexican cattle entered either at Mexicali, Nogales, or Agua Prieta, and the far larger trade was at Agua Prieta. Agua Prieta was under the command of Plutarco Elias Calles, a general who supported Alvaro Obregón, and Carranza, and he surmised Calles would be hostile to him or any other ex-*villista*. However, the governor of Sonora, José Maytorena, was an ally of Villa, and perhaps that could be exploited. The figures he secured from customs officials told him that far more cattle were arriving at Juárez, Ojinaga, and Columbus, and that he could only supplement his contracts at the Arizona points.

Green thought to himself, "If Villa moves west to Sonora, like Angeles wants him to, there'll be plenty. But until he does, I'll just have to get the cattle at Juárez and ship them across."

Arriving in El Paso on the morning of the 22nd, Green went directly to the customs pens to find Jimmy Berger and told him of the deal he had made with the Californians. Green said that Jimmy could have half of it if he would handle it. Jimmy readily agreed, and thought he may have some contacts to work with in Nogales and Agua Prieta that could yield a few cattle.

"You get your ranch deal at Roy all buttoned up yet?" Jimmy asked.

"Yeah, Jimmy, I got it all done before I went to California. All I need now is cattle to stock it. You haven't heard of any yearlings coming in, have you?"

"No, I haven't, Green, but if you're out of pocket, I'll buy what comes in for you, if you want me to."

"Please do, Jimmy, but keep them good. That country needs good cattle, not trash."

"I'll do it that way, Green," and Jimmy was off.

The next couple of weeks, Green spent all his time buying what few young cattle went into El Paso, Presidio, and Columbus, New Mexico. He was putting them out on burnt-up wheat and oat fields around El Paso, and he had over 1,500 out by the end of March. He couldn't move them north because it was still cold and occasionally snowing around Roy, and grass had not come there, but his cattle, if not getting fat, were doing all right where they were. The El Paso newspapers were covering events in Mexico closely, having re-

180

porters on the scene. Green devoured every printed word and was visibly worried about the way the fighting was going. This also worried Mercedes, as she was determined to keep Green out of it.

Green had no great desire to go back to the fighting, but his loyalty was to Villa, Angeles, and the Division of the North. He talked to Sam Ravel about it, and Sam was of the same opinion as Angeles, that is was a mistake to fight in the south, where Obregón had a short supply line and Villa had a long one. Rather, Angeles counseled, they should consolidate control over the north, from the Sierra to the coast, then force Obregón to bring his forces north to confront the Division of the North, where it had the advantage of familiar ground and short lines of resupply. Villa wasn't buying. He was consolidating his forces around Irapuato, while Obregón was preparing a defensive position to the east, at Celaya. This was in the Bajio, a wide open plain of irrigated farm land, well suited to Villa's tactics of *golpetazo*. But Villa's artillery had been cut in half when Zapata lost Puebla, and his supply of ammunition was sparse. He had, in fact, established a shell factory in Torreon, but production was low and the quality of the shells poor. Just the same, Villa was getting ready to fight.

Angeles had been in Torreon, checking on the ammunition and other things. While testing the new batches of shells, one exploded, causing his mount to fall and broke Angeles' leg very badly. When this word got to El Paso, Green knew he had to see him. He could leave the next morning on the train out of Juárez.

Green's announcement to Mercedes that night provoked a furious retort.

"Green, you promised me you were through with the revolution! You are going back on your solemn promise to me and everyone else."

"*Querida*, I am just going to see General Angeles in the hospital at Torreon, far from any battle. I will come home in a few days."

"Green, I think I am going to have your child ... I can't afford to lose any more family. I just can't!" Tears ran down her cheeks in painful anguish.

Green was taken aback by this tearful announcement of imminent fatherhood. He took Mercedes in his arms and held her. Then, very quietly, he said, "*Mamacita*, I didn't even think about that. This is the most joyous news of my life. When will it be?"

"The doctor thinks sometime in the middle of October, but it is too early to tell; however, I am sure. Please don't go back to the war, for our child's sake," she pleaded, still sobbing.

"I promise I will not rejoin the revolution, under no circumstance. I am just going to see Angeles, because it looks like Villa is destroying the division. But I swear to you that I am through with fighting and will not rejoin the division for any reason."

That seemed to satisfy her. She dried her tears and patted her belly and said shyly, "When will you go and when will you return, my *papacita?*"

"I'll be leaving in the morning and should be back in five or six days, counting travel time. Don't worry, the rail line and Torreon are well secured, thanks to Angeles."

"Well, you go, but don't forget your promise," Mercedes said solemnly.

CHAPTER 35

Torreon Military Hospital

Torreon, Coahuila / April 9, 1915

Green went directly to the hospital from the railway station and found Angeles in his private room, reading dispatches.

"How goes the war, *mi general?*" he asked.

Angeles looked up and said, "Green, what are you doing here? You swore to quit the fighting!"

"I have quit. I just came to see you, and get caught up on what is happening."

"It is not good, Green. Villa attacked Obregón at Celaya and got whipped good. Without enough artillery to prepare, he attacked Obregón, who was well dug in and behind barbed wine. We lost a lot of men. The best of the division, I'm afraid. If only Villa had not trusted Zapata with all that artillery and the good shells. This stuff coming out of here is bad. The powder is very volatile. A premature explosion is what put me here. If, if ... so may ifs ..." Angeles trailed off, still obviously in pain.

Before Green could respond, his friend continued. "Green, I have a list of things here. Will you take it to Ravel? It is chemicals I need to make the ammunition, and I need them fast. We are not getting things out of Ravel like we were. Will you try to find out why?"

"Yes, General, I will. Is there any news of the 3rd Regiment? I heard it was sent to Zapata at Puebla."

"Yes, it was, but only the regimental and battalion officers went with it. The gunners were to be supplied by Zapata. All the officers were killed or captured and then shot. Bustamante is, of course, dead and all the others. What a waste," said Angeles, sadly.

"What about Sergeant Major Etienne de la Garza?" Green asked.

"I kept him here. He is over at the factory, trying to do something about the quality of the shells."

"Good, I'll drop by to see him. General, would you be mad if I tried to get him to go back with me?"

"Green, de la Garza is a good man, but he is a *gringo*, and I would be sad to see *gringos* dying in a lost cause. We Mexicans, because it is our business, may do so, but I hate to see others doing it. Besides, unless we can get the materials, he is of very little use to the revolution. Yes, you can take him, if he wants to go.

"You go ahead now, Green. It is good to see you, but I must go to Celaya to try to talk sense to Pancho Villa. Right now, he is the only hope of the revolution."

"General, you're in no shape to travel. You can't even get up the steps of the train," Green said.

"I know, but for the sake of Mexico, I must try one more time to get Villa to see the whole picture." Angeles winced as he shifted his cast in the bed.

"General, for what it's worth, cast my vote with your own when you talk to him," Green added, leaving.

Green found the munition factory in several warehouses down by the railway tracks. He walked between the warehouses until he heard Etienne.

"No, *pendejo*, you weigh the powder into each little sack. Don't just fill each one. No wonder they won't shoot straight."

Green entered the warehouse and saw the big Cajun berating a small Mexican vigorously.

"Hey cousin, what you do down here in Mehico?" yelled Green, aping the Cajun accent.

"Green! Where did you come from?" he yelled over the noise of the powder workers.

"I have come from El Paso. I came to see General Angeles, and he told me you were here."

"I am here, Colonel, to try to show these *pendejos* how to make cannon shells out of scrap and trash nobody would even try to use. They are terrible, and more dangerous to our troops than to the *carrancistas*. Our division is torn apart from Celaya, but Villa is still trying to fight. I think it is lost, and I wonder what I am doing here," Etienne said, looking dejected.

"Look, I asked General Angeles if I could take you back with me. He said he doesn't want any more *gringos* to die for a lost cause. He said it was best for you to go. Will you come with me now? I have a ranch up at Roy, New Mexico, just east of Wagon Mound, where we were snowbound. I need a man there, if you would go. But if you still want to soldier, the United States Army is recruiting everyone that will sign up. Either way, it is better for you. Please come," Green pleaded.

"Green, I want to go. I want to go very badly. But if I leave here now, these people will all blow themselves up. Do you know I have to beat them every day for trying to smoke here in this warehouse, with all the powder? I can't leave them to commit suicide. But just as soon as some people show up to take care of it, I will come. I need to get away for a while anyway. Also, I have to tell Villa that I am through, or at least tell Medina or Angeles. Don't worry, I'll be in El Paso soon. Villa's days are numbered, and I don't want mine to be."

"Well, I'll be waiting for you in El Paso, my old friend."

Green walked across the bridge about 3:00 in the afternoon, picked up the latest paper, and went home. On his way he saw Mercedes in the corral at the livery with her filly, Minerva. Mercedes saw him coming through the gate.

"Minerva, here comes a handsome *caballero*. Greet him properly," she said to the filly and touched her forefeet with the training whip. The filly stretched out her forefeet and lowered her muzzle to the ground in the equine curtsy.

"Very nice, ladies," said Green. "She's coming along nicely, isn't she?"

"We both are, *mi colonel,*" said Mercedes, patting her belly, and then kissed him warmly.

"Let me put her up, and I will walk home with you." Green nodded and waited outside the livery until she came out.

They walked arm in arm down the street, content in each other's company. Mercedes said nothing until they were seated in the house.

"Green, I knew you would come back, because you have never lied to me," she said, "but tell me, what is going on below the Rio Bravo?"

"Villa was beaten badly at Celaya but is still full of fight. I saw General Angeles, broken leg and all, and was leaving to try to talk sense to the chief. Get him to disengage and move north to rearm and reorganize. He doesn't think he will have much luck, though. I also saw Etienne, and I tried to get him to come with me. Angeles said it was all right, but he wouldn't. He's running a munitions factory in Torreon. He said he is afraid if he left now, the workers would blow the place up. He said he would come as soon as he could turn the place over to someone. I expect he will be here inside of three months ... He is tired of the war."

"I hope he comes soon. He is a good man," she said.

Later that night, they lay side by side in their bed after making love. Mercedes said, "They say that we can do this until you feel the baby's fingers grabbing for your *'chile.'*"

Propping himself up on an elbow, he said, "For a well-reared young girl, Mercedes, you seem almost depraved."

"Yes, my *gringo,* but isn't it fun?" she said, pulling him back onto her body. Though he was tired, Green didn't get to sleep until much later that night.

The first stop the next morning was Ravel's store.

"Sam, I have a list of things that General Angeles wants badly. He says things are coming down slowly from here. Is that true, and if so, why?"

"Green, it is true. The federal authorities here are really tightening up on everything. I think it is politics, myself. The people in Washington want this thing over with, and they hear Villa is losing."

"Don't they realize that Carranza is being supplied by the Germans, who I hear would like Mexico to get to fighting us? And they'd be more successful with Carranza than Villa," retorted Green.

"Green, don't ever try to make sense out of politics—it won't work. All I can tell you is the government is tightening up on military supplies, or even anything that might be considered useful to the military."

"Well, Sam, Angeles is sure anxious for that stuff. Maybe you could try some other suppliers. It's mostly chemicals anyway."

Green went on to ask, "Sam, I haven't checked lately. I know some steers have been shipped west. Have the collections been coming in all right? I'd hate to have to go to California to collect."

"They are coming in fine, Green—a little slower than other places, but that's California. By the way, Jimmy went out there yesterday to see about it. We sure picked the right guy. He's a worker and plenty smart, I think."

"Yes, he seems to be. I think after I get set up permanently up north, I'll sell out to him, but I need to see his finances before that," said Green.

"Don't start talking like that again. You know we need you on the border, not sitting on your front porch in Roy."

"Well, it's gonna happen, whether you like it or not. But I'll keep a whispering interest down here always. By the way, I found out I'm going to be a father," announced Green.

"That's wonderful, Green! When is the happy event?"

"Next October, I think. Mercedes doesn't show it yet, but it won't be long."

Green went over to the customs pens and found, to his surprise, that a large number of cattle had arrived, consigned from Villa to him. There were over 3,000.

Several of the traders greeted him, wanting to buy as many of the steers that he would let them have.

"I'll need to sort them, boys, and see what's here. You'll all have a chance, but I need some, too."

He sorted all that morning, and by noon he had 800 big cattle for the California contract, over 1,200 yearlings for himself, and 1,150 that he sold to the traders over lunch. After lunch he secured transport for the California cattle, loaded them, and made arrangements to move his own out. Tired and dusty, he arrived home just before dark to find Mercedes dressed in one of her prettiest dresses.

"Green, we had a call from the Bagwells. They are here in El Paso and we are to meet them for dinner. You must hurry and dress," she said brightly.

"Mercedes, I have been sorting cattle all day, and coupled with last night's activity, I'm all in. Can't do it."

"Go take a bath and dress. You'll feel better then. I have already accepted, and you know you want to see the Bagwells. Besides, we haven't been out in nearly a month, and I want to do something besides eat, sleep, and ..." She trailed off, with a grin.

"All right, but let's not make a habit of this," he said and went off to the bathroom.

After a hot bath and shave, Green did indeed feel better. He dressed and was ready by 7:00, and they got to the hotel on time. Mr. Bagwell had made reservations at one of El Paso's best restaurants, and they all got in Green's automobile and went out.

Green noticed that Marva Bagwell did not look well. It came out during dinner that the reason for the visit was to see some doctors. Green told Mr. Bagwell that he had about 5,000 yearlings bought already and asked him how many more he really needed.

"Green, if you don't need to run anymore, it might be a good idea just to come with those the first year. There's a couple of pastures that could use a vacation, or light stocking, and you could really see for yourself what the place will do and still not press it and get into trouble if it turns off dry."

"I think that sounds fine, Mr. Bagwell. I can get plenty of steers yet, but while I'm finding out about the ranch, a few less would be easier to work with. When should I start with them?" Green asked.

"Judging from the way the country looks, it should be just right in about two weeks. But you could start anytime now."

"I'll wait the two weeks. Would you tell Sol Weeks to expect them in two weeks?"

"Green, if I were you I'd tell him myself. He works for you now, and I wouldn't want him to think that I am still in charge. It's a hard transition for us both, but he's been with me for fifteen years, and he really needs to know that you are the boss. That's mostly for your sake, Green, and his."

"Mr. Bagwell, as usual, you're right. It's not good for a man to be unsure about who is in charge. Just tell him that you ran into me, and I asked you to alert him. I'll call next week to tell him the exact days and numbers, or rather to consult with him about what's the best to do."

"I'll tell him that the cattle are coming, Green, but Sol's a ranch foreman, not a manager. You need to give him exact orders about what to do. He'll do it, and do it well, but he needs to be told. He's that kind of a man," said Bagwell.

"Marva, how long will you be staying in El Paso?" Mercedes asked. "We'd like you to come to dinner at our home if you're going to be here for a while."

"Honey, we'll be here for four or five days while the doctors do their tests. And yes, we'd love to come out to your home one day."

The conversation of the night before had its effect. On his arrival at the border the next morning, Green found an additional 3,000 cattle in from Coahuila and Durango. He started sorting as they were still being unloaded and did not finish until 1:30. He sorted off an additional 600 steers to go to California and sold all but 200 yearlings to eager traders, clamoring to buy. After he had loaded the cattle for California, he decided he'd better talk to Jimmy Berger, so he put in a call to him in Mexicali.

To Green's surprise, the call went through quickly.

"Jimmy, I shipped 800 yesterday, and 600 today, and if my figures are right, that's nearly 4,000 out there. How are things going?" Green asked.

"Not too good, Green. These fellers have been having a bad time. Most of it's their own fault, as they don't know 'come here' from 'sick 'em' about cattle. To start with, there's no fences, and everybody's cattle is in strawberry patches and alfalfa fields that belong to some cattle owners and some who don't own cattle. There's cattle that have to be driven over a mile to water every day. These guys think steers are like dogs that you can tell to stay and they'll stay there. They'll turn down any more cattle coming, because they don't know what to do with the ones they've already got. You got any ideas, Green?"

Green thought about it, and said, "Yeah, Jimmy, I can think of some things to get us out of this mess, but these farmers can't all be that ignorant about cattle. There must be some of them that know."

"Oh sure, Green, I didn't mean that we had 2,500 steers in one bunch wandering all over the valley. Most of the cattle are behind fence. There's only about 500 steers wandering around. I didn't mean to scare you, but some of these guys are really ignorant, and those are the ones these next 1,400 are supposed to go to."

"Jimmy, go across the border and hire some vaqueros to herd

what cattle are running loose, and then go hire some kids, little ones. Most of them know about herding steers, and you can put them with these Mexican steers. They are used to it, too. Find a place where you can turn these 1,400 out temporarily, even if you have to herd them in the desert. I'll catch the first train out of here and should be in sometime tomorrow. Listen, do any of those farms have electricity?"

"Yeah, Green, about half of them. Why?"

"I've seen some temporary fences put up pretty cheap, with one electrified wire, and it works. It's pretty good in cases like this in that they can be taken up and moved pretty easily, and they don't cost much," Green answered.

"I haven't ever heard of it, but there are a lot of electrical lines here. Most of the pumps run off it."

"Well, try to get those kids and men. We may have to swallow that cost, but I think we can salvage this deal yet. I'll see you to-morrow, Jimmy."

"Good, Green, I"ll be waiting. I already have the vaqueros. I've been using them to drive the steers from here to the farms, so we already got them," Jimmy Berger said before hanging up the phone.

Green called home and asked Mercedes to pack some things for him, explaining that he had to go to California to straighten out a wreck. She was none too happy, but complied and brought his bag. She kissed him goodbye as he caught the train on which he had booked the 600 steers.

CHAPTER 36

Mexicali, California / May 2, 1915

reen had put in several hard days, but everything was finally all right. He had to go to Los Angeles to find out about electric fences. A company there was able to ship directly to an implement dealer in the valley. Most of the temporary fences were now up and working. Green discovered that the steers would try the fence when they first found it, but once one steer was shocked, they all stayed behind it. With the help of the Sonora vaqueros, Green and Jimmy got all the strays and the 1,400 cattle from El Paso sorted out and placed on the farms. Some were eating sugar beet tops, some carrots, and others fed on cabbage, Brussels sprouts, and garbanzos, but all seemed to be doing well and gaining weight. It looked like the deal was going to work.

During the work, the *caporal* of the vaqueros approached Green one night.

"Señor Dunigan, are you the same man, the *cañonero* of the Division of the North, that they called Colonel Verde?" he asked.

"Yes, that is right. I am that man," Green answered.

"Colonel Verde, my name is Praxides Balbuena, and I want to ask you why you send these cattle all the way from El Paso. There are many, many cattle just like these just south of the border in Sonora. Why not buy them there?"

"Well, I don't know the *rancheros* there, for one thing, Praxides, and the *carrancistas* control Sonora, or maybe they are *obregonistras*. Whatever they are, both are fighting the Northern Division of Villa now. I would think that if I stuck my nose across the border right now, and they found out I was a *villista* colonel, no matter that I am now retired, they would shoot me," answered Green.

"Colonel Verde, I was a *villista* also, and I can move around. You could do it also."

"What were you, Praxides?"

"I was a corporal in the cavalry," he announced with pride.

"There are a lot of ex-*villistas* who are now on the other side down there. I can't take the chance."

"What if I got the cattle and brought them here?" Praxides asked.

"Have you got the money to buy them? I really can't deal in stolen cattle. If they are confiscated I could handle them."

"If I had the money, I would not be working as a vaquero. I would be watching the *chicas* on the beach at Guaymas, no?"

Jimmy Berger had been sitting there, listening, and he spoke up. "Green, perhaps I could go down with Praxides and buy them, and we could bring them in that way."

Green thought about it until he finished his coffee. "Let's try it. You and Praxides and your crew go down there and buy the cattle to fill out the rest of the contracts here. If it works, we can go on a permanent basis. On this deal, we split the profit equally, unless you need to draw a salary, Praxides. If you do, you get ten percent."

"No, Señor, I do not need the money that bad. I would rather share the profit. It will be more."

"That doesn't seem right, Green. You're putting up the money and you have all the risk," said Berger.

"Jimmy, you'll find there's plenty of risk to everybody. If they find out that Praxides Balbuena is an ex-*villista*, they'll probably shoot both of you against the nearest wall. Believe me, you two have plenty at risk—mainly your lives."

"Well, I guess it's all right. We'll see how the three-way split works. Okay with you, Praxides?" asked Jimmy.

"Seguro que sí, compañeros," he retorted.

192

They shook hands all around to seal the deal, and Praxides Balbuena went to tell his vaqueros they still had jobs.

Green and Jimmy sat around for quite a while, saying nothing, until finally Green asked, "Jimmy, can Praxides read and write?"

"Yes, he can, and he can figure good, too. I think his father was a head vaquero on a *rancho* down there," Berger answered.

"Jimmy, I think I know a lot about Mexico and Mexicans, and I think he is a good man, but you handle all the money until you know him as well as you know your own brother. Remember, down there you are completely at his mercy, so don't confide in him completely. It just might save your life if you don't let him know everything."

"I think that's right good advice, Green, and I'm going to follow it," vowed Jimmy Berger.

"Have you set up any way to get money over here?"

"Yessir, there's a little bank in Brawley that corresponds with the bank in St. Louis, and all the arrangements are made. I even talked to Ben Davidson last week. He said to tell you hello, and to call him," answered Berger.

"Well, I think I will, Jimmy. I'll call him from El Paso when I get back. Maybe he can come see me at my new ranch."

"Green, you know, I pastured 4,000 yearlings on the Bagwell place about three years ago. I was running them for a big auger out of Kansas City. It is sure good country. If you ever need extra yearlings, I'll be glad to furnish them."

"I'll keep it in mind, Jimmy. Thanks. I'd better turn in if I want to catch that early train from Yuma. Good luck and be careful, *compadre*." They shook hands again, and Green left to go to bed.

On the way back to El Paso, Green thought a lot about Praxides Balbuena, his new Mexican partner, particularly in comparison to Cesar Dominguez, Green's old *segundo* in Chihuahua. Praxides was educated, to a certain extent, in that he had the equivalent of a tenth-grade education, provided by a school on the *hacienda* that he was raised on, similar to the arrangement at Herradura. He also was smart enough to know that a partnership share was worth more than a salary, so he could use figures to his advantage. Cesar could read and write a little and could add and subtract, but that was about all, so Praxides was considerably ahead in that category. Both had varying degrees of loyalty. First, to the job at hand, and also to their subordinates, then to their superiors. Green couldn't figure how this translated into loyalty to him or Jimmy, from Praxides, but he thought it was loyalty to his profits more than anything.

What concerned Green more than anything was that his new partner might just go south with the money. This had happened too many times to everyone in the past. Green had always guarded against it by dealing with honest people and keeping pre-delivery payments small. He would write Jimmy about it, but he hoped that both of them had read Praxides right.

Green had kept up with the news from Mexico because it was important to the border newspaper readers. The war in Europe had crowded news of the revolution out of most of the papers in the U.S.A., but those next to Mexico still carried it in detail. A big battle was going on at Leon, west of Celaya, and it looked like Villa was being beaten badly again. But since Sonora was under the control of the Obregón-Carranza faction, the news could be a bit shaded. Green hoped so.

Arriving in El Paso, Green had time to visit Sam Ravel before going home. Ravel confirmed that the Sonora reports were more or less true, that Villa was being beaten, although Obregón had lost an arm in the battle. Villa had at one point surrounded Obregón's army but could not hold. Cavalry charges would not break the Yaquis in trenches behind barbed wire and machine guns. Green also learned that the cattle arriving at Chihuahua ports were down to a small dribble. His California venture would pay off well, if it worked.

It was 6:00 when Green reached his house. Mercedes welcomed him warmly, then stepped back to look at him.

She said, "You are one dirty *gringo!* If your clothes in the bag are as dirty as the ones you're wearing, leave the bag here. Get out of those clothes and take a bath. We have plenty of time before supper."

Green did as he was told and stayed in the bathtub for a while, soaking the dust out of his hide. Mercedes surprised him when she came in, as she usually did not intrude when he was in the bathroom. She looked sad.

"Green, I have some bad news. Marva Bagwell died two days after you left. She died fairly quickly of kidney failure. I went to the ranch for the funeral. Mr. Bagwell was so sad, and he looked very lonely. I think you'd better go up there as soon as you can."

"Well, I guess you're right. I have to get those yearlings moving soon, but I'd better go on up, first. I would imagine that it hit the old man hard. This on top of everything else."

"It did, and he told me he wanted to see you as soon as possible."

"I'll go tomorrow. You know what time the S.P. leaves in the morning?" he asked.

"Yes, it leaves at 8:30. I'll pack you a bag tonight," she said and shut the bathroom door.

The next day Green rented a buggy at Roy and bought some flowers as he passed through town. On the way to old Mr. Bagwell's house, he placed the flowers on the fresh unmarked mound of dirt in the ranch cemetery.

"Green, I hadn't expected you so soon, but I'm glad you're here. We saw you drive in and it was mighty nice of you to put flowers on Marva's grave. Give your rig to Antonio and come on in," he ordered.

Green gave the buggy to the nice-looking Mexican lad, and went in the house.

"Mr. Bagwell, you can't imagine my shock when I got in from California night before last and got the news."

"Green, your wife really helped me through the whole thing. She came up on the train with me and Marva's body, and took care of the house, and all the guests during the funeral. I wasn't much help with anything, but Mercedes just took charge. I'll never be able to thank her for all she did. Oh, Green, excuse me, this is my son, Jim, in from San Francisco."

"I wish we could have met under happier circumstances, Mr. Dunigan, but I'm grateful for all you and your wife have done."

Jim Bagwell was tall, but stooped and thin, and about Green's age.

"Jim, call me Green, and I wish I had known how sick your mother was. I'm glad Mercedes was around to help."

They sat in the parlor and a woman brought in a tray with whiskey and glasses.

The old man spoke first. "Green, I think I'm going to move. I'll just rattle around in this place without Marva, and I don't have anything to do here anymore. I kinda think I'll move to Santa Fe. I've got a lot of friends there, and we'll be able to talk about the 'good old days' and such, like about Billy the Kid, and Pat Garrett, and the rest. Maybe even write a book about it. In any case, I don't think I'd like to stay here without Marva."

"You certainly have the right to stay here," Green said, "and I'd consider it an honor if you did. But you do what you feel like doing, and if Santa Fe doesn't suit you, you come on back and live here. It won't put me out none."

"Why don't you think about it a few days, Dad, and make sure?" said Jim.

"I don't need to. I see Marva in every room. We wanted to stay here, and the Dunigans were nice enough to respect our desires, but Marva and I knew it wasn't right. I don't think we'd have stayed even if she'd lived. It's Green's ranch now, and he don't need an old fool around to second guess him. No, I'm going. But I'll come back to visit, and I still want to be buried beside Marva," he said, with finality.

"Your plot will always be right there with Mrs. Bagwell," said Green.

"Thank you, Green. I know the place is in good hands, and I wish you luck with it."

Green could see tears in his eyes, so he got up to pour another round of drinks.

Jim Bagwell spoke up. "Dad told me that you had been fighting in Mexico with Pancho Villa?"

"Well, I am a retired soldier now. I quit the revolution, and fighting, forever."

"Well, I'd stay retired, if I were you. This war in Europe may kill all the people in the world before it's over," Jim said.

"They're doing a pretty good job with that in Mexico right now. In the last thirty days, Villa, Obregón, and Pablo Martinez probably had between 25 and 30 thousand casualties, and it's getting more barbaric. Obregón just penned up all his *villista* captives and machine-gunned them. They had quit killing the captures, and now Obregón starts it again. They may run out of bodies in Mexico, if this year's rate stays high. A lot of villages you pass through got nobody living in them anymore."

All the men shook their heads soberly, in sympathy for the Mexicans who had suffered so much tragedy.

Jim looked at Green. "Tell me, what kind of a man is Villa? In San Francisco, everybody calls him a bandit because he took a big ranch away from the Hearsts, and in San Francisco, the Hearsts are very powerful people."

"Jim, I think that Villa, in concert with Felipe Angeles, is the only one who can bring order with justice to Mexico. He is a good general, but what makes him important is that he is like the soul of Mexico, wanting the nation to give him only his proper share. The rest of them all have a personal ax to grind. Villa really is representative of all the people, with the exception of the Spaniards and the Chinese, whom he hates and kills on sight. The sad part of it is that I think Villa is beat. He took such a beating at Celaya, and now at Leon, that he won't be able to be a factor. The U.S. is looking at Carranza as the victor, and will probably recognize him soon, which leaves little hope for peace in Mexico. Carranza is just another dictator, like Díaz or Huerta."

"It's a sad story, isn't it?" said Jim Bagwell.

Mr. Bagwell spoke up. "Green, I've invited Sol Weeks to eat supper with us, so that you can tell him what you want to do with the yearlings. He'll be here in an hour, so if you want to clean up, go on up and do so."

"Well, I could use some cleaning ... See you in an hour."

Everyone was assembled in the parlor when Green came down. He poured a drink, shook hands with Sol Weeks, and found a seat next to him.

"Sol, I've got about 5,300 yearlings to send to you next week. I used my old brand, the mashed "O" on them all, but I want to keep the ranch brand, the running B, for use later. They've all worked, dehorned and ready to go. All you have to do is put them out. You got enough help to do it?" asked Green.

"I got five men here, and that's enough unless they're wild. What kind of cattle are they?" Sol asked.

"They're good Mexicans, mostly Herefords, a few shorthorns, and a few Angus, but they work gentle. It's been my experience with these Mexican cattle that most of them have been led more than driven, and they handle like a bunch of saddle horses."

"I think we'll be all right. I generally keep the cattle on hay in the pens for a day or two to let them calm down, and then put them out. They seem to do well that way."

"I think I'll send them up in three shipments. I'll sort them for size. From what I've seen, there will be about 1,500 big ones, cattle that'll weigh close to 500, and there will be about 1,200 small ones weighing 350-375. The balance of 3,000 will be in the middle, at 400-425. Put those big ones out on the best grass, so I can move them early, if I need to. I think the small cattle can be put along the river, in case we have to carry them over. And the balance, do as you see fit. Will that work for the grass here?"

"I believe it will do just fine. If you could ship the big ones and the little ones first, and wait two or three days before you come with the main bunch, it would help."

"I'll load the bigs and the littles on Tuesday and the others on Friday. They'll be here a day later. That way, you can put the main bunch out on the following Monday. That suit you, Sol?"

"Just perfect, Mr. Dunigan."

"I'll be here on Monday to help. I'll need a horse, but I can bring my own saddle."

Jim Bagwell cut in. "Green, I have a good handmade saddle here. I'd count it a favor if you'd accept it as a gift. My cowboying days are over, I'm afraid, but I'd like to know my saddle was still here, in good hands."

"Jim, I'd be honored, and I promise it'll be taken care of properly."

"Time for supper, gents," said Mr. Bagwell, and they all stood.

On the way to the dining room, Jim said to Green, "I'll be around the next two weeks, and would like to help if it's all right with you. It'll be my ride into the sunset—my last days cowboying. And I'd like to do it here."

"Jim, I'd be glad to have you, anytime," Green assured him.

CHAPTER 37

Torreon Military Hospital / June 3, 1915

reen was impressed by the work of Sol Weeks and his crew. They were good hands and knew cattle very well.

On his return to El Paso, he checked in at Ravel's, where Sam had a wire for him that had just arrived. It was from Etienne:

> Vicente Herrera is here. Badly wounded. Come at once.
> Etienne de la Garza.

Green ran home as quickly as he could, grabbed a bag, and started throwing clothes in it.

Mercedes came in about that time. "Green, what are you doing? Are you leaving? You just got home!"

He handed her the wire, and she blanched as she read it. "Let me get a bag. I am going, too," she said.

"No, Mercedes, you are not going. If Vicente is still alive, I will bring him back here. If not, I will take him to be buried at Herradura, and I don't want you to see what it's like down there. It's horrible. If you can do anything, I'll wire you, but I won't risk you getting into any fighting. And don't worry, I am not going to re-join Villa."

"He is my brother ... he needs me," she said sulkily.

"He is also my brother, and he would not let you come if he knew it. And I won't let you go." There was no more argument. Green took his bag and ran for Juárez, just catching the train for Torreon.

The ride to Torreon took about thirty-six hours. Green hurried to the hospital, and, once there, was directed to a ward on the third floor. He spotted the huge Cajun sitting on a bench in the hall.

"Etienne, how is Vicente? Is he here?"

"Yes, he is here, but he is in terrible condition. A big piece of shrapnel hit him in the lungs. They got out most of it, but there is a piece lodged close to his spine that they were afraid to try for. The doctors can't take much time, as you see this place is clogged with wounded. We lost over 10,000 men in Leon."

"Has a doctor seen him? I will take him to El Paso if he can stand the trip," queried Green.

"That one over there, he operated on him this morning. He can tell you," Etienne said, indicating a man in a bloody smock twenty feet down the hall.

Green rushed over. "Doctor, I am Colonel Verde. My wife's brother, Colonel Vicente Herrera, is here and I was told you worked on him. How is he?"

"He is in grave condition. His lungs are torn. We didn't get all the steel and bone chips out, and he has lost much blood. He hasn't much of a chance," he said gravely.

"Doctor, I can take him to El Paso, where he can be treated and cared for. Could he make the trip?"

"He is in the hands of God now. I don't think he will survive the trip, but I am also pretty sure he won't survive here. We have to spend most of our time trying to save those we think we can save. You understand?"

"Yes, I understand. I will take him. If he gets there, maybe we can save him."

"Take him, Colonel, and this, too." The doctor handed Green a syringe of morphine. "Go with God," he said as he walked wearily away.

Green and Etienne found a stretcher and gently loaded Vicente. He groaned a bit but was otherwise unconscious. They loaded him on the train for El Paso, via Chihuahua City, and left.

200

They were two hours out of Chihuahua when Vicente opened his eyes.

"*Ah, mi cunado Verde*. Take good care of my little sister. She is the last of the Herreras." He lapsed back into unconsciousness, and died an hour later.

On arrival in Chihuahua City, Green and Etienne carried Vicente Herrera's body to an undertaker. They said they would return in twenty-four hours with a wagon to transport the body in a coffin. They then left to find a wagon and team. It was a little farther to Herradura from Chihuahua than from Parral, but handling on and off the train would be eliminated, and they didn't particularly want to be around Parral.

Green wired Mercedes about Vicente's death. He told her that he and Etienne were taking the body for burial at Herradura. He forbade her to come, and reinforced that order with a warning that the countryside was full of deserters from all the armies. Green thought that he and Etienne might need help, so he looked up Cesar Dominguez and had him bring a couple of people along to present a stronger party to anyone thinking about waylaying them.

The party left Chihuahua City the next morning, Etienne driving the wagon with Vicente's coffin and some supplies.

The passage to Herradura took four days. During that time, the travelers spotted several groups of five to ten men watching them, but had no trouble. Green felt he had been justified in hiring Cesar and his men as guards. Midafternoon of the fourth day, they spotted the ghostly outline of Herradura. Green had not been with Vicente and Tomas when they came after Orozco's raid, so he didn't know what to expect.

When they went through the wall, with its great gates lying in the dirt, the damage became evident. Many of the roofs of the buildings had been thatch-cut from the sedge grass present in the nearby Conchos River vega, and all had been burned. Only a few corrals and shacks had been made of lumber, the vast majority being stone or stucco. These were still standing but were scorched from the fire, and many large pieces had flaked off. Weeds and cactus were rampant in the once well-manicured grounds, but a few paths and a couple of scrawny chickens spoke to the fact that there was some life there. The only part of the *hacienda* that looked populated was the *campo santo,* as there were many graves.

The little group took the wagon up to the main house and transferred Vicente's coffin inside. There the group became aware of the senseless cruelty of the raid. All of the furniture, rugs, and decorations had been piled in the center of each room and burned. Tears welled in Green's eyes as he surveyed the vandalism.

"We'll stay here tonight and bury Vicente tomorrow," Green ordered, and the designated cooks moved their utensils to the kitchen to cook supper.

After eating, Green and Etienne took a lantern to see the rest of the house. They had trouble gaining the second and third stories, as some of the stairway had been burned, but they made it. The upper stories told the same story—complete and mindless destruction of a beautiful and historic building. However, being made of stone, the shell of the house was still intact and could be rebuilt.

They found the door to Don Tacho's office and library. Being mostly of wood and paper, the entire room was destroyed, including all of the books. The stone was completely blackened by the fire, but Green located the fireproof safe that Vicente and Tomas had found intact. It was behind a bookcase and was not found by the raiders. The brothers evidently had emptied it and left it open. Green wondered if the original grants of Herradura had been there and rescued by the brothers, and how he could find them. He had been through what little Vicente had on him, and it wasn't there. Vicente probably had the papers somewhere safe, in a bank or with a lawyer. Green would try to find them, but he wanted to get out of this area pretty fast, or the revolution, which was around Aguascalientes now, might catch up to him.

In the morning they took Vicente's body to the *campo santo* to be buried. They were in the process of lowering the coffin into the grave when Cesar Dominguez noticed they had company.

An old Mexican couple had appeared at the gravesite, and the man, who was brown and wizened so as to appear almost like an old monkey, spoke. *"Quien es?"*

"Vicente Herrera," answered Green.

"The last of them, I think," he said. "May we stay to pay honor to the family?"

"Surely you can. May I ask who you are?"

"I am Mercadio Gomez, and this is Sarita, my wife. We were the only ones left here after the massacre," he said slowly.

The coffin was lowered and Etienne said a prayer before they covered the grave.

"If it is all right, I will carve a marker for Vicente," volunteered Mercadio Gomez.

"It will be much appreciated, Señor," said Green.

"Señores, if you would come to my house, I have a little coffee. I would be most appreciative if you would partake of what little I have," Mercadio offered.

They all went to his house, a small one that actually had a roof made of tin. The old man explained that he had covered it below the parapet, so no one would know. He also explained how he and the old woman hid from occasional visitors who would pass by. For all purposes, Herradura was vacant.

Coffee was passed around and they all drank. Mercadio Gomez looked at Green and asked, "Señor, are you not the one who used to come and buy Don Tacho's steers?"

"That is true, *viejito*," answered Green.

"I heard that you became a colonel with the Division of the North, that you were called Gringo Verde, and that you married Don Tacho's daughter, Mercedes. Is that true?" he asked.

"Yes, that is all true, but I am no longer a soldier, and Mercedes and I live in El Paso. I came here to bury Vicente, among the other Herraduros," Green said, gravely.

"Is Mercedes the only Herrera left?" asked Sarita.

"Yes, the older sister, Otilia, left for Spain with Porfirio Díaz."

"Que lastima ... que familia valiente," said the old woman.

"Will you stay here, Mercadio?" Green asked.

"It is my home. Where would I go?"

Green pulled out a handful of *bilimbiques,* the money Villa used, and gave it to him.

"Here is some money. When the fighting stops, Mercedes and I will return, at least to see the graves. Watch them for us, please."

"I will be here, Señor. I was born here, and I will die here," he said, and Sarita nodded in agreement.

Green left the wagon and team with the couple and headed for Chihuahua City.

In Chihuahua, Green learned that Villa was in Torreon, with

203

what was left of the division, and was reinforcing Zacatecas. Urbina was in Chihuahua. Green had never been very fond of Urbina, and the feeling was mutual, so he decided not to stop.

Rodolfo Fierro had been on a wide-ranging cavalry raid that had actually come close enough to Mexico City to cause Pablo Gonzales to abandon it, but he was returning to Zacatecas now. He had disrupted Obregón's supply line, but not enough to cause him to stop advancing. Etienne was torn between staying and going north with Green. He was finally persuaded, and they boarded the train to Juárez. He could also see the end.

CHAPTER 38

El Paso, Texas / July 4, 1915

It was about 8:00 in the evening when Green and Mercedes returned home from the *fiesta* that Sam Ravel had thrown to celebrate Independence Day. They had enjoyed barbecue and some music and dancing but did not stay late because of Mercedes' advancing pregnancy and the heat. Etienne had gone with them, but had stayed. General Pershing had been there and had asked Green about Villa.

Green had answered, "Villa's been beaten up pretty bad, I'm afraid, but the people will still follow him. He may be able to come back, but not if he insists on contesting Obregón every chance he gets."

"That's what I heard, Colonel. I still think he is our best friend down there. That Carranza is a slimy bastard in my book," said Pershing.

"General, please call me Green. I am retired and no longer have any connection with the revolution in Mexico. I am only a border cattle trader, and that's what I'm gonna stay."

"I think you're wise, although I wish Villa had some people like yourself and General Angeles to advise him."

"General, I think that you understand, better than most, what is going on. I know that you just gave the best description of Don Venus that I have heard."

They both laughed and had one more drink before Mercedes appeared, saying she would like to go home. They had said their good nights and left.

Green had noticed that his friend Etienne de la Garza was at loose ends. He was glad to be out of the fighting, but he didn't know what to do with himself. He had found a room for himself and was helping Green with the cattle, but he wasn't happy. Green remembered that Etienne had mentioned that he had found a good woman in Mexico and thought that was the trouble.

Green asked, "You said you had a good woman down there, Etienne. Do you miss her?"

"No, Green. I thought she was good, but she ran away with a barber in Torreon. I guess she was just tired of the war, too."

"How about going to my ranch in New Mexico? I have to go up there next week. Why don't you come with me?" asked Green.

"Sounds like a good idea. Maybe I could do some fishing. I'd like that."

"I'm not a fisherman, but I hear there's some good trout in the streams and in the Canadian River. We'll be leaving next Wednesday. If you can't find any, I'm sure we can borrow tackle up there," Green answered.

The trip was made almost without incident—only two flat tires on the way. Green and Etienne arrived at the ranch late in the morning, in Green's new Ford. Sol Weeks met them at the big house.

"Sol, this is Etienne de la Garza, an old friend of mine who just left the fighting in Mexico. He wants to just loaf for a while and do a little fishing. We got any on this place?" asked Green.

"Oh, sure, there's lots of trout in the creeks. I fish a little myself, and I can show him some good places. Nobody else here ever messed with fishing," said Sol, smiling at the prospect of a fishing partner.

"Well, you just do that. He's a little short on equipment. El Paso don't have much for sale. Maybe you could fix him up."

"I got plenty for everybody, Green. You want to fish, too?"

"No, I just want to take a quick look at the steers, and I've got to head back. Jimmy Berger's not due in for another two weeks, and some cattle are coming in. I'll just get Etienne settled in ... By the way, Sol, you heard anything from Mr. Bagwell?" Green asked.

"I got a letter just last week. Says he got a nice place in Santa Fe and has been traveling around in the mountains some."

Green took Etienne into the big house, where they ate lunch, and then Sol and Green left Etienne to fend for himself as they toured the ranch, looking at the steers.

"You know, these yearlings are sure doing it all," Green observed. "The big ones look like they'll be ready to sell the first of next month. I'll have to get working on that."

"They'll do as much if you don't sell them until fall," answered Sol.

"Yeah, but they might get fat, and I sure don't want that," said Green.

Sol Weeks looked at him quizzically, and Green laughed.

"I learned a long time ago from a master cowman, my father, that steers are always worth more to a feeder or grazer than they are to a packer," Green explained. "The other guy always has a way he thinks will squeeze a little more money out of them before he has to sell them to the killers. Besides, we can loosen up the smaller cattle, and they'll do a lot of catching up. You watch—all the cattle we sell will weigh about the same. We sell these, scatter the little cattle out on their pasture, and they'll weigh with them and the big bunch at the end of the season."

"Sounds fairly radical, Green, but if you say so, we'll do our best here. We've had a pretty good season so far, and those vacated pastures have really come on. How about taking the little cattle there, out of the river and saving it, in case you get some cows, or something you need to winter here?"

"That's a good idea, Sol, but let them have the pastures we vacate when we ship, too."

"Sounds like a good plan, Green," Sol responded, figuring he had learned something new.

It was late by the time Green and Sol had finished their look at the cattle, so Green decided to sleep there and get an early start in the morning. At dinner Sol tried to tell Etienne about the joys of fly fishing, but all he did was confuse him.

"All I do is put a shrimp on a hook an' throw it in the bayou. Dis de way I fish—catch some trout, perch, and stuff," said Etienne.

"Well, fly fishing is more like hunting. The fly is tied to the hook and you put it right in front of the fish, but it don't sink. He bites it on top, and these trout are real fighters," said Sol.

"Mebbe so I need a bigger rod and reel."

"No, you use real light tackle. You have to wear these fish down. You don't just wrestle them in."

Etienne looked puzzled and said, "Okay, Sol, you teach me."

Green had his mind elsewhere. "Sol, if I might want some cake, is there a source anywhere close?"

"We used to get it from a mill over in Texas—Lubbock, I think— and we still can, so far as I know. I don't think there would be any problem."

"Have you ever fed cake to cattle here, when it gets dry?"

"No, but I know some ranches up close to Clayton have, and they got along all right."

"Well, I'll leave you and Etienne to your fly fishing. I probably will leave before you get up, so I'll say goodbye now. I'll be back in about three weeks, but call if you run out of fish to catch."

Sol was drinking coffee in the dining room when Green came down about 5:15. Green got a cup and sat down.

"I'm glad there isn't much to do here. Now that you've got a fishing partner, it sounds like you'll be at it full time," Green said.

"I'll take care of the cattle, Green. Don't worry about that, but there really isn't much that needs doing, and I'm going to have fun fishing with Etienne."

"Well, I hope he takes to it. He needs not to think about fighting for a while. He's a warrior, a born soldier, and if he gets bored I'm afraid he may go join one of the armies in Europe, or maybe ours. They're taking in a lot of people."

"Well, we'll try to see to it that he doesn't get bored, even if I have to put him on horseback."

Green left for El Paso, and arrived midmorning the next day. He went straight home to see Mercedes, as she had been in mourning ever since she got his wire from Chihuahua.

"Mercedes, I'm home!" he yelled as he passed through the front door.

She came out of the kitchen, and he could see her eyes were puffy from tears. She came meekly into his arms and kissed him.

"Green, can't you get a job where you come home every night? In the last two months you have been all over the world. I miss you so, and now you are all I have. I think you go because I am so fat and ugly." Her eyes were brimming with tears.

"Mercedes, you are the most beautiful woman I have ever known, and you get more beautiful each day that brings you nearer the birth of our child. I know I have been gone too much lately, but I don't have to go anyplace for a while, and I will be here for you."

Mercedes dried her eyes and hugged him. "Will you stay for lunch, today?" she asked.

"Yes ... I don't need to go to customs until this afternoon. What's for lunch?"

"Just sandwiches, that's all I have here, because I don't usually eat lunch," she said.

"You'd better start. You must eat for two now. I don't want my baby to be skinny."

"Mama Rosenda says that I should not gain too much weight, that the birth will be easier, and it will be easier to get my figure back. Liz Villa says so, too," she retorted.

"You been going to a *curandera*, not a doctor?"

"Both, *mi gringo*. Don't you know Mexicans trust *curanderas* of esteem?" she asked.

"Yes, I know that, but Americans use doctors, and I thought you wanted to be all American."

"Green, I can never lose my *mexicanismo*. Too much tradition, too many years. I can never forsake the land of my blood."

"You know, I am glad to hear that. There is much value and much to love in the history and traditions of Mexico. That is one of the reasons I like El Paso, because of its Mexican heritage."

"Green, we should talk about what to name the baby, don't you think?" she asked.

"I've been thinking about it some. What would you like to name a baby girl?"

"For a little girl, I would choose naming her after your mother.

209

None of her grandchildren have been named for her, and she is such a wonderful woman. I do love her very much."

"That would be nice, but your mother won't have any grandchildren but ours. Marisol is a beautiful name."

"No, we can use it later. Remember, we are going to have many children, if you can keep up." She smiled.

"Okay, Amanda for a girl, but what does your *curandera* say it's going to be?" he asked.

"She thinks it will be *macho,* but she won't tell me why."

"Well, if it's a boy, I want to name him Felipe Angeles Dunigan. The general is the finest man I have ever met, next to my father, and I would like to honor him," said Green.

"That is very nice, Green, but I would like to name him after you, Adrian Green Dunigan y Herrera," she said.

"That can wait, too, maybe for number six or seven," he said, laughing, and Mercedes joined him.

After lunch, Green went to the customs office, where 323 big steers had come in from Villa. They looked suitable for the Dunigan operation, so he shipped them to Jack at Cotulla, except for two cripples that he sent to the packing house.

Green went to Sam Ravel's store to find out the news.

"Green, it's still bad. Villa is in Torreon, having been thrown out of Aguascalientes and Zacatecas, but I doubt if he can hold it. He has lost most of his equipment and many soldiers. He will have to fall back on Chihuahua soon. I don't even know if he can hold there. Wilson just called for a conference of all leaders in Mexico, and everyone said yes, except for Don Venus, who, as usual, said he was the 'Lider Maximo,' and for the U.S. to butt out. Same old thing he always does, but it's still working for him," explained Sam. "How is Mercedes taking Vicente's death, Green?"

"Well, he was the last one. I think she had thought about it so much, though, she had kinda written him off as already killed. But she is still pretty broken up. She is the only survivor, really. She had an older sister, but she left Mexico when Don Porfirio did, and Mercedes doesn't even recognize her. It's all very sad, Sam. Even Herradura is a ghost place, as we saw when we buried Vicente." He paused to consider the future. "Sam, how is the U.S. feeling now?"

"I think that Wilson is getting ready to recognize Carranza. General Scott, and I think Pershing too, favor Villa, but Carranza looks like he's winning, and they don't want any problems on the border, 'cause everybody thinks we're going to get mixed up in the European war. If the U.S. recognizes Carranza, Villa is finished. I won't be able to get a round of ammunition for him."

"That's terrible, Sam. Don Venus won't change a thing from the way Díaz and Huerta ruled, and the whole revolution will have been for nothing," Green said solemnly.

Green checked his accounts with Ravel, then phoned Jimmy Berger, who was still in Kansas. After nearly an hour, he finally got him on the line.

"Jimmy, how are you? How are things in Kansas? You coming back pretty soon?"

Berger chuckled and said, "I'm doing fine, Green. It's a little dry here, but looks like a real good corn crop, and I'll be back in about two or three weeks. Any more questions?"

"No, Jimmy. Didn't mean to ask those all at once, but I need to ask one more. I've got about 1,300 yearlings at Roy that I want to come with soon. The first week in August. They'll weigh a little over 750, but not 775. You got anybody up there to buy them?"

"A man was asking for cattle just yesterday. These would probably fit the bill, and I can sell them to him, I think. He's a big farmer. He put up a good bit of silage, and he's picking a big crop of corn. Ought to fit him like a glove," Berger said.

"Sell them, and get $15 down and a five percent cut, Jimmy, and let me know when and where to ship them."

"I'll do it, Green. I think he'll want to receive the cattle and will come down there."

"I'd prefer it that way, Jimmy. Draw up a contract and get the down payment, and we'll set the delivery date for August 6. That's a Thursday. Tell him I'll arrange for cars."

"Okay, Green, I'll probably come back with him and catch a ride with you to El Paso."

Green hung up the phone. He would call Sol and tell him the date. They had nearly three weeks to prepare.

CHAPTER 39

Roy, New Mexico / August 5, 1915

Jimmy Berger and Anton Langer came in on the 5:00 train. Green met them and took them out to the ranch for supper. Both were shown to bedrooms in the big house and told to come down for a drink before the meal.

Jimmy came down first, and Green asked him, "Mr. Langer looks like a banker, Jimmy. What is he all about?"

"Well, he is a kind of banker, Green. He is buying the cattle for a group of farmers. I don't suppose any one farm will get more than 200 steers. He is the main banker in Liberal, and they've got a hell of a corn crop there this year. He has told his farmers to keep their corn and run it through cattle, and they pretty well have to do as he says. I think the deal will work, all right, but there is a certain amount of coercion in it.

"Langer came down there about two years ago and bought the bank. He is originally from Indiana—Crawfordsville, I think. He's changed the habits around there. You know, most of that country grew wheat and a little corn. Now it's corn and a little wheat. He has financed most of the wells for irrigation, and the country is fairly prosperous. But those farmers owe a lot of money, and almost all of it to him. His bank has certainly grown, and the farming is sure better, but they all are carrying a lot of debt."

Etienne poured Jimmy a drink and introduced him around. Sol was present, as was Praxides Balbuena, who had been in El Paso checking accounts and accompanied Green to help.

When Anton Langer came down, it was quite a contrast. All of Green's people were dressed in working clothes, khakis and duck-ins, whereas Langer was in a suit with a vest, celluloid collar and tie, and a watch and chain across his vest. Green introduced him to everyone and poured him a drink.

Dinner was announced, and they all sat down to a meal of steak, potatoes, and beans.

"My, this is good steak. You slaughter your own, I presume?" asked Langer.

"No, we never eat our own beef—our neighbor's sometimes, but never our own. It's too tough," said Green. Everyone chuckled except Langer, who looked aghast.

"Mr. Dunigan, do you mean to say that you steal cattle?"

Green looked at him quizzically and said, "Mr. Langer, that is the standard response to a tenderfoot question. No, I didn't steal it, I bought it in El Paso. The part about the neighbors is just kind of a joke, but I've been places where it is practiced zealously."

"Well, I hope I am dealing with honest people," said Langer.

"I hope so, too, but you'll know in the morning, won't you?" said Green.

Green could see Langer was a supercilious bastard with a dead buzzard's sense of humor. He did not try to engage him in any more conversation. After coffee, everyone went to bed, as they were leaving before daylight for the delivery.

Green told them, "The cook will call you at four, and coffee will be ready. Breakfast at four-thirty, and we leave before five, except for Jimmy and Mr. Langer. You can get up anytime, but we'll have the cattle in at a quarter to eight."

Jimmy spoke up. "Green, I thought I would help the crew, so you big augers could stay together, and maybe get a little more sleep."

Jimmy had aced him. It was the custom for the owner to take care of the buyer, and Jimmy had called him on it. All except Langer grinned, knowing what Jimmy had done, and so Green didn't even try to fight.

"All right, Jimmy, take my horse," Green said, thinking, *I owe you one, Berger, and I'll get even one day.*

"Mr. Langer, I hope you brought some rougher clothes. It's pretty hot and dusty in those pens," said Green.

"No, Mr. Dunigan, these clothes will be quite all right," he responded.

The next morning Green got up with everyone but Langer. He had told the cook to let Langer sleep until 6:00. Green had waited, and he ate breakfast with the Kansas banker. They drove to the pens and arrived just as the cattle were being penned. Green had told Sol Weeks exactly how he wanted to do the delivery, which was more or less standard.

Entering the pens, Green said, "Mr. Langer, we have a good alley below the scale, and you can make your cut there. Jimmy can help you, unless you want him to check weights with me. Sol will be there, too."

"I believe I can make the cut all right, and I'd like the weights checked by Berger."

"Okay. Sol, you and Etienne help Mr. Langer make the cut. How many did you count in?"

"A thousand two hundred and sixteen steers came in, Green. That's three less than I booked, but I think I know where they are," Sol answered.

"Close enough. Tell the boys I want fifteen head per draft, and put the cuts in that second pen down the alley."

"Mr. Dunigan, the contract was for 1,200 cattle—no more, no less. The extra cattle are not in the deal," ordered Langer.

"It's fine with me," answered Green, as he and Jimmy Berger headed to the scales.

"Where did you find this idiot, Jimmy?" Green asked.

"He's the only one I could find that would give eight dollars a hundred," Jimmy grinned.

"I'd rather sell 'em for six to someone who knows what he's doing," said Green. "No, I really wouldn't," he added, smiling.

Green and Jimmy started weighing the cattle, and found they were weighing heavy, about 780. However, Green wasn't worried, as he knew the heavier cattle would come first. They had weighed about 200 when Green noticed they were not getting down the alley very fast but in fact had backed up against the scale where no more could be weighed. Green left the scale and made his way where Langer was telling Sol and Etienne which steers to cut.

He said, "Sol, turn these weighed cattle into that big pen. You all are not taking the cut out fast enough, and I had to stop weighing."

Sol made his way through the cattle to Green and said, "Boss, he's cutting every steer out that'll weigh over seven and a half. He's cut out over thirty, and there ain't seventy in the big bunch. You said he had a five percent cut, but he's taking about a thirty percent cut."

"Well, this'll have to be straightened out, but for now, just let him keep on. We have pen space where we can weigh them all. Use those two big pens here to let them in, and when we're through weighing, I'll bring Jimmy to sort it out. Can you keep count on what he cuts and what goes through?"

"Yeah, my boys always keep count, but I recheck them myself."

"Okay, Sol. Just keep doing it the way he wants. It's not really hurting us unless we have to quit weighing, and it's my guess that's what he's trying to do. But he's not going to get it done, so it'll hurt him. Just make sure he doesn't stop the weighing," Green said, and went back to the scales. "Jimmy, you got to straighten that old sonovabitch out. I think he's trying to shrink these steers, but I'm not going to let him. He's making better than a thirty percent cut on them. Doesn't he know better?"

"I don't know, Green, but he knows he's only entitled to a five percent cut, plus unmerchantibles. I pointed it out to him when he signed the contract. I'll straighten him out, but let's get back to weighing cattle," responded Berger.

Green and Jimmy Berger were both good weighmen, and the whole herd was over the scales before 11:00, with the exception of the last sixteen that Langer had not wanted. These were put in a small pen, out of the way. Green and Jimmy then checked on the progress of the cut, and it was not good. Only about 500 steers had been sorted—300 accepted and 200 cut. Green examined the cut carefully. To him, it appeared the whole criteria was only weight. He and Jimmy climbed up on the corral fence and watched what was going on. Langer was cutting the cattle based on one reason—weight.

At a break, when more cattle needed to be brought up for cutting, Green called a halt, and he and Berger went to talk to Langer.

215

"Mr. Langer, you know this cut you're making is only costing you time and money. You're cutting forty percent and you only have five percent coming. I looked at them, and didn't see but one unmerchantible, a loopy-jaw steer."

Sol broke in. "Mr. Dunigan, there are four unmerchantibles, a one-eye, a woddy tongue, that loop jaw, and one lame steer."

Green turned back to Langer. "Mr. Langer, all this is doing is causing shrink on the cattle that are to be weighed back, and will make the cattle sold weigh more, don't you see?"

"Mr. Dunigan, the contract calls for the cattle to weigh 750, and I'm cutting out every steer that looks like he may weigh over that, and I am entirely within my rights!" said Langer, smiling smugly.

"No, Mr. Langer, the contract says the cattle will weigh between 750 and 775, and you may cut out, over and above the five percent, any steers that weigh 800. I know because I wrote it," interjected Jimmy Berger.

"Mr. Langer, the cattle's shrunk weight is 764 pounds apiece, well within the limits imposed by the contract, so this whole cut is just costing weight," Green said evenly. "I suggest you bring back the cut, and do it to reflect the five percent, and get on with it. No cowman in his right mind would allow you to do what you're doing."

He turned to Jimmy, who handed him the original contract, and read, "The cattle are estimated to weigh between 750 and 775 pounds, and the buyer is allowed a five percent cut, plus unmerchantibles of the cattle presented for sales. Any individual steer that weighs 800 pounds or over is to be cut out as unmerchantible."

Green checked the signature page, and it was signed and notarized properly.

"Well, that isn't the governing document. This is!" said Langer, handing Green a similar document.

Green turned to the relevant language and saw that it had been altered, just by scratching out reference to anything over 750 pounds, and substituting 750 for 800 in the top weight limit. Then he turned to the signature paper and saw his signature had been crudely forged but properly notarized. He looked back for more changes and found the shrink increased from three to six percent. He showed these to Jimmy silently.

Jimmy sighed, and said, "I knew he was tricky, so I wrote the contract tight, but I had no idea he would do this."

"Mr. Langer, the contract that is in our possession governs this transaction. If you will abide by it, we can complete the business at hand. If not, we will turn the cattle out. It's up to you," Green said.

"Mr. Dunigan, I have this contract, and it governs. You will deliver the cattle now, and under its terms, or suffer the consequences of a long and expensive lawsuit!" Langer said triumphantly.

Green looked at Langer, who would not meet his eyes, then spoke. "Sol, put 'em back together, and turn them out. This deal's over with. Mr. Langer, I'll give you a ride back to the house, so you can collect your belongings."

"Dunigan, you present me with the rest of those cattle, or you're in for trouble!" he yelled.

Green continued walking, and the cowboys started mixing the cattle to drive them home.

Green was sitting in his car when Langer finally came out. Nothing was said on the way to the ranch. When he stopped at the house, Green said, "The train north leaves at 2:30. I'll get someone to drive you over."

"What about my down payment?"

"I'll give you back half, $9,000. This whole deal has cost me more'n that, but I'll swallow it. Serves me right for dealing with a blood-sucking banker," Green said.

"You'll give it all back, or you'll never move another animal in the state of Kansas, and I happen to know you do a lot of business there!" Langer said loudly.

"Langer, you ain't even going to get the $9,000 back if you don't shut up." Green turned on his heel and walked into the house, as Langer shouted orders and threats at him.

After Langer had gone upstairs, Green phoned a lawyer he had used at the county seat, told him the story, and told him to watch the courthouse until Langer left. Then he told Jimmy to take Langer to the train, and gave him the check for $9,000.

CHAPTER 40

El Paso, Texas / September 3, 1915

reen had been waiting three weeks for the other shoe to fall. He expected Anton Langer to try something, and he had, finally. He sued Green and tried to attach all of the Dunigan cattle in Kansas. Green was served, all right, but Langer was unable to attach any of the cattle, most of which were in Chase County, near Emporia. The people in Chase County had been dealing with Texas drovers for a long time and were not about to let any legal trick work be done by bankers, even if they were from Kansas. They had some help from John Dunigan's lawyer.

Soon after the failed sale of the yearlings, Green told Jimmy Berger, "Langer is going to try to do all sorts of things. I'm gonna need a good lawyer in Kansas."

"I think I know a good one. I've heard of him all my life. His name is Frank Goodwin, and he loves to sue railroads, banks, and Republicans—and he's good at it. He's from Hutchinson and knows all about livestock and farm law, although I don't know how many cases he's had in New Mexico, but I'll bet he's been involved," said Jimmy Berger.

"Sounds like my kinda lawyer. Will you call him for me? If he'll agree to represent me, make an appointment for me a week from today, okay?"

"Sure, Green. You want me to go with you?"

"Well, I think I can handle it, but it's your stomping grounds and you are a party to the suit, so maybe it would be best."

"I'll let you know as soon as I do, and I'll make the train reservations."

"Thank you, Jimmy. I would take you out of this suit, but if your lawyer is the right man, we may cross-sue and get some money, so it might be better if you stay in. Agreed?"

"Yeah . . . I'd kinda like a chunk of that sonavabitch myself."

Green and Jimmy entered Frank Goodwin's office promptly at 10:00. Goodwin was a tall man in his mid-sixties, with a full head of graying hair and black snapping eyes. He rose as they entered and bade them be seated after shaking hands. He looked at Green, and asked, "What can I do for you, Mr. Dunigan?"

"You can represent me against a no-account banker named Anton Langer, from Liberal, Mr. Goodwin."

"Jimmy told me about the case. Of course I'll need to know more. Have they served you with papers yet?" Goodwin asked.

"Yes, and I have them here. I'll leave them with you." Green handed the papers to Goodwin, who studied them. "Mr. Goodwin, have you done much legal work in the cattle trade?"

Goodwin laughed and said, "Yes. One of the first cases I handled when I came out to Kansas was to defend old man Shanghai Pierce against a Texas banker, name of Danny Sullivan. You know them?"

"I know enough to say you'd be well versed in the trade," countered Green.

"If you don't mind my asking, I've heard of a John Dunigan from Texas, a big cattleman. You any kin?"

"Yessir, my father," answered Green.

"I've heard nothing but good about him. I hope you take after him," said Goodwin.

"Well, my father and I are in business together. As a matter of fact, Langer tried to attach some of his cattle in Chase County, but he didn't get it done. I hope I take after him," Green said, smiling.

Goodwin was still studying the papers that Green had given him.

"Aha!" he said and grinned widely. "He's made a big mistake, gentlemen. Langer has accused you of various things that, if not true, we can hang a countersuit on, if you want to. Do you just want to get this suit out of the way and over with, or would you like some measure of monetary revenge?" Goodwin asked.

"I think the latter, Mr. Goodwin. I don't do that much business here, but Jimmy does, and this could hurt his reputation. As for me, I took an immediate dislike to Langer, and he did damage me some, so I'd like a piece of the bastard, too," Green said evenly.

"What about juries there?" Jimmy asked. "Doesn't Langer have most everybody tied into his bank?"

"Don't worry about it, Jimmy. There are plenty of good folks in Liberal that he doesn't have his hooks into, and more that are hooked. He's already started foreclosing on a bunch of farmers that he lent money to. Don't worry. I can still get a good jury in Seward County," Goodwin explained. After glancing at the documents again, he said, "He accuses you of the theft of $18,000. Tell me about it."

"The $18,000 was a down payment he made on the steers, or $15 per head. After the blow-up, I gave him a check for $9,000, or half. I figured he had cost me more than that, and by the terms of the contract, I wasn't obliged to give him anything. He hasn't cashed that check, so far as I know. One other thing, this is the original of the contract. He has a copy and he forged my signature on it and made changes, and I saw it. The same man notarized the copy that notarized the original, and more of the changes were initialed. Here is the original . . ." Green gave him the contract.

"That all sounds fine. How much money you want to get?" Goodwin asked innocently.

"Oh, I don't know, Mr. Goodwin. I'm told some lawyers handle cases like this for a piece of the award. You want to do it like that?" Green asked.

"I will, if you want, on contingency fees. It has to do with the merit of the case. You have a pretty good case here, I think, and my fee would be fifteen percent, about," he answered.

"How about we call it this way. Jimmy will be damaged the most, so let him have half. I'll take twenty-five percent and you can have the same. I'm sure you can think of some appropriate numbers to sue Mr. Anton Langer for, under those percentages," Green said.

"I'm sure I can, Green, and I'll enjoy it. You know, there's several kinds of people I don't like. Railroaders, bankers, Republicans, Yankees from New England and New York, and Texans. Since you only qualify in one category, we're going to get along fine. Now, let me read these papers, and we'll have some lunch down the street when I finish," said Goodwin.

After he finished reading both the contract and the suit papers, his eyes alighted with the relish of the forthcoming battle.

"We've got him, we've got him! I can rip a substantial chunk out of him. Could maybe even get his bank, but I don't want it. I can tell you this—his bank may be substantially short of capital when I get through with him," Goodwin said with a flourish, his black eyes flashing.

After they had lunch, Green and Jimmy Berger left to inspect the cattle that the Dunigans had left in the Flint Hills, around Emporia. It was a short ride, and the two of them chatted as they rode the rails through central Kansas.

"I sure think we got the right man for this job, Jimmy. I really like the old man. Reminds me a lot of my father," remarked Green.

"Yes, I think so, too, but I think you're giving me too much of the money we stand to get. You're the one he's after, and the one that stands to lose the most, if we lose."

"Jimmy, that's wrong. You trade a lot in that area, and if he were to win, it would hurt you bad. Even if we win, he's going to try to put you out of business in southern and western Kansas, if he can. Besides, you can use the money to buy more of an interest in our deals, and I'll end up with it anyway," Green said, grinning.

"Well, if it goes that way, maybe it'll be all right."

Changing the subject, Jimmy asked, "How many steers you got left here, Green? You must have shipped most of them by now."

"There's only four or five hundred left here, I think. Just the ones that we'll sell to feeders within a month. My brother Jack is going to pick us up at Strong City, and he'll know."

A little before 5:00 they alit at Strong City, and were met by Jack Dunigan. Green and Jack, who had not seen each other since January, hugged and welcomed each other. Jimmy was introduced, and they piled into Jack's car, heading to a couple of nearby pastures where the Dunigan cattle were.

Green asked, "Most of them get fat this year, Jack?"

"Yeah, over nintey-five percent go to the killers this year. I guess it's the best we've done. I did feed cake to a couple pastures in August, and they did better than before."

"That's been recommended to me on yearlings on the New Mexico place by more than one source. There's probably a lot to it," added Green. "Have you seen Mother and Dad lately? How're they doing?" asked Green.

"Saw them three weeks ago, on my way up here. Dad's doing just fine, especially for an eighty-year-old, but mother has been ailing and doesn't look good to me. She's lost weight and her skin has that papery look to it. I think something's the matter with her."

"I haven't seen them since New Year's. I hope nothing is wrong with her. I don't know what Dad would do if she died," Green said.

They saw small numbers of cattle in several pastures before they went into Emporia, and finally Green asked, "Jack, aren't you about ready to close up shop here?"

"Yeah, next week I plan to ship all the cattle that are fat and concentrate the others for sale to feeders."

"Wouldn't it save time and labor to just clean out everything, ship them to Kansas City, and let them sort and sell the fats and feeders?" asked Jimmy, tentatively, not wanting to anger the more experienced men.

"Well, I call that a good idea," said Jack, with Green nodding agreement. "That'll save a lot of time and money, and those commission men will have to earn their money with a little sweat." All three men chuckled, as none of them had much use for market-bound brokers.

CHAPTER 41

El Paso, Texas / September 13, 1915

After staying overnight and having a long visit with Jack, Green and Jimmy caught the train to El Paso. Green toyed with the idea of going by way of Refugio, to see his folks, but he decided he'd better get back to Mercedes, as her time was coming soon. Green knew he had to be there when the first pains of labor hit her. Jimmy had to button up the last of the cattle in California anyway, so they boarded the train for El Paso.

It took almost three days to get back to El Paso. Although they had sleeping accommodations, they were plenty tired when they finally arrived at El Paso. Jimmy wasn't looking forward to another train trip, but he had to leave in three days to complete their business with the California farmers.

Green went straight home to Mercedes. He found her in the living room, with her feet in a pan of cool water, dripping sweat. She rose unsteadily when he walked in briskly.

"Verde, be glad you haven't been here the last few days. I have been miserable. I feel so ugly, and your son has been very active. He kicks me all the time. And the heat. It is worse than Chihuahua," she said, hugging him tightly. "My ankles are all swollen, and so are my feet, and they hurt. That is the reason for the foot bath. Oh, I hope he comes soon." She said, managing a weak grin in her misery.

"My pretty little *mamacita*. It is good to see you. I know you feel awful, and this heat doesn't help, but the child will come soon. Didn't your *curandera* tell you so?"

"Yes, the doctor says two or three more weeks, but I think the old woman is right. I couldn't stand this misery a whole month. Maybe we won't have fifteen children if this is the way it's going to be," she moaned.

Green stayed home with her the rest of the day, not going to Ravel's to check in, but he called Sam and also Hipolito Villa, and the news was not good. Villa was headed west, into Sonora, which was what he should have done, what Angeles advised him to do, but back in the early spring. Villa had not moved then, and now he did not have much of an army to move. But at least he was trying to fight on his own terms, not Obregón's, Green decided. It was a start.

Green went down to Ravel's store and checked his accounts the next morning. There were a few cattle coming into the customs pens, but they were calves, and small ones at that. No big cattle were coming, but it didn't matter to Green. He had done everything he wanted to do for the year already. He had sold his New Mexico cattle and didn't get hurt too badly. He had lost some weight on the steers that were involved in the fiasco with Langer, but everything else was all right. If he had completed Langer's deal, he would probably be in the market for some of the calves coming in now, but he decided to winter the smallest yearlings on the ranch, as an experiment, so he didn't need anything until spring.

Sam Ravel was there but was busy, so Green didn't bother him until lunch time, when they went to eat together.

"Sam, I see Carranza's people are back in Juárez. Where are you crossing Villa's supplies?" asked Green.

"I'm not, Green. The Americans aren't letting much stuff get to me, and now I got no way to get to him. But to tell the truth, it's been about six months since I've been able to get the stuff he needed and wanted."

"So the Americans are really cutting him off?" Green asked.

"That's what it looks like to me," Sam answered.

"Well, I don't guess it makes a lot of difference right now, since he is moving out, but he has always been supplied through the border here, for the most part."

"Well, I think that the Americans thought he was the best bet to win the revolution, but since he has been losing, they've changed their minds. What they have always wanted was for the trouble to stop, no matter who won," Sam added.

"Yeah, the U.S. liked Huerta, who was worse than Díaz, who was one they adored. Now they're gonna get Carranza, who is as bad as either of them and is reviving *gringo* hatred worse than Santa Anna. Maybe it's reversed from what Don Porfirio said: 'Poor America, so close to Mexico, and so far from God,'" intoned Green.

"Green, as a merchant, I have to do what can be done. If I can't sell to Villa, I gotta sell to Obregón or Gonzales. Villa's finished, but I still have to do business, with whoever has the money," said Sam.

"I understand your point, Sam, but I don't see it that way. I still think Villa can raise half of Mexico to follow him, and I have invested a lot of time and some blood in his cause, and I think he is still the best bet to pacify Mexico on a permanent basis, particularly if Angeles is with him. I'll still do what I can for him, short of going back to fight."

About that time, a small Mexican boy came to the table. He was flushed and breathless.

"Señor Verde! Come quick! Your wife is having a baby! Mama Rosenda, La Curandera Avila sent me to find you," he blurted out.

Green grabbed his hat and yelled back at Ravel, "I'll get back to you later, Sam!"

He ran all the way to his house, following the boy. When he entered, he almost ran into Señora Avila, who said, "What are you doing here? We have work to do. Your wife is already having pains. Don't get in the way."

"We have to get her to the hospital. I'll get a buggy," said Green.

"It is too late for that. Besides, we can do everything a hospital can do. I have my helpers, and everything is ready. This is woman's work. You just stay out of the way," she commanded.

Green heard Mercedes cry out, and he ran into the bedroom. Mercedes was in the big bed, with two women attending her. She was sweating but otherwise seemed to be all right.

"Mercedes, are you all right? I want to move you to the hospital right away."

"I am fine, and these fine ladies are taking good care of me. I want my son to be born in his home, like I was. I will be fine right here. Don't worry, La Curandera Avila says everything is going just fine."

"Señor Dunigan, I have birthed hundreds of babies in my time. The baby is placed correctly, and there will be no trouble, I assure you. Go down to the corner and have a drink, like all Mexican fathers, and keep out of our way," the woman said, firmly.

He looked at them all and asked, "You're sure?"

"We are sure. Now go!" Mama Rosenda ordered.

Green went, but only to the porch, where he sat in a rocking chair. He looked at his watch—it was 2:30—and he timed the intervals between Mercedes' screams. The time between was four to five minutes, so he knew he had plenty of time to wait. He walked down the street to a small bar and had a cold beer, and called the doctor to tell him what was happening. He calmed Green's fears.

"I know Señora Avila. She has probably delivered three times as many babies as I have, and knows what she is doing. I kind of suspected Mercedes was seeing her, but she could be in no better hands, Green. Don't worry," he reassured Green.

Green felt better and had another beer. About 4:00, Green felt he'd better get back, so he walked home. He was quickly run out by the women, and he returned to his self-exile on the porch.

He read, first the newspapers and then a book about the war in Cuba. He was surprised how closely his remembrances followed the action. He surmised that because he was a scout and courier, he had seen more of the big picture than most soldiers see. He was interested in the events of the native revolution, which he knew nothing about, and how it affected the campaign.

Later that afternoon, the screams from the labor were becoming so frequent that Green could no longer concentrate. He put the book down and looked up to see Sam Ravel and Etienne de la Garza coming up the street to visit.

"Are you papa yet?" asked Etienne.

"No, but it shouldn't be long. The pains are pretty close together," answered Green.

They sat down and Sam produced a bottle of Kentucky whiskey, pouring three drinks.

"Here's to your first child—a son perhaps," toasted Etienne.

"The *curandera* says so, and I think Mercedes wants a son, but I don't care," Green responded, lying.

"Of course you don't care," said Sam Ravel, grinning, and they drank.

Green felt good but watched himself. He didn't want to be drunk when his child was born. Soon the cries were almost continuous, and Green got up to check, but was shoved back onto the porch by one of the women, who said, "It won't be long now, be patient."

A little after 5:00, a new sound was heard: a baby crying. All three got up and went into the living room. The *curandera* came out of the bedroom and announced, "Your son has arrived, Señor Dunigan, and your wife is fine, but exhausted. He is a fine, big boy and, as you can hear, has a loud voice. You can see him and your wife soon, just as soon as we clean up."

"How big is he?" asked Green.

"I have no scale, Señor, do you?" she asked.

"I do. I have a scale for weighing beans. I'll go and get it," said Sam Ravel, and he ran out.

"Bring a tape measure, too," Green yelled as Sam ran from the room.

Green sat down in a chair. He felt weak, but wondered how Mercedes felt. He was exhausted, but highly keyed up, elated, and proud.

In a few minutes he was let in to the bedroom. Mercedes was still groggy but looked beautiful with her jet black hair spread all over the pillow.

"Ah, *mi colonel* Verde, how do you like your son? Isn't he beautiful?" she said, uncovering the tiny face swaddled beside her.

Green gazed on his son. A red scrunched face bellowing like a calf on the end of a rope and topped with jet black hair was in the bundle.

"He is indeed handsome ... takes after his mother."

Sam and Etienne came in the room, carrying the scale and tape. The *curandera* took the baby, unbundled him, and laid him on the brass scoop to weigh him. She measured him at the same time.

"Seven pounds, seven ounces, and twenty-four inches. He will be tall and husky," she said. She took him back to Mercedes and said to the men, "Get out of here. The baby is hungry and needs to be fed, and the mother needs to rest. We will be here until morning

227

to see to everything. Go on out and get drunk," said Mama Rosenda.

Green knelt by Mercedes' bed and kissed her hands. "Thank you, *mi alma*."

"Are you going to name him after your hero?" she asked.

"If you agree, yes," Green said.

"I agree. Tell them," she ordered, smiling.

Green turned to everyone in the room. "Ladies and gentlemen, I have the honor to present to you—Felipe Angeles Dunigan y Herrera."

Everyone beamed at this announcement. It didn't surprise Etienne and Sam, but the *curandera* and her ladies seemed highly pleased that a *gringo* named his son after a highly respected Mexican. They almost clapped, but instead the *curandera* ran them out.

"Go now . . . Go out and celebrate the birth of a beautiful child," said Mama Rosenda.

As they left, Green felt a great weight lift off his shoulders. They stopped at the corner bar and had a celebratory drink with the regulars. Green was being very careful not to get drunk, but the whiskey tasted as smooth as glass going down. The three of them then left and went down to the hotel to find some of their friends.

In the bar of the Paso del Norte, they ran into Jimmy Berger and five other border traders having a drink before dinner.

Green said, "Boys, I am here to announce the birth of my son, seven and a half pounds of fightin' fury. His name is Felipe Angeles Dunigan y Herrera. What do you think about that?"

Congratulations, hand shaking, and good wishes passed all around. Green was popular in the border fraternity, and all were happy for him, although very few of them knew Mercedes.

A newcomer from Colorado asked, "How come you named him after that meskin general?"

"Because he is the finest man I have ever known," Green looked him straight in the eyes when he spoke.

The man downcast his eyes and said nothing, but the others were patting Green on the back and shouting.

A bottle of champagne was ordered and toasts were drunk, then supper was ordered and eaten. His companions urged him to stay, but at about 10:30, Green left them, catching a taxicab home.

He was very quiet entering his house, not wanting to disturb anyone. One of the *curandera's* helpers was dozing in a chair in the parlor, and a dim light shone through the open door to the bedroom. He tiptoed through the door to see his little family. Mercedes was asleep, and looked like an angel. The baby was in a crib beside her bed, and Green gazed at the sleeping boy for a long time. He was so proud. Then he remembered he had not informed his parents. He sneaked out of the house quietly and drove to the telegraph office to send a wire to John and Amanda Dunigan.

Felipe Angeles Dunigan y Herrera was born 5 P.M. Stop.
Weight 7 lbs. 7 oz., length 24 inches, black hair. Stop.
Mother and baby both doing fine. Stop.
Love, Green.

CHAPTER 42

Ciudad Juárez, Chihuahua, Mexico /

October 6, 1915

Pancho Villa was in the same office that Green had first entered when Villa had taken Juárez in May 1911, when he was fighting for Madero. This time, however, he did not have to wait to see the general. He was recognized by everyone as "Gringo Verde" and ushered in.

"Verde, I have missed you!" shouted Villa, embracing his friend in a crushing bear hug. "What are you doing here?"

"I have come to see my old friends, *mi general*," answered Green.

"Sit down! You want a drink ... some coffee?"

"Coffee, if it's not too much trouble."

"There is always coffee around Villa. Chocolate, never, but coffee, always," said Villa, grinning.

"So, what brings you back to the great revolution?"

"I did not come back, General. I am a father now, and, as you know, my wars are over."

"A papa! What is it, Green, a girl or boy?" Villa asked.

"A boy—Felipe Angeles Dunigan y Herrera—born last week," Green answered.

"That is nice. Have you told Angeles? He is in Washington, trying to help us. To no use, I am afraid. I think Wilson is going to recognize Carranza," Villa said, sadly.

"I sent him a wire. Hope it got there."

"Felipe told me not to fight Obregón down there, and he told me not to send those guns to Zapata. That is where all these bad things started. If I had only listened to him, I would be in good shape. But he said I had to win the revolution by myself and lead Mexico to peace. I cannot do that. I am an ignorant man." Villa was almost in tears.

"*Mi general,* you possess the soul of Mexico. You are probably the only one who can bring her peace. Avoid battle until you have built up the division again. All Mexico will join you. Do as Angeles said."

"I have the division marching to Sonora, but if the U.S. will not supply me, what can I do?" Villa asked.

"Go to the coast. You know the Germans will sell you guns. That Von Papen has already been to see you. He's willing, but he probably wants you to scare the U.S., so they'll stay out of Europe. It might not be a bad deal."

"I am a friend of the U.S., Green, and I don't like the Germans. They are not interested in the welfare of Mexico, only themselves. They would like to get us in a war with the Americans, to keep them from fighting in France. We have fought the *gringos* before. We lost badly, and we would lose worse now. We cannot trust the Germans, but we might get some supplies from them. You think so, Verde?" Villa grinned evilly.

"I think it could work, *jefe,* but don't fight any battles until you are stronger," said Green.

"You are smart, Verde. I have sent Angeles to Washington, to try to keep the *gringos* on our side. Why don't you come back as my adviser, and you can help with the guns, too?" Villa asked.

"Chief, I have promised Mercedes not to rejoin the war. If I did, she would come here and kill us both. I am convinced of that."

"All right, but I sure could use you," said Villa wistfully.

"Use Medina. He is plenty smart and is a patriot," Green suggested.

"Medina died at Zacatecas, didn't you know?" said Villa.

Green paused and answered sadly, "No, *jefe,* that's a shame. He was a very fine man. Maybe you better bring General Angeles back, for he isn't doing you much good in Washington."

231

"Maybe I will. I think he will do me more good here, but I need this border open, and he is the only one who can keep it open for me, and that is of the highest importance," said Villa.

The interview was over and Villa had made up his mind.

Before Green left, he asked, "Anything I can do, *jefe*? I'll be in El Paso. Just send word ... anything but fighting."

Villa acknowledged that and Green left for the other side, not feeling reassured.

Two weeks later, the U.S. State Department extended de-facto recognition to the Carranza regime and embargoed all shipments of war supplies to other factions. It was a hard blow to Villa, and he abandoned Juárez for the moment. He moved the Division of the North, or what was left of it (9,000 men and two artillery batteries), through the Canon del Pulpito, a terribly rugged pass through the Sierra toward Sonora. Early winter weather struck the passage and his losses were heavy—most of his artillery, 3,000 men, and many horses. But he had escaped Obregón and was in Sonora. He could block the Sierra passes and pick off the *carrancista* garrisons one by one, if he used his head.

Green had been busy up north at Roy, selling his cattle and generally getting ready for winter. He had not sold his little steers and was going to winter them in the vega of the Canadian River, and was busy moving them, selling the rest. He returned to El Paso on November 1. As he was leaving the train station, he was surprised to see a formation of revolutionary troops marching toward the station. He knew enough about them to know they were Manzo's Brigade from Juárez. Everyone around was curious and stopping to look.

Green walked up to a railroad conductor and asked, "What's going on, we being invaded by the Mexicans?"

"No, we are just transporting these troops to Douglas, to reinforce Agua Prieta against Villa, who is attacking there. We're taking some army searchlights, too," the conductor said.

Green caught a trolley for Ravel's store and once there told Sam, "They're letting Carranza use the U.S. rail lines to reinforce Agua Prieta. Villa is headed into a trap."

"He already knows, Green, but he's going to attack anyway, I

232

think. I heard about it yesterday and told Hipolito, and he sent word to Pancho. But he will attack anyway, at least that's what Hipolito thinks," said Ravel sadly.

Villa did attack Agua Prieta. He ran burros and mules through the mine fields, and once they got past, Calles turned on the army searchlights and slaughtered Villa's soldiers. Badly beaten, Villa turned, like a wounded bear, and attacked the *carrancista* garrison at Hermosillo, and was again beaten badly. Villa was reduced to his 1910 status: a Sierra bandit with a small band of followers. Just before Christmas, 1915, the last vestiges of the once great Division of the North left Chihuahua City and melted into the Sierra.

All of the reporters who followed Villa around left and returned to the States. The war in Europe occupied the daily papers now, and Villa was pretty much a memory already.

Green had a lot of time on his hands and stayed close to home. Not many cattle were arriving. The baby was growing every day, and he spent a lot of time with him. He and Mercedes talked about going to Refugio for Christmas, as they had the year before. They had a standing invitation, reinforced by Amanda's letters wanting them to bring the baby.

"Couldn't we maybe have him christened there?" Green asked.

"That would be very nice, Green, very nice indeed," Mercedes answered and added, "I will write Amanda tomorrow and we can plan to leave on the tenth, and stay until after the New Year."

CHAPTER 43

Refugio, Texas / December 28, 1915

reen poured himself a glass of brandy, to cut the grease. There had been a great feast at the Dunigan ranch, and he had eaten everything that was offered him: roast duck, roast quail, a rack of venison, sweet potatoes, dressing, and a good many other things he couldn't recall. The baby was sound asleep in his crib, having been christened at mass that morning. The dinner had been a family affair, including Etienne de la Garza, who was now the godfather to little Felipe. Kathleen, Green's sister, was the godmother. Since Refugio had been established by Irish settlers in the 1820s under Mexico, most of the population was Catholic, and the mass was well attended by all of the old Irish families, who were mostly in the cattle trade.

The ladies retreated from the dining room as the men poured their brandy and lit their cigars. When finished, the men unbuttoned their coats and vests and stretched out on couches, chairs, and rugs. Pretty soon, the noise emanating from that area resembled a sawmill, and Amanda and the other ladies rolled their eyes at the din.

"I told you, if you let them alone they become wild things, uncivilized and unable to function in polite society," Amanda said.

Mercedes, Kathleen, and Lucinda just laughed.

Finally, the snoring became so loud that it woke the baby. Mercedes marched into the living room and shouted, "You woke the baby with your loud snoring! It is rattling the windows and doors! Get up and do your snoring in a barn somewhere, but don't wake my baby again."

Green knew enough not to argue, and the rest knew if they protested it would only bring their own wives into the fray, so they got up and went outside.

"How're your dogs this year, Dad?" asked Jack.

"Let's go see them," John Dunigan replied, and they walked back to the kennels. "I'm trying out a couple of setters this year, and they seem to be all right."

There were ten pointer dogs in the kennels, in addition to the setters, and when the men approached, they set up major barking and howling. John Dunigan would stop to greet each dog in turn. They were all sleek, with no fat on them. It didn't take long for the barking to subside, once they left the kennels.

"Why don't we go to town, boys? I have an errand to do," John suggested.

They secured a buggy and were off to Refugio. John drove directly to the hardware store. He went directly to the store owner, followed by his sons and son-in-law, and asked, "Simon, you got my guns ready?"

"Yessir, John, they just got in yesterday." The man produced two nice little Parker 20 bores, with remarkably short stocks. Dunigan looked them over and handed them back to the boys.

"They ought to do just fine. I'll need a case of 20 bore shells, too."

Green spoke first. "Dad, I can't shoot this—it's too short for me."

"Me, too, Mr. Dunigan," said Bill Foster.

"Well, if they're too short for them, they sure won't fit me," said Jack.

Grinning, John Dunigan turned to them and said, "You boys don't catch on very fast, do you?"

Green recovered first. "Those are for your new hunting partners, Mercedes and Kathleen, aren't they?"

"Yes, and I'll get one for Lucinda, if she ever shows any interest." He nodded at Jack.

"I don't think she will, Dad, she doesn't like to kill things. She

235

even gets after me for killing snakes around the yard," said Jack, smiling.

"Well, I'm very happy with my new hunters, so I'm equipping them," their father said.

"I'll trade you my genuine Spanish Mauser for your London guns," ventured Green.

"Humph," answered John Dunigan.

"Jack, you, Green and I better do some investing in firearms, if we are going to be able to use those fine dogs," said Bill Foster.

"Simon, you got any of these cute little things in stock?" Jack asked.

"Sure, Jack, I got Parkers and Ithacas and Foxes, and some others," he said.

"You got any in full-grown sizes?"

"All you want."

The three of them went over to the gun rack and selected proper quail guns. Green, because he shot ducks a lot, got a 16 bore Ithaca, so he could do both.

They piled their purchases in the buggy and left for the ranch. On the way home, John Dunigan said, "It's about time you fellows bought your own guns. You been using mine for too long."

"We like yours, Dad," Jack said.

"I guess you do, but those guns are too fine to be used up by the likes of you three."

When they got back to the ranch, the three young men took their purchases into the house and showed them to the ladies. Mercedes and Kathleen were properly impressed, but asked why they weren't supplied also.

"Well, we had to buy them so's we could hunt quail, too. You two have been hogging all the dogs and places, and we like to hunt, too," said Jack. "Besides, you can use Dad's guns."

"You selfish pigs. All we shoot is quail. You three shoot everything around, and those big guns of Papa Dunigan's kick," pouted Mercedes.

Just then John Dunigan entered the house and said, "Kathleen, you and Mercedes come here, I have something for you," and he gave them their presents.

The girls were quite surprised and pleased. They kissed and hugged John and stuck their tongues out at their respective husbands.

236

John said to Lucinda, "I'm told you don't like hunting, so I didn't get you a gun. I'll make it up to you, soon."

"That's all right, you have already been more than generous. I'm just glad my sisters can hunt with you, Dad, and don't have to go with those ruffians all the time."

After a lot of good-natured banter, Kathleen and Mercedes claimed John to go hunting the following day. The boys said they didn't need all the dogs, but they could try out their new guns, also. Small wagers were laid to make it more interesting.

After breakfast, the two groups loaded up a lunch and chose dogs, each buggy ending up with six. Spare dog kennels were loaded on an extra buggy. Michael O'Grady, a keen hunter himself, acted as guide and buggy driver for John and the girls. Seth Cottrell, Abner's son who normally trained and cared for the dogs, took out the young men. Territories were assigned, and all agreed that everyone had to be back by 4:00 P.M.

Quail were abundant that year along the Aransas, and the day was ideal, about 50 degrees and overcast. A light shower had fallen that night, so the humidity and scenting conditions were nearly perfect. The boys crossed the river and headed west while the girls headed east.

Both parties carried picnic lunches and both returned home by 4:00, as agreed. John Dunigan and the girls had killed sixty-eight quail, and the men sixty-three. The men were properly abashed and were subjected to much ridicule the rest of the day and night, until bedtime.

As Green and Mercedes retired to their bedroom, Green was still prickly about the ragging he and the other men had taken. He did not speak as he undressed and prepared for bed.

Mercedes, in her nightgown, said, "Green, don't be angry. We were just having fun. Come here, give me a goodnight kiss."

Relenting, Green kissed her, and found himself entangled in her arms.

"Come, *mi amor.* We'll compete in something I know you are the champion of," she said, pulling him onto the bed. She pulled her gown over her head and stood before him naked. "I know a game where you are always champion. You want to play it?"

Green thought she was more beautiful and desirable now than ever before. Motherhood had rounded some angularity of her body, and the whole was now more sensual.

He said, "Well, show me how to play this game of yours."

She did, and when she was through, Green was convinced her enhanced sensuality was not skin deep. It went clear through to her very bones.

The Christmas visits were great times for the Dunigan family. Renewing old ties, doing things together, and competing in a friendly manner served to make it a strong bond. Kathleen's husband, Bill Foster, came to think of the Dunigan family as his own, as did Mercedes, and to a certain extent, Lucinda, Jack's wife. Even the grandchildren were in on it, and it was a great source of pride to John and Amanda.

After New Year's, when each family left to go back to their own homes, there was genuine regret that the holidays were over.

CHAPTER 44

El Paso, Texas / March 9, 1916

reen had scrupulously avoided mentioning the revolution or Villa. In January the Lopez brothers, lieutenants of Villa, stopped at the train at Santa Isabel outside of Chihuahua City, took a bunch of American mining engineers, and killed them. Feelings had run high in El Paso for a few days, but eventually were forgotten. Green had stayed low key, except in the market, as light Mexican yearlings started coming out in large numbers. Green bought most of them, both for his own ranch and for Jack, as his sources inside Mexico said that there weren't going to be many big steers coming out. Green had been especially aggressive lately, because he was filling out the numbers for his New Mexico ranch.

Green and Sam Ravel were sitting in the latter's store when a Western Union boy ran in with a telegram. It was from his manager in Columbus, New Mexico:

Raid out of Mexico this morning. Stop. Store badly burned and warehouse emptied. Stop. Presumed to be Villa's men. Stop. Wire instructions. Stop. Louis Wolper.

Ravel read Green the wire.

239

"Villa wouldn't do that, it's not his way," Green responded. "I'll bet he wasn't even close to Columbus last night."

"I agree," Sam said. "He wouldn't attack the U.S., even though he was plenty hot when they recognized Carranza. He's mad at me, too, because I haven't delivered what he's already paid for, but if he was to do something, he would walk in here and shoot me before he would attack a town across the border."

There was a knock on the door and Green yelled, "Come on in, it's not locked."

The door opened and in walked Lieutenant Patton, General Pershing's aide, looking very much the soldier.

"Hello, Lieutenant . . . haven't seen you for a while," Green said affably, shaking hands.

"What can we do for you?" asked Ravel.

"General Pershing wants to see Colonel Verde, or Dunigan, whatever your name is now, and he wants to see you right away," said Patton crisply. "I am to bring you."

"This have anything to do with Columbus, Lieutenant?" Ravel asked.

"I presume so, although the general did not confide in me his reasons. He just sent me, so if we can go . . ."

"My horse is over at customs. I'll go and get him," said Green.

"I'll follow you," Patton almost warned.

"Suit yourself, Lieutenant."

Green got his horse and accompanied Patton out to Fort Bliss, which was a hive of activity. Horses and men everywhere, wagons criss-crossing the parade ground, and orders being bawled to troops.

"Pretty busy out here, isn't it?" Green remarked to Patton.

"We had eighteen men killed at Columbus, and over a hundred horses stolen, besides arms and ammunition," Patton volunteered, "and I think General Pershing already has orders to pursue Villa and capture him."

Fat chance, Green thought to himself.

Green was ushered into Pershing's office by Patton. Pershing was pacing back and forth like a caged lion, picking up papers and throwing them down again. He turned when they entered.

"Colonel, Villa attacked Columbus about four o'clock this morning. Did you know that?"

240

"Sam Ravel got a telegram about it, just before your aide arrived to fetch me. I might add that I am no longer Colonel, just a civilian," said Green.

"I was not implying that you had anything to do with it, Dunigan. It's that you were very close to Pancho Villa, and he has attacked the United States. I have orders to go into Mexico and bring him back," explained Pershing.

"General, I don't think Villa had anything to do with that raid, and neither does Sam Ravel, and he got his store burned up."

"He was identified as being there, and all the raiders were yelling 'Viva Villa,'" Pershing stated.

"They said the same thing when the Lopez brothers killed those mining engineers at Santa Isabel, and Villa wasn't even close. You let Huerta and Felix Díaz run around here all fall and did nothing. Now some fool claims Villa was at Columbus, and you are going to invade Mexico. It's all wrong, General."

"Right or wrong, I have my orders. I need a guide for the expedition, and I want you!" Pershing said.

"General, Villa is in the Sierra, and I have never been there. When I was with Villa we were in the central plains, nowhere near the Sierra. I wouldn't know how to find him, and if I did join you, my life wouldn't ever be worth a plug nickel in Mexico, and that's where I make my living. No, General Pershing, I won't join you," Green said with finality.

"We can enlist you at the convenience of the government," said Pershing tentatively.

"General, I've told you that I have no knowledge of the Sierra, where Villa is, so I would be of no use to you. Secondly, I have a great deal of loyalty to him, and I wouldn't betray him under any circumstance."

Lieutenant Patton chimed in. "He is an enemy of your country. Doesn't that make a difference?"

"I believe Villa to be a friend of the U.S. He has been an abused friend lately, but still not an enemy. I just don't believe Villa was at, or had anything to do with, the Columbus raid."

"We could force you to come. I have that power," Pershing announced firmly.

"General, I know some people in Washington. My father knows many more who are more powerful. We would fight every step of

241

the way. It would do nothing but bring harm to you, and to no purpose. As I stated before, I know nothing about the place you are going, and even if I did you cannot force me to do what you want. I am on Villa's side in this, and I think you are doing the wrong thing. You are never going to catch Villa if he doesn't want to be caught. All you are going to do is create more ill will toward us in Mexico, where there is enough already."

Pershing, who had his own doubts about Villa's involvement in Columbus, thought that Green was probably right. He decided that there was more to lose by forcing Green back in the army. Patton, on the other hand, was ready for any kind of conflict, as is the case with true warriors, and he was not ready to relent.

"General, we need this man. Conscript him," said Patton.

"Lieutenant, when you have served as long as I have, you will learn to protect your flank from politicians. We will not force Mr. Dunigan to do what he doesn't want to do. Find someone else," ordered Pershing.

"Watch out for people who say they will guide you, Lieutenant. Villa inspired either great loyalty or great fear in most people. Neither of those will be of much use to you," said Green.

"Dismissed, Lieutenant," said Pershing to Patton. "Mr. Dunigan, could you stay for a moment? I'd like to ask you something." Patton saluted and left. "Don't think badly of the lieutenant—he means well. And I think he will be a good officer, with a bit of seasoning," explained Pershing.

"General, that young man is a warrior and will never be content until he is in battle. I know, because I have been around many of them. I was a good soldier, but never a warrior. They thirst for battle as a drunk does for whiskey. Mark my words, he will be a good soldier."

"Well, for his sake, I hope so. He will get his battle, too, for we are headed for France as straight as an arrow aimed at a bull's-eye. I hope we can be ready in time, with trained men. But tell me, you mentioned the Germans several times, as trying to get the revolution to spill over on our side of the border. Do you know this is true, and how are they doing it?" asked Pershing.

"Germany is shipping most of the war supplies to Carranza through the port of Vera Cruz. You must know that money for Huerta and Díaz is direct from Germany, and I know that Villa has been contacted by German agents, promising to supply him. Of course, they can't get to him, unless he takes a port, most likely on the West Coast. Villa told me this himself, and you certainly must know of Germany's involvement with Carranza and the late dictator, Huerta."

"Well, I have sent a great deal of information to Washington about this, but you can never tell what they are going to do. I think that they just want the revolution to be over, no matter who wins, and they think they will hurry this along by sending me and my troops into Mexico."

"You're going on a fool's mission. The *rurales* couldn't catch Villa, and they tried hard for eight or ten years before the revolution. All you are going to accomplish is get some of your troops shot, and some blooded for the European war. But remember, there is no cavalry being used there, and that's all you are going in with." Green rose to leave, and said, "General, I want to thank you for being reasonable toward me. I appreciate it."

"I know it wouldn't have done any good to force you. I admire your loyalty to Villa, but I must admit being puzzled by it," said Pershing, smiling.

"*Adiós,* General."

Green walked out and joined Sam Ravel at lunch, downtown. He told Sam what had transpired.

They were surprised to see Etienne de la Garza walk up. He had been in El Paso about a month, having spent most of the year at Green's ranch, and he had spent the last three weeks visiting his home in Louisiana.

"Well, Etienne, how are things down in the bayous?" asked Green.

"It's okay, I guess. It don't seem like home no more. Guess I been in the desert too long."

"Well, what are you going to do now? I know you're not going to fish for the rest of your life," asked Ravel.

"Well, that's what I want to talk about. What you all think about me goin' back to the army? I miss the soldiering, and it look like we got us a good war in France now. Should I join the French, or go back to the U. S. Army?"

Ravel spoke up. "Ain't no use to go to France. We'll be in it soon enough."

"That's what I tink. Mebbe I go out to Fort Bliss and join up," said Etienne.

"Don't do that," Green advised. "I just got back from there, and they tried to make me guide Pershing's troops that are going into Mexico after Villa. Somebody raided Columbus last night and it's been blamed on Villa, so the U.S. is sending four regiments to catch him. If you enlist there, they'll try to make you do it, and Villa will think you betrayed him. And you know what happens to those people ..."

"I wouldn't do that. But if I enlist, maybe they make me do it, no?"

"They sure will, just as soon as they find out you were with Villa. If you're going to enlist, better go out to San Francisco, or back east, where they might not know. Better still, join the navy," advised Green.

"No, I don' like de water. My foots swell up bad when I just visit in Louisiana."

"What about the marines? They'll go to France, and they are a real professional outfit," suggested Green.

"Well, that's not a bad idea. Where do I join up?" asked Etienne.

"My advice is to go to San Diego. You would be a good way from El Paso or Chihuahua," advised Green.

"Well, I guess I go there now," said Etienne. "I'll see you fellers after de war."

Green and Sam shook hands and said goodbye, and de la Garza left for his new war.

That night at dinner, Green told Mercedes of Etienne's departure for San Diego, and about Pershing's trying to dragoon him back into the army and his escape.

Mercedes looked grim. "If the *gringo* army tries to take you after all you have been through, I will personally slit the throat of the *gringo* general," she said.

"I know that, *mi alma*, and I warned him. I think that is why he let me go."

"He was well advised to do so," said Mercedes without irony.

"*Chica*, why don't we plan to spend the hot weather up at the ranch at Roy? It's much cooler there, and I don't really have much to do here in the hot weather."

"I would love to go, and Felipito would, too. Can I take Minerva?"

"Yes, you can take Minerva. You haven't been doing much with

244

her since the baby came anyway. I may even send her up with the cattle, for the men up there to make sure she still remembers her training. I'll contact Sol to make sure everything is ready for us. Do you want to take anyone from here?"

"Yes, Green, I would like to take Conchita, to help with the baby. She is so good with him. Maria can stay here, to see to the house. I'll work something out with her," said Mercedes.

Green and Sol Weeks had worked out the stocking for the ranch, and in the second week of May, Green shipped 6,500 steers to him, including the filly Minerva, and made the trip himself. The following week, Mercedes, Conchita, and Felipe, the baby, who was by this time called "Fito" by one and all, traveled up. The roads were better now, and Mercedes made it in two days.

As soon as they were settled in the house, Green noticed that Mercedes was critical of everyone and everything. Nothing seemed to suit her, and it stayed that way until they went to bed that night. It was unlike her to be so disagreeable, and Green was puzzled.

The next morning Green dressed quietly and went to the cook-shack to eat with the crew. He was going to ride out later but wanted to talk to Sol about a few things first. When the crew left, he went back to the big house, thinking he might invite Mercedes to ride with him. He had gotten to the second floor when he heard her. She was throwing up. Green was mightily relieved, for now he knew her bad humor was from pregnancy. He waited a little while for her to get over the nausea, and then asked her about the ride.

"Oh, Green, that would be nice. Is Minerva available?" she answered cheerily.

"Yes, she is. You get dressed and I'll have her brought over," answered Green.

They rode for more than three hours, and Mercedes seemed just as interested in the condition of the cattle as Green. The pastures were lush as the first growth of the spring was in full surge, and the cattle were putting on flesh fast. Minerva behaved herself, as did her rider, and they had a pleasant time.

When they were in sight of the house on their return, Green asked, "When is the baby due, *mi alma*? I can always tell, Mercedes."

"The doctor says February, but Mama Rosenda says it will be mid-January."

"Well, the *curandera* was right the first time."

"I think she is this time, too."

"What does she think it'll be this time?"

"She's not too sure yet, but she thinks a little boy again."

That night, during supper, Green had a phone call from Jimmy Berger, telling him that their lawsuit was to begin on Monday of the following week.

"This is Langer's suit versus you and me, Green. Our cross-action won't come up until this one is over with. Anyway, Goodwin says there's no rush, but you should be here for court Wednesday," said Jimmy.

"Okay, Jimmy, tell him I'll be there Wednesday."

"Green, how's Pershing getting along in Mexico? Has he caught Villa yet?" Berger asked.

"The only thing that's happened so far is our troops got run out of Parral by a mob led by a woman. Three soldiers were killed. Otherwise, they just ride all day and haven't even seen Villa," recounted Green.

"You want me to get you a room or anything?"

"Please do, Jimmy, and arrange for Frank Goodwin to have dinner with us Tuesday night," Green instructed. "I'll be in on the last train from New Mexico that afternoon."

"See you then," Jimmy said, hanging up.

CHAPTER 45

Liberal, Kansas / June 2, 1916

reen had caught the train that morning in Tucumcari and arrived in Liberal at about 4:30 P.M. After checking into the hotel, he cleaned up and met Jimmy Berger and the lawyer, Frank Goodwin, in the lobby and they proceeded to a restaurant for dinner.

"Well, Mr. Goodwin, how does it look?" Green asked.

"Green, I've got a good jury and I believe that's all we'll need. Our primary witness will be Langer's clerk, who notarized the contracts, and he'll have to lie in his teeth bad enough to be convicted of perjury for us to lose. Langer may force him to, but it'll be to our advantage, but I don't think he'll risk jail for Langer, and we'll have him," said Goodwin.

"I am going to try to combine both cases in one, but I don't think I will get that done, but in any case, it won't hurt us. Langer will be the first witness, so I'll want you in court to point out where he does not tell the truth, but in no case do I want you to say anything to the whole court, just to me. You understand?"

"Yessir . . . you don't want me to call him a liar, you want him to prove it," Green said.

"Exactly right, my boy," said Goodwin, grinning. "And that goes for you also, Jimmy."

When it was all over with, two days later, the jury found that Langer had altered the contracts, had not dealt in good faith, and had suborned the notary public. He was awarded nothing. Green and Jimmy Berger were ecstatic about going forward with their cross-action. Goodwin dampened their enthusiasm.

"Even though we whipped the hell out of him, this may not carry over into our case. He may appeal, although I did not see any error in the proceedings. There may be other factors, such as the many foreclosures he has made lately, which must affect his banks' earnings. A long appeal might buy him time. Also, he might want to settle our case, as it looks pretty good now, but he may not have the money. It'll be three or four days before the dust settles. Just you hold on to your horses," Goodwin cautioned.

"Well, thanks. As far as I'm concerned, I'm going back to New Mexico and leave it in your very capable hands, and that includes settlement," said Green.

"Me, too," echoed Jimmy.

"Wait a minute, boys. You have to be in on any settlement. You may want something other than what I want," said Goodwin.

"Whatever we can get is what we want. We think you can get more out of him than we would ask, probably," said Jimmy, with Green nodding agreement.

"All right, I'll be in touch," said Goodwin.

Jimmy needed to get to California to buy steers for the farmers, and Green had work to do in Roy, so both departed Liberal that weekend, leaving their lawsuit in Goodwin's capable hands.

Green spent the night in Tucumcari and drove back to the ranch the next day. There was little to do as all the cattle were stocked and doing fine.

That night he asked Sol Meeks to dinner, and when they finished eating, Green said, "There is one thing about this ranch that I don't like, and that is that we still call it the 'old Bagwell Place.' I'd like to give it a name of its own, but I don't want to hurt Mr. Bagwell's feelings and will check it out with him. But you, Sol, and Mercedes should have a lot to say about it and I wondered if you had any suggestions."

Sol spoke up. "Boss, way back yonder, this ranch was once called the 'Canadian River Ranch,' maybe by the first Anglos that owned it, and lots of people used to call it the 'Ranch B' not so long ago."

Mercedes interjected, "Green, you know what I would like to call it. Herradura."

"Mercedes, trust me on this. You're going to get Herradura back, at least a big part of it. So we don't really want to call this place that name, at least not yet. Canadian River Ranch is all right, but what do you think of this? You remember when Tomas and Vicente and I were in our first battle together, when we took the guns from the *federales* and later on we named the battalion after it?"

Mercedes nodded. "It was San Andres, wasn't it?"

"Why not call this place 'Rancho San Andres'? Sounds sufficiently grand, doesn't it?" asked Green.

They both agreed. "I'll go see Mr. Bagwell over at Santa Fe, and if he doesn't mind, we'll name it Rancho San Andres," Green said. "The reason I want to do it is that I want to start a cow herd here and I want them to have a distinct identification. Sol, you design a brand kinda like this . . ." Green made an "SA" on the tablecloth with his pencil. "Make sure no parts of the iron touch, so it won't blot. Anyone else using anything like that around here?"

"Well, Sam Andres uses a block 'SA.' His place is only three miles from here, and his reputation is none too savory," said Sol.

"Well, that's out then. Maybe . . . Sol, did I ever tell you about Brindy Polaris, that lead cow of my father's that led the herds to Montana?"

"No, I don't think so."

Green proceeded to tell him the story of the drive and of the stock of her calves that they had at Refugio. He even told about the cow that had licked Mercedes' belly to bless the baby, at which point Mercedes blushed. So did Sol.

"I'm going to get some heifers out of those cattle to start our own herd, and breed them back to Hereford bulls, so it'll be a long-term project."

"Well, why not name the ranch 'Polaris'?" asked Mercedes, who still disliked any memory of the war.

"That's not a bad idea," Sol said, and Green agreed.

"Well, that's settled. As far as the brand is concerned, what about a small star with wavy lines under it—like brindle? Something like this . . . Anybody around here using anything like that, Sol?"

"Nope, none that I know of, anywhere," he said.

"Well, make it up, and if Mr. Bagwell agrees, this place will become known as 'Rancho Polaris.'"

Everyone seemed pleased, especially Mercedes, who felt she was becoming more of a Dunigan. Family ties were most important to her.

The remainder of the ranch business being settled, they had retired to the living room when a knock sounded at the front door. Green answered it and found a boy, delivering a telegram for Green. He asked the boy to come in and have some refreshment.

"Mr. Dunigan, thank you. You know we usually don't deliver this far from town, but Mr. Potts, the agent, thought we better deliver this one right away."

"Bad news?" asked Green.

"I'm afraid so, sir," said the boy.

Green opened the telegram and read:

My beloved Amanda passed away at 3 P.M. today. Stop. Funeral will be in 3 days. Stop. Kathleen already here. Stop. Others coming. John Dunigan

He handed the wire to Mercedes, who read aloud as her eyes misted over.

Green spoke, "You had any supper, son?"

"No sir, I been on my horse since five, coming straight here."

"Sol, get them to feed this boy and find him a bed. He can go back with us in the morning, as we'll be catching the first train out," ordered Green.

They caught the 6:30 train the next morning. After changing at Amarillo, Fort Worth, Austin, and Victoria, they finally arrived at Refugio about midday two days later. The funeral was scheduled for 10 A.M. the next morning at the ranch. All the Dunigans were there except little Felipe. The reunion was somber.

John Dunigan had aged considerably since their last visit but was still vigorous. Kathleen, Lucinda, and Mercedes took turns making sure he was not by himself. Kathleen, as Daddy's little girl, was especially vigilant, and everyone helped to keep him busy.

The funeral was a big one, and many old friends came to visit at

250

the house afterwards. The family wasn't left to themselves until just before dark, when the adults gathered in the living room.

John Dunigan was the last to enter, and he had a box in his hand.

"Just before Amanda died, she told me she wanted each of you to have a specific piece of her jewelry, and I have it here. Kathleen gets the sapphire necklace, Lucinda gets the diamond bracelet, and Mercedes the ruby ring. She thought these were the pieces each of you admired the most. So here they are. This was Amanda's wish. The rest of her stuff, I'm going to keep for a while, but it'll be accounted for, if not before, in my will. She was very specific, though, about these three items." He handed them out, and each recipient burst into tears in turn.

Then he left them to sleep, or mourn alone.

Green spoke. "Dad and I have talked about his will some. As you know, Jack is to get the Cotulla ranch, and he bought the New Mexico ranch for me. I don't really know what he's going to do with this place, except that if he divides it amongst us, Kathleen will get the part with the house, and he'll equalize with stocks and bonds, or cash. I think the only reason that the whole ranch isn't going to Kathleen is that you live in Brownsville, and Bill isn't in the cattle business, and the fact that it is really home to all of us, having grown up here."

"I think he wants to keep us together, as much as possible, too," said Kathleen, "as do Bill and I. And I think Bill has something to say about that."

Bill Foster took the floor. "As you know, a lot of land is being plowed up around here. Major woods land south of here, the Taft ranch east of Corpus, and a lot west of Sinton. My family's firm, Foster and Company, is going to open an office close by to expand service to this area, and Kathleen and I have talked with my father about me coming up to handle it and maybe moving in here with Papa Dunigan. But we wouldn't even think about it unless Jack and Green agree that it would be desirable, and that Papa Dunigan wants us to."

Green looked at Jack, and they nodded.

Jack said, "Bill, I think that would be wonderful, if you can get the old man to agree. For what it's worth, it's a better thing than either one of us could imagine happening."

Lucinda and Kathleen spoke up to say the gifts of jewelry had been unequal. Kathleen's necklace and Lucinda's bracelet were worth a whole lot more money than Mercedes' ring.

Mercedes said, "It could not have pleased me more. I had always loved that ruby ring, and you remember when my brother put the necklace on you, because it matched your eyes, Kathleen. And Lucinda, that diamond bracelet looks so much better on you than either of us. Amanda well knew what she was doing, and I am deeply touched. It is of no consequence to me that the other pieces are more valuable. If I had had my choice of all of them, I would still choose the ruby ring, and I shall cherish this gift, and the giver, for the rest of my days."

"Well, that's settled. All we need now is for Bill and Kathleen to talk to Dad about moving up here. I'll leave that to you two, but if you need to, tell him that Jack and I approve," added Green.

To everyone's surprise, John Dunigan was delighted by the idea of the Foster family moving in with him. Although this wasn't to occur for three months at least, John started planning where and how his routine would be changed.

The next night at dinner, Mercedes had an announcement. "I want to tell you that early next year, another half-breed will be joining the Dunigan clan."

Everyone shrieked with delight and congratulated them, and John Dunigan remarked, "We're all cross-breeds here. I might be the only pure-bred, but, being a black Irish, there's some evidence of African ancestry back there. Anyway, the mother of this child is so beautiful that any issue is going to be outstanding. Besides, everybody is talking about cross-breeding to get the best of every species, and so far as Green is concerned, it's got to be an improvement."

"Speaking of improvements, Dad, I want to establish a small cow herd at Roy, and I wonder if I can get some of the Brindy Polaris heifers as seed stock," Green said.

"Sure, son. You can have as many as you need. These cows are pretty long-lived, and I really dont need any replacements this year. I believe I could send you as many as a full carload, Green."

"That would be just about right for me too, Dad. Would you just pick 'em for me and send them on when you please?"

"Sure, Green. Be happy to."

CHAPTER 46

El Paso, Texas / October 17, 1916

Green had been very busy, settling all the things left up in the air over the past five or so years. He had retitled his Ranch "Polaris," and gone over all the changes in land titles that needed doing. He had also registered his new brand, and branded his carload of heifers with it when they arrived from Refugio. He and Jimmy Berger, along with Praxides Balbuena, had at long last eliminated the sell and buy back provision in their dealing with the California farmers. The farmers now knew enough to sell the cattle themselves.

He had just received letters from Refugio, from Bill Foster and John Dunigan, which informed him that the Foster family had moved to the Dunigan ranch, and all was going well. The Langer suit had been settled for $50,000, and the money divided. Green had been paid off by Jimmy Berger, so that Green ended up with most of the money. For all intents and purposes, Green was debt free and was very happy that his life had taken on a more settled character.

Mercedes was faring much better carrying her second child. The climate at Roy, although it got hot during midday, contrasted greatly with the stifling heat of El Paso, where it was always hot and never rained. Felipe, their first child, was learning things every day and becoming the pleasure that children usually are.

Cattle were quite profitable in 1916, as the drought of 1914 was history, and the war in Europe was expanding markets everywhere.

It had been a quiet year in Mexico, with the U. S. Cavalry hunting Villa. It was all he could do to dodge them, and Obregón and Pablo Gonzales had consolidated Carranza as the power in most of Mexico. Zapata was still a factor in Morelos and the surrounding country, but he rarely ventured far from his stronghold. There was talk of a new constitution and elections in 1917, but that was in the future. There were still many small factions fighting and raiding in Mexico, and it was not a place for casual travel.

Although he missed the hustle and bustle of El Paso, Green was content at Roy. He stayed in El Paso from October to May and came back for about ten days or so in mid-June. He didn't need to stay on the ranch all the time, as he had ascertained that Sol Weeks ran an excellent operation.

Jimmy Berger had taken over most of the trading in California, with Praxides Balbuena, and had developed sources of cattle for them mostly in Sonora, Baja California, and western Durango and Chihuahua. Consequently, Green didn't need to send them west from El Paso and Columbus anymore. They had also been wintering light steers on the Arizona desert each winter, and this was good for Green's New Mexico ranch, as he had a ready supply of light steers every spring. Green had leased several neighboring ranches at Roy to expand this operation. He reckoned that when he got everything stocked he would be running close to 15,000 yearlings. He also figured his exposure was more than he wanted, so he started advance contracting of a portion of them, a relatively new thing for him.

The Dunigans returned to El Paso the first week of December, not wanting to get trapped by the snow that sometimes fell in northern New Mexico. A few cattle were arriving from Mexico, and Jimmy Berger had his hands full in California and Arizona, so Green was doing all the work around El Paso.

Green liked to be at the center of things. Trading cattle was built on good, current information, and it was much better in El Paso than at Roy. Besides, Mercedes was due soon and she wanted to be near Mama Rosenda in El Paso.

Many old Mexican families passed through El Paso about this

time. These were people who had fled before the revolution and were returning to reclaim their properties, now that it looked like Carranza was in charge. Green thought they might be premature, especially since Carranza had alienated much of his support by his intransigence, but none of them had asked for his advice.

After the new year, almost no cattle came in from Mexico, but other events kept the area busy. At the end of January, U.S. troops were ordered back by President Wilson. It would be April before the last troops left Mexican soil.

In mid-February, Green went out to Fort Bliss to see General Pershing. A few days before, Germany had announced its policy of unrestricted submarine warfare in the Atlantic. Green was shown in to the general's presence by his aide, the same stiff-as-a-ramrod Lt. George Patton.

"Well, hello Colonel— I mean Mr. Dunigan. Here to tell me I told you so?" asked a smiling Pershing.

"No, General, I just wanted to find out what was going on down there."

"Well, of course you know that we never did find Villa. Came close a couple of times, mainly due to our Apache scouts. They were a lot better than any of the ex-*villistas* we used. I remembered your advice, and it turned out right."

"Was the expedition any good? Do you feel like you improved anything down there that will help you in France?"

"Yes, I think so. We found some organizational shortcomings that we corrected. We had some airplanes down there, and I think we learned how to get information faster and better by using them. Of course, most of the force was cavalry, which you know is of no use in Europe, but I got some troop officers to realize the deadly nature of machine guns, and that's going to help us."

"It looks like it's not going to be very long, does it, General?" asked Green.

"We'll be there this year, I think. My biggest problem is going to be to keep the allies from wasting us, like they have been doing with their own troops for three years now. The American people will never stand by for the kind of casualties that the French and British have taken. I know they'll just try to use us to replace the men they have lost, trying to trade lives for territory. We have to reinstate mobility into this war if we're going to win it. We can't just throw more bodies into that grinder. Villa's attacks at Celaya and Leon at least taught us that the tactics they are using in Europe won't work and can eat up whole divisions in the process."

"General, I don't envy you. There's a hard road ahead, and I think the only signposts to successful tactics may have been in Mexico. Maybe if you study Villa at Zacatecas and Obregón around Guadalajara, you may find some answers," said Green.

"We'll sure need some new thinking, all right. You were at Zacatecas, weren't you?" asked Pershing.

"Don't even think it, General. I'm not coming back into any-body's army," Green said stonily.

"Oh, I just thought you might help with the training. I could get you a direct commission as maybe a lieutenant colonel," said Pershing.

"General, that's how I got mixed up with Villa. No, I won't, and you can't make me. But, if you are serious about it, get General Angeles. He was the brains in Villa's campaigns, at least those that were successful."

"I'm afraid that would be politically impossible, although I'd like to. Even if I could, he probably wouldn't come until Mexico's troubles are over."

"I think you'll find the people you'll need already in the U. S. Army. You'll just have to look down deep. They're there."

"I hope you're right, Green."

"Hell, General, they're around. You got one of them right here in your office."

Lieutenant George Patton blushed but said nothing.

Pershing said, "I hope they're all as easy to find as he is."

Green soon excused himself and went back into town to check his accounts. Although he owed more money than he liked, prima-rily due to expanding his yearling operation, he would reduce his debt considerably in the next two years. He would have time to re-trench before the next market downturn.

That night as Green had his first drink before supper, Mercedes suddenly jumped up and ran to the bathroom, calling for the nurse, Conchita.

In a little while, Conchita came back and said breathlessly, "Señor Dunigan, La Señora says to call Mama Rosenda quickly, for the baby is coming."

256

Green called the *curandera* and then drove over to pick her up. She had secured two helpers who would ride with them. When they got back to the house, Mercedes was in the bedroom and seemed to be calm. Mama Rosenda examined her and told Green to stick around, as the baby was coming easily and the delivery would be short. Green went to the kitchen and called Sam Ravel.

"Sam, you still got that bean scale? Mercedes is birthing now, and it looks like it will be fairly quick."

"I'll be over in fifteen minutes, Green," said Ravel.

Green could hear Mercedes' cries and tried to enter the bedroom, but Mama Rosenda stopped him. "This baby is coming fast, and we are very busy," she ordered. "We do not need you getting in the way. We will call you when you are needed." She firmly closed the door.

When Sam showed up with the bean scale, they sat down to have a drink and talk.

"What are you going to name this one?"

"If it's a girl, Mercedes will name her Amanda, after my mother. If it's a boy, I'd kinda like to name him after her brothers, Vicente and Tomas, but it'll be her choice."

They talked for over an hour, and then at 8:30 a new sound was heard—a newborn crying.

Mama Rosenda appeared at the bedroom door and said, "You have a new son, Mr. Dunigan. Everything went fine and both mother and son are in fine condition. You may come in in just a little while. I'll call you."

"Another boy, Green, isn't that wonderful!" Sam said. "You seem to be breeding your own cow outfit. Girls are great, and they love their daddies, but boys can do all your work when they grow up."

The *curandera* finally came to the door and signaled Green to come in. Sam picked up the scale.

"Just Señor Dunigan now. I will come back for you and your scale," said Mama Rosenda.

Green entered the bedroom, just as one of the women placed the little bundle next to Mercedes. He kneeled next to the bed and took one of Mercedes' hands and kissed it.

"How do you feel, darling?" asked Green.

"A little tired, but wonderful! Say hello to your son," and she pushed back the blanket to reveal the baby. He seemed larger than

257

his brother, but with the same black hair and his mother's green eyes. He wasn't red like Fito had been, and his skin had the same dusky tinge as his mother's.

"Señora Avila, would you ask Conchita to bring Fito in to meet his brother, and ask Sam to bring the scale?" Green asked.

Conchita brought the boy in and put him on the bed so that he could see his brother. He gazed at him with wonder, but then crawled over and hugged Mercedes. Sam had come in and set the scale up on a table.

The two men put the baby inside the brass cradle to weigh him. He yelled like a panther when his skin touched the cold brass. He was weighed and measured at eight pounds, five ounces and 25¼ inches long.

"He's a bigun', all right," said Sam.

"All right, you have done enough . . . out, out both of you! Go get drunk like you're supposed to," Mama Rosenda shouted.

Sam and Green went downtown to the hotel for supper, passing on the news to some friends they met. At 11:00 Green got home and looked in on his sleeping family, then went to bed.

Green awoke before 6:00 the next morning and heard noises of activity all over the house. He was able to gain entry to the bedroom, to find Mercedes suckling the little boy, who seemed very content. Mercedes, as usual, looked beautiful with her long, jet-black hair spilled all over the pillow.

She smiled as he entered. "Good morning, Papa. Your new son will greet you as soon as he satisfies his hunger. Señora Avila will be here around eight to finish the papers, so we must select a name for this big boy."

"What do you want to call him?" Green asked.

"I think Adrian—after you."

"That would be nice, but Kathleen and Bill Foster have already honored me thusly, so I would like to name him after his uncles, who have not been so honored and will not have children of their own. Let's call him Vicente Tomas."

"Green, this boy is an American. We must give him an American name, not Mexican."

"Okay, we'll call him Vincent Thomas or Thomas Vincent, whatever you like. But your brothers were not only my comrades but my best friends, too, and their memory should be preserved," Green said firmly.

"All right. The boy will be named Tomas Vicente Dunigan, and we will call him Tom. But the next child must have an American name. Do you agree?"

"Yes, *Mamacita,* I agree. Now I will get out of the way and get working to support my big family."

CHAPTER 47

El Paso, Texas / March 30, 1917

reen, Sam Ravel, and Jimmy Berger were sitting in the Del Norte Hotel bar discussing Mexico and its continuing tragedy.

"You know," Sam said, "this thing has been going on since the strike at Cananea, over ten years ago, and there has been major fighting since 1910. We all know how horrible it has been. I read an estimate the other day that said almost half of Mexico's population has died during this revolution. You'd think they'd be worn out and just quit. But Zapata is still going strong, and there have been battles in the southwest, below Guadalajara, and the Yucatan, and no end in sight."

"Yes, and there isn't going to be an end until Carranza quits insisting that he is the government and *lider supremo,*" countered Green. "His contribution has been to pit the real leaders against one another, and he is still doing it."

Jimmy Berger wasn't adding anything to the conversation because he didn't think he knew much about it, but he finally spoke up about the intercepted telegram from the German foreign office— the celebrated Zimmerman telegram that was in all the papers. "Do you really think the Germans meant that they would back Mexico in a war with us? Do the Mexicans really think they could get all their territory back?" he asked.

"No, they wouldn't and they couldn't. It was just a ploy to keep the U.S. out of the war in France. I heard some of it two or three years ago in Mexico, but no one, particularly the Mexicans, paid any attention. It now has pretty well ensured our entry into the war. It's only a matter of time," said Green.

Green heard someone say, *"Hola,* Verde, *que pasa?"* He turned to see Etienne de la Garza coming across the room, clad in the uniform of a sergeant of the U. S. Marines. Everyone jumped up to welcome him warmly and then sat back down and secured him a cold beer.

"What brings you back here, Etienne? I thought you would be in France by now," asked Sam.

"Almost. I am on my way to Quantico, Virginia. They are putting together a brigade to go to France, and we're getting lots of recruits to fill it up. We'll be part of the first troops over there."

"The Marines must be building pretty fast. You haven't been gone but about a year and a half and you're already a sergeant," remarked Green. "I thought it took at least five years, normally."

"More like ten, usually. They gave some credit to Cuba and Mexico, and they are short of NCOs, so I got promoted fast. I'm an acting gunnery sergeant and I'll probably be made permanent when I'm assigned in the brigade. The marines are a fine outfit, and I'm glad to be going to war with them," Etienne said proudly.

"Why don't you stay with us—that is, if you don't mind a baby crying once in a while," said Green. "We got another one, not a month old. Name of Tom, after his uncles, Tomas and Vicente," he explained.

"Sounds like a full house, Green. I'd better stay here."

"No, we have plenty of room. Mercedes will be glad to see a handsome marine. All she's seen lately are broken-down traders. I'll get your bags and we'll go."

Mercedes was indeed overjoyed to see Etienne. She refrained from mentioning Tomas and Vicente, which Green appreciated.

The next day Green took Etienne with him to inspect some yearlings in a cut-over wheat field. While they were there, Etienne asked, "Green, I follow the news about the Americans chasing Villa and I know they didn't catch him, but where is he? Is he still alive?"

"I talked to Hipolito, Pancho's brother, this week and he had word that Pancho is still in the sierra. He almost died from a wound in his leg, but he got cured. Still alive and kicking, I guess."

"Those were sure some times, down in Mexico with Villa. I wish he could've won," said Etienne, wistfully.

"Looks like we wasted a couple of years for nothing, but I learned a lot down there," said Green.

"Me, too. But I learned a long time ago that fighting just for the love of it finally gets too nerve-wracking, and even boring. At least in France we'll be fighting Germans. I never did like Germans."

"Most French people don't, so you come by it naturally," Green said.

"It'll be nice to speak *francais* again. I hope the natives can understand Cajun."

"You'll make out, Etienne. You always have."

Green was making coffee the next morning when Etienne came down. It was still dark outside.

Mercedes came into the kitchen in her robe and slippers and said, "That coffee really smells good. Can I have some? The baby was hungry and I just finished feeding him."

"Just a minute, *alma mia,*" said Green.

They all had a cup of coffee around the table.

Mercedes said, "Like old times in Chihuahua, huh?"

Green and Etienne smiled and nodded, then Etienne asked, "Mercedes, I didn't get to see the little one last night. If he's asleep, could I slip in and take a look if I'm really quiet?"

"Sure. You probably couldn't wake him with a *pistola,* but try to be quiet anyway," she replied.

Etienne went into the nursery and spent about three minutes, then came back to his coffee. "He is a handsome child, with his mother's coloration, is he not? He will be a devil with the ladies some years in the future."

"Thank you, Etienne, I'll remember that," said Mercedes.

Green and Etienne stayed around the customs pens most all that day, and he left the next day for Virginia, to report. Green was sorry to see him go, but he knew his friend was not going to get killed in the war. Etienne knew how not to get hit.

Fort Bliss, as one of the major army posts in the country, was bulging with people. The army, just like the marines, was quickly mobilizing, as if a declaration of war was already a fait accompli, and El Paso was full of soldiers from dawn till night, every day. It seemed as if El Paso had been painted olive drab.

Green was annoyed that his shipping had been complicated enormously by the traffic in troop trains. The horse and mules market had exploded around El Paso—particularly mules, which were bringing $200-$250 even for sorry ones. He complained to Sam Ravel, who was profiting handsomely from the run-up in prices.

"Goddamnit, Sam, you'd think they could find the mules some place closer to where they need them. Don't they raise mules in France, or England, or in Missouri or Kentucky, or anywhere else?"

"Hold on, Green, you know that they're fighting over most of France, and they're buying Missouri mules faster than they're buying them here. It's just that they need so many, and so many have been killed or used up in the war."

"Well, it's a hell of a note. Respectable horse dealers becoming high-volume mule thieves, and everybody's looking the other way."

"Green, I warned you about sitting on your front porch at Roy and viewing with alarm all the changes that the war is making. It's going to change more, but to a man such as yourself, it's opportunity knocking on your door."

Green was silent as he digested Sam's statement. He recognized the truth of it, in that he had passed many deals that would've been profitable to him, because he just didn't want to get involved. He sat musing for almost thirty minutes without speaking. Sam Ravel eyed him quizzically.

Finally, he broke the silence. "You may be right, Sam. Anyway, I'm going home to eat lunch and talk to my wife about this."

Mercedes was delighted but surprised to see Green come home for lunch, and they sat in the dining room and had a pleasant meal.

"*Alma mia*, you remember I told you that Villa swore to me that the Herreras would keep most of Herradura, but he still hasn't made peace. I do know that many of the leaders who have made peace have been rewarded with grants and such. Of course, Villa is still fighting and probably won't quit until Carranza behaves, but it won't be long. I think as soon as he gives his parole, he will get a place and will make sure that Herradura is put in your hands."

He paused. "Mercedes, with this war, and what the revolution has done, there is much opportunity on both sides of the Rio Bravo. I think I want to take advantage of it, but I'll have to spend some time in Mexico," Green continued.

Mercedes gazed at Green for a time, then got up and went to her room. He heard drawers opening and closing, and then she came back and sat down. She handed him what looked like a ring case, and he opened it to find a squashed bullet.

"I saved that. The doctor gave it to me after Tierra Blanca. I saved it to show to you if you ever talked of going back. You want to hunt for another one, Gringo?" Tears were in her eyes.

"No, I'm not going back to fight. I promised you that. What I had in mind was to occupy and protect Herradura from squatters, and to start rebuilding it for you."

"Green, although I love Herradura, I would not want it if there was a chance of losing you. No, I don't want you there," she sobbed.

"Mercedes, Villa is the only one around there now, and I won't stay if it's dangerous. What I had in mind was to recruit some people to start putting it back together. I'll not be there much, but what we need to do is to occupy it while Villa is still active, so he can put it under his protection. And then maybe we can hold on to it, when things get somewhat back to normal."

"Green, we have plenty of land, two fine boys, a family. I do not need Herradura. And if you were to die there, I would never go there again. Green, you don't need the money. Why do you even want to think about it?"

"Because it is your heritage, and the heritage of a valiant and wonderful family that I would someday like to say I am a part of," Green said solemnly.

She thought for a long moment. "If you do not take any ... any chances, you can go and do it. But please be careful. You're all I've got left, and if I lost you, I would die myself," she said.

"You have two fine boys to take care of, and I expect you to do it. Besides, we aren't through yet," Green said, grinning.

This cheered her up a bit, and she looked at him hungrily. "You want to start now? I am ready."

CHAPTER 48

El Paso, Texas / April 7, 1917

reen opened the paper that morning to find that the United States had declared war on Germany the day before.

"Well," he thought, "it's official now. At least Mexico doesn't have to worry about us coming down there again."

He had been working with Sam Ravel on his plans for Herradura. Sam had a lot of ordnance left over that belonged to Villa but couldn't be delivered because of U.S. prohibitions, and Green thought he might use some for protection as he rebuilt Herradura. He got Sam to transfer six machine guns and two howitzers to a little-used warehouse, where they would be out of reach until Green could smuggle them across. Green then got a permit for a carload of horses to Parral to leave in two weeks. He sent word to Sol Weeks and also to Bill Foster to send young mares that he could use to build a *manada* after he replaced them with local horses.

Soon after deciding to go, Green visited Hipolito Villa. He knew Hipolito had several men he used as messengers to keep in touch with his brother, and Green thought they could carry some messages for him to Parral.

Hipolito recognized Green as he walked into his *cantina* in Juárez.

"*Hola*, Verde!" he yelled. "What brings you to my establishment?"

"Hipolito, I came for news of the great General Villa. Can we sit and talk?"

"Most assuredly so, *mi amigo*."

They sat down at a rear table well away from any eavesdroppers. "What news from Pancho?" Green queried.

"Not much, Verde. He is still in the sierra, but his leg has healed. He got an old *bruja*, a sorceress, to get all the bad spirits out, and it healed quickly. He has about 200 men with him but can call up another thousand when he needs them."

"Hipolito, I am thinking about rebuilding Herradura, and I need to get started. Can you get a message down for me?"

"Oh sure. But I can't keep *federales* or bandits from killing you when you go down there."

"Maybe Pancho could keep them off me, and maybe you could get a message to him about that."

"Maybe, but you'd better tell me what you have in mind," said Hipolito, eyeing him with doubts.

"I will tell you everything, but it must be kept quiet." Green knew that Hipolito had, as his brother's principal agent for the U.S., a very tight mouth.

"Most assuredly, Green. They will not get it from me," he said, nodding.

"Years ago, before I left the revolution, Pancho solemnly gave me his promise that most, if not all, of Herradura would be given back to the Herreras. I believe he will be able to keep his promise in the future. After Orozco's raid, Herradura was unoccupied permanently. I want to get down there and start rebuilding it, so that some politician doesn't get his hands on it until Pancho can deliver. Besides, I can make some money while I am rebuilding, and possibly help your brother. You know me well enough to know that I don't do anything strictly out of the goodness of my heart."

"You do a lot more than most people I know, Green, and you're doing this strictly for Mercedes. You're not too bad a *cabrón*," said Hipolito, grinning.

"I want you to get a message to Cesar Dominguez in Parral that I'll be there in two weeks with a carload of horses. Tell him to round up any of our old vaqueros and any Herraduros he can find. Get word to Pancho as to what I have in mind, just so he'll know."

"Okay, Verde. I'll get the messages down there. Listen, the bridge guard to deal with is named Pico Flores, and he is the sergeant in charge in the mornings, so that is the time to pass things. Pico used to be in the Division of the North, so he will probably remember you."

"Thank you very much, *amigo*. I will see you on my return, huh?" said Green.

"If you return, Gringo."

By the time he had assembled his horses, Green had become well acquainted with Pico Flores, who had indeed remembered Colonel Verde from the Division of the North. Flores had been captured at Leon and had joined the forces of Obregón as a regular. Green had greased him well before crossing the bridge during the morning watch. He had more trouble with the American soldier on the north side, who knew the army was buying enormous numbers of horses, and thought Green might be stealing them. Ten dollars took care of it, and Green led his horses on down to the freight yards, where he loaded each one and tied them in.

The train ride to Parral was quiet. Fear of outlaws kept the passenger load to a minimum, but no outlaw bands appeared. Green did slip out and water his horses when the train was being switched in Chihuahua, but he did it without being seen. The train pulled out for Parral on time, and Green unloaded his horses less than two days after loading them.

Leading his horses down the street, Green came to the *cantina* where he had sent word to Cesar Dominguez to meet him. Inside, he saw a group of men in back who looked familiar.

"*Bienvenidos*, Colonel Verde," shouted Cesar, and welcomed him to the group.

There were ten of them, Cesar and four of his vaqueros, and five of the Herraduros. He welcomed them all and sat down to outline his plans.

"We are going to Herradura to start putting it back together. The first thing will be to gather cattle, if there are any left. I have brought twenty horses, all well-bred, all mares that can be used as a *manada* after we have replaced them. I will take inventory and get what we need on subsequent trips. I don't know if any of you have been there since the raid, but all the stone and brick buildings were still intact. They burned everything else. There was one survivor

267

that we saw when we buried Vicente, old Mercadio Gomez and his woman. Hopefully, they are still there. Of course, we will have to have carpenters and masons and thatchers to do much of the work, and I have sent word to General Villa of my plans. Unless I miss my guess, we will be safe from sierra bandits. When we are well along, we'll be able to hold our own against any group, with the exception of the federal army, and hopefully, our isolation will help us.

"You will be paid, and paid well, but you must volunteer. I know that this is home to half of you, and almost that to the others, but there is danger. Those of you who are not old Herradura can become so if you want," Green finished and sat down.

The men glanced around and nodded. Then Arnulfo Carrasco rose and said, "We will go with you, Señor Verde."

Green and Cesar spent the rest of the day finding a wagon and fixing it up to be the chuck wagon. They bought pots and pans, tents, and other equipment necessary for living under the skies. Three other women wanted to go besides Cesar's wife, and places were made in the wagon, as they would help with the cooking and chores.

Most of the men had their own horses, so Green's mares were just driven when the party left Parral the following morning. The trip was uneventful through several uninhabited villages, and no outlaws were seen. They arrived at Herradura late in the evening of the second day and found it much the same as it had been two years before. Mercadio Gomez and his wife were even there.

"*Viejito, que ha pasado aqui?*"

"*Nada,* Señor. No one has stayed here, although two groups camped here overnight this year, but neither stayed much over a day or so," said Mercadio.

"Did they discover your presence?"

"No, I stayed out of sight," he answered.

"Mercadio, we have come to start the rebuilding of Herradura. We came to stay, although I will be gone from time to time, getting workmen, supplies, and tending to my own business. There will be a new Herradura much like the old one, but with the changes from the revolution, who knows?"

Mercadio's face lit up like a bonfire.

"Señor, there are many men around who can help restore this place. I will be happy to get them."

"Not yet, Mercadio. The first thing to do is to clean up the place and make an inventory of what we need. We will start cleaning up in the morning, and the day after I want to gather the stock and see what we have," ordered Green.

Everyone turned out the next day and cleaned up debris in the buildings, mostly ashes and burned sticks. Orozco had done a thorough job. Only two hide-covered chairs were found in the old vaqueros' bunkhouse left unburned. After the clean-up, which took all day, things looked better. Green told Mercadio to get some help to wash everything down, so they could tell what was damaged and what was just discoloration from smoke and exposure. Green and the vaqueros were going to inventory the livestock for the next few days and wouldn't be around.

Green's job consisted of counting the cows carrying the horseshoe brand of Herradura and throwing the other cows back toward their home range. He also sorted the unbranded cattle that appeared to be Herradura's produce and drove them back to the headquarters to be branded.

After branding, castrating, and processing the stock, Green found he had turned back about 858 cows that were branded, had branded 585 more cows and heifers, for a total of 1,435 females, and had about 400 steers of various ages that could be marketed. Since it was still early in the year, he turned the steers out also, to be marketed in the fall or next year. Although Herradura had a normal cow herd of over 15,000 head, the counts had not surprised Green, except that he had feared that all of the cattle might have been gone, lost, strayed, or stolen. He would contact the neighbors next week and maybe organize a general roundup, which might produce a few more cattle, but that could wait, for their horses were pretty well worn out and needed a few days' rest and they had found only seven of the old Herradura horse stock. Green put the vaqueros to work fixing up the corrals and pens, which they needed for day-to-day work. The cowboys knew things were changing in the cow country, and their duties would change as well.

Green had determined to use the Herrera money to restore the place, and there was plenty. Mercedes was heir to over half a million in Texas banks. Probably very little money was left in Mexico, but Green had brought $3,000 in gold with him and several million pesos in *bilimbigues* and other revolutionary currency, and he had no idea what it was worth, if anything.

The following day Green, Cesar, and Mercadio started to make a list of the things that needed to be done and what supplies would be needed. The first thing to be done would be to make the place habitable. A list was made, consisting of lumber and tiles, many sacks of plaster, plus foodstuff for at least three months. Mercadio knew of several workmen who could do the construction and would move to Herradura for the time needed to do the work. Mercadio also knew of a family of thatchers who could cut, weave, and place all the roofs. There was plenty of material in the vega for them to work with.

Green took Mercadio and two more men with two wagons to Parral to get supplies. On the way, Mercadio secured the services of five artisans, who, with their families, would move and begin work at Herradura within a week. Green still had to find some farmers, because he wanted to make Herradura as self-sufficient as it was before, raising at least wheat for bread and corn for cattle feed. He would need at most five farmers, and there were plenty of those roaming around, but mules, oxen, and tractors were scarce. Green put these items down as things to be done later.

Several pressing items remained on Green's agenda for Herradura. The general roundup of the area needed to be set up and an inventory of furniture and fixtures to make the place livable. Also, he needed to make contact with whatever lawyer the Herreras had used and to track down all the grants and titles pertaining to the land, as well as any bank accounts that might have money in them.

Green and Cesar left the next morning to arrange the roundup. They took a packhorse, as they planned to be gone several days. They knew they would find some of the places abandoned, but it was much worse than expected. Out of nine *ranchos* they visited, three of them were completely abandoned, and four of them had caretakers living there who were only barely existing. The two that had people in charge had only two vaqueros apiece, headed by a *caporal* or major-domo. All told, only seven people were around to help with the gathering of the cattle.

Undaunted, Green went ahead. In three weeks they gathered

almost half a million *hectarias,* but it produced few cattle. Only 2,000 cows and heifers were returned to their home ranches, but Green picked up 150 more Herradura females and 200 more steers and bought all the other steers and bulls, about 300, which he took back to Herradura and branded. He sent checks to those whose whereabouts he knew, and would inquire about the rest. That gave him over 900 to market in the fall.

Green had decided to make Cesar Dominguez the *caporal* of the outfit and to have old Mercadio Gomez act as major-domo during the reconstruction, which was agreeable with them. Three of the vaqueros had moved out and taken up residence at three line shacks, to throw the Herradura cows back on their home range. The carpenters and plasterers had arrived and were at work, under the watchful eyes of old Mercadio. There had been a start on the rebuilding, and Green was satisfied for the moment. He would have a good report for Mercedes.

CHAPTER 49

Herradura / April 20, 1917

hree days after Green returned from the roundup, the lookout on the big house rang the alarm bell. Green alerted everyone and went up to see a group of about five mounted men approaching from the west. Using his binoculars, he saw them well enough to decide that it was probably Villa coming with a few of his men, so he was not really surprised when that turned out to be the case.

"Gringo Verde, will you not welcome your old *compadre,* Pancho Villa?"

"*Sí, como no, jefe. Mi casa es suya!*" yelled Green as the dust enveloped him.

Villa and his men dismounted, and Green led them to the cookhouse for some coffee.

"Verde, Hipolito sent word that you intended to reoccupy Herradura for your wife. I haven't been able to secure it yet, but Pancho Villa promised to do so, and Villa keeps his promises. I have tried to quit, but Don Venustiano wants me dead first," said Villa.

"Well, I think sooner or later it'll happen. I came down here to start rebuilding this place. Maybe I'm jumping the gun, but I wanted to keep it from falling completely down, and I trust you, *jefe.*

I know it will happen. It's just a matter of time. And besides, as far as I know, the title is still held by the Herrera family. I'm really just trying to keep one of Don Venus' people from stealing it in the meantime."

"The only danger is if you get it fixed up nice, some *politico* might try to steal it. But it is pretty far away from anywhere, and those *cabrónes* don't like to leave town. And they should not bother you if they know I am watching, and I have put that word out."

"Many thanks, *jefe*. I don't think I'll be bothered here for a while."

He showed Villa around and told him what he was doing. They then talked of the days when the Division of the North was strong.

"How is your wife, Green? Do you have any babies?" Villa asked.

"We have two little boys now. The first I named Felipe Angeles, and the second for their uncles, Tomas and Vicente."

"You are almost a Mexican, Verde, and Mexico should be proud to have you as a citizen, helping to rebuild."

"I don't think Don Venus would agree," remarked Green.

"Ay, that *pendejo*. He has no vision for Mexico, only for himself. He is an intelligent man, but too selfish. Still, Mexico has survived worse. Huerta, for example," mused Villa.

"*Jefe,* you know you have a certain amount of ordnance that you have paid for with Sam Ravel. I got him to put six machine guns and two cannons in a warehouse at Columbus, and I mean to bring them here. I want them for defense here, but if you need them, they are of course yours."

"I don't think I can use them right now, but they may help if I need to duck in here sometime when the *rurales* are after me. If the revolution starts up again, I may need them. I hope I don't. Mexico doesn't need any more guns. It needs schools and teachers and some years of peace."

"Amen, *jefe*, amen," said Green.

Villa stayed for a couple of days to visit. He told Green how the *bruja* had cured his leg wound and how this same old woman had cured him of a social disease some years earlier. The day before he left, a forlorn monk on a donkey wandered in, looking like he was starving, which he was. Villa wanted to shoot him, but Green talked him out of it, saying that all the victims of Pascual Orozco's raid had never been properly blessed. Villa finally relented. They had a memorial service and also hallowed the ground of Herradura's *campo santo*. They fed the monk, provided him some food and water for later, and gave him a bed. Green wanted him to say mass in the small chapel there on the ranch, but Villa was very dubious.

"Gringo, you don't know what these priests have done to my people. The church has stolen millions from Mexico. All these priests are good for is to marry the girls who want to be legitimate before they make love to a man. I'd kill them all. They were worse than Chinamen."

"*Jefe*, you can talk like that, but you know the people. A blessing from a priest means a lot to them. They have very little else of value in their lives. You know, you might stay for mass. All the things you have done, it wouldn't hurt to be a little closer to God when you go. There is a bad place you could end up in," Green said, grinning.

"I know I am going there already, so it won't do any good for me to go to mass. Anyway, the church would probably fall down on me, and that one of yours looks like it's ready to fall. I don't want to tempt God," said Villa. "Besides, I am leaving tomorrow for Parral. You want to go with me? You'll be safe."

"*Sí*, I would like to go. I need to find some of the Herrera records and such. I think Vicente got all the original papers after Orozco's raid, but I never found where he stored them," replied Green.

"Maybe he took them to his family lawyers. I don't know exactly who that might be, but the oldest and biggest lawyers in Parral I know to be the firm of Saltos y Perez, and that is where I would start looking. Of course, they might have used lawyers in Chihuahua, but I will bet that that firm will know who represented the Herreras, whoever they are."

"It's a starting place, at least," said Green.

The trip to Parral was pleasant, although the weather was starting to get warm, and they parted on reaching Parral. Villa didn't say, and Green didn't ask, what his business was there.

Green went directly downtown to the offices of Saltos y Perez to start his search. He was directed to the office of Geronimo Saltos, a man in his middle to late sixties, a gentle-looking man with white hair and a white beard.

A secretary ushered Green into the office. Rising, Saltos greeted him.

"Geronimo Saltos *a sus ordenes,* Señor Dunigan."

"Señor, I am here inquiring about the legal affairs of the Herrera family, my wife's people."

"Señor Dunigan, Don Tacho was both a friend and my client. I know all about you and your friendship with all the Herreras, and of course your service with the Division of the North. Don Tacho had very little in the way of legal problems, as the family was generally the law in and around Hacienda Herradura. Tell me, how can I be of service?"

"*Licenciado,* our business, of necessity, must remain confidential. Since you seem to know about most of what has happened, you can see the reason," said Green.

"All lawyers are pledged to confidentiality, Señor Dunigan, even in revolutionary Mexico, and I, knowing the circumstances, am completely pledged," vowed Saltos.

Green continued. "My wife, Mercedes, is the only survivor of the Herrera family, except for an older sister, Otilia, who went to Spain when Díaz went there. She probably couldn't make a claim on Herradura even if she wanted to, in a Mexican court, so I am going on the proposition that Mercedes is the sole heir. I am down here, quietly taking possession and rebuilding it in her name. What I am seeking from you is any knowledge of Herrera property. I know Vicente opened a hidden safe after Pascual Orozco's raid and found its contents untouched, but I do not know what was in the safe, except for some money and jewelry. What I am seeking are the grants and titles or abstracts of the *hacienda* particularly, but any information would be welcomed."

"Señor, Vicente Herrera brought most all of the important papers pertaining to Herradura to me for safekeeping about four years ago. I have examined those papers and they are all the original title documents for the *hacienda*. There were some ledgers and bank statements, but the bank account was with the Banco Sembrador here in Parral, showing a balance of 20,000 pesos, I think, and that bank is no longer in operation."

"*Licenciado,* when I served with the Division of the North, some had trouble with my name, so they called me Verde. If it suits you, please do so yourself," Green said.

Saltos nodded.

"Most of the monies were kept in the United States, and I think

I have located all of it. It is a considerable sum, so my wife is quite wealthy. But I would appreciate your advice on what bank to deal with down here now, as it will cost much to restore Herradura."

"Señor Verde, are you sure you want to restore the property? Much land has been expropriated by the revolution, particularly the better properties that have been kept up," Geronimo Saltos explained.

"Well, that is a possibility, and a risk we will take. But there are other factors. I must ask; are there any problem areas in the documents you are holding, and is there anything needing to be cleared up that we can?" asked Green.

"Well, we probably should file probate papers, to legally vest the inheritance to your wife. I can draw up the papers, and she can qualify easy enough. Do you want me to do that, and what shall I do with the papers that Vicente brought me?"

"Please draw them up. Also, I wish you to keep the papers in safekeeping, Señor," Green replied, "and to act as lawyer for us in all matters in and around Mexico."

"I will be happy to do so. Will you need anything else?" Saltos asked.

"Yes. I'll need to use a local bank. Which one would you recommend, knowing that I will have to transfer monies from the U.S.?"

"Banco Parral has the necessary connections both in Chihuahua and El Paso and is well thought of," answered Saltos.

"I will use them, and will channel all legal questions through your offices in the future." Green had found a lawyer. "One more thing . . . I have bought some cattle from the neighbors of Herradura. I have a list of the places and the monies I need to get them, but I don't know where the owners are or if they're still the owners. These cattle were caught when we rounded up the general area. I wonder if you could see that the money ends up in the proper hands?"

"I will do my best, Señor Verde, but with things as they are I cannot guarantee success."

"I understand. Here is the list of the cattle and the places we thought they came from. I will be back with a check when I get the banking arranged and you can deliver it to the owners."

"I will do so, Señor Verde. I am glad to meet someone who will try to carry on for the Herrera family. They were fine people—some of the best in Mexico. I would be sad to see the things that they put so much effort into disappear," Geronimo Saltos said, looking genuinely sad as he ushered Green out of his office.

Green then found the Banco Parral and spoke to a bank officer who had known the Herreras. After opening an account, Green explained that he would be drawing on accounts in Texas banks and wouldn't keep much money there until things were well settled in Mexico. The officer understood, and was very helpful. Now Green had some of the requisites of a commercial operation: a lawyer and a banker.

On his way back to Herradura, Green rode hard and fast, and as he entered the eastern end of the valley that enclosed Herradura, he was confronted by three of the seediest-looking bandits he could have ever imagined. They were dirty, unshaven, dressed in rags, and barefooted. One led a puny burro, and the leader held a revolver that looked like one discarded by Maximilian's troops.

"Hands up! Give us your horse and your guns, or I will shoot you!" declared the one in front.

"You are addressing Colonel Verde of the Division of the North. Put away that broken pistol, or I will turn you over to General Villa to be cooked over a slow fire," said Green, smiling.

The leader looked woundedly at his broken pistol, then dropped to his knees and pled.

"*Por favor, excellencio,* do not give us to the great General Villa. We are just poor starving revolutionaries who have nothing. No food, no family, no horses, nothing. We have only this burro to help us carry water. Have pity on us, Colonel."

"Do you want work?" Green asked.

"If we can get something to eat, *sí,* Señor," he answered.

"What can you do?" asked Green.

"Andres Mendiola and myself, Juan Alberdi, were farmers. We used to farm in the Laguna before the war," he said, indicating the man alongside him. "Pepe Gomez was an *arriero,*" indicating the man holding the burro.

"How long since you have eaten?"

"The night before last," said Alberdi.

Green opened his saddlebags and got out some dried meat and tortillas for them.

"If you men follow me to Herradura, I will give you work plowing the fields there, and I will take care of you. You'd better do it, because you'll never be good enough bandits. The next man you stop might kill you."

They followed him to Herradura, where Green told Mercadio to find them a place to stay until they were strong enough to work as farmers.

Green had set priorities to the work. First, the inside of the smaller buildings, and then the outside. The big house and the outside of the wall were to be the last to be refurbished, as not to give too good of an impression from a distance. Green didn't want to tempt any invaders.

Five old Herradura families had drifted in since he had reactivated the place, but only one was a farmer. The thatchers had arrived and were busy making the thatch, although none of the structures had been roofed yet. It wouldn't be long.

Green yearned to go back to El Paso. He had gotten the job started, and everyone knew what the program was. He missed Mercedes and the boys, and certain tools and equipment that he needed couldn't be had in Mexico at this time. Also, he needed to get his ordnance down to Herradura.

Green and Cesar Dominguez had a long powwow and agreed upon a plan. Green was to go back now, and Cesar would bring the steers to Ascensión mainly by rail from Parral. Green would meet them in Ascensión and cross the steers at Columbus, New Mexico. All of this was to take place in September. There would be a herd of cows and heifers, crossed into Mexico at Columbus, to be taken back, via Parral, to Herradura. Green would also recruit some more vaqueros, as he would need them to come back. His ordnance would have to be smuggled during this time, but Green thought he could get the breeding cattle permitted to cross legally. There were other problems, but Green thought he could work them out by September.

Three days later, Green and Cesar rode off to Parral.

CHAPTER 50

El Paso, Texas / July 9, 1917

aving arrived earlier in the day, Green was by midafternoon working out his plans with Sam Ravel and Jimmy Berger.

"Sam, I want to cross the border into Mexico with substantial seed stock. Cows mostly, some good heifers and plenty of bulls. What are my chances?" asked Green.

"I'd say pretty good. There are permits available for breeding stock, and Mexico City is promoting rebuilding of herds."

"Do the cattle have to be registered or anything like that?" Green inquired.

"No, they have to be inspected to pass as 'good or above average' quality, but this can be handled and there shouldn't be any trouble at the border. I can get the *permisos* and arrange for the inspection beforehand. Where and when do you want to cross?" he asked.

"At Columbus around the middle of September," said Green.

"And how much other stuff will you want at Columbus, besides the two cannons and six machine guns?" asked Ravel knowingly.

"About 10,000 rounds of ammunition, forty Mausers, and a hundred shells for each of the Howitzers," grinned Green.

"How you get that stuff across is your problem, Green. I don't want to get caught dead around it," said Sam.

"Don't worry, Sam, I'll get it across somehow. Just make sure I have the cattle permits in September."

"You'll have them. Have I ever failed you?"

"No, and I don't expect you ever will, Sam. You have been a true friend."

Ravel grinned broadly. It was difficult to get compliments out of Green Dunigan.

Green changed course a bit, and asked, "Jimmy, think you can fill the order?"

"Well, I dunno. Exactly what is the order? I know the date, place, and more or less the time. What I don't know is how many, what kind, and how old?"

"I want 500 bulls, pure-bred, or registered, makes no difference, from yearlings to threes or even fours. About 500 good Hereford heifer yearlings to twos, and 1,500 cows. Good commercial ones. Basically Hereford ... Nothing over five years old, and as few of them as possible. Is that an order you can fill?" Green asked.

"You bet, Green, and it won't be too hard, I don't think. I have a pasture north of Columbus, and I'll start concentrating them there. They'll be easy to inspect there, too."

"Go to it, Jimmy. By the way, I need to talk to Balbuena. Is he around?" asked Green.

"He'll be here next week, if that's soon enough," said Jimmy.

"Yeah, that'll be fine. I'll see you all next week." Green got up and went to the train station to catch a ride to Roy.

Being at the Roy ranch was always the best of times for Green. Everything he enjoyed was there: Mercedes and the two boys, cool weather, green pastures and fat cattle, and a feeling of accomplishment. He spent most of the time with his family but found time to ride the ranch and see his cattle doing well under Sol Weeks' careful management. Sol was good at fixing things before they became problems. His only failure was his inability to catch a trout of more than five pounds on his fly rod.

To Green, and to Mercedes, Rancho Polaris was their Eden of tranquility. Green could remain here the year round and be happy, but he knew that his life had to have more meaning than watching the grass grow. He had been a part of too many exciting adventures to relish going to seed on his front porch.

Of course his biggest project at this point was the rebuilding of

Herradura. He was enthusiastic about it as he recounted all the details to Mercedes. She, too, was excited about it.

"Oh, Green, it all sounds so wonderful. When am I going to be allowed to see all this? After all, I am the owner, am I not?"

"Yes, of course, *querida*. But give me a year to do it before you go. I want it to be just like it was before when you first see it."

"Green, I want to be a part of the rebuilding. I want to go sooner. After all, I am the owner, Gringo," she said.

Green knew to back off whenever she called him that. Her *mexicanismo* was still strong, and he knew that he would have to accede to it, sooner or later.

"I will let you go down as soon as I can. Your house has only one table, one chair, and one bed at this point. You need to get the furniture together so it will be livable when you go," Green pleaded.

"And how do I do that, Gringo? I want a Mexican house, not a washed-out American one, and I must get furniture for it in Mexico," said Mercedes, her green eyes flashing.

"*Querida*, I want our next child to be born in Mexico, at Herradura, so that any citizen inheritance problem will be helped. But things still aren't stable enough in Mexico for you to go yet. I would be breaking my vows to your family to take you."

Mercedes was silent for a moment. "Green, since both you and I want our next child to be born in Mexico, I think we'd best get started on it." She took him by the hand and led him upstairs, unbuttoning her dress as she did.

Green stumbled into the cookshack at daybreak. He got his coffee and started talking with Sol about things on the Rancho Polaris. Green's 12-13,000 yearling steers were doing well, as were his small cow herd, numbering only about 75 or 80.

"You sure were right about those cows," Sol told Green. "In the pasture they break up into herds, from ten to twenty-five cows apiece. All you have to do to gather them is to ride around, and the boss cows will take them to the round-up ground, where the big boss cow will take them wherever you want. Two men is all it takes to get them to the pens. We haven't seen all that many calves, as the oldest of the cows is about four years old, but those we've seen have sure been good."

"You think we got a good enough seed stock, Sol? I can get more heifers in the fall, if it would speed up stocking."

"It wouldn't hurt, boss. Can you get another load in the fall?"

"Sure thing, Sol. I'll talk to Dad in the next two or three days."

Green stayed out of the house and out on the ranch all day. When he got home at dark, Mercedes had on her slinkiest dress, and a lewd twinkle in her eye.

"Ah, *mi patron,* come in and put your feet up ... you must be tired." She kissed him, and it was definitely not a peck on the cheek.

"Now, Mercedes, I'm hungry and sleepy. We're not going to have another night like last night. That's for sure. I'm getting too old for that," said Green stiffly.

"*Amor,* you're better than any young man. But tonight will be good. Quality, not quantity. Come, supper is on the table."

They sat down to supper in the dining room. As they were finishing, he talked to Mercedes about Herradura—the repairs, the help, and the herds.

"By September I will have spent about $20,000 of your money on this," he said. "I will buy some more cattle in September, and you can get furniture and stuff for the big house. I guess that it will take between $150,000 and $200,000 all told, to put it back in shape. I'm hoping that you will get half of the farmland, and I'm only going to work the western half of the vega. I figure it will take about three years to have it back in working order, producing cattle at about half of what the whole place used to do. The cattle will cost about $80,000. I think we can breed up from there. So, I will spend about $100,000 of your money this year. That will leave you $400,000 with another $100,000 to be spent in the next two years. You'll have $300,000 in U.S. banks to do with what you want.

"In view of all of this, if I were you, I would take $300,000 and invest it, put it out at interest. It'll earn a good amount, and you can have a separate income to do what you want from time to time. The other, I'll use it as is needed, but what's left after next year, I'd invest it along with the other. Of course, any profits from Herradura will be all yours."

"Green, you know I know nothing of these things. Why don't you set aside what you need for Herradura, and invest the rest for me? Along the way, we might set up some trust funds for the children ... and the others we will have," Mercedes said, smiling.

"*Mi amor*, I am not a callow youth anymore. My strength is limited! Besides, I need a glass of brandy to fortify myself," Green pled.

"I'll have one with you, and you needn't worry—I won't overtax you tonight. Last night was different because you had been gone a long time," said Mercedes.

Mercedes told Green that she wanted to look at the cows from Refugio that they had on the ranch, and suggested they have a picnic. Green had a day before he would return to El Paso, so he set a buggy for the next day.

Mercedes put the picnic basket in the back of the buggy, and they started off toward the river pasture, where the cows were, about 9:00 in the morning. It was a pleasant two-hour trip. The midsummer high and warm, the green pastures and fat steers along the way—all seemed to add to the contentment of Green and Mercedes. For nearly the first time, Mercedes talked about her mother and father, and her brothers, remembering the good times, and laughing gaily like a teenager. Green, too, was content, seeing his successful operation yielding happiness for him and his family.

They found a pretty motte of cottonwoods by the river and stopped to spread a blanket.

While they were eating, a small group of about twelve cows walked by on their way to the river for a drink. One of them stopped and walked over to them. She was a red cow with a white face, with just a hint of the black stria that came from her brindle forebears, but her wide, low horns marked her as a direct descendant of the Brindy Polaris line that she came from.

Mercedes arose and walked to the visitor. "Brindita, thank you for coming to see us. We beg your pardon for taking up your place, but you see, we are friends, just as your mama was my friend. I hope to see you again soon."

The cow wagged her head, then turned and walked back to her little herd.

Green looked at his wife. "You were trying to get her to lick your belly, like at Refugio, weren't you?"

"There are things between women you *machos* don't understand, Gringo. But yes, she knows, and I know," said Mercedes softly.

CHAPTER 51

El Paso, Texas / August 16, 1917

Back in El Paso, Green sought out Praxides Balbuena at the customs pens.

"Praxides, are you busy? I need to talk to you," asked Green.

"I'll be through here in about a half hour, Verde. I'll meet you over at Riley's," he responded.

Riley's Bar, adjacent to customs, was not elegant, but it served as a watering place for those in the border trade.

Green found a table and ordered a bottle of beer. He was on his second when Balbuena joined him.

"Praxides, do you know Columbus well?" asked Green.

"*Sí*, Verde, I've been all over that part of the country, both as a *villista* and as a trader. I would not be bragging to say that I know the country from Deming to Ascensión as well as anyone," he answered.

Green had become increasingly comfortable with Balbuena since the formation of their partnership with Jimmy Berger. He proceeded to reveal his plan to smuggle the arms he had secured from Ravel to Herradura.

"I want to transport a bunch of guns from Columbus to Herradura. I figure I'll take four wagons with false bottoms, maybe five. What I had in mind is to load them on the railroad at Ascensión, take them to Parral, and then overland to Herradura. I'm bringing some steers up in September, and will take some breeding stock down with the same crew, the same way. You got the picture, Praxides?"

"Yeah, I think so. You want me to drive four or five wagonloads of stuff to Ascensión, load them on flatcars, unload at Parral, and drive them to Herradura. It's not easy to cover the tracks of wagons loaded heavy, but I can if I can join the herd quick enough. The cattle will cover them after that. I'll use six mule teams to pull the wagons, and take along one extra team. About eight men should suffice, and I've got them over in Agua Prieta. We can trust them. You'll have to supply the wagons, though," answered Balbuena.

"Can you find five or six teams of good mules? They're scarce as hell around here," asked Green.

"I have a bunch located up at Silver City. All I have to do is pick them up."

"If you or any of your men want to go to Herradura and even stay there, that is possible. But if they don't, they can leave us at Ascensión. I still need hands at Herradura."

"Well, my boys are all vaqueros originally from big *ranchos,* but they are like me. They like hustling around. They make more money, but I'll ask them. As for me, I like the job I got with you and Jimmy. By the way, we've both been working on your contract. I've already sent 300 cows, 150 bulls, and 50 heifers to Columbus," Praxides said, grinning widely.

"That sounds great, Praxides. You have the men and mules at Jimmy's place in Columbus September the first. I'll meet you there then," said Green.

They ordered lunch and ate, then parted, Praxides to the pens and Green to Ravel's.

"Who am I greeting now, the great Colonel Verde, the trader Verde, or the *hacendados* of Herradura?" asked Ravel.

"I guess all three, Sam. I keep getting mixed up in my glorious past and even more uncertain future," said Green.

"What's up?" quizzed Ravel.

"Sam, I need you to fix some wagons for me to take all that ordnance to Herradura in false bottoms. Then fill up the wagon beds with wire, windmill parts, and tools that are used on a ranch. You understand?" asked Green.

"Sure, used to do it all the time. We even would use the gun carriages for wagon wheels. I think I can do it with about four wagons. When do you need them?" he asked.

"The first of September will be fine," Green answered. "Just the wagons. I've got the mules and drivers, Sam."

"Same old Green. Don't trust anyone. By now you must know I'm on your side," Ravel said grumpily.

"Sam, I trust you deeply. It's just that I like my own people to do the illegal stuff. It's safer for you, and it keeps them committed to me."

"Green, I'm an old hand at smuggling into Mexico. But I appreciate the consideration."

"You got the cattle *permisos* and inspection arranged, Sam?" Green asked.

"Yeah, the inspectors will be at Columbus on the third of September. Pick 'em up there. And, if I may be so bold, they are well greased, so there won't be any trouble," responded Sam.

"Thank you very much, Sam. You know I appreciate it. There is one more item. Mercedes needs furnishings for the big house at Herradura. I know you have warehouses full of the good stuff you bought out of the revolution. We'll buy most of what we'll need from you, and we'll need a lot. That *cabrón* Orozco burnt everything down there. There were just two old cow hide chairs left. I measured all the floors and windows for Mercedes, so she can size it all out."

"I'll be glad to get rid of it, Green, and I'll take care of the whole thing," Sam said.

"No you won't, Sam. She wants to buy it, because she feels a little like she's looting it anyway, and she has plenty of money. Just take care of boxing and shipping it, and have it in Parral by October first. But I emphasize—charge for it. She needs to feel like she owns legitimate stuff, not loot from the revolution," Green insisted.

"Okay, Green, I will do it right."

Having time on his hands, Green decided to go to Juárez and visit Hipolito Villa.

"Ah, Verde, how goes the world? Are you happy with the new little boy?"

"*Sí*, Hipolito, I am very happy, and I bring you greetings from your brother. He is well, and seemingly content," answered Green.

"Seemingly is right. He will never be content as long as *carrancismo* rules in Mexico. But, as long as he is free and alive, I am content. Pancho worries about Mexico. He should be like me. I just worry about Hipolito."

"Well, I guess someone has to worry. Me, I'm with you. I will worry about Green."

"Yes, Green, and Mercedes and the children and Herradura. Also all the Herraduras' neighbors. Yes, I have heard about you. Paying good money for cattle that the owners have abandoned," Hipolito sneered.

"Well, I don't want to have any trouble crossing these cattle out of Mexico, so I went the extra mile," explained Green.

"How can I serve you, *mi colonel*?" asked Hipolito.

Green explained that he wanted to find out how Hipolito had smuggled goods out of Columbus, New Mexico, as he was quite experienced in this procedure. Most of the smugglers, he learned, crossed the border fence about eleven to twelve miles west of Columbus and then headed for Ascensión. That was pretty much what Praxides Balbuena planned to do, except that he intended to head more easterly, to join with the cow-herd sooner. Green asked about army patrols on both sides, and Hipolito said he could get a schedule for him.

Green spent the next few days checking on details with Ravel and Balbuena, and he shopped around for someone to buy his steers that were grazing on Rancho Polaris. He found a trader out of St. Louis who could buy them all, so they discussed price and terms and Green made a date to show him the cattle the following week at the ranch. He wrote letters both to his father and his brother, telling them what to expect to get from the fall movement of cattle, and asked his father to save him a load of heifers from the Brindy herd.

With no further pressing business in El Paso, he caught the train to Roy and got to the ranch in time for supper with Mercedes and to visit with his sons. Fito was walking and talking now, although unsteadily and unintelligibly, while Tom was just looking cuddly in his crib. Green played with the children for nearly an hour before they were taken to bed at 8:00, then settled down to a cigar and a glass of brandy with his wife. They chatted about the ranch.

Mercedes said, "Green, I have been out to visit the cows since you left and I have formed a fast friendship with the cow I named Brindita."

"Has she licked your belly yet?" asked Green, laughing.

"No, but we are friends, and it is much the same. But I want you to take her to Herradura when you take the other cattle. Maybe a few more," asked Mercedes.

"I can't do it this time, *querida*. Maybe later. All the arrangements are made, and they don't include any Polaris cattle," Green said, trying to put her off.

"Green, it is only ten cows, and it can be easily done if you really wanted to, and I would be most grateful," she said, her eyes twinkling merrily.

Green argued with her for quite a spell, not wanting to introduce anything new into a set deal, but eventually he gave in.

Over breakfast the next day, Green told Sol Weeks to pick up the little bunch of cows that stayed by the cottonwood motte on the river and take them to Columbus. Sol said he knew the bunch and would truck them to Columbus, if he could find a truck.

"Okay, Sol, just see to it. Mercedes and I had quite a tussle over it, but she won, like always. Don't send any that have a calf."

"Well, they are sure a nice little bunch, and I hate to lose them. Did you ask your dad to send some more heifers?" asked Sol.

"Yes, but I think I'll try to get a bunch more, now that Mercedes has stuck her oar in. She's liable to try to get the whole bunch, and we'll never get a cow herd started here," said Green.

"Now, boss, don't worry. We all lose battles to the ladies. We'll get our cows started here soon enough," reassured Sol.

Two days later Amos Speed, the steer buyer, came, and Green spent the whole day showing the cattle. Although Green had not known Speed, he knew of the firm he represented. In the interim since their first meeting, Green had called Ben Davidson in St. Louis to check him out, and Ben gave him a clean bill of health. Green told him to come down if he could, and Ben said he would try.

Speed liked the cattle. They talked about price and delivery and settled on 18¾ cents per pound. There were about 300 carloads of cattle, and Speed said he would like to get them in three deliveries.

"That's fine, Amos. I'll want $15 per head down, and since I do the biggest part of my banking in St. Louis, I'll just get my bank to draw on yours on each shipping day. I'll wire them the figures, and they can draw a draft, and you can wire your bank to honor it. Sound okay?"

"You know, Green, I've heard about the Dunigans ever since I was a tad, but I had never dealt with any of you. I had been told that your deals were always buttoned up and neat as a pin. Now I can see that what I was told was the whole truth. I couldn't ask for anything better. You want me to write up the contract, or will you?" asked Speed.

"Well, I have a kind of standard contract that I use, and I can have it by morning."

"It's a pleasure doing business with a professional."

At the house, Green introduced Speed to Mercedes and showed him to a bedroom upstairs.

"Wash up and come on down and we'll have a drink before we eat," Green said.

Their guest came down the stairs and they had a drink or two before sitting down to a lovely dinner. Mercedes used her good china and silver, as they had not had a houseguest in a long while. Mercedes, in a stunning red dress and jewelry, looked like a queen. Amos Speed was suitably impressed. After they were settled with cigars and brandy in the parlor, Mercedes made an excuse and left them alone.

Speed asked, "What bank do you use in St. Louis, Green?"

"The National. Ben Davidson has been my banker for twelve or fifteen years. Do you know him?"

"Yes, I do. Not well, but I know him. He's good at financing cattle deals."

"I was his first cattle customer. My father had dealt with Gerard Alton for thirty years, so when I needed some money, naturally that's where I went. Ben had just started with the bank then," Green related.

"Well, it's a small world. Ben's folks had a ranch close to my folks in the sand hills. I've known him a long time."

"Amos, I'll have the contract ready first thing in the morning. What time you want me to call you?"

"Whenever you get up, Green. I'm usually awake before day, so I'll be waiting."

Just before dawn broke, Green knocked on Amos Speed's door. They walked over to the cookshack for hot boiled coffee and breakfast.

Green handed Speed the contract he had drawn up to cover the sale. Speed looked it over, agreed with its provisions, and signed it. He gave Green a check for $100,000 to seal the deal, as was normal practice in the cattle trade. Green then gave a copy of the contract to Sol Weeks, so he would know how the cattle were to be delivered.

Sol said, "Green, I pretty well understand the trade, but I also know you are not going to be here. Are you going to get anyone to help me, or am I on my own?"

"I can get Jimmy Berger to come up, if you want. He's a good weigh master and understands things, but you're still the boss till I get back," said Green.

"No problem, boss. Jimmy Berger would be a lot of help."

"Okay, I'll get him up here," said Green. "Amos, you going back to El Paso, or St. Louis?"

"I need to go back to St. Louis, Green. These big deals need some face-to-face explanation to the big augers, to settle them down."

"You can catch the S.P. at Roy at noon today. You'll join the Santa Fe up the line, but I don't think they'll have sleepers till you catch the train coming from Denver at La Junta," explained Green.

"I'll be all right. I've slept many a mile on those hard benches, and I expect I'll do more in the future. Such is steady fare in a trader's life."

"We'll leave about 10:30. I have to catch the 3:00 train back to El Paso myself," said Green.

Green had a lot of packing to do. He would go on to Herradura with the cow herd and wouldn't be back until the yearlings were being delivered. Mercedes decided to go with him, to secure the furniture and fixtures from Sam Ravel. Green liked the idea.

They were a bit late leaving for the train but got there in time to

290

put Amos on the noon northbound. Green and Mercedes got on the 3:00 southbound, and it was dark by the time they reached their house in El Paso. Everything was ready for them, since Mercedes had called the housekeeper from Roy. They had a late supper and went to bed.

The next day was spent in Sam Ravel's warehouses. Mercedes had a field day, buying rugs, beds, chairs and tables, curtains, even kitchen utensils and a set of china. She looked at some paintings but bought none, as they were too "French" for her. All of the furniture was the heavy, Spanish colonial style, and all the rugs were oriental. She pretty well filled the list that Green had given her and even found enough doors to close all the rooms in the house. Most of the items were in Juárez warehouses, and what wasn't could be gotten across. Green asked her to tag all of it, as to where it went, after she came back to El Paso in September. In the meantime she would look her list over, and if she needed anything else she could get it then. Sam was very courteous about everything, and told her it would be ready to be tagged when she got back. The whole list came to $12,000, and Mercedes gave him a check for $15,000, saying that was more like the time value. Sam accepted her assessment, thinking to himself that it couldn't be replaced for $50,000, but revolutions usually didn't come more than once in a lifetime.

When they got back to the house, there was a message from Jimmy Berger, who invited them to dinner at a fancy restaurant downtown. Mercedes called Jimmy and confirmed the date, to meet him at the Normandie restaurant at 7:00.

Green and Mercedes bathed and dressed, and caught a jitney cab about 6:45. As they approached downtown, the traffic was tied up. Traffic jams in El Paso were pretty rare, and as a policeman walked by, Green asked, "What's the trouble, officer?"

The cop, a red-faced Irishman, responded, "'Tis the temperance ladies, bless them, havin' their parade," he answered. "More and more. It looks like they're going to try to dry up the country while our brave boys are off fightin' the Huns. I don't think the boys are goin' to like it," he replied.

The traffic started to move a bit later, but it was 7:30 before they got to the Normandie. As Mercedes walked into the dining room, all eyes were turned to her. Green marveled at how she had become more beautiful after each child.

Jimmy rose to greet them, seated Mercedes, and said, "Green, you'd better start packing a gun. Men are liable to try to kill you just for a chance to court your wife."

Mercedes blushed. "It wouldn't do them much good. If anyone killed Green, I would have them taken to Mexico and staked out over an ant hill," she said evenly, and Jimmy knew she meant every word.

"What a woman," he said to himself.

They ordered dinner, Green having a steak and Mercedes some fish, but Jimmy ordered snails and lamb chops, as well as a bottle of wine.

Green chuckled and said, "That's quite an order for a feller that grew up on jack rabbit and hominy."

"You're sure right about that, Green, but this French food sure beats it," said Jimmy, grinning.

"Yeah, the French have never had decent meat, so they sauce everything up, and the result is fine. Me, I like food that is good to start with, minus all the sauces," Green said.

They had a lovely dinner, and finished off with dessert and coffee.

Over coffee, Green asked, "Jimmy, when the cattle from Mexico get in, will you handle them for me? I want all the older steers, the twos and older, to go to my brother Jack at Cotulla, and just sell the yearlings. I would do it, but I'm afraid I'm going to be busy moving everything south. So if you take care of the incoming cattle, I sure would appreciate it."

"I'll be glad to, Green. When do you expect them?"

"About three weeks ... at Columbus."

"I'll take care of it, Green," he said.

"Good. Now I need one other favor, Jimmy. I've sold my yearlings for delivery, starting September 20. I don't think I'll be back by then, so could you go up and help Sol with the delivery until I get back? I think he can do it all right, but he feels like he needs help."

"I got nothing going around that time. I've got some big steers coming in at Nogales and Agua Prieta about the end of October, but I'll be free, and I'm glad to do it."

"Thanks a lot, Jimmy. I'll be back before it's over. Sol will really feel a lot better, and so will I. I'll send you a copy of the contract over in the morning," Green said as everyone rose to leave.

292

He spent the next two days finding out about U.S. and Mexico Army patrol schedules and what routes to avoid. On September 12 he loaded five horses on the train for Columbus and got aboard himself. Unloading at Columbus he rode to Jimmy Berger's pasture to look at his cattle before the Mexican inspection the following day.

CHAPTER 52

Ascensión, Chihuahua / September 15, 1917

reen met Cesar Dominguez as they drove the herd from the railroad to the lake there, to water the cattle. Cesar had eight men with him from Herradura, and the herd of about 1,000 steers handled easily. Cesar's outfit was ready for the trail, so after watering the steers, they were headed out to Columbus. It was a short drive, and they arrived early on September 17. Jimmy Berger was there to receive them, and Green sent Cesar and his bunch to the southbound herd, which had already passed customs and were on the Mexican side. Green helped Berger sort the steers for a while and asked, when no one was listening, when Praxides and the wagons had left.

"About 11:00 last night, Green. It seemed about the best time to miss all the patrols, and he must have, because there's been no commotion about it here."

"Well, that's good. It'll put him joining us tonight, I guess. By the way, Jimmy, who got the yearlings?" Green asked.

"Sold them to the CS. Got twenty-three and a half cents for them," he said, smiling.

"Good sale. Jimmy, I'll be gone until about the first of October, but I'll get Praxides back as soon as I can. I'm sorry to use him so, but there isn't much going on in California now anyway. I'll see you at Roy as soon as I can get there."

"Good luck, Green." Jimmy waved goodbye.

Green joined his herd and put it on the trail. Praxides Balbuena had sent three men to help, making a total of thirteen horsemen, including Green. They made good time and were about twelve miles south of Columbus when they bedded the herd down at 7:00. Green had been seeing a small dust cloud to the west from about 3:00 on. He guessed it was Praxides' wagons, dragging brush to cover their tracks. Sure enough, the wagons arrived about 9:30 and wanted supper, which Green had saved for them.

"No trouble, Praxides?" asked Green.

"No, Señor. I don't think anyone even saw our tracks. They may have seen our dust, but there is always dust. I'm gonna look up our back trail after I finish, just to make sure. I led all our spare horses behind, so it would look like someone moving horses. As far as I saw, there wasn't a trace of wheels, and let me tell you, Verde, those wagons are heavy. No problem now. We'll go in front, and the herd will wipe out our tracks."

"Sounds good. I won't wait up for you," said Green, yawning.

All the wagons moved ahead of the herd as they left for Ascensión at daybreak. They arrived late the next day and put the herd on water at the lake. Green rode in to make sure about the train. They waited for it all the next day, but it did not arrive until after nightfall. It was late on the 19th that they finally got everything loaded and left for Parral. From Parral, it was three days to Herradura.

Green gave explicit instructions to Cesar, Praxides, and old Mercadio about where to put the cattle, supplies, and arms, and gave orders to Praxides to take the wagons back to Parral and pick up the furnishings that Mercedes had bought from Ravel. After that, he was free to leave, although he and his men were invited to join the growing number at Herradura. Green left the following day for Parral, and on to Roy.

While boarding the train at Parral, Green saw several crates from S. Ravel consigned to Herradura, so he spoke to the freight agent and told him to expect Praxides Balbuena to pick them up in the next few days. The freight agent was happy to know how to handle such a large shipment and thanked him. Green boarded the train bound for Juárez, and, on arriving, crossed to El Paso. He caught the train to Roy, arriving at Rancho Polaris just at dark on September 30.

As he entered the house, he was greeted by his sons, squealing delightedly at their father's return. Green gave them some toys he had picked up in Chihuahua, and they took them off to play. He then went into the kitchen, expecting to find Mercedes, but she wasn't there.

"Where is the señora?" he asked.

Maria Rincon, who was cooking, answered, "She is with the vaqueros, where she has been for the last two weeks, *patrón*."

Green turned to Juan Rincon, who was butler, gardener, plumber, and everything else in the house. "Juan, will you go down to the corral and invite Sol Weeks to eat with us? I need to visit with him. From the amount of food you are cooking, I would imagine Mr. Berger and Mr. Speed generally eat here at night?"

"*Sí*, Señor, and usually Mr. Weeks also. There is plenty," said Maria.

About fifteen minutes later, Mercedes came in, leading Jimmy Berger, Amos Speed, and Sol Weeks. She ran to Green and kissed him.

"Welcome home, *querido*," she said, smiling.

They all washed up and joined Green in a drink before supper.

"Well, how is the delivery going?" Green asked.

They all spoke. "Just fine, Green." Then they allowed Sol to elaborate, as it was his job to do so.

"Boss, we just finished shipping the second trainload, so 8,000 have left, and we can start tomorrow on the rest. But I was gonna let the boys have tomorrow and Sunday off, if it's all right with you. We've been working straight through, and our ponies are kinda wore down. Everything went fine, except we had to regather some of the steers. Fence got broke between the Gusting Pasture and the trap, and about 500 got loose. The train we just loaded was a day late, too, but we're still on schedule, and no sign of a norther. I told the men to wait around till I talked to you before they left the ranch, if you want to go ahead tomorrow," Sol informed him.

"Let 'em rest, Sol. A day in town will do them good. But we'll go straight through when we go back on Monday, and tell them to treat any ponies that need it before they leave."

Sol stepped out to tell the men, and Green asked, "Jimmy, what are they weighing?"

"Overall, 8,000 of them weighed net 786. They're pretty damn uniform, too," answered Jimmy.

"Suit you, Amos?" he asked Speed.

"To a tee, Green. I sorted the first delivery big and little, because I had sold them that way, but I didn't need to on today's shipment. They're all going back to Indiana, to stalk fields."

Green gazed at Mercedes, and she looked back, pixielike. She looked just like she had when he had brought her out of Mexico in 1913. Slender and lithe in her country clothes, she seemed more beautiful than ever.

Conchita came in to announce that supper was ready, and she began to corral the children to get them ready for bed. The adults all went into the dining room to eat a simple meal of fried steak, beans, squash, and biscuits.

All the men could see that Green was somewhat upset, and all guessed the reason. Each in his turn was lavish in his praise for Mercedes as a vaquero.

"Boss," Sol Weeks said, "you been holding back on me. The señora is just about the best I've ever seen around cattle—and I mean ever! I seen a lot of hands, but she is the best. She thinks like a cow brute."

Amos Speed chimed in. "Green, your wife knows more about moving cattle without stirring them up than anybody I ever saw."

Mercedes was eating up all the praise and silently laughing at Green. She knew what he was upset about. Green had figured out that she might be pregnant—and she was, about three months—but she wasn't showing. She knew there would be plenty of pillow talk that night, but for now, she was enjoying the compliments.

After finishing dinner and coffee, the men began going up to bed. Green told Sol that he wanted his and Mercedes' horses dropped off at the pens.

"I'll drive her and Amos over, and we'll help you pen the cattle, but we won't be there to help gather."

Sol looked at him mockingly, and said, "Boss, I don't know if we can gather 'em without our top hand."

"You'd better be able to, because she ain't gonna be there!" Green said, his composure eroding. Mercedes decided not to join in,

297

as Green did not think this whole thing funny. She followed him upstairs like an obedient wife.

When he had closed the bedroom door, Green turned on her. "Mercedes, what in hell are you trying to do? You're pregnant, aren't you? Are you trying to lose the baby?" he asked angrily.

"Calm down, *querida*. Yes, I am pregnant, about three months, and I visited the doctor and Mama Rosenda when I was in El Paso. I asked them specifically if riding would be harmful, and they both said that it wouldn't be," she explained.

"They thought you were talking about riding for an hour or so. Not all day for three weeks, running hard cattle work!"

"Mama Rosenda told me that I was carrying this child, as with all of them, easily and securely, and that she was amazed that I was such a good carrier. She told me that to cause me to abort I would probably have to be shot in the belly. Also, she told me that the old woman who taught her was still practicing in Parral, and that she would write to her to expect me. She said that she was the most revered and famous *curandera* in northern Mexico, and I can have the baby there with no worries."

"All right, but I want you to take it easier, starting tomorrow. You can quit showing off . . . I know you're good," he said.

"Green, I have never told you this because I didn't think it was that important, but just as Abel and Sulema Castro half raised you, I was taught in my childhood by a master. A man named Calixto Munoz was at Herradura when I was young, and he was an expert horseman, and my father chose him to teach me. He was a strange man in that he had learned his skills as a *gaucho* on the Argentine pampas, and had left there because of his involvement in some kind of rebellion. He knew ways to handle horses that I have never even heard of. His method of gentling a young horse is called *dominar*, and is practiced by the old-timers on the pampas. They hold the horse's head and talk gently to them, finally forcing them to lay down, and the trainer lays down on them, still talking after an hour or so. They both get up, and from that time on, the horse has complete confidence in the man, and will do anything that is asked of him. I can do this also, and did it with Minerva. Watch me work her tomorrow. My father let me work with this man for over five years, and he taught me all that he knew about horses and cattle. We tended 5,000 cows by ourselves during that time."

"You don't have to tell me about all that. I've seen you in action. All I want is for you not to extend yourself so much that you might miscarry," said Green gently.

"Don't worry, *mi amor*, I know my limitations, and I won't overtax myself."

Green drove Amos and Mercedes to the pens just after daylight. Amos waited at the scales, and Green and Mercedes rode out to help pen the steers.

Green didn't like to do any specific job at deliveries, so that he could watch the overall flow. It was going along well: Mercedes was cutting the steers into drafts of twenty for the scales, Jimmy and Amos were weighing them quickly, and Sol was getting them away from the scale and taking out any defective animals. Green paid particular attention to Mercedes' job, which was usually very difficult, as it was to start the steers moving, count twenty, and stop them. Usually one or two would get by and have to be cut back. Green rode up to where he could watch, and would count along with her. What was different was that her black filly, Minerva, was always facing the twenty-first steer, so she never had any trouble. Mercedes had imposed her rhythm on the steers. Green finally gave up trying to discover how she was doing it and went on to other chores.

The cattle were all weighed by two and then were turned out to water to await the 2,000 that would be weighed the next day. The defects were weighed back and subtracted from the good cattle, and the outfit was back at the cookshack for lunch by 3:30. After lunch, everyone scurried away to take a nap.

Green was almost asleep when Mercedes walked in.

"How did you like Minerva's counting, *mi patron?*" she asked.

"Don't try to tell me that. She's not counting ... you're signaling her when to move."

"She *does* count, Green. You watch her."

"No, Mercedes, you may not realize it, but you are signaling her when to move. I've watched horses that were supposed to think, and there was always a signal from the rider. I don't want to talk about it ... I'm trying to take a nap," Green stated firmly, rolling over and pulling up the sheet.

299

"Oh, *querido*, I want to talk to you. Don't go to sleep yet," Mercedes said sweetly.

She kissed the back of his shoulder and started touching him in sensitive spots. Unable to resist, he rolled over and took her in his arms.

The following day was pretty much the same, except that Green, just to be ornery, changed the draft from twenty to twenty-four, so he could see how Minerva reacted. She didn't miss a count, and Green proved, at least to himself, that Mercedes was, however imperceptibly, signaling her.

After the cattle were all weighed, they gathered steers weighed before and took them all to a trap adjacent to the railroad pens at Roy to turn the entire 4,000 loose. They left the horses in the pens, throwing them some hay, and everyone got to ride back to the ranch in the truck or Green's Ford.

The next morning, everyone returned and penned the cattle. They were early; the train was not due in until 9:00. It arrived on time, and they started loading. They broke for lunch cooked by the ranch camp cook and shared by the Polaris crew, the railroaders, and various visitors from town.

By 4:00 the cattle were all loaded, and the train left. Green and Amos Speed settled up the payment and wired the information to their respective banks. Amos stayed in town to catch a late northbound train. Everyone else returned to the ranch to get a good night's sleep.

Jimmy Berger went back to El Paso the next day, and the cow outfit was busy repairing tack and treating galls. Mercedes and Green were left pretty much to themselves for the rest of the week.

Mercedes was adamant about getting to Herradura soon. Green still feared for her safety but gave in. They made plans to spend the first two weeks in December there. She wanted to take Fito and Tom, but Green put his foot down.

"We have to get the place in shape first, *querida*. They will have plenty of time to see it and get to know it later."

The Dunigans moved back to El Paso the first week in December, to keep from getting marooned when the snow came. Roy was nearly deserted that time of the year anyway. Cattle were starting to move from Mexico, even though the numbers were small. It showed that a bit of normality was returning south of the river, and even though the numbers were small, the traffic kept Green busy.

One of the first things Green did after they moved back to El Paso was to cross to Juárez and visit his old friend, Hipolito Villa. Green informed him that he was going to take Mercedes to Herradura the coming month, and Hipolito looked troubled.

"Verde, you have been very lucky. Do not press it. There are a lot of outlaw gangs from everybody's army, not just the Northern Division, and some of them are pretty strong. I wouldn't take her now."

"You don't understand—but you should, Hipolito. Mercedes, when she makes her mind up, is going to do what she wants to. I want you to get word to Pancho that we are coming down, and we want him to come to see us. We'll be there from the third or fourth of December until the fifteenth. Will you send him that message?" Green asked.

"Of course I will, Verde, and Pancho will try to keep you safe. But he is not controlling Chihuahua as he did, and you must realize it."

"I do. Also, I'd like for you to get a message to Cesar Dominguez to meet us with four men and some horses in Parral on the second."

"Consider it done, Verde. And good luck."

CHAPTER 53

Herradura, Chihuahua / December 3, 1917

They had left El Paso on the first and spent a bit of time in Parral with Licenciado Saltos, signing probate and other papers. Only one small incident marred their trip. Between Chihuahua and Saucillo, a band of five outlaws had attacked the train, but the combined fire of the army guards and the passengers drove them off, with two of their members hit.

Mercedes frowned at the two cannons and the machine guns when they first rode into Herradura, but she didn't say anything. She was very disappointed with her first look at Herradura. Green had left the outside walls unpainted, to discourage *politicos* and bandits, and it still looked drab and spotted. However, when they got inside she brightened up, as a great deal of the repairs had been completed.

All the furnishings had come tagged with where she wanted them, but she spent the whole of the next day moving things around to suit herself. Green sent her some help but managed to be out of the way all day, looking at cattle with Cesar. He had noticed that the monk was still there, looking considerably less forlorn. He asked Cesar about him.

"Oh *sí*, Verde. He is still here, and he is holding masses. He even started teaching school. He is a most welcome addition to Herradura, but I don't think the church knows where he is," said Cesar.

"How many attend mass, and how many children go to the school?" Green asked.

"About twenty grown people and most all of the children attend the school and mass, also."

"Where does he eat, Cesar?"

"Mostly at the camp, but the families have him for dinner two or three times a week. As you can see, he is getting fat," said Cesar. "I allowed him to eat in the camp at first, and I believe he helps being here. If you don't think so, I will stop feeding him."

"No, Cesar, we will keep him here as long as he can stay. Herraduros need God's comfort like everyone else, no matter what the *politicos* say. Besides, we need a teacher. I hope he is a good one."

"I don't know about that, but I do know the children are learning to read and write, and also to cipher."

"Good. Let's try to keep him here."

The two of them rode to the vega, where the farmers had put in sixty-five acres of wheat. It was green and looked healthy.

"In the spring, they plan to plant about 250 acres of corn, fifty of beans, and some to squash, chiles, and onions," Cesar said. "With what they have ready, and about fifty acres we have been cutting hay off of, I think we will be well fed. Also, I have bought a load of goats, and one of sheep, but the people brought chickens, and some even brought sows. We brought in seven or eight good milking cows, but I think we need more. We feed them the hay we cut in the meadow and I purchased a little feed. There is enough milk for the children, but not really enough to make butter or cheese. We are really in good shape, considering we have only been here for six months."

"You certainly are. How much longer will the carpenters be here?" Green asked.

"They have about one month's more work, and they should be through. There is one thing we have not talked about ... We need a really good set of working pens, with a branding chute and a dipping vat, and maybe even a scale. We can build most of it out of what we have here, but it will need some cut lumber, concrete, and iron fittings. I would like to do it while they're here."

"I'm glad you mentioned that. I, too, want to have a good, big set of pens here, where we can do anything. I will draw up what I think we need, and you do the same, and we will work out how to lay it out," said Green, and continued, "Cesar, do any of the carpenters or plasterers know anything about electricity? If we had electricity, we could do all sorts of things here."

"I'll ask 'em, boss, but electricity is pretty rare outside of cities in Mexico," answered Cesar.

Green returned to the big house at 6:00. When he walked in, he was seized by a sense of deja vú. He expected to see Don Tacho and Doña Marisol at any minute. Mercedes had it looking so much like the old house that it was almost eerie. Only the ancestor portraits were missing, having been burned.

He heard some noise at the top of the stairs, and walked quickly over to see Mercedes in a lovely gown, regally descending the staircase.

"Ah, a handsome *caballero* come to call. Dinner will be ready soon," she said.

"How do you like your castle, *patrona*?"

"It is very nice. Almost as I remembered it," she answered.

They had dinner in the large dining room. The big table was lit by candlelight, and there was even wine. Mercedes had hidden some in the rugs from El Paso.

"It was ghostly coming in here, Mercedes. I expected to see your family coming in any minute. There are changes, but to me it is the old Herradura. I don't know how you did it, but it is just like the old place," Green said.

Mercedes replied, "I had only my memories and your measurements to go on, but I, like you, feel it is the same. All it really needs now is some pictures, or maybe better, some wall hangings—*serapes* and such."

"Whatever it needs, I'm sure you will find it." Green smiled.

The next day, as Green, Mercadio, and Cesar were talking in front of the big house, they looked over to see an apparition coming through the front gate. A young man, thin to emaciation, on a sway-backed horse, also thin to the point of weakness, had entered and was dismounting at the water trough. The three walked over.

Green said, "*Bienvenidos a Herradura, viajero.* Where do you come from?"

"I come from Durango. I have seen no one in two weeks since I was robbed by *bandidos* in the desert. I followed this horse for two days before I caught him at a waterhole, which saved both our lives," he said.

"You don't appear to have eaten much lately. Could we presume to ask you to eat with us?"

"You could indeed. I have had nothing but a few berries and some desert lizards."

"Come with us, then. Cesar, see that his mount is cared for," Green ordered, and they walked over to get a plate.

The stranger ate like a man who had never tasted food. On his third plate, he paused for a moment and said, "Please forgive my manners, señores. I was so hungry, but I am beginning to fill up. My name is Romulo Ortiz, and I am a painter of pictures. I was an engineer before the revolution, but I cannot find work, as I was a follower of Villa, and he is out of favor now."

Cesar began, "We know all about Francisco Villa. Most of the men of this *estancia* followed him. You may have heard of them. They were called Herraduros, after this place. Also, your host was the *gringo* Colonel Verde, of the artillery." He nodded at Green.

"Indeed, Colonel, I was a lieutenant in the third brigade under Colonel Bustamante. I was sent there when we went to Puebla and the *zapatistas* left us to be slaughtered by Obregón. I have heard many fine things of you, even though I came to the Division of the North late," said Ortiz.

"Señor Ortiz, are you looking for work, either as an engineer or as a painter?" asked Green.

"Very much so. I need to find some work to earn a living. I will work very cheap, because until five minutes ago, I had been starving for a long time!"

"Do you know anything about electricity?" queried Green.

"Yes, I had electrical engineering classes when I studied at the polytechnic before I joined the revolution. I am a civil, not electrical, engineer, but I can do simple electrical engineering."

"If I wanted to have electrical power here, in this compound, could you tell me how to do it, and what kind of a generator I would need?"

"I believe I could figure that. I would have to have a lot more information from you, but I assume it would be given."

305

"What about your painting? What kind of pictures do you make? Portraits, landscapes ... ?"

"Señor, most of the work that I have done is murals—painting walls. However, I can paint on canvas, anything you might want."

"You seem to be educated. Could you help teach in our school here?"

"Of course. I have never done it, but I took lots of liberal arts before I settled on engineering."

"Señor Ortiz, I think we can keep you busy here for some time, at least until Mexico becomes more stable and you want to get back to larger things. To begin with, we would provide you with food, clothing, and housing, and a small stipend, and we can go from there."

"I would very much like to start with what you have indicated I might be doing," said Ortiz.

Green turned to the old man and asked, "Mercadio, can we put this man in with our monk? I think there is enough room."

"Sí, Señor Verde, there is plenty of room. I will get a bed for him. Señor Ortiz, you will take your meals here."

"One more thing, Señor Ortiz, can you do portraits from old photographs? You see, the Herrera family portraits were wiped out by the revolution, but we have a few photographs. Could you work from them?" asked Green.

"Sí, I can do that, but I will probably need some help from people who knew them well."

"There are those people here, and they will help you. Mercadio, can you get Señor Ortiz some clean clothes?"

"Sí, and bedclothes and such."

"I have a few things to do, but I'll find you later this afternoon. Ask Mercadio for what you need," said Green, who walked off with Cesar.

The two of them went over the cattle counts for some time, Green informing Cesar that his plan was to raise the calves at Herradura, overwinter them there after fall weaning, then ship them to Polaris in the spring. They would summer them there and sell them in the fall. All of this assumed little or no income for Herradura for quite a while, but Mercedes' reserves should be sufficient to tide them over. The last herd had nearly replaced all the money they had spent so far.

306

Green went back to the big house to talk to his wife. She was sitting in a chair in the entry hall, staring at the blank walls.

"Mercedes, what are you doing?" he asked.

"I am looking at these blank walls, trying to decide what to do with them," she answered peevishly.

"I may have a solution. A starving artist wandered in today, and we fed him. I told him we could probably use him. I'll bring him over in a little while for you to talk to. He is also an engineer, and I thought maybe, if you think it would be good, we could look into putting in a generator to electrify this place . . . if you agree?"

"Green, what would I disagree with? If it is good, then we should do it. We do not have to burn candles just because Don Tacho did. Go ahead and bring this painter to me before I go blind looking at these bare walls!" she ordered.

Green sent for Ortiz and told him to find Mercedes at the big house.

Romulo pulled himself together and walked up to the big house. When he located Mercedes, he said, "Señora, my name is Romulo Ortiz. I am a painter of pictures. How can I serve you?"

"Come with me, Señor. I have many walls to cover . . ."

"Señora, some of the finest things done now in Mexico are murals, many with depictions of the revolution. Would you be interested in such art?"

"When the revolution started, Herradura was like heaven to me. There were six of us in my family, and we were very happy here. I am the only one left. The revolution took my family, my home, all my friends and neighbors. I have only my husband and my two sons, soon to be three, as you can see. No, *maestro*, I do not want pictures that remind me of all that I lost," she said, almost in tears.

"Do you have any old pictures of your family, of the old days here? I can work with them if you like. I could perhaps paint a history of Herradura in murals on these walls."

"We have some pictures of my family and some of Herradura before the revolution."

"Señora, let me have the pictures and I will try to sketch out the murals for you, and you can decide if you like them. I will need to talk to old Mercadio, and some of the others who remember Herradura from before the revolution. It will take about two weeks to make the sketches, and I will bring them to you."

"I believe that will do, *maestro.*"

Ortiz later conferred with Green about what he intended to do, as well as talking at length with Mercadio Gomez and some of the other old Herraduros. He spent a lot of time out on the range and around the river, looking at the more spectacular landscapes. He also had several long conferences with Green about engineering prospects.

"Señor Verde, I have been looking at the river, next to your fields, and I believe I have found a spot to put in a small dam that would serve two purposes. It would impound water to irrigate the fields you are now farming, and it could serve to power a generator for electricity. Of course, the larger the better—but the larger, the more it would cost. I believe that an earthen dam that would produce a lake on about 150 acres would be sufficient and would not really disturb the flow of the river. Of course, it would be necessary to wait until July or August, when the river is at its lowest flow, to do the work, but that would give you time to check the design and get the equipment ..."

"You're way ahead of me, Romulo. I was just thinking about lighting, but the idea of irrigation and generating by water passed me up by miles. Have you thought about cost?" asked Green.

"Yes. I estimate that the dam can be put in, and power brought to within the walls, for about 30,000 pesos, gold. Most of the dam would be dirt, but the generator emplacement and the overflow by-pass would have to be concrete."

"Yes, I can see that. Can you work up the plans for me so I can get them checked and find the generator equipment?" Green asked.

"Señor, I need surveying tools and drafting tools, of which I have none, nor do I think I can get them in Parral. They would have to come from Chihuahua or El Paso."

"Make up a list of them, and also the paints and stuff you will need for the big house, and I'll have them shipped out of El Paso this week."

"You will have it this afternoon," Ortiz said.

That night, Green told Mercedes of Ortiz's ideas, and his proposed electrification project for Herradura.

"Papa used to tell me about a place where he thought he could put a dam and have a lot of water for irrigation," Mercedes mused. "He took me there one time ... I wonder if it is the same place?"

"Why don't you get him to show you? It probably is. Has he shown you any sketches yet?" asked Green.

"Just a couple, and I think they are very nice. Scenes with cattle and vaqueros, and crops with farmers, and with sometimes Papa and Thomas in the background, and Vicente and Mama. I told him I didn't want anything about the revolution, but he found out about you and Villa and Angeles, and I think he will try to get me to approve it. Maybe I will, I don't know. I do think the murals may be spectacular here."

"Romulo says the dam, generator, and wiring to get electricity here will cost about 30,000 pesos, gold. The other expense would be wiring and fixtures here within the wall, and I don't know how much that would be."

"Green, I still have only spent, over income only, $70,000. We have plenty left. Go ahead with it. It will make it so pleasant here," said Mercedes.

CHAPTER 54

Herradura, Chihuahua / December 7, 1917

hree days later, Pancho Villa came to call. As he and seven guards rode through the gate, he yelled at Green, "*Hola, Verde!* You got this place looking good. You better watch out for those *politicos!*"

"*Jefe,* it's good to see you. Nobody has caught you yet," said Green.

"No, Verde, and nobody *will* catch Villa, unless that *cabrón* Obregón turns loose his *yaquis* on me. I think he keeps them around to scare Don Venus," Villa said, laughing.

"Cesar, show them where to put up their mounts, and take care of them." He turned to Villa. "Come on, *jefe.* Mercedes is here, wanting to see you."

"Are you so sure of that, Verde?" asked Villa, eyeing him closely.

"Of course ... All Mexico loves Pancho Villa!" retorted Green over his shoulder.

They ambled up to the house and, on entering, encountered Mercedes and Romulo Ortiz, looking at Ortiz's sketches.

Ortiz stood at attention. "General Villa, Romulo Ortiz, *a sus ordenes.*"

Villa nodded, then Mercedes curtsied and said, giggling, "*Mi general,* Mercedes Dunigan y Herrera, *a sus ordenes.*"

They all laughed. Ortiz explained he had been with the artillery sent to Zapata and massacred at Puebla by Obregón.

"I am very sorry," said Villa solemnly. "It was my worst mistake, and all my best men told me not to do it, including Colonel Verde and General Angeles, but the fault was mine."

"We were looking at some sketches that Señor Ortiz is making, to make murals on the walls here in the house. Would you like to see them?" Mercedes asked, and handed them to him.

Villa looked at them, and as tears welled up in his eyes, said, *"Que lastima, que familia valiente."*

Mercedes handed him the last sketch, which was the largest. He looked at Mercedes and asked, "You are going to have this painted on your wall?"

"Sí, mi general," she answered.

His eyes brightened. "Look, Verde, it's got you and me and Angeles. Even Bustamante and this young man, Ortiz."

Green looked at the sketch, which pictured a command conference he remembered just before the attack on Zacatecas. All the principles were in the foreground, with the Division of the North deploying in the background. It was a picture of glory, and it made Green feel proud.

"Señor Ortiz, somewhere you should paint in the *soldaderas*, being led by the best of all, Mercedes Herrera," Green suggested.

Mercedes blushed and Villa smiled.

Green had begun a subtle campaign around Herradura to establish titles, and it was succeeding. He wanted Mercedes to be called *patrona*, himself *jefe*, Ortiz to be addressed as *enginiero*, Cesar as *caporal*, the monk, Brother Anselmo, as *padre*, and old Mercadio as *gerente del sitio* (director). These were venerable titles, describing both function and hierarchy, and tended to stabilize the life around Herradura. Green thought that he had pulled off a neat trick, putting Mercedes at the head of everything but himself as the executive in charge. It seemed to be working, as everyone was cooperating.

Mercadio organized a *fiesta* that night, in honor of Villa. Several kids were slaughtered for an *asado*, or barbeque, long-silent guitars, violins, and trumpets were unearthed, a cache of potables was raided, and tequila, pulque and mescal flowed freely. There was dancing and singing at the Hacienda Herradura for the first time

311

since the departure of Vicente and Tomas Herrera for the revolution. Green and Villa danced with Mercedes and the other women. Years later, Mercedes would mark this *fiesta* as the real beginning of Herradura and the end of the revolution that had so affected it.

Green told Villa about the monk starting the school, and Ortiz's plan for irrigation and electrification.

Villa said, "Verde, you are doing what Don Venus will not do. You, a *gringo,* are helping Mexico in ways no Mexican *politico* will. You are now more of a Mexican patriot than any Mexican I know. You know, Verde, I have collected many books. I have saved them from places that we have burned and looted. Would you accept them as a gift for your school?"

"*Sí,* but only if you write on the fly leaf an inscription that reads, 'For the students—Francisco Villa!' Will you do that, please?"

"I will do it proudly, Verde," said Villa, "and I will send the books very soon."

Green signaled for Brother Anselmo.

"Padre, General Villa is going to send us many books for your school. Can you put them to good use?"

"Of course! And many, many thanks, *mi general,*" said the monk, and he walked away.

Villa grimaced and said, "Verde, you are trying me. I do not like to give things to priests. I would rather shoot them."

Green smiled. "I know that, *jefe,* but he is a teacher, doing good work, and you, of all people, must realize that Mexico will have the church, because the people believe, no matter what the *politicos* do or say."

"I suppose so, Verde, but the church has done many bad things to my country."

"The church is made of people, *jefe,* and people do bad things, just as you and I have."

Villa shrugged and went off to dance. Green and Mercedes watched the *fiesta* until after midnight, when they went to bed.

Villa and his men stayed on for two more days, resting their horses and generally enjoying themselves. Green and Villa rode around Herradura, and Green made pointed references where he thought the lines should be drawn when the new Herradura was patented. Villa took all this in and asked Green if he wanted to go with him and his men when they left for Parral. Green, sensing

312

safety in numbers, and also wanting to get Mercedes back to civilization, said yes, that he would, if he could get "La Patrona" to leave.

Mercedes really did not want to leave. The sole reason she wanted to stay was to watch over the painter's work, which Green knew risked a confrontation. And besides, Green said, "I have to get brushes and paints and a whole list of things from El Paso before he can start, and you need to see the doctor and Mama Rosenda now."

She agreed to go with Villa and his men to Parral after Green told her, "Mercedes, Villa is still the most feared man in Mexico. Anytime we are seen with him protects us and Herradura more, you understand?"

"*Sí*, Verde," she said quietly.

They arrived on December 18, just in time to prepare for Christmas. A few days after they got back, Green found a civil engineer, one Theodore Miller, and gave all of the information that Ortiz had compiled.

Miller asked, "This is quite a lot of information, Mr. Dunigan. What do you want me to do with it?"

"This work was done by an engineer in Mexico who hasn't been practicing lately, due to the revolution. I want you to check it and tell me if it is or isn't correct," said Green. He explained the whole project and asked Miller to evaluate it from a cost standpoint.

Miller nodded. "I believe I can do that from this information. One thing I haven't seen is the name of the river. What is it?"

"The Conchos River, which flows east out of the sierra in southeast Chihuahua, near Parral."

"I will look at it, Mr. Dunigan. Give me four or five days, and I will have an answer for you."

Green then went to Ravel's store to check in.

"How are things in Chihuahua, Colonel Verde?" asked Sam, extending his hand.

"All right ... we're getting the old place fixed up right smart," Green said, taking Sam Ravel's hand. "I got a new list of stuff for you to send down ..." He handed over a list of Ortiz's needs.

Ravel looked at the list and said, "I'll be damned. I just saw an invoice the other day. Where did I put it?" He turned, searching his desk. After a minute Sam took out a piece of paper and handed it to Green. It was an invoice from 1913, and was notated "as per order of Major Verde." It listed all the supplies that Ortiz wanted for surveying and drafting.

"I remember now, Sam. I ordered this stuff after Torreon, to be accurate with the guns. I had forgotten all about it, but I don't remember picking it up. Is it still here?"

"Yeah, it's out in the warehouse, still crated up. Transit and level, drafting board, and nearly everything else on the list. You can pay me the invoice price and I'll deliver it. These paints and things I don't have, but there is an artist supply house down the road, and I can get all of it here by tomorrow. This third list, I don't know much about. But from the three lists, it looks like you're going to dam up a river, build an electric generating plant, and paint pictures on the dam?"

"Close, Sam, close." Green told him all about Romulo Ortiz and the project, and the murals for the house.

"Sounds like a jack of all trades. Does he perform surgery, too?" asked Sam.

"No, but he helps teach in our school. I also have a monk who holds mass and teaches school. Sam, there are lots of people wandering around down there, refugees from the revolution who can do all sorts of things and will work for just room and board."

"Looks like you're trying to make Mexico over by yourself, Green. I know there was plenty of Herrera money, but you'll run out pretty soon trying to power and beautify all of Chihuahua."

"Don't worry, Sam, there's still plenty. I'm watching it," said Green. "Ship the two lists on down for me, will you? Mercedes and I are going to Refugio for Christmas with my family—the boys, too. We've got plenty of time on the generator, and that stuff, so just look around and price it, will you?"

"Sure, Green. I'll have something for you when you get back from Christmas."

Green called the engineer, Miller, and told him he would be back after New Year's, and they would get together then. Having tied up most of the loose ends, Green, Mercedes, the boys, and Conchita caught the morning eastbound, arriving in Refugio late on December 23.

Everyone in the family had already arrived: Jack and Lucinda, their children, as well as the Fosters, who were in residence permanently. The paterfamilias, John Dunigan, was the most effusive in greeting the grandsons he had never met, as were all the uncles, aunts, and cousins. This had little effect on Fito and Tom, but they were glad to be the center of attention.

Genuine affection and amity were the hallmarks of the Dunigan family reunion over Christmas. Jack and Green, having independent lives, were bit players to the Fosters, who had returned to the family home, and, according to John Dunigan, were contributing most of the well-being of the extended family. Certainly the ranch was running smoothly, and John was enjoying himself more, now that Bill and Kathleen were tending to most of the day-to-day management of the ranch.

Mercedes' advancing pregnancy did not allow her to go hunting, so John contented himself by taking his grandchildren. Jack, Green, and Bill did the same, but got in a lot of hunting with themselves. The only sour note of the reunion was the absence of Amanda, but everyone felt better after a memorial service at the ranch *campo santo*, which John Dunigan, and not a local priest, led.

For the past year, John, Jack, Green, and Bill had remained in close touch, through letters and the telephone, as had the ladies. If anything, Amanda's death had fostered a familial spirit that brought everyone closer together.

Mercedes, having lost all her kin, was an enthusiastic convert to the Celtic Dunigans and was the biggest promoter of family solidarity. It was with tears in her eyes that her child was to be born at Herradura in Chihuahua.

John Dunigan reassured her emphatically. "Honey, we don't care where it's born. It will be a Dunigan, and that's what's important."

Green and his family arrived back in El Paso on January 3, 1918. Not many cattle were arriving, so Green had time to explore his project in depth with Theodore Miller.

In his office, Theodore Miller explained, "What your information has shown me is that the project is probably feasible and cost effective, especially since it services two objectives—irrigation and electrification. It could be better if you had some other customers, for both products, but I estimate the costs at $50,000 gold, and that's assuming outside contractors for most of the work. Not having seen the site, I would say the biggest danger will always be the dam being taken out by a big flow of water. The flow estimates you gave me were quite large, and what little information I got about the river seemed to confirm them. What I think you have here is a major dam site, able to produce water and electricity several magnitudes over and above what you are thinking about. Of course, I would need to see the site to confirm that."

"You are probably right, Mr. Miller, and I have seen the site. The problem is that such a dam must, of necessity, be a governmental project, and Mexico cannot even feed itself at this time. What I really want to know is, if we do this, would it preclude doing a proper dam at some later date, under government auspices?" Green asked.

"I don't see that as a problem. It might even help. You could build a big dam on the base of your smaller one, or right in front of it. It shouldn't be a problem."

"Thank you very much, Mr. Miller. I am glad I came to you. And if I ever have any similar problems, I'll be back," said Green, leaving.

Mercedes had a pretty good idea, after conferring with Mama Rosenda, about when the baby would come. Even the doctor pretty well concurred with the estimated date, April 13. Green then proposed to leave March 20 for Herradura, and everyone acquiesced in that date. Arrangements had been made by Mama Rosenda to have her teacher, Señora Mondragon, to provide a *curandera* to go to Herradura with them. It was decided to take the boys and Conchita also.

Green tidied up affairs around El Paso, visiting Rancho Polaris and Sol Weeks, who went with him to see the steers he had on the desert in Arizona that were slated to go to Roy in May.

Having tended to his business, the Dunigans left for Parral on May 20, picking up Aurelia Gonzales, the midwife, and arriving at Herradura on March 25.

After depositing Mercedes, the midwife, and their baggage at the big house, Green went in search of Romulo Ortiz. Instead, he ran into Padre Anselmo.

"Tell me how your school is going, *padre*. Did you get some books from General Villa?"

"Oh yes, *jefe*. We got three large crates of books. I do not have room for all of them, and many of them are pertaining to subjects the children have no knowledge of, or any foreseeable need for. Many of them are very finely bound and are very old. I have taken the liberty of placing them in the library of the big house for now, and would like to leave them there, if you have no objection," he informed Green.

"That'll be satisfactory, *padre*. We'll keep them for you," Green said.

"Please don't call me *padre*. I am just a monk, not a priest. It is not proper," said Anselmo. "Call me Brother or Fray, please."

"I know that you are not a priest, but the people here call you *padre*. They feel better about it," said Green. "By the way, does your abbot, or bishop, know you are here? And if so, do they approve?"

"I have written to my superior and told him what I am doing, and he has answered, telling me to stay here, as I am in a safe place. But he agrees that I am overstepping the limits of my religious authorization. So I guess I am to stay here and do what I am doing, at least until it is safe."

"Is there anything you need, *padre*?"

"Well, *jefe*, we could use some paper tablets for the children to work on. Paper is kind of a precious commodity here."

"I'll have some sent in. Anything else?"

"There are a lot of things, but we can make do with what we have," answered Anselmo.

"Make a list of what you might need, if you could have everything you want. We will get those things that are most necessary as money becomes available. All right?"

Anselmo nodded and went on his way. Watching him, Green made a mental note to get material so he could wear a decent robe. His was badly tattered.

Green found Ortiz at the blacksmith's shop, beating on some red-hot iron.

"*Jefe*, I am glad to see you. Did you and *la patrona* have a good trip?"

"Yes, we did, *enginiero*. How is everything going? Did you get the things I sent down, the surveyor and drafting equipment?

"*Sí*, and I have put them to good use. My original setting and figures are still valid, but I have proved up my original calculation."

"Romulo, I had an engineer in El Paso check your work. He told me it was good. He also told me that the site could be used for a major dam. I asked if this structure would preclude putting a big dam there and he said no, that the big dam could be put right on top of it. I brought his report, and I'll give it to you tomorrow when I get unpacked."

"I think that this site could be for a major dam, *jefe*, one that

317

could provide much power and water for several thousand acres, but I did not think a private landowner would want to build such a structure. Those are usually reserved for governments. However, our dam, as designed, would not interfere with such a project, should it be undertaken in the future. As it is, the dam could probably supply water for 700 to 800 more acres than you are planning to farm. It might be a good selling point to keep all the old vega, renting it out to some groups of farmers, or maybe even like an *ejido*. Anyway, I'd really like to see the report, because the river flow is dwindling and I think we can start work within two months. That's what I'm doing here, designing some of the center structure that will control the flow," explained Ortiz.

"I'll get you that report in the morning, Romulo," said Green, as he saw Cesar crossing the yard.

Green had a brief chat with Cesar, who reported on the cattle and related the histories of some new families that had come to Herradura since Green had been there. Cesar had built the working pens he and Green wanted, and had finished most of the fencing for the traps they would need. They both knew it would be a year before the cattle started really producing, so they had time to get ready. Cesar had bought a few cows from nearby owners or traders—but less than 400, so they still needed more. It would be quite a while before they were fully stocked.

The big house, built in the Spanish colonial style, had wide verandas all around and thick stone walls, so that it was cool, even in the hot summertime. Now, in late spring, it was extremely pleasant, with cool breezes wafting lightly through the house. Ortiz had been busy decorating the walls, and Green studied the murals closely. There were four murals in the entry hall and parlor, scenes from pastoral life on pre-revolution Herradura. Green recognized the images, not only of Don Tacho, Doña Marisol, Vicente and Tomas, but of many vaqueros and others who would not return from the revolution. Mercedes must have had many photographs, or perhaps Ortiz remembered them from the Division of the North. However he did it, Green thought Ortiz's representations were attractive and representative.

Mercedes entered the room and asked, "How do you like them, Green?"

"I like them, and I like the idea of murals instead of paintings and portraits. I think that it is more Mexican, and it gives more life to the people depicted, as well as warmth and a sense of history to this house."

"Have you seen the big one upstairs, the one about the revolution?" she asked.

"No, did you allow one?"

"Yes, and I like what he did. It ties Herradura to the revolution, and it was certainly a part. Come, I will show you," and she took him upstairs.

They mounted the circular staircase, and as they turned on the stairs, the long wall at the top came into view. It was nearly completely covered by the mural, painted in the vibrant colors of native Mexican art, and was dominated in the middle by the image of Villa on his famed mare, Siete Leguas. Studying it, Green thought it depicted the deployment of the Division of the North before Zacatecas. Angeles, Medina, Vicente and Tomas, and even Green himself were in it, and on one flank, in the van of the *soldaderas,* was Mercedes. Green thought it wonderful.

"What do you think, *querida?*" he asked, unsure of her reaction.

"I like it very much. As you know, I did not want to be reminded of that war, but Romulo persuaded me that the revolution was very much a major part of our history, and I allowed it. I think it really is very good."

"Do you like the others?" asked Green.

"Yes, I like them even better, for they remind me of the good years. He told me he wanted to do three more, and I told him to go ahead. After he is finished, I want you to send word to Villa. I think he will like it—particularly the picture of Siete Leguas."

Mercedes was very active in the next five days, inspecting and ordering improvements done. But after about two weeks, she quit leaving the house. She felt her time was near, and although she didn't take to her bed, she stayed close to Aurelia Gonzales, the *curandera.*

Green was spending a lot of time out on the farther reaches of the ranch. Grass was high, and the cattle were fat. Many of the cows he had brought in had calved, and most were heavy with calf. He would have some production this year.

In his mind's eye, he could see waterings in many places, but they would have to be wells, and a few tanks, but mostly wells powered by windmills. He didn't know how deep the water was on Herradura, so he would have to investigate. There was only one well on the whole place, in the compound, and it was only about 150 feet deep. But that well could be feeding out of the river. He made up his mind to seek advice in Parral.

Juan Verde Dunigan y Herrera was born on April 13, 1918. Mercedes had an easy delivery, although the baby was about the same size as Tom. To Green, birthings were now old hat, so he just sat around and drank good cognac and smoked a cigar until the *curandera* told him he could enter the room. Mercedes looked beautiful as always, and he kissed her.

"How do you like your son, Verde?"

"He is fine, just like the other hooligans. He will make a good vaquero."

The baby was christened three weeks later at the Herradura chapel by Padre Anselmo, and the service was followed by a *fiesta* that night. Villa found out about it and arrived for the *fiesta* but not for the christening. The rumor was that he still shot priests on sight, so Padre Anselmo kept an eye on him until he left the following day. Villa brought the baby a present: a magnificent black stallion, four years old, said to be a full brother to the famed Siete Leguas.

A week later, Green packed everyone up to go to El Paso and on to Roy. In Chihuahua, Green found a man who knew something about water. The geologist, Pedro Regalardo, told Green that generally, around the Conchos River, wells within two miles of the river found water at 120 to 150 feet. Farther away, there was an artesian sand that could be tapped about 650 feet, but it would flow without a pump. Green was ecstatic. He inquired about well drillers.

Regalardo said, "Used to be one here and one in Parral. The one here was killed, but I don't know about the one in Parral. They were both cable tool drillers, and their rigs were pretty well used up. You'll probably have better luck looking around Tampico, in the oil fields."

On arriving in El Paso, Mercedes, Conchita, and the children went directly to Roy, but Green stayed in El Paso to finalize orders for the equipment needed for the dam and the generating plant. He and Sam then went to the customs pens to find Jimmy Berger.

Jimmy had just finished sorting five carloads of steers for

California. He turned to Praxides Balbuena and said, "Send these to Carver at Brawley. Can they go out today?"

"No. No cars until tomorrow, and maybe not then," said one of the railroad men.

"Well, just keep them here until you can load them, Praxides," ordered Jimmy.

Praxides nodded, waved at Green, and ran the steers down the alley, to a pen with some feed in it.

"How's it been going, Jimmy? You getting many cattle?"

"Some, but not enough. I still have to fill your brother's order for Cotulla. Why don't you stir them up down there, Green?"

"They are bringing out everything that can get out. You know every army down there was financing themselves with stolen cattle. It's probably a good thing, too. If they hadn't come up we'd have been short, as much meat as is being sent to England and France for that war."

Green found a letter for him when he arrived home. It was postmarked March 12, 1918, A.P.O. Europe. The return address read: "Gy/Sgt. E. De La Garza, 1st Marine Brigade, 2nd Division, A.E.F."

Green opened and read it as fast as he could. Etienne's script was almost illegible, but he got through it. Etienne explained what had been going on in Europe these past months, how the American units had been bloodied piecemeal by inserting them in French formations all last summer through January. Then he told how Pershing had finally formed them back into U.S. formations, and under his command, just in time to meet the big German offensive. Etienne was effusive in his praise of the American troops, particularly the Marines.

He wrote, "We held a forest against the Germans so long that the French named the woods for the Marine Brigade."

His long letter ended on a plaintive note: "I think this will be my last war, old friend. I'm gonna retire when I get home. You got something I can do out west? I don't want to go back to the bayous. Your old comrade, Etienne."

Green was delighted to hear from his old friend and wrote him a letter telling him to come on back, as he had the perfect place for him. Green had in mind the post of major-domo at Herradura.

CHAPTER 55

Herradura, Chihuahua / July 17, 1918

At the dam site, work was going along at a furious pace. The river, as always at this time of the year, was down to a trickle, about three feet wide and five inches deep. The earthen part of the dam, built from both sides reaching for the center, was nearly finished. Fifteen teams of small-footed Spanish mules and *fresnos,* dirt buggies, were carrying dirt in and packing as they came away. They were working on a small dam that would hold the flow while the dam center, mostly steel and concrete with the gates and generator, was emplaced.

Ortiz had the whole countryside working on the dam. It looked like an anthill. Green knew that it all had to be done by muscle and hands, and it was a race against time to hold the river flow until the center of the dam was in place. Five small cement mixers were going, and about twenty wheelbarrows waiting, plus all the *fresnos,* to carry the cement to the dam. As the framework was settled into the trenches for it, the cement was hurriedly poured, in a race against the rising water behind the temporary dam. Romulo Ortiz was confident he would win the race, but Green was skeptical; however, Green never dreamed Ortiz could recruit the workers that were there.

Ortiz was everywhere. He would let about ten men rest at a time but kept rotating them. No one stopped to eat, and about 3:00 P.M. Green rode back to the cookshack to have the cooks prepare a big meal for everyone about dark.

When Green got back to the dam, at 7:00 P.M., it was still a beehive. He saw that they still had two feet on the mini dam. Just before the last light of the day, Ortiz cut off the cement mixing, and the last work was done by lantern. The water had only risen about two inches.

Green asked, "All finished, Romulo?"

"*Sí, jefe*. It is built. We will have to remove the forms tomorrow, but it is done," he said proudly.

"I didn't think you'd make it. Where'd all these people come from?"

"They are always here. I just called them out of the hills. You can always get them if there is something worthwhile being done. I have promised them a *fiesta,* and that is what they have come for. Also, they are curious to see if it will work. If it does, it is the first irrigation in this part of Mexico."

"I told the cooks to be ready for a big crowd, and they were already busy. But did they know how many are to be fed?"

"*Sí, jefe,* I had already told them. And I got plenty to drink. It's liable to last all night. I'll be up all night, checking to see if it holds—but it will hold," stated Romulo. "I feel so proud of myself, and for you, and all Herradura. Do you know, I even had all vaqueros working there, with their hands!"

"Romulo, I too feel proud, but mostly of you. It was always yours to do or not to do," said Green quietly.

There was eating and drinking, singing and dancing all night long. At one point, Green heard the verse from "La Cucaracha" about himself, the same one he had heard at his wedding. Green left after midnight, but the party was still going strong.

Green could never stay in bed after daybreak, but today was special. After a cup of old coffee, he saddled his horse to see the dam. Picking his way out of the compound, he had to dodge many sleeping bodies left over from the night before.

Romulo Ortiz was already there, with a few men, removing the

323

forms from the inside of the dam. He said, "I'll leave the outside forms on for another day, but it seems to be strong enough. I mixed it fairly dry."

"Well, the little dam is still holding, but not by much. It'll overflow by noon. We'll probably know then," said Green.

The dam held. And by September, they had finished digging the canals, so that they could water the wheat crop to bring it up. The dam did not fill up until the following spring, during the runoff. The work of electrification of Herradura was progressing but wasn't quite finished.

One day Green stopped Ortiz on his rounds and said, "Romulo, I owe you something. You have done marvelous work, and I have paid you a pittance. I have not been fair to you."

"*Jefe,* remember, I arrived here destitute, without hope of advancement. You took me in and gave me a chance to practice my engineering and my painting, to hone my skills. There is no work for a man like me, yet you have fed and clothed me. This dam, and the murals—people will hear about them and see them, and I will have plenty of jobs, either from the government or from individuals, who see what you have done. I do not plan to stay here forever, and I will move on when they start to do things again in Mexico. But for now, my life is probably better than any practicing engineer in Mexico. Don't think you are not giving for value received." He turned to another subject. "*Jefe,* when we finish with the wiring, Padre Anselmo wants me to do a mural of the crucifixion in the chapel. Can I do it?"

"Sure, do it. And if you want to do them anywhere else, just go ahead. Just use your judgment. Don't put murals on the milking shed. When you get free, I want to do some surveying. I'll tell you about it tonight. Come to supper."

"I would be honored," replied Ortiz.

He and Green ate a quiet supper and talked about the dam and other projects. Green told him about Villa's promise on Herradura and asked Ortiz to survey the half Green thought they would retain, also about locating fences where Green thought they should be. They also talked about water, and Ortiz was informed of what the geologist in Chihuahua thought. In talking and poring over old maps of Don Tacho's, Green gave Ortiz the outlines of his future plan for Herradura.

Ortiz was delighted. He would be drawing a master plan for the property, and he had a lot of ideas. Green was skeptical about a lot of them, but kept quiet. Romulo Ortiz was a well-directed and talented man. If his plan was too idealistic or grandiose, Green still had his veto: the financing. Green figured to let Ortiz have his head; Green's hands were still on the bridle reins.

The plans to bring Etienne down as major-domo were discussed, and Ortiz was positive. He told Green that whenever Mexico became organized again, and commerce began to be normal, that he would go. But, as of now, he would remain as a major participant in the improvements at Herradura.

Green stayed around for several days, checking on cattle. Their numbers were rising faster than he had thought they would because Cesar Dominguez had bought quite a few cows from traders, and probably thieves and neighbors. The cow herd was approaching 4,000. Green told Cesar to slow down and only buy the best. He said to be on the lookout for calves, to bring in the fall, that he could summer at Roy.

Green left the next day for Roy, after looking again at the dam. Ortiz was seeding it with grass to prevent erosion. Water was barely covering the foot of the dam, but there was no leakage. He bid him goodbye, and rode off.

On his way to Roy, Green stopped off in El Paso and ran into Amos Speed, who inquired about his yearlings.

"Amos, from what I hear, they're going to be lighter this year, as it has been dry. But if you want to contract them, give me a figure and come up to look."

"Green, I'll give you a dollar and a quarter more than I gave last year," he said.

"Come on up next week, Amos, and we'll have a look. I'll have had time to feel the market by then."

"I'll be up next Wednesday night."

Green went to find Sam Ravel. He and Ravel talked about well drilling, which Sam didn't know much about. "Why do you want to know about wells, Green? You think there's oil at Herradura?" Sam asked.

"No, Sam, I'm thinking about how I could carry about 2,000 more cows down there, if there was plenty of water. I was told water wasn't too deep close to the river, but farther out there was an artesian sand about 600-700 feet deep. There isn't anyone around down there, but they talked about drillers around Tampico, working in the oil fields. I just thought you might know."

Sam Ravel, as Green knew, hated to admit ignorance on any subject, so when he said he would find out more, Green knew he would investigate.

Green spent a day on the stockyards talking with the traders, including Jimmy Berger. The consensus was that yearlings were selling about steady with last fall, but there was some news of higher contracts for fall. He decided that Speed was bidding on the market, and he would sell them.

Green was happy to be back. Fito and Tom toddled to him and hugged him, and Juan smiled from his crib. Mercedes was overjoyed that he was home.

Fito was walking and talking, mostly in Spanish. Tom was walking and crawling and making noises, and Juan just smiled. Mercedes wanted to hear about all the things happening at Herradura, and Green filled her in. She had taken care of all the legal work, and Juan had dual citizenship, in Mexico and the United States.

Amos Speed arrived, saw the cattle, and bought them for September delivery. They both thought the cattle would weigh about thirty pounds a head lighter, so the price was fair. Green took a check in return for the contract.

The summer passed quickly. In September the yearlings were shipped, and the Dunigans, all of them, including Conchita, went to Herradura.

On the way from Parral, Green said to Mercedes, "I believe I'd better get an automobile for down here. It's a long ride from Parral, and I believe a car could drive over these roads. They're not bad, and it'd save a lot of time."

Mercedes' eyes narrowed as she spoke. "Gringo, we have plenty of time. In Mexico, time is nothing, and you should start realizing it. Doing it this way we can see the country better. No, I do not want a car."

"You're the *patrona*. But maybe a truck?" Green ventured.

"No, no, no. I want no vile-smelling car messing up the pure clean air. We got along for a hundred years without them, and we do not need them now." La Patrona had spoken.

Green shut up. He liked the idea of not running pell-mell to every new device. The two-day ride from Parral to Herradura was indeed always pleasant and invigorating. If La Patrona didn't want cars and trucks, he could get along without them.

The lights were working at Herradura when they arrived, and the entire compound blazed at night. Mercedes was not quite sure this was progress, but she was overjoyed with water pressure in the big house. Once they were settled, Green set about choosing some mounts for Mercedes, and found an old gentle one that Fito could learn on. He also designated a vaquero to act as groom and assistant. One of the older Herraduros, Narciso Cantu, was chosen. He also told Cesar Dominguez to be on the lookout for a small horse, maybe a Shetland or Welsh pony, that Fito could ride when he tired of the old plug chosen as his first mount.

The news they got from an occasional newspaper or from their radio set indicated that the war in Europe was winding down. Green was anxious, for he needed Etienne at Herradura more than ever.

The family stayed there most of the winter and spring, leaving only for their annual reunion at Refugio for Christmas. They went north to Roy when the Herradura yearling moved, and that was in May. Green stocked the New Mexico ranch about 80 percent with cattle from Herradura, either raised there or bought from neighbors. He was headed in the right direction, and probably could integrate the two operations in the next two years.

Carranza was still in charge of Mexico, but the government was shaky. Obregón was his main strength, and in April 1919 they managed to trick Zapata into a meeting and were able to assassinate him. That left only Villa still alive—but out of the government. There was talk of friction between Obregón and Carranza, and, as Pablo Gonzales was already gone, this would take away Carranza's control.

In July, Mercedes announced to Green that she was going to have another baby, pretty close to the end of the year. This made everyone happy, but she added, "Green, I think we have a big enough family now, don't you?"

"Yes, my love, four is enough. I just hope this one is a girl."

"Maybe *la curandera* Avila can tell us. I'll stop and see her in El Paso when we go south," said Mercedes.

"I'll order a buggy for you from Parral to the ranch," said Green, smirking.

"It'll still be easier than riding a car, Gringo," she spat back.

Green figured that the projected date of the birth would preclude them from spending Christmas at the homeplace in Refugio, so he invited Jack and his family, the Fosters, and his father to come down in October. He wanted to show them Herradura. He also invited Sol Weeks and Jimmy Berger at the same time. Green thought he might organize a bear hunt or a hunt for bighorn sheep to entertain them.

They arrived on October 12 and stayed for ten days. There were *fiestas* and *asados,* deer, bear, and sheep hunts, *charreadas* and rodeos. Mercedes, Kathleen, and Lucinda, joined by John Dunigan most of the time, spent their time in the compound, admiring the big house with its murals, the chapel, and the other buildings, but they reserved one day for a picnic by the lake, which was nearly full. They were joined there by the men. Jack got a bear, and Bill Foster killed a desert bighorn, but all of them bagged at least one mule deer. John Dunigan got chummy with Cesar, Sol, and Jimmy Berger, and they spent a lot of time with the cattle.

It was a joyous time. The Herraduros melded with clan Dunigan, and would hold together for years.

Mercedes dropped one more jewel into the bowl. She told them that the *curandera,* who had always been right, forecast the birth of a girl this time. Mercedes announced that she would be named Amanda.

Amanda Marisol Dunigan H. arrived at precisely 2:00 the morning of December 21. Green was deeply delighted as he gazed upon his daughter. Weighing only six and a quarter pounds, she was petite, as compared to the birth weight of his male children.

The community of Herradura held a *fiesta* at the christening of Amanda six weeks later, and all came to the chapel to see the little girl. She was allowed to attend the *fiesta* for only a short while, until bedtime. Villa, although invited, did not come. He sent his regrets and a silver cross and chain. It was a beautiful large cross, and very old, sixteenth or seventeenth century. Another spoil of war, no doubt.

Two weeks after the arrival of the new year, 1920, a letter came from Ravel in El Paso. It said that Etienne de la Garza had arrived in El Paso, and Ravel had moved him into Green's house to wait.

Green left immediately to bring his friend down. He found Etienne looking much the same, but with a haunted look that had not been there before. He also had a limp, from a bayonet wound not fully healed.

Etienne explained. "A week before the war was over, we were attacking, east of the Meuse River. The Germans were scraping the bottom of the barrel, as far as men go, and an old German got his bayonet through my leg. He couldn't pull it out, and I cut his whole damn head off. My knife was sharp. It tore up my thigh some, but it'll be all right in a couple of months. I can do anything that needs doing.

"Green, it was a hard war," he continued. "Even you can't imagine the amount of artillery used. Sometimes over 500 guns per mile of front. I saw too many good men blown to pieces, and I want no more of war. I hope this is the last one."

"Don't worry. Mexico has had enough of war. They won't fight again, although there is skirmishing from time to time. We have nearly rebuilt Herradura to its old state, and I think you will like being major-domo there. We have a lot of good people, and many old friends. Villa even visits from time to time. You'll like it there, being a hero, and all," Green said, eyeing three rows of ribbons on his chest.

Etienne laughed. "Green, you'd be surprised what they give medals for now. Most of these are foreign, and given to the entire brigade or division. I am prouder of my gunnery sergeant's stripes than anything else. What is most important is that it is over and done with. No more."

"Etienne, get some clothes you can travel in, at least to Chihuahua. They ain't too fond of American uniforms in Mexico these days. We can pick up some more clothes in Chihuahua or Parral. You'll also need weapons."

"I got my .45 from the Marines, and I've still got my old Spanish mauser. Will they be all right?" he asked.

"They'll be fine, but bring some extra ammunition for the automatic. No one down there has it. We'll go across and catch the 9:00 train out of Juárez in the morning."

The next morning they were safely aboard the train before 9:00. They stopped in Chihuahua for two days, to buy clothes for Etienne, and from Parral they rode Herradura mounts and led a pack horse.

They were only about five miles from the compound when Green told Etienne, "Don't turn and don't look. There are five horsemen on that rise to the south, and they look like *bandidos*. If they start after us, hightail down the road. I'll drop back and keep the packhorse up, but if I yell, you stop, unlimber that mauser, and shoot to kill. We probably won't have to because I think we can out-run them. These horses are all grain fed, and I doubt theirs are. I'll just say go, and you go. Got it?"

"Okay, Green. I'd just as soon outrun them. I've had enough killin'."

Only a quarter of a mile later, Green yelled, "Go, Etienne!" and Etienne went. They were about 250 yards ahead of the bandits, well out of range, and all but one of the bandits were losing ground. Green had dropped back and quirted the pack horse into full speed, acting as rear guard.

The one bandit was gaining on them, evidently riding a good horse. When he got inside of 150 yards, Green pulled up, pulled his mauser from the rifle boot, and spilled him off his horse. Soon Green heard the machine guns from Herradura open up. After the gun's strike kicked on both sides of the still pursuing *bandidos,* they pulled up and retreated.

Green and Etienne slowed to a trot then, and the fallen bandit's horse caught up with them, following them through the gate.

"You got quite a fortress here, Green," Etienne remarked.

"Yeah, has to be. Still plenty of *bandidos* around. No harm done, and I think that pony is a keeper. He was gaining on us."

Cesar took their horses, and Green told him to put Etienne's things in the major-domo's cottage by the front gate.

Etienne was greeted like a long lost brother by Mercedes. He marveled at all that had been done since he had been there, when they brought Vicente's body. He looked at the big mural of the rev-olution and said, "Everybody's in it but me."

"We didn't have a picture of you, but maybe Romulo can paint you in from life," said Green, chuckling.

Etienne was quickly into the swing of things, organizing every-thing. He and Romulo Ortiz got along well, and Ortiz, being kept busy with the surveying Green wanted done, took time to show Etienne all about the dam and the generator. Etienne knew a lot about water, and he started improving the irrigation system. By the first of April, when Green usually started arranging to ship the steers to New Mexico, Etienne had taken over most of that detail work. Green wasn't much more than an observer that year, because Etienne and Sol Weeks handled everything. Green had done an excellent job setting things up and training people. He had become redundant to his own operation.

Mercedes saw what was happening, and how it frustrated Green. For all of his exciting life, he didn't think he was old enough to retire. Green was less of a trader than a rancher these days, but that was a natural progression.

The Dunigan family followed the yearlings from Herradura to Rancho Polaris, and Green was very active in the work to stock the Roy ranch, as was Mercedes. It had been several days since he had read a paper, but on May 25 he opened the El Paso newspaper of May 22 to the headline that blared "Carranza Dead." He read the story and determined that Obregón had broken with Carranza, and if Obregón had not actually pulled the trigger, he was probably responsible.

Green packed his bag and told Mercedes, "I have to go to El Paso. Things are breaking fast in Mexico, and I need to keep up. I won't go into Mexico before telling you, *querida*."

Things were moving fast indeed. Adolfo de la Huerta was appointed provisional president by the convention, and there was little or no opposition, as the presidential election was to be in the fall. De la Huerta immediately set out to close down the revolution. Going all over Mexico, he got all the faction leaders to declare for peace and disarm their forces.

The Division of the North was given a general amnesty at Chihuahua and was disbanded. Villa was given a 25,000-acre *hacienda* near Parral called Canutillo, and he, with forty of his *dorados*, became farmers on July 2, 1920.

After Villa had ensconced himself and his men at Canutillo, Green sent word to Mercedes to come down so they could see him. He also sent word to Romulo Ortiz to meet him in Parral with the maps he had surveyed.

It was July 25 before Green and Mercedes got to Canutillo. Villa greeted them grandly, and insisted they stay a few days there. Doña Luz was in permanent residence and put them up in the main house. All the *dorados* were busy. Four tractors were going in the fields, and it was quite a sight to see—the gold-encrusted sombreros twinkling in the sun on top of tractors.

"You see, Verde, we Mexicans are all farmers at heart. Such ferocious fighters as the *dorados* plowing in the fields," said Villa.

"*Sí*, I had no troubles finding all kinds of people. As a matter of fact, we took in all comers for a while, but eventually had to stop it. They were eating us out of house and home," said Green. "*Jefe*, I've brought some maps I've had made of Herradura. As you know, before the revolution, Herradura was over 250,000 *hectarias*. Because of pressures for land reform, we, Mercedes and myself, felt that 100,000 *hectarias* would be enough to get clear title to. You remember your promise, and I presume you talked to de la Huerta about it, but we wanted you to know that 100,000 *hectarias* would be fine with us," explained Green.

"I did talk to Fito about Herradura, and he too wanted to make it smaller," said Villa. "He said it would not look good to confirm the *latifundias* at its original size. We argued, but he has a point. I think he will be overjoyed to confirm the title of 100,000 *hectarias* to you."

"The maps that I have, and will give you, show the original and the 100,000 that we think is right. It was surveyed by a registered engineer that we took in, the one who painted the murals. He built a dam on the river, and we can irrigate the 500 acres in the vega we kept, plus maybe a thousand more. He also put in an electric generating plant. We have lights and power now. Romulo Ortiz did it all. He made a showplace out of it."

"Verde, this is even more reason to settle the title on you. Give me the maps. I will see Fito in five days from now, and he will do it," Villa assured him. "I know the Herreras had plenty of money, but are you going to break your wife? All this had to cost a lot. Are you really a spendthrift?"

"No, *jefe*. So far I have spent less than 150,000 gold. Ortiz came to us destitute but will accept very little pay. Many people helped us for free, just to be a part of the effort. It shows, however, what can be done to improve the lot of Mexico, if the *politicos* will just stay out of the way," said Green.

"I wish there were a hundred Verdes and Ortizes in Mexico. We would recover quickly. Fito de la Huerta is a good man, too, but I think that Obregón is going to be the next president. Anyway,

Verde, you have my thanks, and the thanks of many Mexicans. We are proud to call you a Mexican!" Villa said, his chest swelling.

"You must come and see it, *mi general*. Bring Doña Luz and come to see us next week. We are going to stay a couple of weeks before we go back," invited Mercedes.

The Villas did visit Herradura. Villa recognized Etienne and welcomed him back, and wanted to know all about the war in France. Doña Luz admired the artwork and invited Ortiz to come and paint at Canutillo. He said he would be happy to, in about three months. Green was glad to hear this. He was feeling guilty about all the things Ortiz had done for very little pay. Green spoke to Mercedes and they agreed to give him 5,000 gold pesos as a parting gift.

The Dunigans left for New Mexico after ten days, but they would return in November.

CHAPTER 56

Herradura, Chihuahua / September 1918

In September, a large packet was forwarded to "Señora Mercedes Dunigan y Herrera" from Mexico City, with many official seals and stamps. Inside was a many-paged patent to the agreed-upon 100,000 *hectarias* of Herradura.

Its preamble was in correct, flowing Spanish, saying, "In recognition of the valiant services to the Republic of the Herrera family, including Colonel Verde Dunigan, etc., then the confirmation of title upon Mercedes."

Obregón was elected president of Mexico in the fall, and Mexico seemed to settle down to rebuild. There was the occasional *pronuciamiento* from a local *cacique*, but it usually was quickly settled. The *rurales* reappeared, and in their heavy-handed way were pacifying the countryside. But the people approved, and helped, the result being many fewer bandit gangs. Green removed the machine guns from the wall but left them on top of the big house.

When the Dunigans returned from their annual Christmas visit in Refugio, things were quiet in and around Herradura. Just before they moved back to New Mexico, Mercedes announced their fifth child would be born in November. She was happy about the event, but protested vehemently that it was absolutely the last.

The year 1921 was a reasonably good one in the cattle trade. Green had balanced his Herradura production to Rancho Polaris capacity but was more active on the border and in Mexico, bringing in about all the cattle used in the Dunigan operation in Cotulla and Refugio, and on even to Kansas grass. Jack and Bill Foster had expanded their operations to where they sent over 10,000 steers off Kansas grass every year; however, they had lessened their liability by buying much smaller cattle and growing them at home before sending them north.

Green, on the other hand, had shrunk his operation down to 8,000 yearlings, all from Herradura or its neighbors, and had opened a lively trade in breeding heifers in Mexico. He had the best cattle in north central Mexico, and his heifers were in high demand.

Herradura had changed little, but a small pueblo had risen, based on the vega land that had once belonged to Herradura but had not been confirmed the year before. Green sold as much water as he could to the *campesinos* and participated in several projects with them. He also sold excess electricity to them, and the pueblo had been named Marisol, at his suggestion.

Mercedes had the child on November 5, 1921, and instead of choosing a family name, Green reached back into the mists of his Celtic ancestry and named the boy "Finn Foster Dunigan y Herrera."

They took the baby, along with the other four, for Christmas at Refugio. It was a joyous time, and the children, being younger than those of Jack and Lucinda and the Fosters, were very popular. Green sent them out to spend two days with Abel and Sulema Castro, and this earned him everyone's favor. The hunting was excellent that year, and there was scarcely a meal that did not include game.

A new project was in the works. John Dunigan had been coerced by all of them to write down his memories of earlier days, and with Kathleen as his secretary he bent to it with vigor. Before they left, Green read over a hundred pages, mostly about the trail drives. He would finish it a week before his death, in April 1922, but it would not be printed until 1924.

Green and Mercedes returned to Herradura on January 7, 1922. It was a year of consolidation, accompanied by a market crash in cattle of heroic proportion. Although all the Dunigan ranches survived, it was not a good year for cattlemen. Romulo Ortiz left in February to go to Villa's at Canutillo, and Padre Anselmo was ordered to a monastery in June. They had to find another schoolmaster, as attendance had grown to over forty with children from the pueblo. After several false starts, Green found a man in his sixties who had lost his whole family to the revolution. He had been a teacher before and had been in Obregón's army. His name was Aristides Chacon, and he was steeped in Latin and Greek, literature and history. He dearly loved two things: children and Mexico. Mercedes was very fond of him, and had him to dinner at least twice every week.

To take care of the spiritual side, Green had conferred with the bishop of Parral, and a priest visited every other month on an irregular basis. Priests were still enemies of the revolution.

When they returned from John Dunigan's funeral in April, the Dunigans went directly to Roy. The summer was pleasant, and Sol had found some small horses just suited to Fito and Tom. Mercedes spent a lot of time on Minerva with them.

The year 1922 ended as it had begun, but with less money to divide, and with the absence of John Dunigan. The Dunigans moved with the cattle to New Mexico, and the boys were glad to get back to their favorite ponies.

The next year started as just another year until a telegram arrived on July 21, from Ravel:

"Villa assassinated yesterday in Parral. Burial in three days at Canutillo. Doña Luz unharmed. Sam Ravel."

Green yelled to Mercedes to begin packing. They caught the first train out, raced across the border for another, and arrived at Parral at noon on July 23. Green hired a buggy and got to Canutillo by nightfall. They found Doña Luz Carral de Villa devastated by Villa's death, but comforted by the visits of so many of Villa's old comrades. She was tearful as she greeted Green and Mercedes.

"Why, Verde, why? Pancho was through fighting. He had made peace. Why did they have to kill him? He didn't threaten anyone."

"Doña Luz, he could raise an army overnight, that is why. The politicos could never feel safe as long as a man of Villa's strength lived. And they killed him because they hated him, as the common people loved him," said Green somberly. The assembled mourners nodded in agreement.

336

There was no priest at the burial. An ex-captain of the *dorados* delivered a short eulogy at the small Canutillo *campo santo*. At the end, Green reached down for a handful of dirt, which he sprinkled on Villa's coffin. He said, very sadly and very slowly, "This is what Francisco Villa lived for, fought for, and died for. Those of us here, who knew him best, must never dishonor it."

Historian, Yale graduate, and U.S. Marine officer
KERRY MCCAN is a fifth-generation South Texas
cowboy and rancher. He is the author of *Brindy
Polaris,* the authentic story of a nineteenth-century
cattle drive.